LIKE NO C

MW00587420

A Novel
Larry Eisenman Center

LIKE NO OTHER BOY

First edition. June 9, 2020.

Copyright © 2020 Larry Center.

ISBN: 978-1393708537

Written by Larry Center.

Table of Contents

"Oh! What things unspoken trembled in the air."
—Johnny Mercer, A Handful of Stars.

Chapter 1

"The Voice in my silence." –Helen Keller

IT WAS A SATURDAY AFTERNOON at the San Diego Zoo, a beautiful day with a pale blue sky. Tommy and I were standing in front of the zebra exhibit. The zebras were running around and nipping at each other, kicking up dust, tails swishing. But instead of watching the zebras, Tommy stepped away from the enclosure and looked down at the ground. He made his usual droning noise that sounded like a motorboat engine, then put a hand to his mouth and gnawed on his knuckles. They were already reddened to the point of almost bleeding. He was eight-years-old and still biting himself. I watched him and winced. As his father, Chris Crutcher is the name—nice alliteration, I think—no matter how much I'd seen him do this, it still hurt to see my little boy harm himself.

In the distance, a lion roared as if he were trying to remind himself of his own kingliness.

"Wow! Look at those zebras, Tom-Tom," I said, hoping to squeeze at least a drop of interest out of him. I was always trying to make Tommy pay attention to something in the real world, anything, desperate to get him to look and respond. "See their stripes? Aren't they cool?" I gently pulled his reddened hands away from his mouth. "Zebras like stripes. Strange, huh? If they see stripes painted on a wall, they'll stand next to the wall. Is that crazy or what?" I'd just read that on a sign nearby. It was an abstract idea to present to him, I knew, but I did it anyway.

Smells of espresso, popcorn, and grilled hot dogs filled the air while crowds of people swarmed around us. Tommy chewed on his hands again, the backs turning wet with saliva that glistened in the bright afternoon sun. He'd been biting himself, self-abusing like that for nearly three years and nothing we'd tried, none of the therapies, seemed to be able to make him stop. Frustrating wasn't the word.

"Wouldn't it be cool to ride a zebra? I sure think so," I said, still trying to draw Tommy out of himself.

I stepped closer to him and knelt down to his level, bringing my face close to his, but Tommy's foggy stare continued to wander off into the distance. He shrugged and said nothing. This was no-speak, his own secret code. He turned completely away from me and hummed louder. "Ouuuu . . . drrrrrr . . ." Sweat stains dampened the back of his blue shirt. He was being his typical disinterested self. Just another day with my son. I rose back to my full height.

Though his mind was an odd black box, Tommy's face was close to angelic: symmetrically aligned features on porcelain skin, curly, honey-wheat hair, and long lashes that shadowed eyes so big and blue there was little room for the whites. A gorgeous kid, for sure, a potential child model, tall and gangly for his age. He walked on his tiptoes with a kind of pelican strut, head before body, neck outstretched, legs following.

As I watched four young boys gawk and giggle at the zebras, Tommy spun around, arms extended like a propeller, eyes closed. He looked like he was trying to make himself dizzy. The whirring sound he made turned into "beeeeep, beeeeep." Then he stopped spinning and slapped himself on the forehead. Just like that. Thwack. I felt a resonant pain in the deepest regions of my gut that seemed to spread through my entire body; empathy pain. I felt it all the time.

"Please don't slap yourself," I said. "You know that's not right. Come on now, let's have fun here. Zoos are fun."

But Tommy just looked away, still staring into space. He kept to his own planet, my far-away little boy. I felt like his distant moon.

This was our first trip to the zoo and I was on tentative ground. I'd been looking forward to our time together all week, since seeing the ad on TV that had grabbed me: lions, tigers, polar bears, plus some dandy pandas as well—oh, my! Tommy was mine on weekends, thanks to the shared custody agreement after my divorce. Usually, on Saturday afternoons, we went to the park near my house or worked on puzzles indoors, or just kicked back and watched TV. For us, this was quite the unusual outing.

We left the zebras and their antics and shuffled along the winding sidewalk that flowed around the exhibits. I showed Tommy the giraffes, a nosy lamb at the petting zoo, and two enormous elephants that flapped their ears and lumbered lazily around. He hardly seemed to notice them.

Even a unicycling juggler throwing yellow balls into the air didn't stop Tommy from going after his hands again, chomping away at his nails and skin. Wearing a polka-dotted shirt and a great big smile, the juggler stopped in front of us. He tossed balls up and down in revolving circular patterns, catching a ball or two behind his back. It was a show, a real eye-catcher.

"Wow! Look at that juggler, Tom-Tom," I said, pointing. "Isn't he good?"

But Tommy was more interested in a nearby pile of dirt. Moving away from me and withdrawing even deeper into himself, he picked up clods of it, squeezed, and then let them fall. Now his hands, already wet, were a mess. *Great.*

As I reached for a wipe from my backpack—wherever Tommy and I went, Mister Backpack went, too—I noticed a father and son sitting on a bench not far from us. The boy, dark-haired and pudgy, appeared to be around Tommy's age.

"Daddy, a juggler!" the boy said, excited. "Look!"

"He's good, isn't he?" The father fiddled with his phone as he spoke.

"Maybe I could learn to juggle like that. He's so cool! Hey, Dad, can we go see the reptiles next? Please? We learned about them in Miss Wexler's class."

"Sure, son."

Jealousy stabbed me, although I knew I shouldn't feel it. While that kid was having a normal talk with his dad, Tommy was picking up a rock and putting it down, picking it up and putting it down, then crumbling a leaf in his hands. He said not a word. This was his way, hyper-focusing on a particular object and blocking out everything else around him.

The juggler moved on. I swallowed hard. "Okay, Tom-Tom, let's go check out some more animals," I said, trying to maintain my encouraging tone.

"Daddy." Tommy shook his head, looking past me. It had been his first word in a half-hour. "Go. We go." He spoke in what I called brick-words, words that all sounded the same, as if they dropped heavily from his mouth pre-formed, one on top of the other in monotonic units.

"Really? But we haven't even seen the reptiles." I faced him. "Don't you want to see the reptiles? The snakes and stuff?"

"Go. Go. Pleeeeease. Go." Tommy hung his head and fidgeted. He put his right thumb into his mouth, then whirled around. I always saw his persistent hand biting, his spinning, and his motorboat buzzing as sounds that reflected the storms deep within his mind.

"Sure. Of course, we can go." I gave him a smile. I wasn't about to push him past his limit.

Tommy seemed unfazed by the big things in life, like being shared between his parents, living in two houses, and getting emotionally tugged this way and that ever since Cheryl and I had divorced two years ago—my uncivil war as I called it. Yes, he had his fixed routines, but he'd seemed to take the change in his parents' relationship in stride. It was the impact of unexpected sensory experiences—crunchy peanut butter, the label on the back of his shirt, even the sight of the Sunday newspaper in disarray on the floor—that made him whine and pitch fits. These roadblocks could bring the neuron highway of his mysterious mind to a painful standstill.

When Tommy found a cigarette on the ground and reached for it, about to pick it up, I pulled his hand away just in time.

"Don't, Tommy. No! You know better than that." He would have put it in his mouth if I hadn't stopped him. I took a long breath and released it slowly, my eyes landing on a red-haired child eating pink cotton candy, swirls of it like edible clouds. "Okay. Let's go, then. I guess we've seen enough."

"Go . . . Go," he said. His words seemed so disconnected, as if they arose not from his wants and needs and emotions, but from some kind of word-producing system inside his body that mechanically emitted vowels and consonants.

But on the way to the exit, we wound up near an African bird exhibit in a less populated area of the zoo. With Tommy still humming and murmuring by my side, oblivious to the world around him, I followed a long and winding trail. Instead of taking us to the exit, the shade-covered path ended in Primate World, which was set back on its own. Sounds of chimpanzees shrieking in the distance made Tommy stop dead in his tracks. He blinked, then moved forward with caution. He stood higher on his tiptoes and made a soft, inquisitive sound. "Oooouuuuwoooo."

"What's wrong, Tom-Tom?" I asked, narrowing my eyes. I knelt down to his level. "Are you all right?"

Tommy just sucked in a big breath as if he were about to blow out a birthday candle, then shuffled on as I followed behind. Instead of complaining, he headed straight for the exhibit and entered. He seemed suddenly curious. Interested. And I was intrigued.

From a distance of about fifty feet, we could see a single large and hairy chimp, chomping on leaves in the sunlight, separated from us by a thick glass panel. Tommy's face flushed.

"Hairy so much," he said, pointing at the chimp. "Wow."

"Yes. They're cool, for sure. They're chimpanzees. You like them?" I rubbed my chin as I studied him, then glanced at the chimps.

"Wooooow." Tommy clapped his hands. "Woooweeeee. Go. Here."

"Sure." His newborn enthusiasm made me smile broadly. It was just so completely unexpected.

As we made our way down a narrow path shaded by large overhanging trees, we found a group of chimps set behind glass walls, nestled in a jungle-like atmosphere. Large climbing rocks and verdant trees abounded in a field of grass and bushes. It looked homey, like an outdoor chimp hotel. Some of the chimps were playing or cuddling, some lumbered around, and others simply sat by themselves and stared vacuously into space. Tommy pointed at one of the chimps shuffling around near the glass.

"Woweee." He stood unusually motionless and just took it all in. "Wowweee. Cooool."

This sudden curiosity made my mouth drop open. I'd never seen him so engaged and he wasn't biting his hands or anything. A slow-moving chimp shook his head, scratched an ear, and shambled past us, lazily heading for a rope swing. Another chimp stuck out his tongue and then flicked his hands in the air. Tommy watched them all with such focus, his eyes fixated on the animals.

He turned to me and pointed at one of the larger chimps sitting by the window. "She baby in tummy, Daddy." He cocked his head. "She chimpie baby in chimpie mommy tummy!"

"Really? You think so?" I raised an eyebrow and folded my arms across my chest.

"Yep. She baby." He spoke so matter-of-factly as glimmerings of excitement shone in his eyes. "She chimpie baby. Chimpie in there and happy!"

"That's using your words. I really like that." I laughed and stepped closer to him. "But how do you know she has a baby?" The chimp didn't have a protruding belly as far as I could tell, though I was far from an expert.

"Baby! Daddy! Chimpie!" He actually hugged himself and giggled.

I couldn't believe it, this new eagerness of his. My breath caught in my throat as I stepped back, accidentally bumping into another onlooker, a short man with a full beard. Stroking his beard and scratching his head, the man shot me a nasty look.

"Sorry," I mumbled.

The man replied with a grunt as he moved past us. The adult chimp that Tommy had pointed at stood up, screeched, then raised a smaller chimp on to its shoulders with the ease of an acrobat.

"Can you tell Daddy how you know?" I pushed back my Padres baseball cap as I gazed down at him.

But once again, Tommy said nothing. He brought his hands back up to his mouth and nipped the backs of them.

"Tommy, can we please not do that?" I shook my head, hoping he would listen.

It was as if Tommy's brain had gone into loop mode, playing a certain behavior over and over again like a song. In desperation,

I turned to Plan B—speaking cartoon-ese. As a professional voice-over actor in the San Diego area—*Loco Bob's out of his mind with price cuts! Discounts galoooore!*—I could produce a number of cartoon voices—*"That's-that's all, f-f-folks!"* This skill had made me a hit at kids' birthday parties and, to be honest, some late-night adult parties as well.

"Hey, Tom-Tom." I channeled my inner SpongeBob SquarePants and spoke in his goofy, clunky, cartoon voice. "Let's put our hands in our pockets, okay? No biting, okay? You know that would make me sooooo, soooo happy. Pockets please, my little starfish."

"Okay, SpongeBob." The words plopped out of his mouth and I was gratified. Tommy looked down shyly and stuffed his hands into the pockets of his khakis. As he rocked on the balls of his feet, he looked past me and stuck out his tongue, making a long circle with it around his lips, sides, top to bottom. "'Kay."

"Thank you. And," I winked, switching to a deeper tone, "oh yeah, Larry the Lobster thanks you too."

But then Tommy threw me another curveball: he pulled his hands from his pockets and pressed his index fingers against his roughened thumbs, a motion similar to snapping his fingers. He moved them against each other, producing what seemed like a soft, scratchy *flick, rub, flick, rub, rub . . . flick-flick, rub.* I'd never seen him do anything like that before. He knew some sign language—about fifty signs. He'd learned them at school as a way to improve his communication abilities and relieve his frustrations. Of course, Cheryl and I had taught ourselves some signs, as well. But these motions were nothing I could recognize.

"Are you okay, Tommy?" I bent down to his level once again and frowned, worried the new hand gestures could be the prelude to another tantrum. In fact, he'd already thrown a fit this morning over a spilled-milk issue and had nearly split his lip on the kitchen counter. My muscles stiffened. Tommy's tantrums were living nightmares. They haunted my dreams.

Tommy stopped flicking his fingers, cocked his head as if listening to an inner voice. "She baby in tummy. Baby mommy, see?" he said again, pointing at the same chimp.

When he was seven, Tommy had tested at the four-year-old level in terms of expressive language, and typically his days and nights were filled with bouts of prolonged and remote silence, followed by short, sporadic glimmerings of monotonic speech. There were times when he seemed to be improving, then other periods when he regressed, his disordered mind fighting the very basic nature of communication. It was heartbreaking. There was no other word to describe it. But on that afternoon at the zoo, I felt a glimmer of hope. For him, "She baby in tummy," was practically a speech.

He made the sign for chimp—I had no idea he even knew that sign, though I remembered it—putting your hands at your sides and scratching upwards, as if you were an ape.

"How do you know about the baby, Tommy?" I asked.

He tugged at his juice-stained, olive-green T-shirt, folded his arms across his chest, and offered something I was always yearning for—direct eye contact. Though he didn't speak, direct eye contact was gold to me. His blue eyes, which usually skittered and darted around like butterflies, landed on my face and stayed there, holding my stare for several long, spectacular moments.

"Daddy belly," Tommy insisted in his staccato-like talk. "She . . . baby . . . baby belly in tummy." He spoke as if he were lecturing me. I grinned. The mild breeze wafting in from the coast seemed to reflect my elevated mood.

I pointed to a larger window exhibit of chimps down the path. "Let's go over there. I think we can get a better look."

"Okay, Daddy." He scrunched up his face and clapped his hands, then surprisingly doled out a burst of enthusiasm. "Yeah!"

"Wow, Tom-Tom. You really do like these chimps, don't you?"

Again, Tommy nodded vigorously, a serious expression on his face.

Although a crowd had gathered at the glass, I stayed close to Tommy and eased us both to a spot where he could watch the primates without obstruction. I had no idea what to make of his uncanny interest in these creatures, though, I, too, was mesmerized by the chimps and their almost human mannerisms as they lolled around, picked at each other, or wandered in search of a new leaf to mash on their teeth and tongues. Some looked sleepy, some content. Regardless of their actions, they paid no attention to the Homo sapiens on our side of the glass.

But when Tommy started flicking his fingers again, a big chimp with a wrinkled face and dark, watery eyes took notice. He shook his head, then waddled over to where Tommy stood. Again, Tommy made the sign for chimp, curling his hands at his sides. Big Guy's eyes remained glued on Tommy, who placed his hand against the glass, and then . . . damned if the chimp didn't do the same. Hand against hand, boy and chimp. Big Guy bellowed.

The two locked eyes and stood stock-still, focused so intensely it seemed like each was channeling the other's thoughts.

Tommy beamed at the chimp while I watched, stunned, my lips parted. Tommy bobbed his head and, in imitation, the chimp bobbed too, sticking his tongue out. Then the two started swaying together like synced metronomes. When Tommy made another odd, flicking gesture, the chimp rubbed his thick fingers together as well. I laughed out loud. Truly, this was the craziest thing I'd ever seen. Tommy just stood there, an intent look on his face. He seemed so absorbed, so focused, like I'd never seen him before.

Three other chimps shuffled over, using their own hand movements and facial expressions, gawking, stretching their mouths wide. They gestured to each other with large movements of their arms. They eyeballed Tommy and Tommy alone, intent expressions fixed on their friendly faces. One chimp with gray, wispy hair under his chin screeched, flailed his arms, and jumped up and down as if trying to get Tommy's attention. But Big Guy and Tommy ignored him, mesmerized with each other. When Tommy touched the top of his head, Big Guy did the same. Then when Tommy rubbed both of his ears, Big Guy rubbed his ears as well. The bearded man I'd bumped into earlier stood next to me, his arms folded across his chest.

"Now ain't that somethin'," he intoned. I turned away from Tommy and realized we were surrounded by a growing group of onlookers.

"Hey, Brandy," I heard a voice say. I spied a tall woman in a white dress standing next to her black-haired female friend. Smiles had blossomed on their faces. "Look at that kid. The chimps can't take their eyes off that little boy. It's so cute!"

On the other side of us was a lanky teenager with pimples on his chin. He'd whipped out his phone and was recording Tommy's interactions, the way the chimp was imitating Tommy. "This is so rad," he mumbled.

Oh, God. A YouTube moment. I thought about tapping the kid on the shoulder and making him stop. But why cause a scene? Besides, when you were out in public, wasn't privacy a thing of the past? Maybe I should record this, too. But my cell phone was just about out of battery power.

"Whose kid is that?" asked a man behind me as I swung around.

"There's the dad," a woman said in a New York accent. She was short, with black hair and black glasses. She pointed at me. "The tall guy with the Padres cap."

"That's me, all right." I raised my hand slightly and everyone laughed. I felt my face flame up as fatherly pride melted like warm butter in my chest. I stood a little taller, straightening my shoulders.

Tommy flicked his fingers even more vigorously. Then he made the sign for play: hands turned sideways, shaped like the sign for Texas Longhorns, wiggling up and down. Then back to the flicking, which looked as if he were somehow tapping out the primate version of Morse Code.

Big Guy opened his mouth wide and let out a jungle-shriek. He returned the finger flicking, and then wiggled his hands and held them in a way that looked awfully similar to Tommy's "play" sign. Wispy Hair tried to shove Big Guy out of the way, but the big chimp refused to budge.

Tommy and Big Guy swayed a minute more, continuing to gaze at each other, flapping fingers and bobbing heads. Big Guy did a little dance to the beat of Tommy's hand clapping, and then Big Guy clapped his hands and it was Tommy's turn to dance, elbows angled out and knees bent as he hopped up and down. It was amazing. The crowd resounded with laughter and a few Ooos and Aahhs. The teen continued recording, looking amused.

Then just like that, Tommy backed a few feet away from the glass, and the chimps scampered off to their playing, grooming, and swinging around, completely ignoring the humans, as if the show was over. A few kids tried to replicate what Tommy had done, trying to get the chimps' attention. They failed to get a response. I just stood there, keeping an eye on Tommy.

"Play . . . make . . . chimps." Tommy gazed up at me. He made the play sign, then the chimp sign.

"I see that," I said. "I had no idea you liked chimps so much!"

"Do, Daddy. Doooo."

I reveled in another delightful moment of Tommy's lingering eye contact and in the brightness on his face. He seemed unlocked by the experience, transformed.

Before we left the exhibit, I turned around and gazed once more at the chimps, who were still scampering around. They were so human-like, with their contemplative gazes, their self-conscious movements, their gestures. Surely, there was more than a bit of Homo sapiens running in their blood. And were we humans more chimp-like than we realized?

Maybe some of us more than others. I smiled to myself, thinking of the bearded man I'd bumped into, then edged closer to Tommy, who now fidgeted and hung his head, silent as ever. What was Tommy contemplating? His shoes? The shadows that dangled around him?

"Those chimpies really like you, Tommy." I crouched down to his level. A bead of sweat dotted his upper lip.

He didn't say anything, but he gave me another wondrous moment of direct eye contact and I drank it in. Then snot bubbled from his nostrils. I produced a tissue from Mister Backpack, which was stocked with a change of clothes, tissues, band aids, the works, and tried to wipe Tommy's face clean. He grimaced and jerked and twisted away from me, but I persisted.

"Nooo!" He folded his lower lip in defiance.

"Come on, son. Let me just wipe your . . . there," I said when I was done. "Thank you."

"Daddeeee." Tommy rubbed his nose with the palm of his hand, reddening his nostrils. His stubborn refusal to allow me to touch him had always hollowed me out. He pointed back at the chimps. "Like." He spoke loudly, then expanded his arms like wings and made the "like play" sign. "Like chimpies, Daddy. Big lots!"

"Well, that's great, Tom-Tom." I beamed, grinning.

"Chimpies," Tommy said. "Chimpies." He clapped his hands and jumped up and down, excitement flashing on his face.

As we headed away from the chimps, Tommy shuffled along by my side, his hands in his mouth again, walking with that pelican strut. We passed a small sign planted at the edge of the primate area. I stopped to read the words:

Did you know chimpanzees only have babies every four to five years? We are very proud to announce that here at the San Diego Zoo, Wanda G, our newest chimp, is expecting a baby in approximately eight months!

I read the sign twice, blinking rapidly. Damned if there wasn't a picture of Wanda G herself on the sign—the chimp who looked awfully like the one Tommy had said was pregnant.

I stood still, hairs on the back of my neck tingling. How in the world had he known?

WE STOPPED AT THE ZOO Brew and I bought an iced latte, something I really couldn't afford given the dire state of my job situation. But what good was living without an iced latte every once in a while? I mean, really. I tried to interest Tommy in a treat, but he refused.

I found a shaded bench near the lake, where ducks glided past and children played around the edges, their shrill voices rising in the air. Walking behind me and finally catching up, Tommy plopped down next to me on the bench, staring into space as he put one finger up his right nostril and another in his mouth. Was he just zoning out? Or was he contemplating his time with the "chimpies?"

I was, for sure. Tommy didn't have the reading skills to read that sign. It was totally out of the question. And yet he had known Wanda G was pregnant.

I studied my son's face, pensive and twisted with worry—the way he almost always looked. Now he stood, kicked at the ground, then rubbed the side of his head, where the infamous scar was. Two and a half years ago, while Cheryl and I were still barely hanging on to the threads of our marriage, he'd fallen in the yard outside our home and hit his head. We'd rushed him to the hospital, bleeding and nearly unconscious. I'd been out of my mind with fear. The diagonal scar on the left side of his head still remained, along with the painful memory of that awful day, the emotional scar as real as ever.

"Hungry, Daddeee," Tommy said, rubbing his stomach.

"Know what? Me, too."

Ten minutes later, we returned to our bench and I was cutting Tommy's hot dog into circles and squares, throwing away half the bun, and adding exactly two dabs of ketchup. Three dabs would throw him into a fit.

He needed his food sliced into shapes. That was his way. Squares, circles, triangles—the geometric diet.

We'd tried all kinds of diets—gluten-free, non-dairy, vegetarian, even camel milk, and on and on—but nothing seemed to help him. Like all autistic children, his gastric issues abounded—constipation, diarrhea. The works. If only treatment was as simple as choosing tofu over hamburgers, apples over potato chips.

When we finished our meal, Tommy took my plate, and along with his, tossed our trash into a nearby receptacle, then returned to the bench.

"Good job." He'd offered to take my plate without me even prompting him. I was impressed. I had the urge to mess up his hair. Since he always moved away whenever I tried to touch him, I restrained myself. And yet, the distances he kept from me, emotional and physical, his intractable inwardness, had somehow drawn me closer to him than I was to anyone else I'd ever known.

"Want anything else to eat?" I asked.

Tommy just bit his fingers.

"No, Tom-Tom. Not your fingers. You're not that hungry, are you?"

I smiled. He didn't get the joke, this one and only child of mine.

He'd planted his hooks deep inside me, really, ever since he was born, a normal-looking, beautiful healthy baby boy. We'd named him

Thomas after Cheryl's grandfather, who died just a few years ago. I liked the name, solid-sounding, an oak of a name. The delivery went without a problem, and we proudly brought our little bundle of joy home where we had prepared a nursery. Cheryl and I felt blessed. We watched him curl his miraculous little fingers into fists, felt the smoothness of his angelic face, adored his inconceivably perfect nails.

Ever since I'd witnessed him coming into this world, I felt it was my duty, my obligation, to see this son of mine through whatever hardships he endured. If love is the bond between two people, ours was surely made of emotional superglue.

"Tommy? You ready to go, or do you want to see something else?" I tried to get his attention.

Nothing. He looked everywhere but at me.

"Tommy?"

He looked down and scratched at his shoes, messing with the laces. He hyper-focused on them and I just let him go at it. I crossed one leg over the other and simply sat there, not wanting to get up from the bench either. This March Saturday afternoon was just too ridiculously gorgeous, the breeze too hypnotic; seventy-two degrees, crisp and sunny.

Leaning back, I studied the crowds of people roaming past us, herds of them, like buffalo wandering over sun-swept plains of pavement. They formed an interesting display, these zoogoers: the long-legged females with their designer purses, their smartphone-appendages and stylish footwear; mothers leading toddlers by their hands accompanied by paunchy, pale-faced fathers whose twitchy expressions and long faces made them look like they were suffering from ESPN withdrawal; the weirdly tattooed and nose-ringed; the proud, grey-haired grandparents. I smiled. Maybe the *real* zoo existed outside the cages, and the true spectators were the animals, calmly eyeing this odd assortment of human beings who traipsed by. Tommy and I were just two more animals in the pack.

I recalled Tommy's interactions with the chimps again. How was it possible? I would've Googled chimps and children with autism to see if there was any known relationship if my phone wasn't about to run out of juice. I still couldn't get over what had happened.

Still, we'd been at the zoo over two hours and now it was definitely time to go. Too much time out and about was not a good thing. It would lead to fatigue and most likely, a Tommy tantrum.

"Okay, Tom-Tom, ready to go?" I asked, turning to him.

"Beanie," Tommy said. He tossed two monotonically shaped and packaged words out: "Beanie. Me."

I reached into Mister Backpack and withdrew Radar the bat, Tommy's ever present Beanie Baby, and handed it to him. Radar was black all over except for his white flappy ears and looked mostly like a rat with wings. But it was cuddly and soft. Theirs was an intimate relationship. Tommy was always playing with the stuffed pet and at times even spoke to Radar in bizarre, nonsensical phrases.

Tommy zoomed Radar in the air, then snuggled the bat as we trooped through the massive parking lot, joining the rest of the Home sapiens who were checking their phones, hurrying kids along, or sipping sodas.

I glanced at the leather-strapped watch I was wearing: It was 2:45.

The watch was a gift from Cheryl, my ex.

What a ride, my marriage. Yes, we'd had a history all right, beginning with our own version of the Garden of Eden, and ending with Exodus.

As we approached my cringe-worthy blue Altima in the vast parking lot—we were in section CC-12—a security alarm went off from someone's nearby car. The loud, continuously beeping horn startled Tommy, who slammed his hands over his ears, doubled over, and let out a high-pitched scream. Loud sounds almost always threw him into a fit. The doctors had a name for it: hyperacusis, but naming the problem did nothing to solve it. Radar slipped out of his hands and fell to the ground. As the blaring continued, the car's lights flashed as well. Adrenaline pumped through me, my mind in a whirl.

"Ouuuu! Eeeee!" Tommy pounded his feet on the asphalt, the delicate lines of his face all twisted into crooked pathways. "Ouuuu! Stop!"

Passersby gawked at us, some slowly taking it all in while others quickly scurried by.

"Ouuu! Eeeeeeeee!"

"Settle down, Tom-Tom." I crouched next to him and kept my voice calm, trying to find that smooth surface in an emotional undercurrent that only wanted to suck me under. I whispered as gently as I could. "If you settle down, I'll give you a token." I reached into Mister Backpack. "I'll make this one red. How's that sound? Red's your favorite color, right?" I had twelve tokens ready to go. If he earned all twelve, he would be allowed a bevy of sugar packets to play with. He loved playing with sugar packets, arranging them in all kinds of shapes and patterns on the kitchen floor.

But when I showed him a token, Tommy just knocked it from my hand and grew even more upset. The token fell to the ground, an unwanted little orb, spinning away.

He screamed even louder, closing his eyes, his face screwed up into a fierce contortion. "Ooouuu!"

The horn had stopped blaring, but it didn't matter. The residual aftershock lived on. Tommy went berserk now, entering into full tantrum mode, and there was no telling how long it would last. I didn't dare try to move him. Once, I'd tried to pick him up while he was in the midst of a tantrum and he'd poked me in the eye and I'd strained my back. No, it was not a good idea.

This much was true: if raising a child with autism and dealing with all its responsibilities had placed me in the major leagues of fatherhood, Tommy's tantrums had upgraded me to the World Series.

Tommy wailed as if I were beating him. His eyes turned inward and unfocused.

"Noooouuuu!" He doubled over again and started breathing in quick, successive spasms; tiny gulps of air, snot bubbling from his nostrils. "Nooouuu!" My only hope was to wait it out. I felt myself go red in the face as he self-stimulated, shaking and wriggling his fingers in front of his eyes. He bit the backs of his hands, twisted his head side to side. The backs of his hands started to bleed.

"Ooooouuuuu . . ." He ran his tongue around his lips.

"Tommy, please." I spoke gently, making sure I didn't aggravate him anymore than he already was. "Can you stop that? Please?"

I pulled his hands away from his mouth, and he quickly returned them. I clenched my teeth and sighed. Just as I was about to try another token, a tall woman wearing a flowery dress approached us, stepping right into our daytime nightmare.

"Is he okay?" she asked timidly as Tommy proceeded to cry out and slap his ears, then stomp on the ground and scream at the sky.

She was holding her daughter's hand, a child of around four or five, with freckles sprinkled across the bridge of her nose and wide eyes that absorbed Tommy with awe and wonder. The calm little girl sucked on the remains of a green lollipop that matched the color of her eyes while Tommy continued to wail at the sky.

"Is he all right?" she repeated.

I stepped back and wiped my forehead with the front part of my bicep. Sweat dribbled down my sides as if I'd been digging ditches. This was emotional construction. "Yes. Thanks for asking. He's fine, I think. Just overtired. That, plus his autism."

"Oh." She looked suddenly sympathetic and at a loss for words. "I see."

Tommy groaned and then whacked himself across the face, hard. I felt the sting inside my body. Empathy pain, again.

"Tommy," I said, trying to hold onto my calm while the winds of my own Daddy-tantrum crept my way and the woman looked on. "Please. Settle down. Don't you want a token?" Patience, Lord. Patience.

He surprised me when he stopped screaming and studied the new little plastic orb I was holding up. A gagging sound blurted from his throat, then he coughed. He tried to snatch the token from me.

"No, no. First, you settle down," I said, holding the token away from him.

"'Oken." He kicked a foot out.

"Settle."

"'Ooooken! 'Oken!" He wriggled his fingers in front of his face. If I was going to follow the rules of the program, I couldn't give him a token until he stopped fussing. Otherwise, I'd be rewarding bad behavior.

"Well, good luck," the woman said with a sorrowful expression. "Come on, Amy. Let's go."

"Mommy, that boy's crying," Amy said, moving closer to her mother.

"Yes, darling, I know."

"We'll be all right," I said. Then, turning to Tommy: "Breathe, Tommy," I urged as the mother and daughter departed. "Breathe." I felt my face burn with embarrassment. "Breathe. Come on. Please? You can do it. Settle down, Tommy."

But now he gasped for air, lungs heaving. It was as if he were forced to suck in oxygen through a straw.

"Come on, Thomas Crutcher. Breathe."

He started hyperventilating, his back arching, chest heaving, then bent down and put his hands on his knees.

"Breathe!"

"Uhhhhh.... ouuuu . . . eee . . ."

He looked like a person who'd almost drowned. The panic in his troubled eyes when he looked up at me for Daddy-help turned my anger into complete sorrow. I felt totally helpless. What could I do but suffer through this with him? I shoved the token in my pocket, then thought about retrieving the blanket I kept in my trunk for meltdowns, wrapping him up in it and giving him body pressure. Body pressure sometimes soothed him, but it only worked when we caught his tantrum in the earliest stages, right at the beginning. Now it was too late for that.

Finally, Tommy did the only thing he could. He screamed one final time, blew out a gush of air, then held his breath until his face turned red, and then—one, two, three—collapsed solidly against me with one final whine. He wasn't unconscious, just suddenly and overwhelmingly exhausted.

I looked up at the sky and said a thank you—relief at last. I smoothed a hand down the side of my face and exhaled slowly, my heart thumping.

"It's okay, Tom-Tom. It's all okay. You're going to be fine."

"Fine?" he mimicked, finally catching his breath and breathing normally again.

"Yes, fine."

"Fine?"

"Yes. Fine."

"Fine? Fine. Fine? Fine . . . Fiiiiinnnnne . . ." Saliva drooled from his lips down to his chin.

Then a hand went to his mouth. Hunched over and weary, Tommy moped by my side as we trudged toward the car at last.

I nudged him forward. Lines of sweat continued to stream down Tommy's face, which had turned pale. He clicked his teeth together.

"'Oken?" He looked up at me again, his eyes connecting with me for just a second. "'Ooooken?" He stretched out his hand.

"Sure, 'oken." I handed him a blue one, wondering if color might have made a difference. Unfortunately, the desire for the token hadn't been strong enough to intrude on the tantrum. I made note of that to tell the teacher. "It's all yours. Have at it."

He stared at the token and turned it over in his hands. "'Oookennnnnn."

When we finally made it to my car, I buckled Tommy into the backseat with a dusty Radar at his side and exhaled loudly. I slung Mister Backpack into the passenger's seat. My back was hurting. I climbed into the driver's seat and just stared straight ahead for a long moment, hands on the steering wheel. A great wad of sadness filled my gut. I blamed myself, too. I should have seen it coming. I carried ear plugs in Mister Backpack because of his noise sensitivity, but why hadn't I given them to him? This surely wasn't the first time I'd screwed up. I had to be more on the ball. But it wasn't just me, either. What about all the therapies he'd undergone, all the time and money we'd spent? Applied Behavioral Analysis, psychologists, so many so-called experts on how to deal with autism, and this was where we stood: Tantrum City. Gnawing on his hands. Self-abuse.

Tommy started zooming Radar in the air, then hugged the stuffed pet. "Fine . . . fine . . . fine . . . buuuuuu . . . Ouuuuuoooo . . . mmmmm . . ."

I took my pulse, which was still racing NASCAR style, while Tommy was now acting as if the tantrum hadn't even happened, as if the past fifteen minutes had simply disappeared from his awareness. "Fine . . . ouuuuu . . . " He hugged Radar and talked soft, gentle nonsense to his pet. "Ooouuuu . . . goooom . . . treeeeeesta . . . beeeesh . . ."

Sometimes, I wondered if my son even had a sense of the past.

"Well, time for home, Tom-Tom." No sense in wallowing at this point. I started the car, pushing down the accelerator a few times to get the old man cranking. This car suffered from mechanical arthritis, unlike the leased Benz I used to drive when my financial life was hitting on all cylinders.

"'Kay, Daddy. 'Kay."

Keeping the car in park, I turned around and studied Tommy and his reddened hands, the dull distance in his eyes. I thought of something.

"Hey, would you like to come back another day and see the chimps again?" I asked.

"Yes, Daddy. Yes." He gave me direct eye contact.

Bingo. That was the answer I'd been looking for. I turned around in my seat and plugged my phone into the car's charger, then dialed Cheryl's number, excited to tell her what had just happened at the zoo. The tantrum, I would refrain from mentioning. When she didn't answer, I found myself rambling into her voicemail.

"Cheryl, look, it's me. The craziest thing just happened at the zoo with these chimps, I mean, Tommy and the chimps, I don't know. Christ. I don't even know how to explain it all. Give me a call ASAP, all right? It's just totally bizarre. You should have seen it."

I ended the call and sat back in my seat, my mind already flowing around the idea of getting access to chimpanzees on a regular basis so that Tommy could, what? Talk to them?

Yes.

Absolutely.

Chapter 2

A half hour later and with Tommy at my side, I opened the door to my condo on Coronado and stepped inside. My aging fox-red Labrador greeted us as if he hadn't seen us in days, nights, and weekends. Maybe even decades. Max was my anchor, my true companion, and, to be honest, not a bad psychotherapist to boot.

"Hey, Max, how goes it? You miss us? You miss us? Huh?" I said as I placed Mister Backpack in a corner in the hall.

Being hit by a car when he was a pup had left old Max with a maimed right front leg, but it didn't do a thing to curtail his bright-eyed gusto. As Tommy and I shuffled into the foyer, Max nuzzled us and barked, speaking back to us in his doggie way.

"Settle down, boy." He shook not only his tail, but his entire hindquarters, looking up at me with canine reverence. "You missed us, didn't you? I know you did."

"Max, Max." Tommy petted my true companion with gentle caresses, his admiring eyes lingering over the dog. Theirs was a special relationship too. There were times when they would stare at each other so intensely I swear it looked as if the two of them were sharing a secret, and then Max would bring Tommy a toy or Radar from another room. I wondered if there was a connection between what Tommy did with Max and what had happened with the chimps.

Max shoved his nose into Tommy's palm, into his stomach, and then sniffed me as well, taking in huge gulps of olfactory information. He snorted and shook his head.

"Smell us, Max," Tommy said in his robotic way. "Big."

"Yes, I know." I chuckled. "I bet we just blew that dog's mind. He's probably dying to know where we've been." Smiling, I knelt down to Max's level, rubbing his ears. "We've been to the zoo, Max. You should have seen all the animals there. Lions, tigers, and bears." Max barked as if he totally understood. *Sure, of course. I get it. The zoo.* I let him outside to do his business in the backyard.

"TV, Daddy?" Tommy said, hugging Radar against his chest again.

We moved into the den where sailing pictures taken by a local photographer hung on wood-paneled walls and three Voice Arts Awards—ego-boosters that had long ago lost their power to console me—rested on a shelf next to the pictures. I glanced at the three overdue bills waiting for me, sitting on my end table: cable, electric, and phone. A nasty triumvirate. Even worse: I was one month behind on my mortgage, a fact that kept me up at night, staring at my ceiling as I wondered how I was going to come up with the money.

"Sure, TV's fine," I said. The weight of my financial insecurity had been sitting on top of me ever since the divorce. Cheryl had always been the one with the steady paycheck. I used to have a steady job too with a company called Focus Media as creative director. But once I'd entered the up-and-down freelance VO game, where the only jobs I got were the result of my own networking capabilities, it was goodbye steady paycheck for me.

Tommy kicked off his shoes. We sat down on my brown smooth-leather couch.

"Let's see what's on."

I switched on my fifty-six-inch HDTV, which got every channel in the known universe, and scrolled around until I landed on Tommy's all-time fav—Cartoon Network.

Tommy fell into TV reverie, hands at his sides, legs crossed. When he watched, he really watched, totally focused. But unlike most children with autism, he didn't have a single cartoon show he was fixated on. He was flexible that way, surprisingly enough.

"'Tooooon," he said, eyes glued to the screen as *Steven's Universe* was just ending.

Leaving Tommy's side, I went to my bar, which was in a room off the kitchen, and drew a sense of comfort from the bottles of SKYY vodka, Kahlua, and a Napa pinot noir ensconced in my wine rack. I took a towel and wiped the burgundy-colored granite countertop, then fixed myself and Tommy glasses of orange juice, adding a splash of vodka to mine. I needed it after our day at the zoo. My back was still hurting. And that tantrum . . . wow. I went to the kitchen, put together some squared-cheese blocks and crackers on a plate, and brought them in as well. As I sat down next to him, the memory of Tommy's world-class meltdown ricocheted through my mind.

How could I love my son so much and yet, sometimes just want to strangle him at the same time?

"TV time for a while. Just you and me, okay?" I said, as we kicked back like frat pals. I plopped my long legs on the coffee table.

"Daddy. Teeeveeee." Tommy's tongue circled his lips as he rubbed his nose.

The *Justice League* came on, the episode beginning with Hawkgirl, a superhero who communicates with birds, locked in a vault deep inside the core of a distant planet.

"Daddy. Girl." The words dropped from his mouth, one at a time. His ability to express himself was so difficult, it took such effort.

"Yes, Hawkgirl. She's in trouble," I said. "For sure."

Tommy sat there, riveted. Did he empathize with Hawkgirl's lonely predicament, locked up as she was in her own faraway world?

"Hey, Tommy. What do you think's going to happen?" I asked when the show went to a commercial. Max, who I'd let back inside, limped over and curled up on the floor next to us, flicking his tail, his dark, shiny eyes rooted on mine for a long moment. "Can you tell Daddy? What do you think's going to happen to Hawkgirl? Is someone going to save her? Huh?"

Tommy gobbled some cheese and crackers, then once again, fidgeted and flew off into Tommy-space. His silent language echoed and boomed like a bass drum. Then he opened his mouth wide.

"Oooouu. Ooouuu, eeeee, grrrrrraaahhh . . ."

His tongue appeared, doing the infamous around-the-world lick of his lips. "They . . . they . . . be . . ."

"Yes?" I clutched my glass.

But the words that lingered on the tip of his tongue and on the edge of his mind somehow refused to appear.

Tommy used the palm of his hand to hit himself on his forehead. My chest heaved.

"Don't do that, son. That's not good for you. You know that." I spoke as gently as I could.

"No, Daddy. No . . ." Then it was as if he pushed one single word out of his mouth and birthed it: "Saaaaay."

"What?" I leaned forward.

"No . . . saaaaay . . ." He looked stricken and clasped his hands together as he fell into an even deeper silence. His tight grimace suggested to me he truly wanted to tell me something, but found himself unable to express himself. When a tear welled up in his eye, I was stunned. My hand went to my throat as I sat up straight, then set my drink down on the coffee table. Tommy wiped the tear away and my heart lurched in my chest. I'd *never* seen him cry before.

"It's okay, Tom-Tom." I sighed, feeling his pain, so close to him. "It's okay. I know words are hard for you."

"No." Tommy sucked a hand. "No, me . . . saaaaaay." He hugged Radar. He was confiding in me, telling me something as best he could.

"You'll get the hang of it." I swallowed. "I swear you will, okay? I understand."

The truth was, despite all the research I'd done on autism, despite all the therapies and counseling we'd been through, I didn't understand a thing. I wiped my hands on my pants and felt a weight in my heart as large and as ponderous as the moon.

When another commercial began, I changed the channel and suddenly, there I was on TV, my voice anyway. I had to laugh as I took a sip of my drink. I was telling the people of San Diego and surrounding areas about a furniture company's amazingly spectacular tent sale.

"This week only, friends. Prices starting from just five-ninety-nine. If you want the best deal in town on a comfortable sectional . . ."

It wasn't my best work, but I didn't sound half bad. Thirty seconds of fame. Too bad the jobs had mostly dried up. I used to go into the studio, lay down my track in front of the mic with headphones on, and then rush to the next job, flushed with a good income. I even had a few national accounts. But ever since the divorce and my subsequent year-long depression, which knocked me out of the VO scene—I mean, how can you work when you can hardly get out of bed?—I now sat around waiting for the phone to ring. My networking capabilities had really suffered.

"Hey, Tom-Tom, that was Daddy on TV." I touched his arm. "Cool, huh?"

But Tommy only gave me one quick glance, and then started to rock himself.

Leaving him alone, I got out my laptop and Googled chimps and autism. I just had to see if there was any kind of documented relationship. To my surprise, there wasn't a thing on the subject. Totally new territory. No relationship at all as far as Google could tell me. I was surprised. I thought there'd be at least something of interest. I would have to look more later on.

Another change of channels landed us on *Animal Planet*. *Strangely enough, a* group of chimpanzees living in the wilds of Africa filled the screen.

"Wow! Look at that, Tom-Tom. Chimps!" I said.

I sat up straight and watched the action as Tommy clapped his hands and nodded, then pointed at the TV. Once again, in the presence of chimps, he seemed to show a burst of excitement. Max had lifted his head and was staring at the screen as well, taking it in. The dog watched TV all the time.

"Chimpies!" he said without his monotone, a voice filled with enthusiasm. "TV, Daddy!"

"Yes, there they are! They're your friends. Right?" I pointed at the TV and nodded, smiling.

These chimps were using tools to catch ants. They worked as a team, helping each other as they employed long sticks to siphon ants out of the ground. Once again, I was witness to how humanlike they were, so fascinatingly similar to us, yet so curiously different. When the camera zoomed in for a close-up, the eyes of the chimps gleamed with a wily intelligence. They were so active, like ADHD kids before they took their Ritalin. One chimp raised an arm high in the air as if he were waving at the cameraman, just holding it up like that, a chimp hello-wave that wouldn't stop. Hello. Hello. Hello. And hello! A real comedian, that one.

Something shivered through my spine as Tommy scrambled off the couch and inched closer toward the TV until he was no more than a foot away, standing there, mesmerized.

"Chimpies!" He clapped his hands. "They . . . chimpies!"

"You like them, don't you?" I said.

Tommy nodded vigorously, his eyes on fire as he turned to me. "Yes, Daddy! Like!"

Max, who was still watching the TV screen himself, barked as if he was telling us he liked them too.

"Well, I think they like you." My body tingled and my mouth grew dry. While Tommy continued watching, I stepped outside with Max on my heels and phoned Cheryl again. I just had to tell her what I'd seen. Our trip to the zoo today could be a life-changing event. She needed to know. But my call went to voicemail once again. I could only leave another message.

"Cheryl, will you please call me? I have to tell you about what I saw today at the zoo. You won't believe it."

THAT NIGHT, AFTER I bathed him, I handed Tommy first his 5 mg of melatonin, which he downed with a glass of water, then his small dose of Wellbutrin. We stood next to each other in his bathroom. He was dressed in his Care Bear pjs and looked particularly handsome, all clean and fresh.

"Geen," Tommy said. Before swallowing it, he inspected the Wellbutrin tablet, studying it like a scientist. The pill had a perfect line down the middle and a "W" engraved in the marbled surface. "Tiny geen."

"Yes, sir. Green. Just for you. You like green." I smiled.

"Cooooo geeen." He finally swallowed it with water.

Tommy was sensitive to colors, even shades of colors, light green, royal blue, pinks, and reds. That was why I'd wondered if the color of the token in the parking lot at the zoo would have made a difference to him. We were working on a reading book that assigned colors to letters of the alphabet, hoping to improve his phonetics. We hadn't made any breakthroughs yet, but it was holding his interest and showed promise.

I'd painted his bedroom in the colors of his choice, red and bright yellow—gaudy as hell. He seemed to enjoy the process and I didn't want to stymie it. How hard it must be for him, I thought, unable to filter out the world the way normal children did. If colors helped him somehow organize his reality, who was I to stand in his way?

I took a big breath and thought about what was coming next. Maybe I should just let it go for tonight, I thought. But I just couldn't do it. Besides, I had to be as good a parent as Cheryl, who I considered the master parent, and I knew she wouldn't avoid the process, difficult as it was.

"And now it's time to brush, Tommy." I pulled out his purple Cartoon Network toothbrush and dabbed the bristles with white toothpaste. "You get *two* tokens if you brush without a fuss tonight." I grinned at him big time.

"No brush!" Tommy stared at himself in the mirror and pulled a defiant face, his nose and jaw twisted in rebelliousness as he pinched his mouth shut. He shook his head right and left.

"Come on, Tommy, brush your teeth, old sonny boy, you can do it." I mimicked Larry the Lobster, and then switched to Clarence, that pudgy CN star, whose vocal range seemed to oddly dwell somewhere between a man's and boy's: "Your teeth need to be brushed young man. Do you understand what I say?"

Tommy's yellowed teeth reflected the fact that he simply refused to brush. The sensory overload of brushing was too much for him. Cheryl and I had tried everything, from cute puppet shows about how fun it is to brush teeth to emotional arm-twisting of the most severe kind. We had no idea how many cavities he had.

"No brush!" Tommy pressed his lips close. I wielded the toothbrush around in the air, brandishing it. It was man against boy in a battle to the death. He shook his head and stubbornly closed his eyes. He grunted, keeping his lips pinched together. "Mmmmmm . . ."

"Come on, Tommy. Open up for Daddy."

"Nooooo," he said, through his clenched mouth.

But I pulled down on his lower jaw just enough to get the toothbrush to slide in and make a few rounds over his teeth. He bit down on the toothbrush and it wouldn't budge. The damn thing was locked in place.

"Come on, Tom-Tom. Just let me have one good brush. Okay?"

White toothpaste was all over his lips now, but very little had gotten on his teeth.

"Mmmmm." He groaned, refusing to cooperate.

"Please?"

I made one more attempt at getting the toothbrush on his teeth and was mildly successful before he bit down on it again. I yanked on the toothbrush, but he wouldn't let go of it. Max came up to watch. He barked and huffed, looking at me and Tommy, then back at me again, standing outside the bathroom. I couldn't tell whose side he was on. He barked louder.

"Hush, Max."

The hard work broke me. Enough was enough. I stared at myself in the mirror, and the dad looking back at me held a sorrowful expression. Another failed attempt.

My shoulders sagged. "Okay. You win."

Tommy made a motorboat sound as he raced out of the bathroom and headed straight for his bedroom. His usual tactic was to jump into his bed and hide under the covers, waiting for me to come in to the bedroom and tell him goodnight.

So much for his teeth. But I had hope: On Monday morning, we had an appointment for Tommy with Dr. Rahmed Patel, a dentist who specialized in children with autism. I was sure Tommy would be totally uncooperative and pitch a fit when the doctor tried to look inside his mouth. But it needed to be done. I was looking forward to the visit and also dreading it. We'd been put on a three-month waiting list and were lucky to get the appointment.

With Tommy in bed, I stood at the doorway just outside his room. He started using his first finger to scrawl around in the air, as if he were make-believe writing or drawing. I'd never seen him do anything like that before.

I just stood there and watched, and he hummed to himself pleasantly as he continued air-writing.

When I came in, he dropped his hand to his side.

"What are you doing, Tom-Tom?" I stood over his bed and looked down at him.

"Draw, Daddy. Picture."

"Really. Of what?"

"Chimpie." Tommy yawned. He showed no interest in drawing, but he did like to color. I would have to get a book of animals that he could color in.

"Well, we'll get back to those chimps as soon as we can." I leaned down toward him. "Kiss?"

He hesitated, then nodded shyly, and I leaned over a bit more and pecked his forehead. His shampooed hair smelled like flowers. The nightlight's soft glow threw shadows on the wall as Tommy turned his head toward me, curved his lips upward, and held them like that: fixed, rigid, exposing his teeth. It was as if he'd read about how humans smiled or studied diagrams and was doing his best to imitate the process.

"Hair, Daddy." He spoke softly and put a hand to his hair and scratched. One word: "Hair."

I smacked my forehead with the palm of my hand. "Oops. I forgot. Of course. Just a sec." I went to the bathroom and returned with the special black comb I'd bought for him. The words *Tommy Crutcher* were embossed on it in gold lettering. Ever since his mother and I had split, Tommy had me comb his hair before bed. He wouldn't go to sleep until I did it. I loved running the comb through his silky honey-wheat hair, one of the few times he allowed me to touch him.

"How's that? Okay?" I spoke gently.

"Good." Tommy yawned. "Goooood."

I set the comb down on his bedside table, then rested my cheek against his and felt the sweet warmth of his breath on my skin.

"Good night," I whispered, standing at the door, filled with a deep and abiding affection for this flawed being, this work in progress. I felt such strong feelings for this son of mine, my heart melted from the warmth inside my chest. "I love you, Tom-Tom. Do you know that? I love you so much."

"Daddy," was all Tommy said in his monotonic way. Another unit of a word, shaped and molded like the others: "Daddeee . . ."

THE MAIN REASON FOR our marital breakup: Tommy's autism turned Cheryl away from me. That was my explanation, anyway, though Cheryl would probably offer her own version of our not so glorious story. She became obsessed with bending our son back to normalcy, and if I didn't agree with her methods, then she didn't want any part of me either. But it was plain to me that you couldn't bend someone back into a shape that never existed in the first place. We even disagreed on how we should dress him. Cheryl wanted him outfitted like a catalogue model. I was happy when he chose his own clothes, even if they didn't match.

As I went to my bar and poured myself another vodka with a touch of OJ, I let my mind wander, going back in time, and there it was, facing me once again: that morning, the day when we started unraveling as a couple. Yes, I could pinpoint the time. Thinking about it, my head started to spin. I felt a quiver in my bones.

"I want to take him to another psychologist in San Francisco next week," Cheryl had said over breakfast. "What do you say?" She ran a hand through her uncombed auburn hair, unable to hide the circles under her eyes. Four-year-old Tommy sat in the corner of the kitchen, playing with a deck of cards on the floor, totally lost in his own world. "Her name's Susan Adler," Cheryl went on, glancing at Tommy, "and she's got a technique called the Lovaas method."

I remembered how light slanted in through the windows, streaking across our son's face, as Tommy scattered the cards around and then crumpled them up. You could call it playing. He hadn't said a word in weeks and his eyes were always averted, troubled, which broke my heart; our hearts.

"I don't know," I said. A filled-to-the-brim coffee cup sat in front of me, untouched. "He's seen so many therapists already. Maybe we should just give him a bit of a break for a while and . . ."

"A break? A break from what? I swear, Chris." She'd lost weight since dealing with Tommy's autism, her face a palette, shades of pale. "Sometimes you just don't get it. Actually, I don't think you ever get . . ."

Cheryl couldn't continue. My throat clenched as she broke down and sobbed, covering her face with her hands, her shoulders shaking. I reached for her and tried to embrace her, but she moved away. "I'm at a dead end here. We're at a dead end, and I don't know what else to do. Do you? Do you?"

Her plea for help frightened me.

We'd both had too many nights recently, staying up far too late getting Tommy to sleep, trying to train him and seeing progress, and then watching that progress slip away. Our world was unraveling and we had no idea how to stop it.

"Do you have any answers?" She wiped away her tears, swallowed, tried to gain control.

"All we can do is keep trying, I guess. But maybe, if we just accept him as who he is, and just encourage him toward normalcy, I don't know . . ." I looked away. *Clouds of confusion billowed in my coffee cup.*

"Encourage him? I can't just encourage him. I can't do just that. I don't know about you, but I need to do everything I can. I feel like we should take him everywhere, to as many therapists as possible. It's just too much. I'm so at a loss. There's nowhere to really turn, no one who can . . ." She sobbed and broke down again, tears streaking down her cheeks, and for a long moment, she was unable to speak—just like Tommy. Then she looked at me, red-faced, a well of pain deep inside her eyes. Tommy droned along as she said, *"I just want to hold him. I just want to see him smile and hear him say a few words. Is that too much to ask?"*

Just hearing the desperation in her voice, my heart broke like a dam, a river of pain flowing everywhere.

The ringing of my cell startled me and I blinked as the memories faded away, the raw emotions of our problems parenting Tommy still lingering.

Shadows flickered on the walls and I turned on a lamp. I hated shadows of all kinds, real and imagined.

The caller ID read "Marty Ackerman."

"Marty! How you doing?" Marty was a colleague of mine in the voice-over biz. I tried to sound bright and bubbly, but I suddenly needed air. I opened a window in the kitchen, then returned to the den. I blinked.

"Hey," Marty said. I took a deep breath and realized that someone was cooking steaks on a grill nearby, the delicious smell wafting my way. "I've got a job for you if you're interested. It's a spur of the moment thing, but—"

"A job? Are you kidding? Of course!"

Marty had helped me land commercials for a jeweler and a pizza chain when I was still on top of my game. He worked for a large ad agency in L.A., San Diego's more exciting and edgy sister.

"There's this spot for a furniture company, and our voice guy came down with bronchitis at the last minute. The thing is, we're wondering if you could come in tomorrow and help us out. You think that's a possibility? They want it finished ASAP. It's scheduled to run Monday morning, 8 a.m. We have studio time and everything."

I spoke slowly. "Does it have to be tomorrow?" I gripped the phone.

His reply was quick and firm. "Afraid so. Can you do it?"

"What are they paying?" I could still smell the steak, but I had no appetite at all.

"The usual rates. Four seventy-two for a two-hour booking with residuals. They might even kick in an extra hundred."

It was money, not a lot, but I needed anything I could get. I had to keep Tommy tomorrow though.

"Let me see what I can do, Marty. I have my son with me this weekend. I'll have to arrange something if I can."

Hanging up, I weighed my options. Cheryl, an interior designer, was in Santa Barbara with a client, so I quickly deleted her from the list. She wouldn't be back until late Sunday. That left her mother, a slight woman with palsy in her right hand, but she and Cheryl's father were out of town too. Typically, my Plan B was to use a babysitting service, but when I called them, I found out they were all backed up because of unusually high demand. I realized I had no other choice but to turn to the one man who practically invented me—my dad.

The only problem was, at eighty-two, my father was barely able to handle Tommy alone anymore. He'd kept Tommy for me before when I was in a pinch. But now with his occasional dizziness and his high blood pressure, would it be possible?

I was my father's keeper, so to speak. His caretaker. I was responsible for his medicines, taking him to the doctor when necessary, checking on him as much as possible, making sure he was eating enough, the list went on and on. He depended on me a lot. And now, I was depending on him.

"Hi, Dad," I said when he came on the line. "How's it going?"

"What the hell do *you* want?" His rough voice sandpapered my eardrum.

Treat me like a telemarketer, why don't you? "How you doing?"

"Oh, cut the crap. You know exactly how I'm doing. How's any old fart my age gonna be doing?"

I held the phone away from my ear and picked up a paperweight. I felt either like slamming it hard against the table or throwing it through a window.

"Well, that's good. Anyhoo, are you going to need a ride anywhere soon? How's your food supply? Your doctor's appointment's not till next week. But still, just wondering if there's anything you need. How's your back?"

"Stiff as always. Eddie Johnson's coming over to visit for a while tomorrow, the old bag."

"Okay, fine." Dad refused an in-home aide for even one day a week and a move from his house into assisted living was, in his eyes, unthinkable.

"Me in assisted living?" he would say. "Are you serious? I'm not gonna live around all those old people."

Right, Dad.

"So, I was wondering . . ." I began.

When I'd finished explaining my situation, my dad, being the grand old taskmaster that he was, didn't even hesitate. "Look. Last time I kept Tommy my blood pressure went up. I wasn't even sure I could control him. I can't risk it. You're going to have to figure out something else."

"Okay. I understand." My voice broke. "I don't want to pressure you." Before I could say anything else, the phone went dead.

I wracked my brain, but couldn't think of another person. In desperation, I tried Sam Axelrod, a friend and colleague of mine, but got no answer. Nothing. The silence in my condo wrapped around me like a smothering blanket, then it was as if the silence turned into hands and tightened its pressure around my throat. A job had fallen right in my lap and I was going to lose it. Could I take Tommy? The chances of him pitching a fit while I was trying to work were pretty good. No, I couldn't risk it. I texted Marty back: *Sorry.*

He responded quickly: Okay, pal. Thanks anyway.

And that was that. It was a wrap. One more lost opportunity because of . . . what? Fate? Bad luck? A toss of the coin? Why did I always seem to land on tails?

Max was scratching himself in the den and the jangle of his dog collar resounded through the room. I thought about that tantrum again and felt bad. I should have given him his damn ear plugs. Why wasn't I on the ball? No way would I tell Cheryl about our little incident.

When a car horn honked outside, I jumped.

Then I heard: "Daddy."

Tommy stood at the top of the stairs, hugging himself, an anxious look on his face. "Daddeee . . . Daddeee."

"Yes, son?" I called.

"I scare." He crumpled up his chin, his hair still nicely combed, Radar nestled against him under his arm.

"Did you have a nightmare?" I frowned.

"Scare."

"There's nothing to be scared about, Tom-Tom," I lied.

I went upstairs and led Tommy back to bed, fluffing the pillow for him as he slid under the covers. I tucked him in.

"It's all right. Daddy's here." I gave him a warm smile, reassuring him as much as I could.

"Daddy . . . you . . ." Tommy's brick-words seemed heavier than ever with a kind of inherent meaning in them that only he could understand. "Daddy . . . you . . ."

"Right. Daddy's here." I touched his forehead, smoothed it. Amazingly, he let me.

"Stay." Tommy's eyes melted into mine.

"Yes, I'll stay. Of course." I fluffed up his pillow again, then brought over a wooden desk chair that we kept in the corner of the room for just such a purpose. "Night chair," Tommy called it. I sat next to him as he turned on his side, the chair creaking as I shifted in my seat. The quiet of the room, the soft glow of the nightlight, the few children's books scattered on the floor. It felt so intimately familiar, as if I'd lived in this room for lifetimes as my son's guardian angel.

His emotional nightlight.

"Daddy," he said, snuggling deeper under the covers. "Daddeeeee . . ."

"I'm here, Tom-Tom. I'm here. You know I'll always be here for you."

This much was true.

When his breathing finally evened out, I trudged downstairs and did the only thing I could possibly do: I opened up my computer and started searching for anywhere in or near San Diego where I could possibly get my son hooked up with some chimps. One-on-one personal time would be best.

Chapter 3

Hope and all its beautiful ramifications arose in the form of the Weller Institute, a primatological research center located near Live Oak Springs, about an hour and a half from San Diego. Tommy, Cheryl, and I headed there for an exploratory visit with the chimps, which was set for 10:00 a.m., March 30th, Saturday, just two weeks after our encounter at the zoo.

I'd talked to Dr. Rachel Simmons, one of the directors, and emailed her a video of Tommy interacting with the chimps. Dr. Simmons proved to be interested and brought up the subject of Tommy meeting with their research primates to their board. A week later, she'd called me and said we'd been granted an hour's visiting time under careful supervision. I was ecstatic.

I'd made the video on my phone when I took Tommy back to the zoo on Sunday, the very next day after our initial visit. I carefully recorded the same kinds of uncanny interactions both with Wispy Hair and Big Guy, the mimicking, the gestures.

At one point during his visit with the chimps, Tommy placed his hand on the glass barrier at the exhibit, matching it with a chimp's hand, and it suddenly reminded me of a sad scene from a prison movie: The inmate presses his hand against the window after talking to his loved one, and then the loved one puts her hand on the window too, both of them trying to connect through a barrier. I couldn't help but ponder the similarity: Tommy and the chimp were each locked up in their own ways.

Now as we drove out past San Diego, the landscape giving way to more widely spaced houses, fields, farms, and reams of giant windmills that would have given Don Quixote a fit, I sat in the passenger seat next to Cheryl, anxiously awaiting the visit. We were in her blue Ford, Tommy in the back with his stuffed animals and a few books, which we hoped might entertain him. Mister Backpack was safely ensconced on the other back seat, next to Tommy.

Traveling on the interstate, we soon passed an entrance to the Cleveland National Forest, which cut deep into the horizon with its imposing tall pines and oaks, its chaparral, all of it melding together like liquid landscape in some impressionistic painting. It was beautiful.

Tommy continued playing with Radar and Monkey, his new pet, as Cheryl continued driving along. He'd gotten Monkey from the dentist, where, during his uncooperative visit, Tommy refused to open his mouth until we threatened him with the constraints of a papoose board. Fortunately, we didn't have to use the restraining device. We'd discovered six cavities. The dentist, Dr. Patel, who had a gentle way with Tommy, much appreciated, told me later he had his own autistic son, a teenager, whose picture he showed me. I saw that same awkward smile on his face that I saw on Tommy's, that far-away look. Dr. Patel said his son gave him a window into autism by telling him that he either hears, or sees, but he can't do both, and that sometimes, he felt as if he didn't even have a body, that he was four years old before he even knew he had a body. Sad, indeed.

Tommy seemed to favor Monkey more, snuggling him close, and letting Radar lay at his side. Every so often he gave us his usual murmuring and humming sounds that resonated with the car's engine.

"We're off to see the chimps," I said with a smile. "Who would have ever thunk it?"

"Indeed," Cheryl said, nodding at me. "I know."

Getting Cheryl to agree to visiting Weller hadn't been hard at all. I was standing at her front door when I showed her my video of Tommy and the chimps, the strange and crazy interactions. She was impressed. "Wow! Look at that! He does seem engaged, that's for sure. If this helps Tommy, I'm up for anything. Zebras. Giraffes. Elephants. Whatever it takes."

"Great. I'll make the arrangements." I gave her a wide smile while inside, I flushed with pleasure.

"You know," she said thoughtfully, "we so often do things my way, all the therapies I mean, so let's try it your way for once. It should be interesting." Her conciliatory tone made me beam inside and out.

Now as we cruised down the interstate, Cheryl told me how she was taking her mother to receive treatment for her palsy, how her dad was in Brazil right now working on designing a new bridge, that a plumber had come to her house just yesterday because a pipe had burst in one of the bathrooms. I told her about my father and how sour he still seemed, and we made a joke about how he should work as the anti-greeter at Wal-Mart. "Get the hell outta here," he'd probably say. "Just go home! All sales are canceled!" It felt so good to hear her laughter.

"How you doing back there, Tom-Tom?" Cheryl asked a minute later, looking at Tommy through the rearview mirror and giving him a bright smile.

"Good. Radar good. Monk good."

"We had fun last night, didn't we?" Cheryl said. The tone of her voice was cheery. "That pizza was great. And you did such a good job on the clown game."

Tommy didn't reply.

We lapsed into road silence as the music played from Cheryl's radio: Sirius XM. Tom Petty. I let out a sigh that filled the car like smoke.

"So, how's work coming, Cheryl?" I asked.

She glanced at me. "Good."

I played with the vent on my side, opening it and closing it several times. Time crawled by. Cheryl looked over at me for a moment, and once again started tapping her fingers to the music.

"Come on, Cher," I said finally. "There's got to be something else we can talk about."

She turned down the radio and gave me a forgiving smile. "Well, actually, I just got this crazy new job if you want to hear about it," she said. "It's really nuts."

"Do tell."

She took a breath, then dove in. "So, these new clients, two guys in their forties, wanted original Trompe L'oeil art pieces all over their house, in their bathrooms, foyer, kitchen, everywhere. You know, art that looks like the real thing, like a baseball sitting in a baseball glove, and you think it really *is* a baseball sitting in a baseball glove, but it's really nothing but clay?"

"Yes. I know. Sure."

"Well, I had to contact all these artists all over the country for samples and they finally settled on this one artist named John Ellison from Sedona. Then I had to make sure all the décor matched each piece of art in every room. They were so particular. I was calling places all over the world. The good thing was they didn't care about the cost. They're techno-wizards, gazillionaires, I think—a gay couple from San Francisco."

"Cool," I said, though the issues of gazillionaires and their designer bathroom needs seemed like life on a far-removed solar system.

"I was shocked. In a good way, of course." She smiled. "It was a bonanza of a deal."

"You're the best at what you do, Cher. Everybody knows it."

"Thanks, Chris. I appreciate your vote of confidence." She looked sideways and our eyes met for just an instant, but it was long enough for me to see the old Cheryl, the woman who had fallen in love with me. I felt a little thud in my heart and the next thing I knew, I was dissolving back in time:

Our first trip together: Cheryl's flowery fragrance wasn't just intoxicating, it was hypnotic. We were flying from San Diego to Vegas for a last-minute weekend get-away before our wedding in the fall. I couldn't wait. This was our pre-honeymoon, so to speak, a little bit of jumping the emotional gun. Why not?

As we descended for the landing, the plane cruised over an explosion of neon lights below, reds, blues, yellows, flashing, too much to take in against the nighttime sky. In Vegas, enough is never enough. The Cabernet I was drinking seemed to have expanded my consciousness. I was high, figuratively, literally. Our hands were wrapped together, she had such soft hands, smooth, dexterous fingers, red nails, knowledgeable hands that knew how to touch me, how to reach me.

The MGM Grand, in all its bedazzlement, appeared below. "I love you," I said. The words just bubbling up and out of me.

"I love you too."

I couldn't believe how happy I was, hearing those words from her. They were like magical incantations. It was as if I was inhaling the white line of happiness like a drug, snorting it up. I trembled with the expectation of what was surely to come, checking into the hotel—We'd gone all out and bought an expensive suite at the Wynn—walking into a gorgeous, finely appointed room, admiring the night's electric neon view as we parted the curtains, the luxurious bed on which we'd come together. Vegas itself was our counterpart in this conspiracy, smiling at us, our witness to the wondrous secrets we shared behind closed doors.

"Do you think we'll have children one day?" she'd asked plaintively, turning from looking out the window and its light-scape of a view to gazing into my eyes. The question came out of nowhere and I was taken aback.

"I don't see why not. Sure," I said. "I'd love to be a father. We've already talked about that, remember?"

"She'll be a lovely child." She gave me a winsome look.

"She?" I asked. My eyes wandered over her cheekbones, the fine line of her straight nose, the beautiful curve of her mouth.

"Or he," she said. "It won't matter, will it?"

"No. Of course not." I laughed. "Just as long as it's healthy." We touched our plastic cups together and then toasted to the thought of what we knew was our rightful future: healthy children, perfect little tykes. I figured two of them, for sure, maybe even three, who knew? Then we shared a kiss that was everything I'd ever dreamed.

Time is a circle. I am, was, will always be, lost inside the circular motion of time.

Fast forward: Tommy was crying all night long. He'd thrown shit on the walls, running naked around the house, barely three years old, and he fell and cut his head on the sink in his bathroom. We needed to rush him to the emergency room, but Cheryl was yelling at me because she thought I was moving too slow, and I was yelling at her because, well, I was just yelling. She couldn't find her car keys, my car was in the shop, and we nearly came to blows as our son wailed on and on . . .

"So, how's the voice-over business these days?" Cheryl asked all of a sudden, breaking through my reverie, my circular, emotional chronology in which time loses all sense of forward-moving linearity. "Speaking of gazillionaires."

"What?" I cocked my head toward her. I slammed into the present as if my emotional time machine had crashed back to earth. My ears felt plugged.

"Just kidding. Seriously, how're things going with your VO career?" She gave me a glance, then looked straight ahead as she drove.

"Oh. Not bad." I ran a hand through my hair while my stomach suddenly turned to jelly. "Could be better, though." I was on the verge of having to find some other kind of drudgery to pay the bills, Uber driving being one such possibility. I was putting off this next step for as long as possible.

She waved a hand in the air. "I'm sure it's fine."

Buzzards swooped over a dead animal in the road. The wide, endless sky above formed a stark counterpoint to how I felt—small and cramped inside the car.

"Birds," Tommy said.

"Yes," I said. "Big birds. So black too. They're called buzzards."

"Buzzzzz," Tommy said. "Buzzzzz."

"So, are you landing many jobs these days?" she asked.

She was pressing the issue. But I didn't mind her snooping. "You know how it is. Busy, then slow, it's up and down. I'm also considering going back to work for Focus."

"Really." She'd been driving with her right hand on the steering wheel, but now she put both hands on the wheel.

"Yep. I talked to Sam Axelrod." Sam was a colleague at Focus Media, where I used to work as well. We'd spoken a few days ago. "Actually, Sam says he might be able to get me back on board. I've been thinking about finding something steadier. You know?" I started tapping my right foot.

"That would be perfect. Hey, listen . . . " She paused for a moment and my ears pricked up. Someone once told me that it's not the words we say that really count, but the silences between the words. That's what we should really listen to. When it came to Cheryl, I had learned to listen to those silences very closely.

"Yes?" I said.

Another long pause, then: "See, there's this new issue I wanted to talk to you about. And I think now's a good time to bring it up." The tone of her voice changed, thicker, more serious.

"Which is?" I asked.

Cheryl glanced at Tommy in her rearview. I turned and inspected him too. He had dropped Radar and Monkey and now looked lost in his own world, his eyes, dark and distant as he put his red and scraped knuckles in his mouth.

"So, there's this place called the Acorn School I've come across," she said. She turned down the radio.

"Okay," I said. "And?"

"It's strictly for children on the spectrum, and they have all this impressive data. It's in Houston. It's expensive, but," the words came out in a rush, "I really feel it might be worth it."

"For Tommy? Houston?" I didn't quite get it.

"In fact, I'm thinking about flying out and taking a look. I checked out their website. They seem to really have their act together. Behavioral therapy, biofeedback training, and something called 'static exercise.' The reviews all say it's extremely effective." She swallowed, turned to me, and gave me a determined Cheryl look, one I knew too well. When it came to finding help for Tommy, she was one-hundred percent all in. As devoted a mother as there ever was. She spoke seriously. "Look, Chris. If this school's as good as they say it is, I want us to consider sending Tommy there."

I said nothing for a moment, just taking it all in. I let my mind absorb the words, then felt them drop into my heart. "You mean we'd all just pick up and move? To Houston? What about your interior design business?"

She was part owner of the business, but brought in probably eighty percent of the sales.

"Oh," she flicked a hand, "I'd sell my half and start over. It wouldn't be a big issue." She took a breath, then put a hand in the air, palm forward, as if she were giving a pledge. "If it would help Tommy, I'd do it. Absolutely."

"I mean . . . Of course," I said slowly. This *was* news. I really didn't know what to think. Did people move halfway across the country with their ex-spouses? Or was she trying to get rid of me? My stomach suddenly knotted up. "It sounds kind of drastic." I forced calm into my voice while my hands turned wet. "You think it would really be better than Hillwood?"

"Hillwood, right." Cheryl spoke derisively. "You mean the school where they wouldn't even tell us he was having a problem with his classmate? That school where he got in a fight? Where he's hardly making any progress?"

Slow progress was the reality. This was true enough. And yes, an incident had occurred between Tommy and another boy with Asperger's. On the playground, William, a smallish kid who had an obsession with turtles was trying to talk to Tommy and play with him, but Tommy'd wanted to be left alone. Tommy pushed William down and a fight broke out between them. Tommy started it. I'd witnessed it while helping the teacher for the afternoon. It was miserable. I'd rushed to them along with the teacher and pulled the boys apart. William had landed a blow to Tommy's head. Tommy had been suspended for the day.

Once Cheryl had learned about the fight, she'd gotten all over the principal and the teacher through vitriolic emails, asking why she hadn't been informed regarding "our son's and that boy's relationship." Of course, she'd added a carefully worded apology as well. The principal had written back promising to do a better job keeping William and Tommy apart.

But could this Acorn School in Texas possibly offer something that much better?

We passed a VW bus, one of those sixties looking things. Sure enough, a long-haired, hippie-looking guy was driving. Probably listening to something like the Grateful Dead. Or Jimi Hendrix. I had to smile. Who said time always moved forward in a linear fashion?

"I'm definitely flying out there," Cheryl said. "Do you want to come with me?"

"Is it a boarding school of some sort?" I still didn't know if she was totally serious about this, or just pondering it, or what? I stared at her profile, her straight nose, high cheekbones, colored with a touch of makeup. It was all a mask. I had no idea what she was thinking.

"No. The children just attend during the day, and then go home. But while they're there, it's totally rigorous." She kept her eyes on the road.

"Look. If this school's worth it, anything for Tom-Tom," I said, ponying up. "I'd never stand in the way of him getting a better education. Never."

"Good." She turned my way and gave me a quick encouraging smile. "So, you'll check it out?"

"Sure. Tommy's what it's all about it. Whatever it takes."

"Takes," Tommy repeated from the backseat. "Tom-Tom. Ouuuu . . . uuuuuu . . . There?" he said. "There?"

"No, not yet," Cheryl said, her voice sweet. "How about reading your book?"

Tommy grabbed the "See-And-Say" book lying next to him and started to look through it.

"Mom. Go. Home. See. Dad. Play. Swing." He spoke the words, one at a time, slowly, carefully, his brow furrowed as he worked hard to decipher the letters.

"Good, Tommy," Cheryl said. "That's wonderful reading! Isn't that right, Chris?"

"The best!" I said, feeling a rush of joy inside.

"Yay, Mommy!" Tommy smiled and clapped his hands.

"You're such a good boy," Cheryl said. "A good, good boy. And you did such a fantastic job with the puzzles last night, especially the ABC one. And you were so nice at dinner, eating with a fork and everything. You should've seen him, Chris. He was really doing a great job!"

"Good boy," Tommy echoed. He clucked his tongue. "Good boy."

"He's such a cute thing," Cheryl said, tossing some hair off her shoulders and adjusting the AC.

"Are you kidding? He's amazing," I said, and then did my impression of Simon Cowell on *America's Got Talent*, launching into a snobby British accent. "This kid floors me. He's got the voice, the moves, the talent, he's going to go far. Comes from Liverpool, does he?"

Cheryl laughed. "Damn, Chris. That's good."

Tommy tried reading a few more words, then forgot about the book and withdrew into himself, sucking on his hands. We'd found it was better to let him go with the flow than to force him back into doing something he wasn't interested in.

Silence once again prevailed. It had a dimension to it, for sure, and it spoke too. Knowing Cheryl as well as I did, our silences were never empty, meaningless phrases. This one said all kinds of regretful things, talked far too clearly: how our marital relationship had spun off the tracks, the pain and the anger that had ensued. It was as if she was trying to tell me: *please, do not bring up our heartbreaking past.*

I couldn't read her mind, but I certainly could fathom her heart at times. No doubt about it.

Still, hanging out with your ex on a road trip is *not* something I would recommend to Yelp readers with anything more than a one-star review.

I played with the vent on the passenger side again. This breaking news about Houston . . . This was a major-league decision. I clasped my hands together. If she planned on moving out of state with Tommy. Wait a minute. She couldn't do that, could she?

What if I said no?

My phone rang. I peered at the number on the caller ID, and blinked: Damn if it wasn't Sam. This could be about Focus.

"Hey guy, guess what?" Sam said loudly in my ear, his voice full of energy and high-voltage excitement when I quickly answered.

"You're changing sexes?" I said.

"Nope."

"Well, I'm surprised. I thought sure you'd said—"

"Shut up and listen, will ya? This is important. Now look. The fact is I just landed you a frickin' Monday morning interview with Ed Ryerson himself. Are you up for it?" His excited voice, pulsating with energy, dug straight into me. I sat up in my seat.

"Really?" I said. "You mean he's giving me a shot?"

"Hell yeah!" Sam's voice grew louder, making sure I understood. "Be there at ten a.m. Sharp."

"Man. Thanks, Sam. I can't tell you how much—"

"Oh, hush." He laughed. "Just be there with bells on. And agree with everything he says. The word is he's very interested."

"Cool," Cheryl said when I ended the call and told her what was what. "That's great news."

"I know." I grinned, feeling a sense of satisfaction balloon inside me. This *was* good news.

Cheryl checked on Tommy in the rearview mirror. I turned around and saw that he'd fallen asleep. Sleep was rescue; sleep was perfection. "You'll take it, right?" she asked.

"We'll see," I said, assuming a nonchalant air, trying to conceal my desperation. "I need to go through the interview first. I have to see if it's a good fit, too."

"Oh, I'm sure you'll do fine," Cheryl said, speaking as if it was a done deal. "You're a real talent. Everybody knows that. You're the best." She smiled at me before returning her eyes to the road. "No one can do SpongeBob SquarePants like you."

Sweet words, indeed.

"And Larry the Lobster, don't forget him," I said, pointing out an extra talent.

"Of course." She winked at me.

Cheryl accelerated and the California desert rose before us, stark pines and scrubby bushes in the distance, lonely-looking and centuries-old across miles of flat bare land. Everything was so wide open here, so free. I let down my window and took a big gulp of clean, unpolluted air. God's country. Lots of room to run. My future life formed a nice fat vision in my mind: So, I was going to meet Ed Ryerson after all. The truth was, I couldn't wait. Job security. I could practically taste it. But what if Cheryl actually did take Tommy to Houston and I landed this job in San Diego? Tommy not being nearby, unable to see him on weekends? I couldn't tolerate it. Just the thought made me queasy.

"So, what's so special about this Weller place anyway?" Cheryl asked as we finally approached the entrance. Cheryl steered into the compound, passing the sign, no security guard, and maneuvered into the large parking lot in front.

"Weller? Are you kidding?" I spoke seriously, as if I were reading the news. "They're famous for educating a chimp who went on to Stanford and got his Ph.D. in molecular biology."

"Not funny, Chris," she said.

I pulled up their website on my cell and scrolled down. "The Weller Institute's been around since 1985," I read out loud. "They study, and I quote, 'the mechanisms underlying cooperation, reciprocity, inequity, and other decisions in nonhuman primates from an evolutionary perspective. Weller also investigates language growth and cognition in terms of nonhuman primate evolution by quantifying and exploring both evolutionary status and biological abilities in chimpanzees."

"I see."

"And here's a tidbit. They also use computer game experiments to better understand how chimps strategize relationships."

"Okay, Einstein. Enough."

"It's a mecca of cutting-edge science. It's considered to be one of the most advanced research centers in the world, according to the National Science Institute."

CHERYL PARKED IN VISITOR parking, and when we all got out of the car, the strident sounds of chimpanzees greeted us immediately. We were definitely in the right place. Did chimps have their own language? Were their varying shrieks and screeches meaningful? Tommy snapped to attention, and I grew nervous and excited simultaneously.

"Chimpies, Daddy!" Tommy said, and he jumped up and down like a kid on a pogo-stick. "Where? Where? Here?"

"Yes, Tom-Tom. They have all kinds of chimpies here. And you're going to meet a few."

"Me, me, go! Go! Now!" Tommy kicked at the ground. "Go! Go!" He gave me direct eye contact. "Want go!"

Cheryl checked her phone and sent a quick text.

Tommy made the sign for chimps, curling his fists at his sides, followed by the sign for "like," a hand touching his chest, then pulling away. I felt the beautiful pull of hope for Tommy and all its possibilities tugging within me.

"Chimp sign?" asked Cheryl, then looked at me with a raised eyebrow as she put her phone away in the small purse she was carrying. I edged Mister Backpack higher on my shoulder.

"That's it," I said.

"Like chimps," Cheryl said, smiling. "Good, Tommy." She nodded. "I see that. Very good."

Cheryl signed back, using the same gestures. I tingled inside, rushing with anticipation. I couldn't wait for her to see Tommy sign with the chimps in person.

As we stood in the parking lot with Mister Backpack slung over my shoulder, three large red brick structures were facing us, all connected by a concrete covered walkway. Clean, orderly, bougainvillea and shrubs were planted around the parking lot. A few cacti as well. We were at least fifteen miles off the interstate and the remoteness of the location gave everything a laboratory feel that made me think of sci-fi stories about chimp experimentation; kind of eerie in the middle of nowhere. Beyond the compound were stretches of more desert and chaparral and a scarce grouping of oaks and pine trees. The climate felt warmer and drier than in San Diego. Entering this new world, I drank it all in with a feeling of sudden trepidation and excitement combined.

"Chimpies." Tommy's eyes lit up like rescue flares. "Chimpies."

Cheryl applied lip gloss in a circular motion and then rubbed her top lip against her bottom one. Her lips turned wet and shiny. "Chimpanzees, here we come," she said, smiling at me.

"We're off to see the chimpies," I sang, mimicking the *Wizard of Oz* song. "If ever if ever a chimp there was."

We both laughed as a warm wind circled us.

"Oh, Chris," Cheryl said, looking around at the buildings. "I can't believe we're doing this. It's really kind of crazy. I mean getting Tommy mixed up with chimps? No one's going to believe this."

"Let's just keep an open mind, okay?" I said.

"Sure. I'm with you every step of the way."

"Really?" I asked, turning to her, trying to measure the depth of her faith in this mission I'd designed ever since the zoo visit.

She spoke sincerely, with resolution in her voice, as she nodded. "Yes, I am. I'm here, aren't I? I'm hoping this could somehow be helpful for Tommy. Anything for Tom-Tom."

It was a mantra we'd spoken more than once.

"Well, let's just see what happens," I said.

With Tommy trudging along by my side, we followed the concrete walkway and entered a spacious front office with two desks, computers, and two women staring intently at their computer monitors. Pictures of chimps in the wild hung on light-blue walls. Philodendrons stood in the corners, green and tall. Large windows allowed bright sunlight in. Tommy stayed as close to me as he could allow himself, about a foot away, biting his hands now. New places always disturbed him and his anxiety became my anxiety. He shook his head and drooled. We'd kept Radar and Monkey in the car to simplify things, but I was now wondering if that was a mistake. My throat constricted and my heart started to thump inside my chest.

"Hi," I said to a blue-eyed woman who was working at a desk near the door. "I'm Chris Crutcher, this is Cheryl Bridgewater, and we've come to see Dr. Rachel Simmons."

"Hi," Cheryl said. "And this is Tommy. We have an appointment?"

"Of course. Just a moment," she said with a welcoming smile, peering at us over bifocals, her eyes stopping at Tommy. "I'll text her and tell her you're here."

We stood around waiting for a few awkward minutes. Tommy grew disturbingly quiet. He scratched his head, then started fixating on the word, "Read."

"Read. Read. Read . . . reeeeeed."

Cheryl and I exchanged wary glances.

"Look at the pictures of the chimps on the wall, Tom-Tom," I said, pointing at them, trying to distract him.

"Read. Read. Read. Ouuuu . . . eee . . . F-Fiiiine . . . Fiiiine . . ."

Then he smacked himself.

"Tommy, no," Cheryl said. "That's not a good thing. You know that."

The exasperated look on her face plus Tommy's slap made my stomach squirm. What could I do?

A minute later, a nearly six-foot tall woman came in through the front door and Cheryl and I stared. Tommy continued making his odd noises. "Breeee . . . Uuuuu . . ." She looked like she could have played volleyball or basketball in college. Just a few lines around the corners of her mouth and eyes, but otherwise, a smooth complexion that said life had been good to her. She was wearing faded jeans and a white T-shirt with a Weller logo printed on it, two blue circles intersected with the face of a chimp underneath it.

"Hi. Welcome to the Weller Institute," she said. "I'm Doctor Rachel Simmons." With a heart-shaped face and cerulean-blue eyes, she formed the picture of an intelligent woman with attractive features; mid-to-late thirties. The bright, easygoing tone of her voice made me feel instantly welcome, even though nervous anticipation was running through me. After introducing myself and Cheryl to her, Dr. Simmons said, "So, this is the famous Tommy." Before we could stop her, she stooped and tried to grasp Tommy's hand, casually reaching for it and expecting a normal handshake as she would from any child. "Nice to meet you, Tommy." She beamed at him.

But Tommy jerked his hand away as if a rattler had attacked. He quickly shoved both hands into his mouth. "Ooouuuu . . ." He propelled around.

"Read. Read. Read. Ouuuu . . . Aaaaaeee . . ."

Dr. Simmons took a step back. "My," she said, looking at us. Her shocked expression quickly turned into a frown, her broad forehead wrinkling.

"Tommy, remember, I told you about Dr. Simmons." I felt my face color with embarrassment. I quickly glanced at Cheryl, who gave me a serious look. "She's the lady who knows all about chimpanzees. She wants to show you around. She's here to help us."

"It's okay, Tommy," Cheryl said. She spoke softly. "The nice lady just wants to meet you, that's all."

I gently removed his wet hand from his mouth as he looked down, shuffling his feet.

"Ouuuu . . . Mmmmmm . . ."

"He gets agitated in new places and with new people," Cheryl explained, her eyebrows knitted.

"We're sorry. We should have told you. He's sensitive about being touched. He actually doesn't even allow it," I added, shifting Mister Backpack around on my shoulder.

"It's all right." Dr. Simmons smiled, accepting our apology, then crouched like a baseball catcher, two feet from Tommy, giving him his distance.

"So, you like chimpanzees, Tommy?" she asked, giving Tommy another bright smile.

Tommy gave her his full blast of cold, chilling silence, hand back in mouth, squirming and twisting his body.

"Well, I like chimpanzees too," she went on. "Did you know chimps have hair all over their bodies except their palms and the bottom of their feet? What do you like most about them?"

"Chimpies," Tommy said all of a sudden, blurting out the word. He made the sign for chimp, that up-and-down hand gesture at his sides. "Chimpies. Chimpies."

"Oh, yes. We have chimpies—lots of them." She watched Tommy flick and rub his fingers together, then make the "like" sign, then, the sign for "play."

"So, he knows signs?" she asked, clearly impressed as she stood and faced us. Her slender hands formed the gestures for "knows signs?"

"Yes, he's studied them in school, he actually knows quite a few," I said.

"It takes away his frustration when he can't speak sometimes," Cheryl chimed in.

"Interesting." Dr. Simmons rubbed her chin as her eyes lingered over our son. "Well, the chimps you're about to meet know signs too. They're in the process of undergoing intensive training. This is part of our experimental protocol." She smiled. "He's quite adorable. You must be so proud."

"Thank you," I said. I was hoping we wouldn't be met with derision by snooty scientists and now I knew we weren't going to be. I was relieved.

"We're very proud of him," Cheryl said. She gave me a smile as she fingered the bracelet on her wrist. "He's the love of our lives." Cheryl drew within inches of Tommy, as close as he would allow without pitching a fit.

"All right, then," Dr. Simmons said. Her tone turned professional. She cleared her throat. "We'll be entering through the observation enclosure. The chimps are stationed in a play yard which is walled off by thick glass. I'll enter their space and then bring them close to the glass so that Tommy can interact with them. We'll see how Tommy takes to them, but we won't allow him to enter the play yard directly, not at first anyway. But he will be able to interact through the glass wall. We're giving him one hour to interact with the chimps."

"Should we keep our voices down?" Cheryl asked.

"That's not necessary, but certainly no shouting," Dr. Simmons said.

As we exited the office and followed her to an outdoor, brick courtyard, where metal tables and chairs were set out, surrounded by cacti in vases, Dr. Simmons stopped walking and turned to us. I felt a trickle of sweat bead down my chest. Chimp noise in the background intensified. Screeches and shrieks, followed by ear-grinding squawks. What if nothing happened? What if the two visits at the zoo had been nothing but flukes?

Tommy stood by Cheryl's side, though still maintaining his distance. Tommy mumbled to himself and hung his head. He kept covering and uncovering his ears and then shoved a finger up one nostril.

"Before we go further into the compound, I need to tell you that this visit is highly unusual," Dr. Simmons said. "Just to reiterate, Weller doesn't cater to the lay public. This is a research facility only. To be honest, I'm actually amazed that the board agreed to your visit. I just wanted to make it clear where we stand."

I nodded. "We're incredibly grateful you've allowed us the chance. This is extremely important for us." I gave her a smile, then turned to Cheryl. "Right, Cher?"

She nodded, hands on hips, looking around. "Absolutely."

"So, how many chimps do you have here at the facility?" I asked.

"There'll be four in the compound for your visit today," Dr. Simmons said. "Mikey, SeeSaw, Rose, and Obo. But we have twelve in total in our facility. The ones we chose for you to view are the most relaxed around humans. Well, one's quite reserved, but we thought we'd bring him out too, just to give him some exposure. The rest are domiciled in a different enclosure today."

"Chimpies," Tommy said and clapped. "Chimpies."

"Yes, Tom-Tom," I said. "Chimpies, here we come!"

Again, Tommy made the sign for chimp, then another sign I couldn't read. Tommy sneezed and snot hung from his nostrils. I took a tissue from Mr. Backpack and wiped his face.

"Noooo!" he protested, rearing his head back. "Noooo."

"We want to be clean for the chimps, don't we, Tom-Tom?" Cheryl said.

"Clean. Clean. Clean," Tommy said. He licked his lips.

I threw the tissue away in a nearby receptacle and the three of us followed Dr. Simmons out of the courtyard, walking through a thick green door facing us, and then entering what looked like a high-ceilinged barn. Warm, moist air intermixed with pungent animal smells, wood chips covered the floor, and bright sunlight streamed through large windows.

We passed through the barn and, going under a covered walkway, we came upon an even larger enclosed area cordoned off with thick glass and brick walls. The roof was covered by wire mesh.

"Here we are," Dr. Simmons said, stretching out her arm. "Welcome to the play yard."

Dr. Simmons led us up a series of winding stairs to the right of the play yard and we came to a level platform surrounded by a guard rail, an observation area that looked down into the compound through the glass. In the play yard, swings and ropes hung from wooden beams above. Two trees in the middle rose to the mesh ceiling. The play yard was about fifty yards wide and long, a large space for chimps to engage.

"They're so cute!" Cheryl said as she pointed at the three young chimpanzees who were hanging on tree limbs, using their amazingly supple arms and hands. They swung from tires, and climbed with the grace and skill of Olympic athletes. They picked up small rocks and stalks of grass, shrieked loudly. Rambunctious play was clearly the norm, except for the smallest one, I realized, who sat in a corner and bit his toes, rocking back and forth. He hid behind a patch of bushes.

"They're really just a bit older than babies," Dr. Simmons said. "But they're very inquisitive."

The three chimps stopped running around and playing with each other, sat back on their haunches and just looked up at us. Eyes blinking. They scratched themselves and then shrieked. They stood about ten feet away from the glass.

But then they quickly lost interest and started chattering and shrieking, pushing and shoving each other like contentious siblings again. I wondered if they were showing off. I smiled when I glanced at Tommy, who was standing rigid as a rock, his hands at his sides.

"Chimpies, Daddy," he said, turning to me and looking me straight in the eyes. I shivered with excitement. "They play." He jumped up and down, then flicked his fingers. He signed: "Chimp." "Like." "Play." And then he made the sign for "run."

Cheryl moved closer to me. "This is so cool," she said softly. "And Tommy really seems to be focused on them."

"I know."

What I witnessed mystified me, the rambunctious human-like chimps with their inquisitive expressions, Tommy's uncanny empathy with them, the sci-fi desert isolation of where we were, Dr. Simmons' apparent empathy with Tommy, and most of all, the fact that inside my gut, I knew I was taking the right direction for Tommy's sake—I just knew it.

"Yes, they play, Tommy. You like them?" Cheryl said, her face coloring.

Tommy nodded, then tossed off several words: "Like. Like. Lots. Mommy. Daddy. Play." Tommy signed the word for play. "Chimpies play. Play."

"I'll go in and settle them down." Dr. Simmons spoke with a serious tone. "Then I'll introduce your son. We'll watch how they react and how your son reacts, and make a determination from there. I'd say the best thing is to go slowly at first, just to get our toes wet, so to speak. This is as new to me as it is to you."

Dr. Simmons walked down the metal stairs, and opened up the door that led into the play yard. Entering their domain, she put on a lapel microphone, then picked up a bucket filled with red grapes and started handing them out as she greeted the chimps.

"Hoooo . . . eeeeee . . . Ka-Creeee . . ." She mimicked the chimps. Her voice came to us via two round speakers that were set up on the observation deck. "You can talk to me and I can hear what you're saying too," she said. "There are microphones on your side as well."

"Cool," I replied. I'd worked with sound systems for forever, and this was a slick setup indeed, with Bluetooth to boot.

Except for the smallest one, who still remained alone in a corner of the play yard, the chimps loped toward Dr. Simmons, all arms and legs, bumping and shoving each other out of the way, a motley crew indeed. They reminded me of school-age children, called in from recess by their teacher. Dr. Simmons patted them all, then gingerly gathered two chimps in her arms, hugging one and stroking the other's head. They all puckered their lips, blinked their eyes at her, looking happily nurtured.

"They're so social," Cheryl said. "I never realized monkeys bonded like that. Did you?"

"They're chimps, not monkeys," I said.

"What's the difference?" Cheryl asked.

"There's a big difference," said a husky female voice behind us. "Most monkeys have tails. Chimps don't."

We turned to find a tall, thin woman also wearing the Weller T-shirt standing behind us. The observation deck connected to an office near the play yard and evidently, she'd entered onto the deck without our noticing. Her big brown eyes exuded intelligence. She had her hands in the pockets of her khakis, but thrust a right arm out to meet us. We shook her hand. "Hi, I'm Marcy Davenport, Dr. Simmons' assistant. I've heard a lot about your son and I saw the video. I must say, it was something to see." Her warm, thin-lipped smile reminded me of a hostess's smile at a party. "Actually," she went on, "just for your info, a monkey's tail serves as an appendage, like another hand. And chimps have a much larger brain-to-body ratio and use tools far more frequently. Chimps are way smarter than monkeys."

"I see." Cheryl laughed. She put a hand to her chest. "My ignorance."

"No problem," Marcy said. "It's amazing how many people don't know the difference."

"Play, Daddy." Tommy said. "Me . . . plaaaaaay tooooo . . . Play chimpies toooooo."

I didn't know if it was his voice, which they obviously heard through the play yard's speakers, or if it was his jumping up and down, but suddenly Tommy caught the chimps' attention. They all stopped and stared up at us on the observation deck. Dr. Simmons turned our way.

"Can we take him down in front of the glass?" I asked Marcy.

"Sure. Of course." She nodded, ushering us down the stairs. "Absolutely."

We walked down the stairs, Tommy between me and Cheryl. As we stood in front of the glass, Marcy joined us. The observation deck I realized held a good vantage point for an overall perspective, but wasn't going to allow us that up front and personal look, and that's what we'd come for.

Tommy immediately pressed his nose against the thick glass wall. He made a few flicking gestures. I caught Marcy's confused expression as she watched his gestures. Dr. Simmons surveyed the scene, rubbing her chin, as the three chimps shambled up to the glass, pushing and shoving each other, then just stood there in front of the glass, their heads bobbing up and down, studying this new boy-creature. A minute passed, then suddenly, the chimps started screeching louder than ever, and thumping their chests.

Then the screeching stopped. A thick silence ensued. A chimp with a narrow face and moist brown eyes stared at Tommy with a playful expression as he scratched the top of his head. He stuck out his tongue. The largest one stuck out his tongue too, then shook his head mightily left and right, while the third, who appeared to be the most jittery, shook his head and pouted his lips, jumping up and down, bouncing into the other two. Then, as if on cue, the three musketeers placed their hands against the glass, and then shrieked and screeched almost in unison.

Just as he'd done at the zoo, the connections began: Tommy put his hand up next to each chimp's hand one at a time. Taking a minute with each chimp. He shook his head slowly, right, left. The chimps couldn't take their eyes off him. They seemed mesmerized. They beat their hands against the glass, then glanced back at Dr. Simmons as if they were seeking her acknowledgement. Again, they touched hands to hands against the glass, then Tommy made the flicking gestures and the chimps just stared, their mouths gaping open, eyes blinking. He signed "chimps," and one of the chimps signed the same gesture back. Then Tommy signed "play," and all of the chimps signed back. Tommy shook his head and the three chimps shook their heads as well. Tommy placed his first finger against the glass and the largest one responded by putting just one of his fingers against the glass as well. Cheryl and I looked on, confused, amazed, our mouths gaping open. I suddenly realized our shoulders were touching, parents, together, looking on. We were divorced, but a strong connection remained. This pleased me and felt good. I couldn't even begin to comprehend the dynamics between Tommy and the chimps. I wondered if the primatologists could help us out.

"Incredible," Marcy said. "I've never seen anyone command their attention like this. It just doesn't happen."

"They certainly seem glad to see him." Dr. Simmons adjusted the microphone on her lapel. "It's just like the video you sent."

"He seems to get along with them so well," Cheryl said. "I mean, it's as if they're friends already. I can't get over it. It's almost like he's talking to them in some incomprehensible way."

"Is it possible to actually bring Tommy into the play yard?" I asked.

"We don't generally allow anyone other than employees into the enclosure," Dr. Simmons said. "But we do have a plan of action for this possibility, which we drew up before your son arrived."

"Chimpies." Tommy said, pointing out into the play yard. "Want chimpies now." He hugged himself, then jumped up and down and clapped his hands.

The chimps shrieked and made gestures, thrusting hands and arms out, whirling them around. I had no idea what they were saying if they were saying anything at all. Then, as if on another kind of invisible cue, the chimps started lunging themselves against the glass, banging against it. The glass shook with their powerful thrusts. Boom! Bang! Boom! I was amazed by their power.

"They're expressing their dominance," Marcy said, pointing at them.

Tommy faced the largest chimp, pressed both of his hands against the glass, and shook his head again slowly right, then left. The chimps stopped banging the glass, just stood there, and then the largest chimp turned his head right, and then left. They both opened their mouths wide, stretching their lips, and held each other's gaze, just like at the zoo.

"Interesting," Dr. Simmons said. She spoke like a scientific observer, completely nonjudgmental. "They're giving us play responses, as evidenced by the minimal tooth exposure." She cupped an elbow with one hand, while tapping her lips with the other.

"Chimpies . . . happy." Tommy pointed at the chimps, then turned and looked at me. Then at Cheryl. "Happy here." He flashed us a smile that reached out and touched my heart. This wasn't the robotic, puppet-like imitation of a smile that he usually exhibited.

When Dr. Simmons stepped out of the enclosure, giving a command to keep the chimps away from her as she walked through the door, she stood in front of Tommy. She gazed down at him, head tilted to one side, as he bit the backs of his hands.

"Well, Mister Tommy," she said. "You certainly have their attention. They don't do this with just anyone, you know."

Tommy put his hands in his mouth. "Oooouuuu . . ."

Cheryl gently guided Tommy's hands away from his mouth. "Oooouuuu . . ."

"So, what do you make of it all, Dr. Simmons?" I asked.

"Well." She took a long breath and furrowed her brow. She stood next to Marcy, who had a look of wonder on her flushed face. "I really would have to study these interactions more closely to come to any real conclusion. Right now, I can't say I have any explanation at all, but if it's okay with you. . ." She paused, framing her thoughts. "I'd be willing to allow Tommy in with the chimps under extremely close supervision for a short time."

"Really?" Cheryl asked.

Dr. Simmons nodded. "I'll be right with him."

"Chimpies. Chimpies. Me chimpeeeees."

Tommy jumped up and down, his shining eyes leaping from me to his mother and back again. To see him so willing and eager to engage the outside world instead of living his normally abnormal interior life was remarkable. It was as if the wall was coming down and a new child of mine was stepping out, the boy that I knew was in there, somewhere, if only I could reach him. Suddenly, I felt that same old ache in my chest for this son of mine.

"What we've planned," Dr. Simmons said, "is using a mini-barrier, which will keep the chimps enclosed, barricaded behind thick glass. But it will allow Tommy greater firsthand access."

"A mini-barrier?" I asked.

"Yes, you'll see. It'll be perfectly safe."

"All right," Cheryl said. "Let's go for it. I think he really wants it. And he does seem to have this instinct, though I have no idea where he got it from." She laughed, turning to me. "Chris, you don't have any chimp in you, do you?"

"Actually, we all descend from these nonhuman primates," Dr. Simmons said seriously, not finding the humor in Cheryl's comment. "P. Troglodytes are our next of kin. They're part of the Homininae subfamily, just like us. Genetically, humans and chimps are 99.9% identical." She turned to Marcy. "Marcy, will you please text Jack to bring in the mini-barrier?"

A minute later, a thin man with a full beard entered the play yard from the opposite side and brought with him the mini-barrier, into which he gently ushered the three chimps, plying them with grapes in the process. It was basically a large, walled-in box made of steel surrounded by thick glass walls, portable, on rollers. The top was meshed for air flow. Each chimp was placed in his own unit inside the mini-barrier. The smallest one still remained in his corner, withdrawn from the rest. I assumed that this one was safe where he was. This chimp seemed completely into himself, isolated, hardly noticing anything, putting his fingers in his mouth.

Once the barrier was in place and the chimps were inside, Dr. Simmons tried to take Tommy's hand.

"Come on, Tommy," she said with a smile.

This time, amazingly enough, Tommy not only accepted her outstretched hand, he did so eagerly, took hold of it without reservation and walked quickly by her side, as if he was leading *her* on. He didn't even panic or back away. Blinking rapidly, I savored the moment and couldn't believe it. My shell-of-a-son was actually reaching out and taking hold of a stranger's hand? Impossible, but there it was. He stood close by Dr. Simmons' side.

"Did you see that?" I said with a throaty laughter, turning to Cheryl. "Did you see him take her hand?" Surely this was a confirmation, a sign pointing in the right direction.

"Yes," Cheryl said. "I can't believe it."

A flush of excitement ran through me.

Standing close to him, Dr. Simmons escorted Tommy through the door and led him toward the three chimps in the center of the enclosure. Tommy strode purposefully, a little boy on a mission. He actually stood taller, his back straight, and he walked with a more flowing stride, less like a pelican.

"Marcy, do you mind recording this?" Dr. Simmons asked.

"Sure." Marcy nodded, then went to a computer panel next to us and clicked a few buttons. The three rotating cameras set up in the play yard emitted a red light, signaling that they were on. "This should be interesting," Marcy said, grinning.

As soon as Tommy entered the play yard, the chimps froze, peering cautiously at Tommy. Had they even seen a human child before? Dr. Simmons led Tommy to meet and greet the tallest chimp. The chimp and Tommy both sat down, face-to-face, new pals, new playmates, across a glass wall. I had to suppress a giggle. This chimp's big liquid eyes seemed more intelligent and curious than those of some people I knew.

"This one's name is Mikey," Dr. Simmons said. "Of all the chimps, he's the most interested in humans. He's a real character." She laughed. "Sometimes I forget he's a chimp, and sometimes I think he forgets he's a chimp, too."

Tommy started swaying and Mikey froze. Even the forgotten chimp in the corner turned to see what was going on, taking his hands from his face and eyes.

Tommy signed: "Boy. Like. Chimp. See. Run."

Then, Mikey made a sign. "Play." I could definitely read it, the first finger of one hand locked around the first finger of the other hand. It was incredible, seeing an animal make a sign that a human could understand, reaching across barriers. What could we learn from chimps? What did they want to say to us? I could only marvel at what was happening. Then the chimp made another sign, wiggling his fingers and placing one palm against the other, but I wasn't sure what he was saying.

"That's the sign for 'tickle,'" Dr. Simmons explained. "It's their fun sign. Mikey's our best signer."

"They're communicating," I said. "It's amazing."

"Incredible," Cheryl said.

Mikey again signed: "Play. Tickle." Then shook his head right and left, then shrieked loudly.

"I must say, they're incredibly responsive to him," Dr. Simmons said. "These chimps typically treat visitors very warily. But with your son, it's totally different. They rarely want anything to do with humans, except the people they already know well."

"That's just how they were at the zoo," I said.

"Chris, you don't think he's going to get obsessed over them, do you?" Cheryl asked, touching my shoulder. "You know how children with autism can get obsessed so easily."

"I know. I know. But I don't think this could become an obsession."

I recalled one of Tommy's classmates, William, a child with Asperger's, the one Tommy had gotten in the fight with. William was obsessed with turtles. That day in the classroom he'd lectured me in length on why turtles sun themselves and the differences between turtles and tortoises. But surely, this was different. Wasn't it? Tommy was communicating with the chimps, becoming alive in their presence. Surely, chimps were way higher on the evolutionary scale than turtles. There was no comparison. No, this was more than obsession. It had to be.

Tommy and Mikey, still facing each other, continued swaying, right and left, back and forth. They became pendulums in perfect sync, the back-and-forth motion of their bodies slightly hypnotic.

"I wouldn't believe it if I wasn't seeing it," Dr. Simmons said. "Completely spontaneous. Completely untrained."

The pendulum swinging stopped, and Tommy and the chimp now sat motionless.

"Ball . . . tree . . . home," Tommy said all of a sudden, words dropping from his mouth, one at a time. And then he signed the words that he spoke. My jaw fell. "Ball . . . chimpie . . . home . . . trees . . ."

What?

"He's talking, Cher. Did you hear that?" I said.

"Yes. I'm not sure talking is what I'd call it. But, God. At least he's expressing himself."

"I really think it's because he feels so comfortable with them. He's able to tone down all that extraneous noise in his mind."

Tommy stared at Mikey for a long while, then swung around and eyed the small chimpanzee sitting in the corner. The small chimp was still rocking quietly back and forth, eyes closed, biting himself every so often.

"Chimpie hurt, Mommy," Tommy called, pointing to the withdrawn chimp. "Chimpie, he hurt bad bad."

"Oh, no," Cheryl said, playing along. "Really?"

"That's Obo," Marcy explained, walking back over to us after tending to the cameras. "He's our toughest case." She frowned as she curled some wisps of hair around her ears. "He was born at another facility where his mother completely rejected him. She wouldn't nurse him at all, and so he was bottle-fed by attendants. She abused him, bit him. They had to remove him from her or he would have been killed."

"How did he end up here?" Cheryl asked.

"He was donated to our program about six months ago. We've been utilizing several intervention techniques to attempt to get through to him, but unfortunately, so far, no luck yet." Marcy crinkled her brow. "He has a toy he plays with, but most of the day he just sits and rocks."

I felt sorry for the little guy. Biting himself? Completely withdrawn? He seemed like a chimp with autism, if such a thing was possible. Holding Dr. Simmons's hand, Tommy headed toward Obo, walking quickly, with long, purposeful strides, pulling Dr. Simmons along. I'd never seen him walk like that. Head up, posture straight, eyes focused and alert. The robotic movement that matched his robotic speech was gone. When Tommy stood less than a foot away from him, the chimpanzee looked up, blinking his eyes at Tommy. Now there was no barrier at all between boy and chimp.

"Chris," Cheryl said, grabbing my arm. "Are you sure about this?"

"Huh?" I hardly heard her. I was too engrossed by Tommy's antics.

"I said, are you sure about this?"

I turned to her and put a hand on her shoulder. I looked out through the glass. "Of course, I'm sure. It's going to be all right, Cher. Let's just trust him. He seems to know what he's doing."

"Okay. You know?" she said. "I really think you're right."

The meeting of the minds continued. Obo scratched a toe. He quickened his rocking back and forth, bit his toes, and then covered his face with his hands. He looked like he just wanted to hide from life itself. I felt so sorry for him.

Tommy drew even closer. Dr. Simmons loomed over them.

Obo glanced at Tommy shyly and then grunted and snorted.

Tommy grunted and snorted right back. Then he let out a cry. "Euuuu . . . Uuuuu . . . uuuurrreeeee . . ." It was incredibly chimp-like, similar to a chimp-shriek.

The next thing I knew, Tommy was sitting down facing Obo, legs crossed. Obo bit his toes and rocked back and forth even more dramatically. Tommy let out another cry and then slowly and carefully reached out both hands and rested them on Obo's shoulders. The chimp allowed the embrace for a moment, but soon squirmed out of Tommy's reach and ran to the other side of the play yard and sat down again, rocking back and forth.

I moved closer to the glass, eager to observe as Tommy hurried after him and stood over Obo. The chimp shrieked. Tommy patted Obo on the head, edged closer, and then, amazingly enough, started to slowly pick through the chimp's hair. Obo seemed to relax, even to enjoy the attention. He was doing this just like the chimps picked through each other's hair. I was stunned. His knowledge of their behavior patterns seemed effortlessly intuitive. Tommy held the chimpanzee's head and grunted, chimp-like; this time his grunt was softer, friendlier.

"Wow," Cheryl said. "He's acting like Obo's caretaker."

"He has such a gentle way with them," Marcy said, marveling.

Tommy yelled at Obo and shook his head. Obo covered his eyes. When Obo tried to run from Tommy again, Tommy put his hands on the chimp's shoulders and said, "No." Then he let out a cry, "Eeee . . . Eeeiiii . . . Ahhhhh . . . Uuuu . . . Oooooo!"

Obo stayed.

As Dr. Simmons continued hovering over Tommy and Obo, another assistant, a young woman wearing jeans and a Weller T-shirt, brought out cereal, apples, and chunks of watermelon for the three chimps. She brought the chimps out of the barrier and stationed them around the base of one of the trees. Mikey made a few gestures, putting one hand in the other and then forming a fist as he moved it up and down.

"He's saying 'drink fruit,'" Marcy said, referring to the watermelon. "And SeeSaw's signing, 'candy fruit.' You see, they actually make up words around the qualities of a food or object when they sign."

"So, they *can* have meaningful gestures," I said. "Amazing. Don't you think so, Cheryl?"

"It really is." She spoke with her eyes open wide.

"The thing is," I said, "if Tommy has the chance to be with these chimps, I'm thinking it might open him up and allow him to express himself with *human* words as well. You see how alive and happy he is? Even his speech inflection changes when he's around them."

"He just seems to come out of his shell," Cheryl said. "This is like a breath of fresh air to him."

We both gazed out into the play yard again as Obo scurried away from Tommy and scampered to another corner of the enclosure. But Tommy let him go this time and, before Dr. Simmons could stop him, Tom-Tom was sitting among the other chimpanzees while they ate, just pulling up a seat.

Dr. Simmons, a broad smile etched on her face, stood over Tommy as he clapped one chimp-friend on the back and squawked at another one, shrieked and shook his head back and forth.

Tommy turned toward Obo, who remained alone in his corner. "Come," Tommy yelled. "Come!"

Obo shook his head. He rocked and began gnawing on a finger.

"For the past two months now, Obo's hardly eaten anything," Marcy said. "We're worried about him. If he keeps on like this, we'll have to intubate him."

Almost as if he'd heard what Marcy had said, Tommy marched over to Obo and waved his arms in the air. Obo hid his face with his hands. When the chimp wouldn't respond, Tommy turned his back on him and pounded a foot on the ground. When he faced the chimp again, he let out another jungle wail. "Eeeeeee . . . uuuuu . . . "

A minute later, chills ran up my spine when Obo stood as if unfolding himself from a long nap, shyly took Tommy's hand, and then shambled toward the group, allowing Tommy to lead him.

"I'm not believing this," Marcy said. She put a hand up to her mouth, her lips shaped like an O, and gasped.

Tommy led the small, disabled chimp forward, step by step, as I watched in disbelief.

"What the hell?" Cheryl said. "He's really taking control, isn't he?" She laughed.

I'd never seen my son so drawn away from his interior self, so happily relating to the world, even if it was the chimp world. Teacher-Tommy retrieved cereal from the food table and offered it to Obo.

"Eat," Tommy commanded. "Ouuuu . . . Eat."

Tommy made the sign for eat, tapping the tips of his fingers to his mouth. Obo scratched his chin. He shrieked one time, shook his head back and forth, and then shyly took a few of the cereal pieces from Tommy's hand and put them in his mouth.

"Eat!" Tommy screeched. "Chimpie! Eat!"

"Oh, my God," Marcy said, her eyes wide. "Look at that!"

Obo's jaw moved slowly as he ate crunching the food. After a moment, he sat down with the other chimps and grabbed some watermelon. He shrieked at Mikey and Mikey shrieked back.

"Good job, Tommy," Dr. Simmons said as she stroked Obo's back. She turned to us and shrugged as her eyes opened wide, as if to say, *I have no idea what's going on.* "You don't know how much this means to us. We've been trying to get Obo to eat for months."

"Obo and chimpie and good," Tommy said to Dr. Simmons, giving her direct eye contact. "He hurt. But he love it now. He love it."

Tommy signed the word for "love."

"I WOULDN'T HAVE BELIEVED it if I hadn't seen it myself," Dr. Simmons said after the chimps had been put back into the mini-barrier. Tommy stood at her side, signing the word for chimps over and over as he looked around the play yard, a rosy complexion on his face.

"Perhaps we could perform a statistical analysis," Marcy said. "Do a study and compare language patterns and behavioral processes between the chimps and Tommy."

"Can we bring him back again then?" I asked, hoping this could turn into a kind of long-term therapy program, seeing in my mind Tommy flowing with normal language, happy and well-adjusted, a boy who had come out of his shell at last. I felt a lightness in my chest at the thought.

"I'd like to say yes right away," Dr. Simmons said, studying Tommy. "But unfortunately, there are regulations we'd have to work through, plus, if he were to return on a regular basis, we'd have to propose a legitimate study. This is a research facility, so everything we do here is based on grant proposals." Dr. Simmons looked at Marcy and then back at me. "I'll tell you what, though. I'll discuss this with the other staff members and write up a systematic schedule and a proposal. How's that sound?"

"Fine. I think that would be great," I said. "Cheryl?" I asked, turning to her.

"Sure," she said. "I don't see why not. I'd love to see him come back, if it's possible."

"I'm afraid our one hour is up at this point," Dr. Simmons. "I'll need to take Tommy out of the play yard."

But when Dr. Simmons took Tommy's hand and tried to lead him away from the chimps, he said, "No go! No go! Stay and play. Want here." Tommy backpedaled away.

Dr. Simmons gave Cheryl and me an unsure look.

"The chimpies are tired now, Tommy," Dr. Simmons said. "It's time for you to leave, okay? Maybe you can come back again. Soon."

"Come on, Tommy. It's time to go," I said. "Come on, son."

"No!" Tommy said. He gazed around the play yard.

"Let's go, Tom-Tom," I called again. "We can come back another time. Let's go home and tell Max all about what happened."

"Tommy. Let's go. The chimpies need to rest," Cheryl called. "We'll come back another day."

Hearing our commands, Tommy stomped the ground as if he'd been cheated out of extra play time, then finally allowed Dr. Simmons to lead him out, her hand gently placed on his shoulder. He didn't move away from her, just strode through the door and marched up to us, feet continuing to stomp the ground and anger lighting up his eyes. Here he was at least showing emotion about something! Wasn't that remarkable in itself?

"Want stay," he said, standing in front of us, Dr. Simmons at his side. A line of sweat beaded his brow and his face was red. His eyes were alive with light. I'd never seen him so awake. Finally, here was something that was pulling him out of his shell and making him want to hold on and embrace it. "Want . . . stay." He shook his head. "Want stay." My heart beat with joy.

"I'm sorry, but it's time to go home, Tommy," Cheryl said softly, kneeling down to his level. "We can come back another day, all right?"

"Wanna stay now."

"Tommy, really, it's time to—"

"Want . . . " His voice grew louder. "Stay!"

"The chimps are like babies and they need their naps," I said.

"No naps." Tommy signed "no" with an extreme gesture. "Want play." Then he signed, "Want play," his arms flailing in anger.

The chimps bobbed their heads up and down and shrieked and chattered, as if they too were discussing Tommy's dilemma. Marcy let the chimps out of the mini-barrier and after a minute, their chattering subsided and they returned to their own world, swinging and grooming each other, shoving and playfully pushing, as if they belonged to one big and gregarious family.

I reached into my pocket for the tokens, but realized I'd forgotten them. Out of the corner of my eye, I saw Obo scamper away from the other chimps, return to his corner, and start biting himself again. There was something about that little guy that just got to me and my heart beat for him in sympathy. He was so locked up inside, just like Tommy. Surely, the two had something in common.

Cheryl, Dr. Simmons, Marcy, and I walked out of the play yard area, pretending we were leaving and hoping Tommy would follow us, but my stubborn son remained glued to the ground. He wouldn't budge. He started gnawing on his hands. Then he pointed at the chimps.

Cheryl and I looked at each other. We knew what could possibly be on the horizon.

"Chris. You're going to have to pick him up," Cheryl said.

I glanced at Marcy and Dr. Simmons who stood silently next to each other. Cheryl and I returned to Tommy's side and I grabbed him around his waist while pinning both of his arms. The negotiating stage was over. With Cheryl next to me, whispering soothing words to Tommy, and Marcy and Dr. Simmons following, I carried him out of the play yard building and through the barn structure like a struggling sack of potatoes. I had no other choice. He kicked and screamed, swinging his arms at me, at one point, nearly landing a hefty punch on my chin. I finally let him down when we got to the courtyard, where Marcy left us, saying goodbye.

"No. Nooooo." He kicked a foot out and sliced a hand through the air.

Dr. Simmons followed us out to the car. Tommy reluctantly walked with us like an angry prisoner. He rubbed his eyes and moaned.

When we got to the car, a full-blown tantrum ensued. Tommy batted himself across the head. He clapped his hands over his ears. He arched his back, stretching every noncompliant moment to its fullest.

"Oooouuu! Euuuu . . ."

Out of the corner of my eye, I saw Dr. Simmons observing this, looking embarrassed and not sure what to do or say, her arms folded across her chest.

The sad thing was that we were so used to this routine, the crying, the flailing of his arms and feet, holding his body rigid and then falling on the ground and kicking his legs in the air. Cheryl and I finally managed to gather him up, this work-in-progress son of ours, and place him in the backseat and strap him in.

"No! Want chimpies!" Tommy cried. "Chimmmmmpppppies!"

We knew to stay calm during a meltdown, and we worked as a practiced team. Cheryl produced a bottle of lavender oil from her purse, and held the bottle up to Tommy's nostrils, forcing him to take some whiffs.

"That's my good boy," she said in her best Mommy voice. "That's my good, good boy. Everything's fine now. We'll be home soon and have some ice cream."

I entered the car from the other side, slinging Mister Backpack inside.

"You're doing great, Tom-Tom." I whispered in his other ear. "You're such a good boy."

"He certainly knows what he wants, doesn't he?" Dr. Simmons said when we'd finally pacified the storm. I was breathing heavily, my heart thundered, and my back hurt. A nice application of Ben Gay was in order when I got home.

"That he does," I said grimly.

"Thank you for letting us come here, Dr. Simmons," Cheryl said. "Let's stay in touch."

"Absolutely. Goodbye. Drive safely. Talk to you soon."

Chapter 4

After my interview with Ed Ryerson, I met Sam Axelrod for lunch at a place called Duff's. A casual-artsy restaurant on Fifth Avenue not far from the water, Duff's was famous for their infinite varieties of martinis, grapefruit gin, pomegranate lemonade, you name it. Jazz music played softly in the background. It was crowded and everyone seemed to be enjoying themselves—everyone except me.

"Well?" Sam asked as soon as we were seated at a corner booth. Sam was dressed in a grey suit with a red tie. His full head of black hair was slicked back. Tall and wiry, built like a tennis player, Sam was one of those high metabolism people who could eat whatever he wanted and never gain a pound. He flashed me a hundred-watt smile, bright as Times Square neon.

I paused before answering, then finally said it. "It's a no." I shook my head. The words fell out of my mouth like Tommy's brick words.

Sam jerked back in surprise. He blinked. "What? What do you mean? I thought sure he was going to hire you."

"They have work for me all right, but it's in Atlanta." I laughed. I had to. It was either laugh or cry. Hopes and dreams take you high, but real-world gravity drops you down fast. Newton wasn't just describing a physical phenomenon. "Ryerson called it a 'slot.'" It sounded like a parking space reserved for something about the size of a clown car."

"Atlanta? Are you serious?" Sam's brown eyes went wide as he leaned forward.

"Serious as rain." I looked past Sam and noticed a well-dressed man and woman staring longingly into each other's eyes, sitting next to each other in a booth. Cheryl and I used to stare into each other's eyes just like that and I had to look away. I bit my lower lip as longing for our own romantic days rained down on me, thinking of what we had and what we lost.

A tall waitress with red hair and bright red lipstick took our orders. I knew the Reuben sandwiches were amazing, but I had no appetite. Still, I ordered one. Sam went for the shrimp salad. Fresh caught. A minute later, the waitress brought us glasses filled with water, accompanied by slices of lemon.

"Food'll be here shortly," she said, shooting us a smile.

"Hey, maybe you should take the job anyway," Sam said, taking a drink of water when the waitress had moved away.

I leaned back in my seat. "I was thinking about it, for sure." I downed my entire glass of water, but my throat still felt dry. I stared at the lonely lemon.

"Why not?" Sam said. "Let Cheryl take over so you can move and get a better job. That woman put you through hell. Remember what she did during your divorce? Put all your clothes in storage and refused to give you the key? You have to think of yourself sometimes."

Sam had a point. To be honest, there had been days when I *did* feel like running, hitting the road for another place, another life entirely. When Tommy was four years old and not yet toilet trained, when he'd defecate on the carpet and then smear his feces on the wall, who wouldn't have wanted to run? That torn, conflicted feeling lived inside me. I was only human after all.

But I also knew a deeper truth, and that truth would not allow me to run.

"I helped bring Tommy into this world, Sam," I said slowly, my hands tightening into fists. "I can't let him down. Leaving him with

Cheryl and moving away, even if I had a good-paying job? I just can't do it. It would be easier to stop breathing. Tommy needs me. And dammit, I need him." I touched my chest as if to remind myself that I still knew how to breathe.

"Ain't no river wide enough, right?" Sam asked, raising an eyebrow. He laid his hands palm down on the table as if they were cards in a game of poker. We both used to wear wedding bands. It was a sad sight to see, that still-visible line of white flesh around his ring finger; one more reminder of my own situation—single and alone.

"Something like that." I nodded and gave him a small smile.

"Well, I think you're nuts." Sam clucked his tongue.

"It's the only way for me. When the going gets tough, dads like me stay put—we don't get goin' at all." I laughed. "Maybe I'm in the minority these days, but that's how I roll."

"Yeah, I see your point. It's called the higher road, dumbass. But you better watch out, 'cause it runs by some dangerous cliffs."

"I know. Trust me."

Sam sighed and moved the salt shaker around mindlessly. "*My* problem was I gave my whole life to my career and was hardly ever home for the family." He finished his water. "And now I'm dealing with a sixteen-year-old who's on probation, and I can hardly make ends meet either. I mean, the biz just isn't what it used to be no matter where you are. It's scary nowadays. It's tough even with a job."

"Ronny's on probation?" I asked.

"Yeah. Marijuana. Isn't it great?"

The food came and Sam dove in, downing his shrimp salad, but the Reuben before me looked too large to fit into my stomach. My appetite was on vacation. I munched on the pickle instead.

When I got home, after Sam saying he'd keep looking around for me, I took off my expensive grey suit and undressed the high hopes I'd fluffed and buffed and primped in my dreams. Nothing. That's what had happened at the interview, though it was good seeing Ryerson again and for a while, talking about old times. His career was a rocket ship. He was Vice President of Focus Media now. My career felt like a sinking battleship.

I threw on some patchy jeans and a frayed dark blue T-shirt, then put on Thelonious Monk's "Higher Ground." I flopped on the couch in the den. I tried to close out the world one mental inch at a time. I was running out of road.

Max limped over and crawled onto my lap, huffing all over me. I'd given him a bath two days ago, and he still smelled clean, his coat silky. He licked my ears, my nose, wetness on my face, plugged my ear with his sloppy tongue.

"What am I going to do, Max?" I asked.

Max gazed at me for the longest time, eyes searching me. He licked me again, caught my nose, and splashed me with wetness.

"I need answers, boy. Got any?" I scratched behind his ears. Max whimpered as he licked my cheeks and my hands. I was sure he was sensing my insecurities, smelling my fears. I got up from the couch and went to my bar, perusing my stock. There was a new bottle of Glenlivet. Skyye, my usual vodka. Some reds. Yes, drown my sorrows in booze ocean.

Why not?

No. Getting drunk was not the answer. I'd watched my father go down that route through the years, all that happy hour business which started to extend to earlier and earlier in the day, as if he kept moving to different time zones. But I had no intentions of going down that same path. Not when I had Tommy to live for.

I turned on the TV instead and mindlessly flicked through about a million channels, and when that got me nowhere, I took a walk with Max. The day was gorgeous, of course. San Diego beautiful, with a slight breeze pushing a few high clouds around. Max was ecstatic, limping along. We wound our way down the island and back, the wind blowing my hair. I felt small against the view of the panoramic blue ocean that stretched before me.

When I returned, I went to my mailbox. A letter from Cheryl's lawyer, Gloria Beaman, stared me in the face. I knew exactly what it was about: The next child support payment was due in five days. I received this letter every single month. Her attorney had no problem with sending me a letter. She had my email address, but still, the letter came, plus the email. She was that thorough. Obviously, it was worth the stamp to her to remind me that I was on her watch list: Gloria Beaman, Atty at Law. I dreaded reading that name. A payment slip was always graciously included in the envelope at no extra charge. Ha! I usually sent the money to Beaman, who forwarded it to Cheryl. In three weeks, I needed to come up with two-thousand dollars. It was a huge amount of money for me to pay. The amount had been adjudicated by the judge when I was still making a good living with all kinds of VO jobs on my calendar. I'd appealed to have it lowered, but the court had ruled against me. I was stuck in the box. The walls were closing in.

BUT NOT COMPLETELY as it turned out; not at all. I finally received what I was hoping for—feedback from Dr. Simmons concerning our next steps.

It came two anxious weeks later as I still continued looking for jobs and coming up empty-handed. In her lengthy email, Dr. Simmons wrote that she'd led a panel discussion on the issue of my son with four of her colleagues, and reviewed the videos of Tommy and the chimps several times. What they found, she said, was "completely intriguing." In fact, she wrote, "We have some decidedly interesting news for you and Tommy, which we are looking forward to sharing."

She put "decidedly interesting" in bold type and when I read the words my heart pattered. I was dying to know what she was considering. I forwarded the email to Cheryl.

Then, before I knew it, it was Saturday, another perfect San Diego day, bright and beautiful, April twelfth, 11:30 a.m., when Tommy and I headed back to Weller. Cheryl had an important client to see the day I was planning to re-visit Weller, so it was just me and Tommy. She told me to report back to her whatever I found and was sorry she was going to have to miss the trip. I was, of course, a bit angry that she couldn't make the time to come, but if that was what she needed to do, so be it.

All excited, I pulled into visitor parking, then Tommy, Radar, and I—carrying Mister Backpack, of course—stood in Weller's administrative office, waiting for Dr. Simmons. I was so glad I'd found her. She seemed caring and understanding, the perfect person to escort us into this strange primatological world.

A short, squat man with a beard told us Dr. Simmons would be with us shortly. Waiting, I perused a photo of a large chimp in the wild laying on a desk as Tommy, standing a few feet away from me, zoomed Radar in the air. I'd decided to let him bring Radar this time for extra support. I shifted Mr. Backpack on my shoulder. When the room's rear door opened, sunlight washed in, and it was as if Dr. Rachel Simmons appeared out of light itself. I felt a rush of adrenaline at just the sight of her.

"Well, now." She strode up to us with a warm smile gracing her face. "Just who I've been wanting to see."

She wore a white lab coat with the Weller logo on it that gave her a more professional look than she'd had when we first met. She bent down to scrutinize Tommy, who moved a step closer to her. My pulse raced.

"So how are you doing, Tommy?" she asked. I watched as her eyes glided over him, almost greedily, as if he were some kind of newly won prize. "Are you ready to have some fun again today with your friends? Obo and Mikey have been missing you a whole lot."

"Chimpies?" Tommy inched closer to her. He handed Radar to me and I placed the stuffed pet in Mister Backpack. "Chimpies see and me see chimpies?"

Already he was opening up and I was delighted. I thought about what Cheryl had said about leading Tommy toward an obsession with the chimps. All I could say was that if this *was* an obsession for him, it sure seemed beneficial.

"You bet! Yes, sir!" Dr. Simmons said, smiling widely. "Are you ready?"

Tommy clapped his hands and that light of curiosity I'd seen on his face during the first day at the zoo switched on even brighter now. I was overjoyed and wished Cheryl was with us to see what was happening.

"Go. Go. Gooooo." He reached out and grabbed Dr. Simmons' hand, pulling on it.

"He touched you again." I marveled at her easy way with him. "He never touches strangers like that."

"Really?" Dr. Simmons' voice rose in pitch. She looked surprised.

"Never. He won't even allow *me* to touch him that much. But you? Right away like that? It's some kind of breakthrough, for sure." My breath caught in my throat. "I'm actually astounded."

We headed toward the chimp enclosure, Tommy strutting between us. I reached for his hand, and for once, he held mine without hesitation. Then he eagerly took Dr. Simmons's hand, and the next thing I knew, we were both swinging him back and forth between us—just like he was an average kid and we were his parents. Crazy. He giggled as we lifted him off the ground, clinging to both of us, monkey-like. I couldn't believe we were doing this, that he was *allowing* us to do this. Warmth radiated through my chest and

I looked over at Dr. Simmons who gave me a bright smile. It looked like she was enjoying this moment as much as I was. I was astounded.

"Fun, Daddeeeee . . ." Tommy said.

We finally let him go once we entered the courtyard.

"Thanks for letting us come again." I meant every word of it. I felt my face flush with color. "I can't tell you how much I appreciate this. I was so grateful to receive your e-mail."

"Actually, there's quite a bit of new information we need to discuss. I'd like to talk to you about some quantitative ideas we are considering," Dr. Simmons said, her voice turning to a more professional, scientific tone. "And I'd like you to meet someone."

When we entered the play yard, passing through the musty barn, I spotted a tall, wiry man in his fifties who wore a full salt-and-pepper beard. He was writing diligently in a notebook, lost in concentration. He was standing next to the glass wall and as soon as we entered, he turned our way.

"Chris Crutcher, I'd like to you to meet Dr. Sidney Evans," Dr. Simmons said.

"Chimpies!" Tommy said, pointing out into the play yard, totally ignoring Dr. Evans. "Chimpies! Chimpies?"

"Dr. Evans has flown in from Portland," Dr. Simmons explained. "He works at the WASHU Institute for Primate Studies and he too has studied the videos of your son. He's come to help us with our research."

"Well, that's kind of you." I shook his hand.

Dr. Evans cleared his throat. "I'm afraid kindness has nothing do with it." He spoke with a sense of highbrow academia, his words all buffed and polished, trimmed and styled as neatly as his red beard and wavy hair. "I'm here to learn all I can about your son. Primatologists all over the world are talking about what's going on here. We find Tommy entirely fascinating."

"All over the world?" I stepped back, shocked.

I recalled the indemnification waiver I'd signed along with Cheryl that Dr. Simmons had emailed me and remembered there was something in it about allowing distribution of research materials, photos, and videos if required. I hadn't thought much of it until now.

Dr. Evans addressed Dr. Simmons. "Do you want to tell him, Rachel, or shall I?"

"Go ahead. You do it, Sidney. Please." She gave him a smile.

Tommy started fidgeting and put his knuckles into his mouth. I gently guided his wet hand away.

I knelt down to his level and tried to engage him with eye contact. He looked at me for about three seconds before averting his eyes. "Just a minute, Tom-Tom. We need to hear what the doctors have to say, okay?"

"Chimpies." Tommy pointed at the enclosure.

"In a minute, son," I said. "In a minute, okay?"

"Son, son, son," Tommy repeated. "'Kayyyyyy. Kayyyyy . . .'" Tommy pointed at Mr. Backpack and I gave him Radar again. He rubbed the pet against his face and smoothed its back, cuddling it. "Oooouuuu . . ."

"Anyway," Dr. Evans went on, "have you ever heard of someone named Carly Yates?"

I gulped. This was getting crazier by the minute. "Of course. You mean the tech billionaire?"

"One and the same," Dr. Simmons said.

"As you probably know," Dr. Evans went on, "Ms. Yates has always been interested in studying animals, but what you probably don't know is she's keenly focused on nonhuman primate research these days."

"You mean chimps?" I asked, blurting the words out.

"Yes," Dr. Simmons said. "Especially chimps."

I'd read about Carly Yates in newspapers and seen her on TV for years. She was a childhood genius who'd bought and sold several tech companies and was worth billions. The last I heard, Yates had purchased several hundred acres outside of San Diego and had established what was known as a land-based "Noah's Ark," rescuing species on the verge of going extinct from all over the world and bringing them together in one place. It was just one of her many philanthropic ventures, saving rain forests, donating money to vaccinate African children against polio, animal rights, fighting against elephant poachers, the list went on and on. I totally admired her, as did millions of other people.

"Dr. Evans is good friends with Ms. Yates," Dr. Simmons said. "In fact," Dr. Simmons went on, "once Dr. Evans reviewed Tommy's videos and we discussed the entire issue, he approached Ms. Yates about your son. I hope you don't mind."

"Really? Well . . . no. Not at all."

"At any rate, Ms. Yates was completely impressed," Dr. Evans said. "In fact, she's willing to donate up to a million dollars toward our research, toward studying Tommy as a child with autism, and how he relates to the chimps at Weller. It would be a rather in-depth analysis, I can assure you that."

"A million dollars?" I gasped as I turned my head to one side. "Really?"

Dr. Evans and Dr. Simmons both nodded jubilantly.

"I . . . I don't know what to say. Of course, I'd have to think about this, and, really, you must realize, I'm here for Tommy's sake most of all."

"We understand that completely, Mr. Crutcher," Dr. Evans said. "And Ms. Yates understands that as well. We totally want to help your son. That's why we think this could be a real win-win situation. We get to do the research on Tommy's uncanny abilities and Tommy gets to interact with the chimps as much as he likes. We also see a real opportunity to improve his communication by directly relating to the chimps. We plan to have a psychologist on staff who specializes in autism to help with Tommy's therapy."

"Of course, he'd only be able to come on weekends as he goes to school during the week," I said.

"Weekends are fine," Dr. Evans said. "We expected as much."

"Sure, weekends work perfectly. Mr. Crutcher," Dr. Simmons said. She continued in her professional tone of voice. "We've formulated a hypothesis regarding your son, and we've actually created a software program that can statistically calculate the signs Tommy makes in real-time and compare those against the gestural behaviors and vocalizations of our chimps."

"Meaning?" I asked, thinking I was getting in over my head, that I would need time to think all of this through.

"Meaning that we'll be able to quantify any actual improvement your son makes in terms of language, plus any new developments in communication that the chimps make as well. You see, Mr. Crutcher," Dr. Evans cleared his throat, "based on what we saw in the videos, we believe your son's communication abilities could possibly close the gaps and fill in our understanding of the cognitive functions of chimps and other nonhuman primates."

Dr. Simmons said, "Not only in terms of language, you see, but in terms of emotional behavior as well. How do they learn? What is the nature of a chimpanzee's thought patterns? What is the extent of their language? How close is it to human language? And how different? What does it mean when a chimpanzee thinks? To look into all these questions using your son's extraordinary intuitive knowledge is actually the chance of a lifetime. We just can't afford to pass this up."

My limbs tingled as I shifted on my feet. I looked down at Tommy. *The chance of a lifetime?*

"Ouuuu . . . Daddy . . . Ouuuu . . . You." Tommy said. He gave me an extra-worried, pensive face as he bit his hands, then twirled around like a Sufi dancer. "You. You. You. You." He moved closer to me.

"Just another minute, Tom-Tom. All right?"

"'Kay, Daddy. Grreeeee... Ouuuuu ..."

"You see," Dr. Evans continued, "we believe your son may actually possess the ability to cross the language barrier between chimps and humans, and for the first time in primatological science, to actually teach us what chimps are thinking and feeling. It's a remarkable possibility. That's the basics of it anyway."

I was totally flustered. Breaking news was coming at me, hard and fast.

"Well, this is all a lot to get a hold of right off," I said. "Of course, I'll have to think this through. But all in all, it sounds tremendously exciting."

I couldn't wait to tell Cheryl. I had no doubt she'd be equally excited.

"Great," said Dr. Simmons. "And now, let's see if we can work some more magic with Tommy and the chimps."

"Chimpies," Tommy said and clapped his hands. He made the sign for chimp, pulling his hands up at his sides. "Chimpies." He looked at me, his eyes lighting up.

I remained in the observation area, watching through the glass wall, as Tommy once again joined his chimp friends inside the play yard. My mind spun with all the doctors had told me.

Under the doctors' careful supervision, Obo followed Tommy around, a shadow at his beck and call. At times the two sat on the ground and simply gazed into each other's eyes, Tommy flicking his fingers rapidly, or swayed back and forth in sync. I folded my arms across my chest as I gazed out at him. My son looked as if he'd found his place in life, as if this was what he'd always wanted and where he'd always wanted to be. My eyes misted over just watching him. I too felt like I'd found the missing piece to the puzzle, a father-detective who'd finally put all the emotional clues together and found the answer. The chimps *were* the answer for him. I just knew it in my bones. An uncontrollable grin spread over my face.

"Ever since Tommy visited with him, Obo's been eating with the gang every single day," Dr. Simmons said as she came up to me, leaving Tommy with Dr. Evans and another assistant who entered the play yard, a lanky woman wearing the Weller t-shirt. Dr. Simmons set her clipboard and recorder down on a nearby table. "His weight's improved, and he hardly sits in the corner anymore. It's basically a miracle."

We watched Dr. Evans taking notes on Tommy and Obo as they played, and Marcy keeping the enclosure cameras trained on them. The other assistant stood over Tommy as well.

"Coffee?" Dr. Simmons asked.

I turned to her. "Sure. Black's fine."

She went into the main office and a few minutes later returned with two mugs as Tommy hugged Mikey and then chased after a ball while the other chimps engaged in a massive play session, romping all over each other, pushing and shoving. A frenetic energy filled the air. Dangerous? Hardly.

"Thanks."

Dr. Simmons and I went up to the observation deck. There were three wooden chairs on the deck and Dr. Simmons sat down on one of them, pointing for me to sit next to her.

"So, what are you thinking about all of this?" she asked, engaging my eyes as she sipped her coffee.

"I'm just floored by it all. I honestly don't know what to think. All I know is the chimps do seem to help him. They somehow draw him out and it's like he's a different kid when he's with them. I just feel that if he can keep seeing them, he could gain so much and hopefully learn to break out of his shell."

"I know. It's totally exciting." She took another sip, nodding her head.

"I'm just wondering about his safety with the chimps, though."

"I can assure you, Mr. Crutcher," she said, "we've discussed the safety factor many times. We've concluded that there's no cause for concern due to Tommy's free and easy relationship with the chimps. These are young chimps, you see, and they've lived in this environment all their lives. They are used to humans around them. So, all in all, we don't believe that Tommy would be in danger being near them. All the doctors are on board."

"That's good to know. It's just something I wanted to bring up."

"Understood perfectly."

We both looked out into the play yard. The chimp named Mikey was hugging Tommy and then Tommy followed Mikey around. They shrieked at each other, Tommy doing an excellent reproduction of a chimp shriek. I could hear it all through the speakers and microphones that had been set up around the play yard, Bluetoothed for listening on the observation deck. I had to smile. Mikey climbed up one of the trees and Tommy sat on the ground, watching him, flicking his fingers.

"We have some additional paperwork for you to review," Dr. Simmons said. "And there's one more issue we need to discuss—your legal relationship with your son. Are you the primary custodian?"

"No. We have shared custody, me and Cheryl."

"You see, from a legal standpoint, for Tommy to participate in this program, we'd need the signatures of both parents."

"I don't think she'll have a problem signing," I said.

"Good. But are you sure?"

"Why?" I asked.

"Well, quite honestly," Dr. Simmons cleared her throat, "Ms. Bridgewater called me and we talked and well, I was sensing some negativity from her, about Tommy and the chimps, that is."

"Really?" I leaned forward, surprised.

"Yes. It seems that she has this school in Houston in mind, and she was thinking about visiting there and seeing if that might be the appropriate place for your son."

"She didn't tell me you'd talked with her," I said, feeling a tinge of anger.

"I didn't think she had."

This news set me on edge. We had argued before over the best therapy for Tommy, and usually, she either won or I let her win. Lovaas. Applied Behavioral Analysis. These were all the standard treatments that Cheryl had wanted to employ. And when we discovered that they weren't as helpful as we'd hoped, she'd pushed forward with other methods, searching night and day for anything that would help. But sometimes I thought her zealous need to help Tommy seemed to go over the top.

But the Acorn School, when the chimps looked so promising? I was totally confused. Had she already made up her mind?

"And what if she refuses to sign?" I asked. I didn't think she would. But now I wasn't sure. My hands grew wet.

"Well, there's still a way to work around that, as shared custodian. You see," Dr. Simmons cleared her throat, "it all depends on the exact arrangement of your agreement. We've actually talked to our lawyers about this and, well, the hopeful part is that if there are certain educational provisions in your agreement, which are in fact typical for the state of California, then you *alone* would be able to sign off on the program. But we wouldn't know for sure until we'd actually looked over your divorce agreement."

"I see. Well, then. I guess you'll need to see a copy."

"Exactly. We'll have our lawyers go over it ASAP. Also, there's one other thing I need to tell you about."

"Which is?"

"If this all comes to pass, there'd be a stipend for you and Ms. Bridgewater as Tommy's parents."

"A stipend?" I gulped.

"Yes, a stipend is fairly standard in all of our research grants. We're thinking something in the order of twenty thousand dollars every three months. Plus, ten thousand dollars to your son in trust for his future education. Does that suit you?" I felt her eyes linger over me, questioning. Was she thinking I would ask for more?

My bills, my condo. This was an answered prayer, for sure.

"So, the money would be split between me and Cheryl?" I asked.

"Yes."

"Well. That does suit me." I couldn't stop the smile that broke out on my face. "I'm not sure how my ex'll react. But still. It sure will help me out. Things have been kind of tight lately." I shifted Mister Backpack. "And of course, it would go to anything Tommy needed as well." I wished that I could afford to give it all to Tommy. Still, this was amazing. I took a thankful breath.

"So, it will help. Good. Let me show you something, Mr. Crutcher." Dr. Simmons's scientific voice kicked in.

"Please, call me Chris," I said, taking a long sip of coffee.

She smiled at me. "Fine. And I'm Rachel."

"Rachel, then."

When our eyes met, it was as if a breeze of understanding passed between us. Blood rose on my cheeks and I saw real determination in her blue eyes. Even though she was a primatologist and was principally interested in chimpanzee research, I felt that she also believed in chimp therapy as a way to helping Tommy—believed in it as much as I did, and this was amazing; she was a professional who was on my side.

"Thank you so much for this," I said, unable to hide my happiness. The lightness in my chest expanded with excitement. I felt like a door had opened at last for Tommy and now I was able to walk him through. On the other side was help, hope, the possibility for a more normal life. Everything.

"Thank *you, Chris.*" She spoke firmly. "*This is the chance of a lifetime for Weller as well.*"

So, we were in this together. Great.

Rachel hit play on an iPad she brought over from the office next to the observation deck and I watched, mystified, as the slow-motion video of Tommy played before my eyes. Obo was fixated on Tommy. But now, the action was slowed down so that I could really see what was going on. I now realized that Obo stood up and went to eat with the others that day because the chimp had locked his eyes on Tommy's hand movements. But it was more than just his hands.

"See?" Rachel said after we watched for a minute or two. "There's a pattern. Tommy signs, Obo nods, but then they just stare at each other for quite a while. See that? See how long the staring pattern is? And then Obo nods again, more staring, then looks right and left, and slowly stands. Tommy flicks his fingers and Obo looks fixated on that gesture, then nods again. We think that that's the point when the communication occurred. It was remarkable. Human to animal. It's never been captured before like this."

"Yes. I see that." It *was* remarkable. I gave a slow, disbelieving shake of my head as I felt blood rush to my face. "But how could it happen?"

"You see," Rachel explained, "a chimp has a far more powerful visual memory in some ways than a human."

"I didn't know that."

"Yes. Their memories are actually photographic and lightning fast. This is a fact. For example, if you show a chimp a pattern of nine numbers in random order that flashes before their eyes in less than two-hundred milliseconds, they can recall those exact number patterns when prompted on a screen. No human brain can come even close to doing that."

"Really." I rubbed my chin, fascinated.

"Yes. It's true. So, that's why signs can be so effective with chimps. They have such wonderful sight memories. They can remember patterns quite quickly. And from what we've seen thus far, watching his interactions and gestures, we believe Tommy has a similar ability. But there's even more to this than just signs, Mr. Crutcher." Rachel's eyes sparkled. "Have you heard of someone named Temple Grandin?"

"The animal scientist with autism?"

"Exactly."

I hadn't connected her abilities with Tommy's, but now, come to think of it. Was there a connection?

"As you probably know, she too has a high-level sensitivity to animals," Rachel went on. "The way she tells it, she doesn't think in words as much as she sees *pictures* in her mind. She intuits what's bothering or irritating an animal and can actually in a way "read" them, understand them. Being around animals changed her life, opened her up to a new world in which she could feel comfortable to express her true self."

"Amazing. So that's why Tommy communicated with Obo? Because of signs plus mental pictures?"

Rachel nodded excitedly. "Yes. Exactly."

I thought about how he'd known the chimp was pregnant at the zoo. Was he seeing pictures in his mind that described their conditions to him?

"Wait a minute," I said, suddenly sitting up straight. "My Dad does something similar as well."

"How so?" Rachel cocked her head.

I told her about my father's unusual gift, how he claimed he saw pictures in his head when he handled the horses on his farm in Georgia as a young boy, when he walked them around and fed them. He'd told me this several times, though I often wondered if he was just making it up. He'd also told me he owned a baseball bat with Babe Ruth's signature. That was a complete hallucination.

"He says he can read horses by the way they swish their tails and their postures."

"Well, there you have it then." Rachel's eyes sparkled. "Tommy's ability most likely has a genetic component, handed down from your father. This is another area we need to explore."

"So, just to get this straight in my mind. Tommy has this unique gift then, part genetic, part neurological, something in the wiring of his brain perhaps due to his autism and his *lack* of normal human speech, that allows him to understand chimp thought through mental pictures and gestures and basic instinct. Is that the gist of it?"

"That's about it. Yes." She laid her iPad on the floor next to her.

"But what about other children with autism?" I asked. "Will they be able to benefit from this research?"

"I think so. It's true that there are documented cases of children with autism benefitting from animal relationships. And we have found that the chimp brain does have similarities to the autistic brain in how it processes speech and language. Thus, working with Tommy, we'll be able to understand this autism-animal relationship better as well, and hopefully, come to understand the nature of autism as a whole."

"That's great. What do you think the long-term benefits of this would be?" I asked, leaning forward.

"Good question. I must say, I can see your son definitely working with chimps in some capacity, that's for sure." She smiled.

Suddenly, I did too. A future with chimps. Why not? Tommy, the primatologist?

"Daddy. Come." Tommy stood at the glass, looking up at me, and beckoned me inside, his voice resounding over the microphones. "Daddy. Obo!"

"What?"

Tommy pointed toward Obo. He clapped his hands and gave me excellent eye contact.

"Would it be all right if I go inside with him?" I asked.

"Actually, we've discussed letting you inside the play yard as well as your son. And we've concluded that we do believe you should be involved. We're thinking you could possibly accelerate the relationships, so, by all means."

When I entered the enclosure, Tommy grabbed my hand without hesitation and tugged me along. "He want see you." Tommy led me over to his best friend. "You, Daddy. He w-want see you. Obo like you, Daddy. He be look at you and I show him you and he like you so much." Tommy pointed excitedly. He flicked his fingers then made several signs: WANT. DADDY. CHIMPS. SEE. He jumped up and down, then clapped his hands. "Come, Daddy! Obo not be shy no more, Daddy. Obo not hurt no more. No hurt him. He like you, Daddy. He want show you here . . ." Tommy scrunched up his red face, wrinkled his nose, and pushed out the word, *"every . . . thing."*

My mouth fell open, jaw hitting the ground as goosebumps dotted my arms. I had to contain myself because I felt tears filling my eyes. Rachel had followed me into the enclosure and I turned to her and beamed. We both understood without saying a thing:

For the first time in his life, Tommy had just produced a real flow of words. At least four or five sentences, all at once. But it was more than a flow. Compared to Tommy's usually primitive level of speech, this was a river, a torrent of consonants, vowels, and syllables streaming from his lips, and most of them made sense. From his lips to my ears. They were not monotonic brick-words at all. This was real speech.

"Come, Daddy. Obo, come. He want show you." Tommy's voice was completely different, inflections and emotional resonances underlining every syllable. My heart raced and blood pulsated in my ears.

Holding him by the shoulder, Tommy edged Obo forward toward me, closer and closer, and Obo obeyed. I knelt down and patted Obo, who made a guttural noise I decided to take as friendly. I grew nervous, my stomach fluttering, until the chimp reached out and gently touched my arm. Then I found myself relaxing. He carefully shuffled even closer, taking his time, lowering his head and softly jabbering. Such a shy thing. His musky body odor surrounded me, pungent and thick, and his breath fanned warm air against my skin. I peered into the dark pools of his eyes. A knowing consciousness radiated out at me.

I laughed when Obo worked his mouth and jaws as if he were trying to speak to me too, the poor soul. Obo placed his hand on my shoulder and nodded at me vigorously. This was too much. The self-awareness in his piercing gaze as he studied me was indisputable. This was far different from Max's doggie look, understanding as it was. This was real consciousness apprising me, real cognitive understanding. This was my ancestor. My cousin. My genetic inheritance. I chilled inside.

He seemed more sensitive and, in a way, more intelligent than the other chimps in the compound, but also far more tentative and afraid. A complicated guy, no doubt about it. He puckered his lips at me and I found myself puckering back as if I were speaking to a toddler.

"Nice, Obo. So cute," I said softly.

Tommy stood back, his hands at his sides.

"See, Daddy? See?" Tommy jumped up and down.

Obo opened his arms to me, exposing his hairy stomach and the broadness of his chest. When I sat down cross legged on the ground, the young chimp whimpered, then slowly climbed in my lap and wrapped his arms around my neck, his strong arms laced with muscle. He cooed. Hardly three feet tall, built like a fireplug, surely this was a courageous act for this sensitive primate. But I knew it was Tommy-inspired. My heart melted. Again, he stared deep into my eyes. Was he trying to tell me something? Was he trying to take me on a journey into his world? If only I could go there. I felt so close to this chimp in one way, and yet, the journey between our two minds was a million years away. Suddenly, I realized that the other chimps, Mikey, SeeSaw, and Rose had formed a circled around us, and were quietly watching. Again, goosebumps dotted my arms.

I looked over at Rachel who, like me, appeared to have misty eyes. Dr. Evans had also joined us, his clipboard at his side, a wide smile on his face.

"Ball, Obo," Tommy said.

Obo opened his mouth wide, sticking his tongue out and encircling his lips with it the way Tommy had always done. Christ! Another similarity. One more dot to contemplate.

"Ball red. You good chimpie, Obo. You like play ball. I do too. We play together. And we have fun here. With my daddy too. Daddy, you like Obo?"

"Yes, son, he's great. I like Obo lots."

Tommy signed again and then spread his arms wide. "He this big great happy. He make me happy. I like that. Yes, Daddy. I love that." Tommy beamed.

I nearly fell back. I was ecstatic. I grew giddy and for a moment, lost the ability to speak myself.

"I hate to get unscientific," Rachel said, dropping her scientific voice completely as she gave me a wondrous smile, "but to put it bluntly, that little boy of yours has so much intuitive knowledge with the chimps that it's blowing our primatological minds."

Dr. Evans laughed, beaming as he gazed at Tommy. "It's true," he said. "It's so very true. We're all literally astounded."

WE ARRIVED HOME TWO hours later and I couldn't stop thinking about what I'd witnessed. Surprisingly, Tommy hadn't put up a fuss when it was time to leave his friends on this visit. I had prepped myself for another stormy departure tantrum, but it never manifested. Talk about being relieved. Now, I placed Tommy by Max's side in front of the TV to watch his new, favorite channel, *Animal Planet*. I did my best SpongeBob voice with that crazy laugh of his: "You stay and watch some TV, Mr. Crabby Patty, I'm going to call your mom. Okay?"

With Radar on one side of him and Monkey on the other, Tommy looked up at me and giggled. I saw the flicker of a real smile on his face and I smiled back. The positive effects seemed to be lasting. How long it would continue, however, I had no idea.

I stood in my kitchen, looking out the window at the bay, and called Cheryl. She answered immediately.

"What's this about talking to Dr. Simmons?" I asked, trying to keep my voice calm.

"Oh, Chris. I don't want to be a thorn in your side. I really don't. But I've been doing lots of research on this chimp issue," she said.

"And?"

"And, well, to be honest, I'm afraid that the chimp angle isn't as good as I thought it might be."

"Why not?" I sighed depressively, staring at a sailing boat in the distance.

"Because it looks like it could make him obsessed with chimps. You know how children with autism can become obsessed?"

"Cher, so what if it's obsession? If it's benefiting him, I don't care."

"Look. I really don't want to argue with you over this. And I know how much you care about Tommy. So, I'm not trying to cause waves over this at all. I mean I love that little boy and only want the best for him. As do you, right?"

"Of course."

"So, we're both on the same page. It's just that I've talked to a few psychologists, including Dr. Landrum, that research psychologist that we both respect from UCLA, you know? And a few M.D's as well, plus others in the autistic community, and they all said the same thing."

"Which is?"

"They all said that if we keep exposing him to chimps, there's a very good chance he'd only use them as a way to hide from humans, that he'd become more like a chimp-boy and isolate himself even more. I don't think I can take that risk. Can you? Do you see what I'm saying?"

I didn't know what to say. My mouth hung open. My pulse raced.

"I mean I'm only saying this because I want what's best for Tommy."

"I know you do. I do too." I scratched my head.

"And besides, that Acorn School, I mean how can you compare a chimp facility with a well-researched program run by professionals who specialize in autism?"

"But you should have seen him, Cheryl," I said. "He was really talking. Words were pouring out of his mouth, well, for him they were pouring anyway, and he was expressing himself so much better. He wasn't just imitating chimps. He was coming out of his shell.

He was so alive there today. His smile was fantastic. He was actually speaking like I've never heard him before."

"Oh, Chris. Let's be real. The doctors told me that when he does that, he's probably just mimicking."

"Mimicking?"

"Yes. Who cares if he talks to a chimp anyway? Isn't he still shrieking and making all kinds of noises and signs too? We need real quantifiable research behind what we do with him. And there's absolutely no research from the chimp perspective. I couldn't find a single article that looked into chimps helping children with autism. Nothing. What if this chimp business actually regresses him? How do we know for sure it won't? Besides," she went on, "chimps are dangerous. They seem cuddly and cute, but the fact is, they've mauled people when they're in captivity, torn their faces right off. I do not want my son hanging around dangerous animals."

"The scientists at Weller don't think it's dangerous for him. Rachel, I mean Dr. Simmons explained that to me completely."

But it was as if she didn't hear me. "Look, Chris." Cheryl took a breath. "The truth is I need our son to be in a real school that has real specialists where he interacts with real *human* children. That's why Acorn's the perfect place for him. They have the best teachers and everything."

"But even if he's improving his speech when he's with them? Even if he's opening up and becoming more alive?" I asked.

"The other day I took him to the park and he actually seemed to be enjoying himself on the swings, and he said a few words too. So, should we start initiating swing therapy as well now?"

"So, you don't see it then," I said, realizing the futility of trying to convince her.

"No. I'm sorry. And I'm not here to make you angry or to cut you down or anything. I'm really not. I just want what's best for Tommy."

"Sure, Cheryl," I said. "I guess we just have a disagreement, that's all. Let's just think about this, okay? There's no rush to make any kind of decisions."

"Well, for me there's no need to think about anything else. Acorn's what I want."

Those last words, before we hung up, really got at me. The more I thought about her responses, the more my nerves started buzzing, my heart thumping. I poured myself a glass of water just to try to settle down. Her mind was made up. There was no doubt.

We'd been through all kinds of "professional" therapies, and not one of them had been able to create the kind of result I'd seen at Weller. Maybe she was the better parent in some ways, the more detail-oriented one, for sure, the one who did most of the interfacing with teachers and therapists, but in this case, I really believed that I was the one who had the answers. I just knew it. We'd always been a team when it came to Tommy, but now . . .

The realization hit me hard in my gut. The truth was clear enough: I wasn't going to be able to convince her that Weller was the right way. Not when she had Acorn on her mind as her primary goal. If I wanted Tommy to continue with his chimp exposure, I was going to have to fight for what I believed in, for that bright look on his face when he was with the chimps, for that eager smile when he was around them, for the stream of words that had poured out of him, fight for his unique ability, fight to make sure that it grew and blossomed. I felt like calling Dr. Simmons and telling what Cheryl was thinking, but decided not to. No reason to bring up a negativity so soon.

Still, after what I'd seen at Weller, there was no way I could let this go. No way at all. I didn't care what Cheryl said. She loved Tommy just as much as I did. But this was more than about that. This was about results. Thinking over what she'd said and the undertone of defiance in her words, my heart hammered and my hands grew slick. It was time to stand up for what I believed in. A new sense of resolve resounded inside me. It was time to grow a set of balls.

After checking on Tommy, who was still lost in TV Land, I phoned an attorney named Mark Hyman, who I'd met through Sam. When I got him on the line, I explained my entire story, how Cheryl was thinking about taking Tommy to Houston for educational opportunities, while I needed him to stay in San Diego because of a new therapy I'd found for him involving chimpanzees.

Then the very next day, I arrived at Mark's office with a pile of notes I'd made and the videos of Tommy interacting with the chimps, and handed them over. Mark rented space downtown in one of those combined office suites. He shared a secretary with other lawyers and, from the twelfth floor, had a window looking out on the water. Mark looked my notes over as I sat across from him, staring out the window. A big ship cruised in the distance. We viewed the video I took of Tommy and the chimps at the zoo.

I liked the way Mark's rigid jaw was set firm as he watched the video. This was a man who knew how to stand his ground, I decided.

"Chimpanzees, huh?" he said with a grin after viewing the video.

"That's right." I knew it sounded crazy, but what could I do?

"Are you saying you have proof your son receives benefit from being with chimps?"

"Well, not exactly proof-proof. Not yet, anyway. But I have other videos showing how he communicates with the chimps, how he's so excited around them, and how he expresses himself better. And this Weller Institute's on the verge of getting a research grant to study him and everything. Carly Yates herself is the donor. There's an amazing amount of potential."

He stroked his smooth chin. "Carly Yates, huh? Interesting. But your ex feels the Acorn School's the best option."

"That's about it." I crossed my legs. "It's this private school in Houston that specializes in children with autism."

"Perhaps you could get an independent psychologist to verify this benefit with the chimps?" Mark asked as he wrote down some notes.

"Are you kidding? I've got research scientists from all over the world studying my son. I'm going to have data out the wazoo. You may be reading about this in the news. It's that big."

"Okay. Got you. Sounds impressive." He leaned forward and adjusted his blue tie. I noticed the wedding band on his left hand. This was good. Married. Stable. I wondered if he was a dad. That would be even better. "At any rate, if your ex does decide to go against you and take him to Houston for this Acorn School, you'll be able to block her as the shared custodian. She won't be able to take him to Houston or anywhere else out of state without your consent."

"Do you think she'll try to sue for sole custody so that she won't need my consent?"

The thought of losing my custodial rights made me shiver inside.

"That's the question. If she sues for sole custody, she'd have to prove that you were a terrible father, or that this Acorn School offers an exceptional opportunity for your son that could be found nowhere else, or most likely, both. But I must say, separating your son from you, the father, is not in your son's best interest right off the bat. At any rate," Mark paused, "you're looking at five thousand dollars for my retainer, one-half up front. If this goes to an actual hearing, there'll be additional fees."

"It won't be a problem at all." I spoke confidently. I would find the money somehow or die trying.

"So, let me explain how this would go down." Mark prattled on about petitions and briefs and how the courts consider a variety of factors when adjudicating relocation of a child of divorced parents—reasons for the move, reasons given for your opposition, past histories between the parties insofar as it bears on motives and so forth.

I could hardly concentrate on the somber beat of his legalese.

"The main thing to remember," he concluded, "is that the court always, and I mean always, goes with what's in the best interests of the child. And an autistic child, well, that's a special consideration, for sure. But taking your son away from his father really does strain things unnecessarily, as far as I can see, especially with his autism. If he's getting good and reasonable services at Hillwood . . ."

"So, would the court see it my way?" I asked, my stomach suddenly roiling.

"That, I'm afraid, is not an answerable question. You never know what's going to happen, sorry to say. I've seen petitions denied that I was sure would be granted and vice versa."

"Well, I have no choice. Let's get on with it. I know Cheryl too well. I bet a million bucks she's already got Gloria Beaman filing with the clerk so that she can take him to Acorn. Once she has her mind set on something she goes after it all the way until she—"

"Wait a minute. Did you say Gloria Beaman?" Mark's brown eyes looked suddenly dark.

"Yes."

He frowned. "Well then, that puts a whole new light on the subject. She's one of the best divorce attorneys in California, represents movie stars, producers. And she's representing your ex?"

"Yep. I'm sure her father's paying for it. He's got the bucks to do it. She used Beaman in our divorce two years ago."

Mark played with his wedding band. "Interesting. She's quite the big shot attorney. Anyway," he shook his head, "let's hope for the best. I'll contact you the very minute I receive her petition."

I was screwed.

Chapter 5

L ife takes strange twists and unexpected turns, does it not? Through the sheer force of Cheryl's insistence, I found myself in Houston. Go figure. But if she was going to visit Weller and consider it, I would have to visit Acorn. Fair was fair. That's how Cheryl put it, anyway, demanded it, put her foot down and everything. Besides, Mark had persuaded me that any case I had would only be bolstered by seeing Acorn with my own eyes. I relented.

On a Friday morning one week later, with Max on vacation at the kennel, we left Tommy with Cheryl's parents—her mother and father standing there at the foyer of their house in La Jolla with sad, tentative faces. It was an awkward moment for us all in many ways. Thoughts of our wedding streamed through me, how Cheryl's father had proudly welcomed me into the family, joking about my vocal skills. A multitude of feelings crossed my heart; regret, sadness; longing for the way it was once upon a time. A song on the radio actually came to mind, one that I heard when I was in my teens, and the words hit home: *If I could do it over, I would do it all again, giving you all the love inside of me, all my love within, if I could turn the wheels of destiny, or turn back the hands of time, I'd travel to the days we love and laughed, and all those starry nights, once upon a time, you were mine.* My hands grew slick. It was all just plain sad.

As if to compensate for our marital dysfunction, we provided Cheryl's parents with gobs of toys and coloring books, way too many.

"Be good, Tom-Tom," Cheryl said. She moved close to Tommy for a hug, kneeling to his level, but he only backed away and looked down. Cheryl frowned as she stood back up. "Well, call us if you need us," she said to her parents.

"Brrrrrr . . . Mommy . . ." Tommy hardly seemed to notice us leaving as he put his fingers in his mouth and studied an area of square light that beamed in through a window. We launched our expedition by taking an Uber from her parents' house to the airport.

The flight was as turbulent as expected, not with the aircraft, but with the emotional winds that blew between Cheryl and me. I wondered what Rachel would think of all this, our going to see this school. Would she approve? We discussed Tommy, we argued over Tommy, and finally, we agreed to disagree and just read magazines. Thoughts of Dr. Simmons ran through me creating a warm sensation inside, the way she lit up with Tommy and the chimps, how Tommy had taken her hand so readily.

We landed in Houston just after 10 a.m. Cheryl and I decided to take a rental car out to the school, which was located on its own campus near an affluent suburb on the opposite side of the city.

Driving past downtown on the interstate, the Houston skyline rose on our right—square and tubular-shaped buildings boasting capitalistic confidence rising to the sky—and I caught a glimpse of the Minute Maid Stadium, home of the Astros. It was all so big and bloated and so un-San Diego. Not my kind of city at all.

"Your Dad's looking well," I said as we drove along. I was searching for something to talk about that we could agree on. The woman I'd once loved, the one whose scarred eyebrow I used to gently kiss, that woman was obviously dead and gone. Yes, I missed our Garden of Eden era, but I had to move on.

"He does." She nodded, realizing, I thought, that we needed to at least stay amicable for Tommy's sake, if not for our own mental health. "He's heading to Peru for another job soon. He won't stop working. I don't think he can. Oh, Chris. Let's not argue about this, all right?" Cheryl said, and she reached over and touched my hand, which was resting on the gear shift. "Let's just do what's right for Tommy. We need to think of Tommy first and foremost."

"Exactly." My chin trembled with sadness, with the history of all that we'd done and undone for Tommy's sake. All that we'd seen and gone through, the doctor's visits, the therapies, one after the other, the hopes and frustrations, seeing Tommy progress for a while, only to disappointingly regress. Autism was such a vicious opponent. Still, her words hit the mark; I couldn't have put it any better myself.

We finally made it to the Acorn School and followed the signs until we reached the visitor's parking lot. We got out and walked around the campus, heading for the main office. I had to smile. No chimps here. The humid heat was oppressive while the clacking sounds of a helicopter above disturbed what looked like a tranquil setting. Anyone would be impressed by the facilities: Brand new red-brick buildings and a tree-shaded quad where children on the spectrum were sitting in circles and actually playing games together—at least some of them.

We entered the main office, a high-ceiling building and stepped into the principal's office. Everything smelled new and fresh. Clean. A tall woman, probably in her fifties, wearing a blue dress greeted us and gave us the proper privacy forms to sign.

"Thank you for coming," she said. "I'm Sara Rice, Ms. Rosengaarden's assistant. Ms. Rosengaarden should be a long any minute to show you around."

"Thank you," Cheryl said as we took a seat next to her desk. Our appointment was for eleven and we were a bit early. Cheryl picked up a brochure that was on the table next to us. I checked my email.

A few minutes later, Ms. Rosengaarden, the principal, entered, a petite lady wearing a black dress with pearls and long, dangling earrings. She was probably in her early forties.

"I'm so glad to meet you," she said, as we stood. She shook our hands vigorously, radiating with energy. A great big smile flashed across her face. "Thank you so much for coming. I hope your flight wasn't too bad. It's quite a drive from the airport. Anyway, I want to give you a tour first of all, and then we can sit down and talk."

"Fine," Cheryl said.

I shoved my hands in my pockets.

We visited a few classes and observed students rigorously engaged in their lessons. The spacious classrooms were stocked with computers, and colorful artwork of all shapes and sizes hung on the walls, along with daily schedules with all kinds of stickers. Class sizes were small, with no more than eight children in each class.

The classrooms were equipped with large TV monitors on the walls and the name of each child was pictured on the screen along with a running count of pluses and minuses accruing in real time. In one class, there was the same day of the week lesson that I'd seen in Tommy's school. I was struck by the orderliness in the rooms and the way the teachers and assistants appeared to have all things under control. It was so different from Hillwood, where a certain chaos seemed to reign, and the special ed teachers had an easily recognized fatigue written in their eyes, though they did their best to maintain a positive outlook.

Acorn, I learned, took students from kindergarten all the way through high school, all affected by varying degrees of autism. Ms. Rosengaarden boasted that sixty-eight percent of the students attended college after graduating from the program. That was definitely impressive—if it was true. How could I find out for sure? I kept my natural suspicions to myself.

The school specialized in a technique called "static exercise," she explained, in which a virtual reality 3-D headset or visor was placed over a student's eyes and the student had to track a dynamically moving series of balls across the screen while sitting still. They had half-hour sessions once a day.

"It improves focus and mental clarity," Ms. Rosengarden said. "The exercises link eye movements with neurological events in the brain, thereby accelerating neuronal connections. The results have been overwhelmingly positive. A software program keeps track of the students' progress on a daily basis."

"Is it available at other schools?" I asked.

"No. We have a patent," Ms. Rosengaarden said. She spoke stiffly. "Only Acorn offers it."

"Interesting," Cheryl said. "Don't you think so, Chris?"

"Sure." My lack of enthusiasm was obvious. A patent on a potential method to help autistic children? It seemed kind of selfish to me. If it was so good, why didn't they give it out to the world?

After touring the grounds, we sat in the principal's spacious office in smooth leather chairs. A colorful Chagall print hung on one wall, a goat with two horns and big, soulful brown eyes, flying through a green and tangerine-orange sky. Why did Ms. Rosengaarden pick that particular print to hang in her office? The painting made me feel even more uncomfortable than I already was. What was she trying to say? For some reason, it bothered me. The one large window in the room overlooked a duck pond and a play yard where children scampered around on a jungle gym and played on swings, pushing each other higher and higher. I noticed that there were hardly any rocking or hand-flapping behaviors with these kids. It looked almost too good to be true. I had to admit it. The place looked downright efficient and result-driven for children with autism.

Chimps or the Acorn School?

I was starting to feel confused.

We learned that Ms. Rosengarden and her husband, a physician, founded Acorn four years ago. They had two children with autism and had been frustrated by the school systems and traditional therapists. They were determined to find a better way.

"So, you see, here are the baseline responses of our students," Ms. Rosengarden said, handing us a professionally prepared brochure with all kinds of colorful graphs. "When they arrive, we track fluency, the number of appropriate versus inappropriate behaviors, and, of course, academic performance. We try to be as exact as possible. Most children come here with very poor scores in all areas. Then, after a time, as you see here on this page," she handed us one colorful sheet, "behaviors and linguistic fluency start to improve. Eighty-five percent of children experience a ten percent improvement in just six months." She spoke proudly.

Tommy improved more than ten percent with the chimps in one visit, for sure, I thought, though I was unable to validate that. But Cheryl was nodding her head with every word Mrs. Rosengarden uttered. This was obviously the Gospel According to Acorn in her eyes.

I'd always admired Cheryl's diligence as a mother. I recalled how she once lobbied the school board for more support materials for Tommy and other autistic children, a tiger for Tommy's needs, calling board members and teachers day and night, showing up at meetings and demanding that the needs of autistic children be met. She never gave up.

And now, the Acorn School. This place wasn't on her wish list—it was on her demand list. How could I even think I had the power to stop her? Who wouldn't like a place like this? Surely, it was the perfect setting to offer hope for a child with autism and give comfort to a parent's desperation.

And yet . . . the chimps.

"As I recall," Ms. Rosengarden said, "you said Tommy's speech is now at the three-to-four-year-old level, yes?" She opened up a file on her computer containing Tommy's test scores, which Cheryl had arranged to be sent from Hillwood and studied it. The light from the screen flickered on her pale face.

"Yes." Cheryl sat up in her chair. "And we can't seem to do any better. He's had all kinds of therapists. We just can't seem to move him forward. It's been *more* than difficult. Isn't that right, Chris?"

I nodded. "It hasn't been easy." My stomach tensed as I sensed the desperation in Cheryl's voice. We both knew the sorrows of seeing our child struggle with even the most basic academic concepts, dealing with resistance and disinterest, fighting back the tears when tests results came back reporting no advancement. Pouring knowledge into Tommy's mind wasn't just a task, it was a Herculean achievement. We used to spend hours with him, just trying to get him to make eye contact, to learn the difference between hello and goodbye, to learn the alphabet.

"Let's see now." Ms. Rosengarden spoke as she stared at the monitor. I doubted if she even heard me. It looked like she was more comfortable hiding behind the screen than talking with the humans sitting before her. I wondered if she didn't have a touch of autism herself.

Ms. Rosengaarden continued. "We have the Briggs Language, the PPVT, the ADI, the Childhood Autism Rating Scale, the Stanford-Binet, the VDOS. Okay. And there's his IEP. Good." She perused the data. "He's been tested quite a lot, I see."

But what about the chimps, the excitement that had burned in Tommy's eyes? How do you test for that? How do you quantify something that's basically intangible, and yet you know with all your heart and soul exists?

"Tested, diagnosed to death, actually." Cheryl pulled a tissue from her purse and dabbed at her eyes. "It's been so frustrating, Ms. Rosengaarden. You just can't imagine."

"Trust me," Ms. Rosengaarden said. "I can more than imagine."

"Yes, I guess you can." Cheryl's eyes moistened. "Of course, you can." Cheryl dabbed at her eyes. "Excuse me." She sobbed, then gave us a bold smile. "I'm sorry. I didn't plan on becoming so emotional." "It's all right. I understand." She gave Cheryl a sympathetic smile. Cheryl gained control after a long, uncomfortable moment, while I dry-swallowed and felt like emotional walls were closing in on me. San Diego was so far away from Houston, worlds away. If Tommy moved to Houston, I would be a far more distant moon to him; probably even out of his emotional solar system completely. I recalled how my parents had left me at camp near Hendersonville, North Carolina, when I was a little boy, way up in the mountains. I'd swallowed back my tears that first night, the world looking bleak and dark. It felt miserable. I was so alone and afraid. I couldn't imagine watching Tommy leave me and go off to another city. It would be crazy hard for him. Already, I felt my hands go slick as my eyes misted over just thinking about that possibility. What would it do to him being so far away from me?

"At Acorn, we find that speech advances along the same lines that correspond to emotional adjustment," Ms. Rosengarden said. "When a child feels safe and relaxed, when they're completely engaged in an activity and excited by that activity, then and only then does a child with autism begin to expand and grow his vocabulary and even his syntax. It does take time, no doubt about that, and lots of encouragement."

But that's how it was when Tommy engaged the chimps. They supercharged his interest level and emotional involvement, and made him feel safe and comfortable. It was as if he was learning human sociability through chimp sociability. They were the best teachers he would ever find.

"We try to engage the child with activities that keep their focus. We often use exercise and storytelling combined, along with a lot of one-on-one therapy. Anything to keep the child interested," Ms. Rosengaarden continued.

"That's the problem with Hillwood," Cheryl said. "I feel that sometimes he gets lost in the shuffle, you know? There are so many kids that it's hard to give him one-on-one attention."

"That's not a problem at Acorn." Ms. Rosengarden's eyes shone. "We keep the children busy every day. It's non-stop. Of course, we give them down time and sensory break times too, but not for long. Soon enough, we're right back at it. We're here to challenge our students and to move them forward every step of the way."

"Sounds good," I said. "But what about the independent research data? You're a new school, after all. What are the studies showing?" I wondered what Rachel would think of Acorn. Would she see it as a good opportunity for Tommy? Had she ever heard of static exercise?

Ms. Rosengarden brought out more brochures.

"These show our research in terms of our school versus other schools. You can see the difference right here," she pointed to a red bar versus a blue bar, "in terms of reading, behavior and emotional intent."

I perused the graphs. How did I know this was even accurate?

"So, what's the cost?" I asked. I looked over at Cheryl who gave me a knowing nod.

Ms. Rosengarden went over the prices, which were listed in black-and-white on a separate sheet. Tuition, sourcebooks, and static exercise fees, which seemed way too high to me. "It boils down to forty-two thousand per year."

I stared at the figures and gulped.

"Daddy'll pay it." Cheryl's eyes glimmered. She was practically salivating. "I've already talked to him. He said it's not a problem. I *know* Tommy will love it here. This is exactly what he needs." She was gushing.

Cheryl had raised the specter of her father's wealth over me before. It made me feel small and left in the shadows, unable to measure up, though I'd never really admitted it to her. I sucked in my breath through clenched teeth.

"To be honest," Ms. Rosengaarden went on, "I hate to tell you, but we only have two more openings left for this year, and so I'm going to need your decision rather quickly. We have four other children who're considering Acorn for this semester, and the only way we can do this fairly is first come, first served. I hope you understand."

"Chris?" Cheryl smiled warmly at me, but the darkness in her eyes belied the emotional undercurrent we were both feeling.

All I could think about was Tommy with Obo and Mikey, his friends, and the liveliness in his eyes, his coming out of his shell and opening up to the world. If I said, "yes," I'd be extinguishing the world that Tommy seemed to thrive in, walling off what he loved best, closing him down.

"Chris?" Cheryl said again. "Talk to me. What are you thinking?"

I took a deep courage-summoning breath and my eyes, for some reason, fell on Chagall's horned goat-animal hanging on the wall, its huge, brown eyes looking not at me, but into me, through me. My head suddenly felt as if two hands were squeezing it as Cheryl leaned forward, waiting, her jaw set. She was daring me to say no. Just daring me.

"Trust me," Ms. Rosengarden said. "I know how hard it is raising a child with autism. Bob and I hardly slept the first five years with our two boys. We know exactly what you're going through. That's why we established Acorn. So that other parents wouldn't have to experience all the pain we endured."

"Of course, we live in San Diego now." I scratched a wrist. "So, we'd have to move here."

"Yes. Cheryl was telling me. That would be a transition, for sure, but you wouldn't be the first family to move here for Acorn. Believe it or not, the children seem to adjust fairly quickly."

The AC fan shut off while I felt like a furnace, boiling within.

"I'm completely impressed," Cheryl said. "Chris? Shall we sign the papers? I'm all for it. I really want you to be a part of this decision. It's all for Tommy's sake. Surely, you understand." She reached over and touched my hand. "You wouldn't want to stop him from reaching his full potential, would you? I know you love him as much as I do. It's in your hands."

In my hands.

Tommy . . . Obo . . . Precious words, verbal diamonds, falling from his mouth . . .

I rubbed my forehead and ground my teeth. I saw in my mind's eye the way Tommy had rushed to his new friends, so free, alive, spontaneous—

"Can we think about it?" I asked.

"Any other day, that would be fine." Ms. Rosengarden drummed her pen on the table and glanced at the clock on the wall. "But like I said, right now I *do* have four other children whose parents want them admitted, and I actually promised to let them know by today. If you don't want the slot for Tommy, I'll have to turn to one of the others."

"I see." Yes, I saw it all clearly now.

I slowly shook my head and rose from my seat. There was only one choice I could make. I gave one last glance at the crazy Chagall.

"I can't." The words dropped from my mouth like boulders, and I knew I was crushing Cheryl with each syllable. "I'm sorry. I just can't agree that this is the best place for my son." I turned to Cheryl. "I know you really want this, Cher. And I'm sure this is a fabulous school. I mean, anyone can see that. But Tommy's different. He's not like the other children." I paused, afraid to bring up the issue that was almost always on my mind. Finally, I took the leap. I spoke directly to Ms. Rosengaarden. "See, it's these chimpanzees, Ms. Rosengaarden," I said. "You see . . ." I cleared my throat. "He seems to have an affinity with them that goes beyond anything that could be accomplished here and I just, well, I just can't see how I can give up on that. I even have a team of primatologists working with him in a study."

"Did you say chimpanzees?" Ms. Rosengarden blinked.

Cheryl's voice turned thick as she thrust out her chest. "Oh, Chris has this fantasy about some monkeys at this zoo, facility, whatever." She gave me her death stare. "It's *crazy.*"

"Well," said Ms. Rosengarden. "I don't know anything about—"

"It's just that I'm seeing real progress with them," I said, trying to plead my case. "When he's with them, he just seems so—"

"Chris." Cheryl rubbed her forehead as if she'd just been attacked by a migraine. "Don't. Please. I'm begging you. Don't be impossible."

The room suddenly swirled around me. "Ms. Rosengarden, I want to thank you for showing me around. It was quite an education." I shook her hand, then headed for the door. "You have a wonderful facility here. You truly do. I'm afraid that I just don't think it's the best place for my son. Cheryl, you can take the rental car back to the airport. I'll call a taxi, or an Uber, or something. Don't worry about me." I gave her a curt smile.

"Chris. Please," Cheryl pleaded, her eyes insisting. "Think about what you're doing."

"I am thinking about what I'm doing."

Cheryl's voice was angry. "Those chimps, it's just not practical. There's no research behind it. Nothing to base anything on at all. It's totally off the wall." Her voice rose louder, echoing in the room. Her face grew red as her eyes misted over. "All they'll do is turn him into a boy chimp. Is that what you want? I thought you said it was all about Tommy."

I spoke quietly, looking her straight in the eye. "It is."

"Ms. Rosengarden." Cheryl fished through her purse, her hands trembling now. "I want to put down the money to hold his spot. I'll write you a check right now for the deposit. The deposit's twenty-percent down, right?" Cheryl turned away from me.

"Yes, that's correct. But maybe you should think this over, if the two of you—"

I exited the office, not waiting to hear the rest of what Ms. Rosengarden had to say, nearly colliding with a maintenance man. The heavy jingle of his keys followed me down the hall.

"Chris, wait!" Cheryl's voice was loud and demanding.

I spun around. Cheryl was standing in the hallway outside the office. Her voice echoed against the tile floor and the walls, which were adorned with colorful pictures the children had created, zany, bizarre pictures, and yet the artwork also revealed a kind of hidden simplicity as well, depictions of life upside down, inside out, emotions surfacing through colors and lines.

"What?" I crossed my arms over my chest.

"Why do you always close the door on me? I don't understand you at all. Can't we at least talk? Can't we at least have lunch and talk about this some more?"

"Fine, Cheryl. If you want." I had no appetite, though I was starving for normalcy in my life, freedom from strife. I felt a bit dizzy.

She stepped toward me. "I do want. And I want to make you understand a few things, too. Chris, please don't act this way. Please. I'm begging you. I just want Tommy to . . ." she choked up, "to have the best chances possible. Don't you see that?" She dabbed at her eyes. "Don't you see?"

"I want what's best for him too, Cher." I spoke angrily and balled up my hands into fists. I wasn't going to be forced and rushed into a decision—no way.

MID-AFTERNOON. HEAT-stroke territory. We found a sandwich shop called Julio's in a retail strip in a suburb of Houston. Two employees were behind the counter, wearing light-green shirts, one taking orders, the other making the food. We sat down in a booth across from a group of lanky men wearing T-shirts who looked like they'd just gotten off a construction site. The place seemed drained of excitement and was just barely holding on by its monetary fingers.

All I could think about was the fact that I still had a bit of power over Cheryl: Since Houston was out of state, I possessed the legal ability to stop her from taking Tommy to Acorn. And yet, I knew, if she won an adjudication through her attorney, by proving that Acorn was in Tommy's best educational interests, and that my insistence on placing Tommy with the chimps might be dangerous, that power might be pulled out from under me. I felt a tightness in my chest.

I ordered a Reuben sandwich, Cheryl, a turkey sub. We paid separately after Cheryl said she'd pay for mine, but I refused to let her.

"Okay, Cher," I said, getting down to business after we'd gotten our food. "I know you're in love with this Acorn place. And I must say, on the surface, it looks great. But how do we even know that what she's claiming is actually true? And that thing about 'static exercise', I don't know, it seems weird to me. If it's so great, how dare she patent it and keep it to herself like that? You know what I mean? It sounds greedy. Have you Googled the concept?"

The pallor in Cheryl's face was even more stark than I'd realized, the accompanying worry lines along her brow underscoring the energy-drained look in her eyes. "I have actually, and there's some excellent research behind it. Look, Chris. Let's talk rationally, okay? All I'm saying is that Acorn has scientific research behind its protocols and Weller doesn't. Acorn specializes in treating children with autism. Weller doesn't. Acorn is designed to give children with autism specialized care. Weller's not designed that way at all. Do you see what I'm talking about? It's really that simple."

Cheryl took a bite of her sandwich.

"But it's not all about research, Cher," I said, trying to stay calm. "I don't care if this place gets an A plus rating from God's Yelp review. I know Acorn might help other children with autism, I'm sure it probably does, Tommy's different. He's in love with his friends and—"

"Wait a minute." She put a hand up to stop me. "Did you say his *friends?*"

"Yes," I knitted my brows together as I swallowed some of my sandwich, "his friends at the Weller Institute."

"God, Chris. Do you have brain damage? Are you serious?"

"Look," I said, taking a long breath. I hardly tasted my food. "All I know is that I've seen Acorn now and I've seen Weller. I've made my decision. I'm going to do everything in my power to make sure that Tommy continues going to Weller. It's like I told you. He was talking with real sentences and everything and the scientists there, they—"

"Right. Talking." Cheryl looked away. "Talking to chimpanzees. Do you hear what you're saying? Do you hear how crazy you sound?"

"He *was talking,* dammit! You only saw that first visit. You should have seen him when I took him back. It was amazing. He was saying all kinds of things. Besides, yanking Tommy out of San Diego and dropping him in Houston would be entirely disruptive to him."

Was this the time to tell her about the research grant? About Carly Yates and what the primatologists had planned?

"Chris." Cheryl softened her voice and then I felt awful as a tear slid down her cheek, which she quickly wiped away. Both her face and neck were inflamed. "Chris. Please. You have to understand, I'll be with him every step of the way. We'd take it slow. He'll have his mother right by his side. I know it'll be a transition, but if the end result's beneficial, why would you want to stand in his way? I just don't get you." She paused, letting her words sink in, nibbled on her food, then pushed the plate away. "It's like you've always tried to stand in that child's way. Every time I wanted to try a new therapy with him, you were always saying, let the kid be, let's just encourage him. Well, you can't just encourage autism. Our son needs treatment."

"I know he needs treatment. I'm not arguing there."

"So, why don't you agree with me? That's what Acorn specializes in, treatment for children with autism. This chimp thing. Good God, are you kidding me? If I told any psychologist what you wanted to do, they'd laugh me out of their office."

"Look." I took a breath. "I haven't told you everything, okay? Weller has created this entire research grant to study him, and there are these primatologists who are extremely interested in Tommy and . . ." Hell, there was so much to explain; too much for now. I couldn't get it all in. I changed tact and played with the coleslaw that came with the sandwich. "Why don't you look at it this way? What if we tried the chimps for just a year? And if there's no more improvement, I'd say Acorn all the way. What's wrong with that? We won't have another chance with Weller—it's now or never while Acorn will always be there."

"But there's no time to waste on those chimps," Cheryl shot back. "These are his formative years, for chrissakes! Every single year with Tommy counts. We can't be playing around." She took a sip of water and then covered her face with her hands.

Then she pulled her hands away and it was as if the curtain came down. A new Cheryl emerged, a woman ready to do battle with me for her son. Her face was flushed, and I was sure I saw swords of light in her eyes. "The truth is, you can fight me on this all you want, but in the end, you need to face it." She gritted her teeth. "I'm taking Tommy to Houston whether you like it or not. I put the deposit down." She leaned forward. "It's done. I have the legal wherewithal to see this through."

I stared at her, not saying anything. Finally: "Not without my permission, you don't," I said. I took a sip of water and put the glass down too hard. "You can't just *yank* Tommy out of state without my permission. There are laws about that. We have shared custody, remember?"

"Actually," Cheryl said, leaning back in her seat now, a mysterious smile crossing her face. "I believe I *can* take him out of state. In fact, I'm almost certain."

I furrowed my brow. "How so?"

She spoke with a wily air as she toyed with her fork. "The truth is, Beaman says I actually have a case. And if you're going to fight me on this, I'll have no chance but to pursue a legal alternative, and I'll win, just like I creamed you in the divorce and took everything but your goddamn balls."

I felt the anger rise up to my throat. "Then let the games begin," I growled in return.

We drove back to the airport in our rental like strangers forced into the backseat confines of a taxi, the silence and fury between us stultifying. Thin clouds flew high above, looking like they too wanted to get the hell out of Houston. Then just as we pulled up to the rental return area and I turned off the car, I received a text that bolstered my confidence. A pathway cleared:

Mr. Crutcher, Weller's lawyers concluded: YOUR signature's all that's needed. Consider Tommy admitted to program. Thank you. Dr. Rachel Simmons.

This was perfect. A thin smile broached my face as Cheryl climbed out of the car, collected her bag, and quickly strutted ahead of me, acting as if she didn't even know who I was.

God, she could be so spiteful sometimes. But if Cheryl was going to put down a deposit on Acorn, then I was certainly going to admit

Tommy into the Weller program. I had just as much rights over Tommy as she did.

Chapter 6

The very next Saturday arrived. Tommy and I were just about to leave for the public library to see a 10 a.m. puppet show, then after the show, we planned to head out to Weller for the first day of our program as devised by the scientists. I was all atwitter with excitement and couldn't wait for it all to begin, to see Dr. Simmons again and the chimpanzees, Obo, Mikey, and the boisterous gang, to watch Tommy's interactions with them. I was so looking forward to it and felt a rush of adrenaline in anticipation.

The downer part was that earlier in the morning, I'd reviewed the latest email my attorney had sent me and my heart had cannonballed into my stomach as I read it. Mark said he'd received a notice from Gloria Beaman about a possible filing against me for custody so that Cheryl could take Tommy out of state—just what I expected but had hoped to avoid.

Now I was in my den, thinking about facing Gloria Beaman all over again and all her legal maneuvers—she'd torn me to pieces last time—putting on my shoes, when Tommy stepped in front of me, dressed in his khaki pants and a yellow T-shirt. He shook his head right and left and cried out: "Oooo . . . uuu. Oooooo . . . Daddy? I hurt. Hurt heeeerrrre, Daddy."

"Huh?" My mouth went dry.

Tommy pointed to the same place behind his right ear where William had landed a blow on the playground that awful day when he'd gotten in that fight. I recalled how he'd wobbled after being hit on the head, and how he'd blanked out for a short while. I'd taken him to the hospital after we left school that day and I'd had him examined. Thankfully, the doctor had said she saw no problems and no sign of a concussion after testing him.

But now I gulped down a stone of anxiety.

"Daddy." His brick word crashed through the window of my heart.

"Yes, son?" I blinked, hands beginning to sweat.

"I . . ." But nothing else followed.

Max limped over to Tommy's side and eerily whined up and down the dog scale of notes in a way I'd never heard before, then barked, raising his head to the ceiling. I stared at Max, then Tommy, then Max again, who rested on his hind legs as if he were suddenly standing at attention or on guard. Surely, he sensed something.

"Daddy, I—Daddy, Daddeeee . . ." Tommy swung his head from side to side.

"Tommy, are you all right?" My voice quavered.

"I—you . . . Mommy." He whispered the words, barely audible.

Then a dazed look came over him, and his eyes rolled up into his head. He turned pale. His body convulsed, and I watched, stunned, as Tommy fell to the floor, hitting it with a hard thud. Walls rattled. It was as if a gun inside my gut triggered and fired. I just stood there watching, not knowing what to do, throat dry.

"Tommy!" I yelled. "What's wrong?"

Lying on the floor in the middle of the den, Tommy's back arched and jolted, shuddering, as if volts of electricity were coursing through his body, his breathing growing rapid and shallow. His body stiffened, relaxed, and stiffened again. Damn if it didn't seem to be a seizure.

Should I hold his tongue? Don't hold his tongue? Could people actually swallow their tongues?

Not knowing what else to do, I scrambled for a pillow from the couch, placed it under his head, and went for my cell phone and dialed 911, returning back to his side, trying to hold him still.

"My son. It's my son," I said, when a woman answered, my voice trembling in panic. "He's having a seizure. I don't know what to do. He's on the floor, convulsing. He's never done anything like this before."

"Your address, please?" the woman said, her voice firm and direct.

"Eight two eight Morningdale, Coronado."

"Thank you. Your name?"

"Chris Crutcher."

"Thank you. Okay, Mister Crutcher." She sounded distant to me, as if she were speaking through a straw, and I wasn't sure if it was the phone connection or the failure of my own hearing or the panic in my mind. "For starters, have you timed the seizure?"

"Should I?"

"Yes. And make sure his clothing is loose and he has a pillow for his head."

"Anything else?"

"I'll stay on the phone with you. Let's just see how long it will last."

It lasted a good five minutes according to my watch, an eternal lifetime of bodily trembles, lip biting, and head swinging. Tommy's body arched high, then fell back, then arched again, gripped in a kind of intermittent paralysis. Max kept pacing and circling, alternating between barking and whining.

All I could do was sit next to him as my heart trilled like a chased rabbit's, hands sweating, breath quickening. Finally, the contortions and the trembling subsided.

"Tommy, are you all right?" I stroked his sweaty forehead, the phone resting against my neck.

He didn't answer.

"Tommy!"

Nothing.

"I think the seizure's over," I said to the dispatcher. "But he looks pale and he's sweating and—"

"How long did it last?"

"A bit over five minutes." I felt exhausted and scared all at once.

"I'll send an ambulance," she said. "If a seizure lasts over five minutes, we always send one. I'll stay on the phone until the paramedics get there."

"It's going to be all right, Tom-Tom," I said, praying it was true. "Daddy's here."

His eyes flew open and he looked straight at me. "Mommy," he said softly. "Mommy, where you, Mommy." His voice was soft, his lips were parched.

"Daddy's here, son. How do you feel?" I said, trying to force myself to be calm.

"Mommy."

And then it happened again. Before he could even rest for any length of time, Tommy seized once more and it was as if my body seized with him: empathy pain galore. I felt terrified. Watching him, it was as if someone was taking a hammer and nail to my heart. Once again, he arched his back, his eyes rolled up into his head, and the convulsions walked up and down his body. Max stood next to Tommy, a faithful guard dog, barking every so often, as if he knew not to move until help arrived.

Waiting for the ambulance to come, I phoned Cheryl and told her what was happening and to meet me at Harborview.

"Why? How?" she said when I gave her the news. "What do you mean, a seizure? Are you serious?"

"Yes," I said. "Totally serious. Do I sound like I'm joking?"

Her voice shook. "I'm on my way."

Chapter 7

Harborview Medical Center. The same hospital where my mother died from cancer. God, it was awful losing my mother like that. She was the cornerstone of our family. Tommy had arrived in the ambulance and I'd followed behind in my jalopy of a car, feeling completely at a loss. The paramedics had taken Tommy into ICU and now, I sat in the waiting room on the third floor, a large room with a TV on the wall playing re-runs of old football games. Four other people were in the room with me, an African-American female holding her daughter's hand, a grim look on the mother's face, and an elderly couple who sat close to each other, lines on their weary faces, looking pale and afraid. We were all in a place we didn't want to be.

I stood and went to the bathroom, then came back and sat down on a green chair in the corner. I mindlessly thumbed through a magazine. But as I continued to wait, I couldn't help it: The memories of my mother's sad fate started seeping into my mind, this hospital, two floors higher, memories coming at me one emotional image at a time, breaking the dyke between past and present . . . and then . . . emotional chronology . . . there I was . . .

My mother sat down with me at the kitchen table, a mug of coffee in her hand. Tommy, about four, was with my father in the den, reading a book together. We could hear the sing-song of my father's voice as he read about a hungry caterpillar. He was able to hold Tommy's attention and even make him giggle.

Chocolate-chip cookies were baking in the oven and the smell filtered through the house.

"I went for my annual exam this week and they found a problem, Chris," my mother said quietly.

She sipped her coffee and I covered her hand with my own. Her hands were wrinkled, worn, eroded by time.

"Maybe it's nothing serious," I said.

She sighed, and then checked the cookies in the oven just as the timer went off.

Tommy came running into the kitchen at the sound of the buzzer. "Ding, ding," he said. "Ding. Ding. Ding."

He knew the ritual. We'd come over many times to eat cookies with my parents. Cheryl was out working, but promised to come by later.

Dad trudged in and scratched his belly. As my mother pulled the cookies out of the oven, he inspected them, smelled them, then said to Tommy, "Hot. We need to wait for them to cool."

"Hot, Pa," Tommy said. "Hot!"

My father sat down with us after pouring himself a cup of coffee. He drank it black, like me—like father, like son.

"Tommy, tell us something the caterpillar ate," my father said.

Ignoring my father's question, Tommy turned to my mother and hummed. "Granna. Play."

We'd gone through this before. While we waited for the cookies to cool, my mother would sit at the piano and entertain us.

"Can you say play, Tommy?" my mother asked. "Can you use your words?"

But Tommy just hummed again and shook his head.

"Oh, all right, if you insist," she said.

My mother loved to perform and didn't need much encouragement. We followed her into the den where the old white upright rested against a wall. It was scratched and dinged, but she kept it in perfect tune. My mother sat down at the piano, flexed her fingers and broke

LIKE NO OTHER BOY

*into "Satin Doll." Then a medley of other jazz hits. She still played well,
even with the arthritis.*

*My father nudged me as she continued playing. "Chris, come with
me. I want to show you something." He spoke softly and put a finger to
his lips as if to say, "Mum's the word."*

"Be right back," I told my mother.

*As she played an up-tempo show tune, Tommy stood next to the
piano, mesmerized. Drinking in the music. His attention to music,
when played live before him, had always astonished me. Music on the
radio? He paid no attention to it.*

*My father led me into his workroom off the garage, turned on a
light, and stepped toward a toolbox sitting on a workbench. Boxes of
various shapes and sizes filled with receipts, checks, and invoices were
piled on the floor. He opened a drawer in the toolbox, then drew a small
dark-blue jewelry box out amongst screws and nuts.*

*"It's our forty-fifth wedding anniversary next week," he said, his eyes
focused on the box. "I bought your mother something special."*

*He opened the box and a beautiful platinum-set sapphire and
diamond ring sparkled before my eyes. It looked otherworldly. He'd
stored it in the toolbox, and I smiled—where else?*

*Upstairs, my mother was singing and playing now: "Camptown
ladies sing this song, do-da-do-da . . ."*

"Do you think she'll like it?" he asked.

*I put a hand on my father's shoulder, which still felt strong. "Are you
kidding? She'll love it."*

*He frowned. "The biopsy came back cancerous, Chris." He turned
to me with tears in his eyes, fingering the box. "I'm going to tell her
tonight. She doesn't know yet. She's . . ."*

My phone buzzed. Cheryl was calling me. My heart boomed. I
broke out in a cold sweat.

"Are you on your way?" I asked, my voice quivering.

"Can you believe it? My car won't start. I'm waiting on an Uber."

"Just hurry, all right?"

"I'm doing the best I can." She sounded nearly panicked.

I finally met the pediatric neurologist. Dr. Eugene Whitaker was in his early forties with thinning black hair. He wore a blue bowtie and a long white lab coat. Short neck. Long, thin nose. We sat across from each other at a polished oak table in a wood-paneled conference room. I caught a glimpse of my face in the table's ultra-shiny surface. The stranger who stared back at me looked openly terrified.

Whitaker studied the screen on the tablet he'd brought with him, and then got right to the point. "Based on our tests, it looks to me like Tommy's had a grand mal seizure, arising from the temporal lobe," he said. His voice was dry, without emotion.

"But I don't get it. He's never even had a seizure before." I spread my hands in front of me. "And he was given an exploratory EEG when he was around three, and then again at five, and there were no abnormalities at all." I dry-swallowed. "I just don't understand."

"Unfortunately, as a child with autism grows and matures," Whitaker explained, "the brain changes in unforeseen ways and a minor undetectable weakness at one age can turn into a dysfunction later on. Actually, seizure activity sometimes occurs so deep in the brain that surface electrodes can't even detect it. Whether this is a seizure disorder manifesting or just an isolated incident, we won't know until—"

Before he could finish, the door to the conference room flew open, and in stormed Cheryl. Finally. As much as we were on the outs right now, I was thrilled to see her.

"Sorry. I got here as fast as I could." She placed her purse on the table, smoothing her tailored blue skirt and silk blouse. Her expression was grim as she clutched her cell so hard her knuckles turned white.

"He's resting in a room down the hall," Whitaker said. "Everything's under control now."

A text alarm went off on Cheryl's phone, but she ignored it. Leaning forward, Cheryl listened as Whitaker repeated what he'd told me, her eyebrows knitted together.

"We've started him on a low dose of Dilantin and we're monitoring his blood levels. We'll do a follow-up MRI at a later date as well."

Dilantin. Another drug. Great.

"He was hit on the head at school about two months ago," I mentioned. "He got in a little fight. Would that have caused it?"

"It's hard to say. It's a possibility, though," Dr. Whitaker said, rubbing his hands together. He looked away as if he were thinking of something.

"A possibility?" Cheryl pursed her lips. "Wait and see? You can't be more precise than that?"

The next thing I knew, Cheryl was covering her face with her hands and her shoulders were heaving. I felt myself disintegrate right there on the spot as well. When does God turn off the pain spigot that He, in all His wisdom, showers down on us?

When?

"That Martin boy, remember he was in Tommy's class last year?" Cheryl turned to me, wiping her face with her hands, the silver bracelets on her wrists jangling, echoing the state of my nerves. "He had seizures and had to wear a helmet. It was awful. I-I can't believe it. I can't take it. I just can't—"

"I'm sorry," Whitaker said delicately. He cleared his throat. "But all in all, let me reassure you, I really don't think this will be a debilitating factor for him once we get things under control. As I was explaining to Mr. Crutcher, children with neurological disorders are at a greater risk than—"

"Doctor?" A blue-eyed nurse poked her head through the door. "It's the Crutcher boy. We need you now."

I was the first one out the door, my heart pummeling against my chest like a wild animal trying to ram its way out of my ribcage. I raced toward Tommy's room, which was far down the hall on the same floor. I heard cries, and then an inhuman squeal that pounded my eardrums.

"Eeeeee . . . iiiiiuuuuu . . .Eeeee . . . "

Two nurses stood next to my son as he twisted, bucked, and jerked. His mouth foamed. It was as if some demon from another world had taken hold of him. His hands curled into tight fists at his sides, and his back arched wildly, completely out of control.

"Eeeee . . .. uuuuuu . . ."

It took me a minute to realize that Cheryl was standing next to me, her hand on my arm and squeezing for dear life. I gasped, feeling breathless, heart knocking.

"Ouuuu . . . Eeeee . . . Mamamamameee . . . Dadadadadadeeee . . . "

Whitaker stood next to the bed, monitoring him, still maintaining his calm. I desperately wanted to help, to make it stop, to fix this problem with some sort of restorative wrench I could pull from my fatherly toolbox. But what could I do?

Spittle flung from Tommy's mouth. He stiffened and then violently jerked. Stiffened and jerked. Then his body fell limp for a moment, but only to mildly jerk again, back arching, hands clenched into fists. For a long moment, his entire body shook, quivered, lay silent, then shook again. Head twisting side to side, his face turned white.

God, make it stop. Please make it stop!

My head buzzed. Large dots floated in front of my eyes.

What seemed like light years later, Tommy's breathing finally slowed, the trembling subsided, and the seizure mercifully ended. I felt like I'd been through a boxing match. I thought I might pass out. I looked around for a chair to sit in, but there wasn't one. I leaned against a wall, clenching my teeth and fists. Fear landed inside me and beat its wings in my chest.

When Tommy drifted off to sleep, a nurse wiped the drool from his lips and the sweat from his forehead. The sight of Cheryl's pale face and the way she wrung her hands . . . My own fogginess and fear . . . It was as if we were worn-out survivors on an utterly fragile boat, two parents completely lost at sea.

Cheryl and I both stepped toward the bed and took turns kissing our sleeping son on the cheek. My heart broke just standing over him. He looked peaceful. Quiet. I stroked his face. Cheryl felt his forehead as if she were trying to read his temperature; parental habit. We murmured soothing words he couldn't hear.

A few minutes later, we were standing in the hallway outside Tommy's room with Dr. Whitaker.

"I thought you had it under control," I said, unable to hide the disappointment in my voice.

"We'll have to increase his dosage." Whitaker's still-calm eyes bore through me. "There's a certain degree of trial and error to these kinds of—"

"Can't you get it right?" Cheryl snarled. "What do you mean trial and error? He's not some kind of a goddamn science experiment."

"Cheryl." I took hold of her arm. "Calm down now. The doctor's doing everything he—"

"Calm down?" She yanked her arm away. "You fucking calm down! I want answers."

"These things take time," Dr. Whitaker said. "I'm sorry. But I assure you, we'll get things under control."

Cheryl glared at the doctor with vampire eyes—as if she were about to take a bite out of his neck.

"Dr. Whitaker, are they . . ." I hated to say the word. "Are the seizures painful for him?"

"Not physically," Dr. Whitaker replied. "Although there can be some pre-seizure head pain and other warning signs such as dizziness or nausea. The body actually goes numb. Sometimes there's an electric-shock feeling when it happens and patients can experience a metallic taste in their mouth and grow disoriented. But there's no real physical pain, if that's what you're asking."

So, it was the parents who felt the pain. And that was fine with me.

Dr. Whitaker relegated us to an empty waiting room down the hall next to the nurses' station. Cheryl and I sat on opposite ends of a putrid-green couch. I sipped bad coffee made worse by the taste of Styrofoam. Cheryl drank herbal tea. She was a take-charge woman, and God knows, the mother of an autistic child has to be, but now all she could do was mindlessly thumb through a dog-eared *People* magazine. I actually felt sorry for her. I alternated between standing up and sitting down, feeling confined and jittery. I was living on thin emotional oxygen and I had no idea we'd be thrust together again, so soon.

There wasn't much to say. No, there was too much to say. Cheryl flipped the magazine's pages while I stared into the netherworld of empty space.

Silence. The dreaded language of our lives.

"Why'd you go off on the doctor like that?" I asked finally.

"Are you kidding me? Why not?" Cheryl placed the magazine on a table and put her face in her hands. She rubbed her eyes, then leaned back and gazed up at the tiled ceiling. "Okay, I was wrong. I don't know. I just got set off. I've got a lot on my mind right now." She turned to me and looked me up and down. "More than you know."

A tear zigzagged down her cheek, a single drop of emotion reflective of the way we lived raising Tommy, always zigging and zagging, day in, day out. We lived in an emotional maze. Cheryl pulled out a tissue from her purse with trembling hands like a rabbit from a hat, white, soft, and fluttery.

"Look, Chris. What if Tommy'd had a seizure when he was out playing with your chimps?"

"Life's full of risks, Cher." I gave an explanatory wave of my hand. "You have to weigh the benefits against the risks. You know he's totally supervised. But you do have a point. We really don't know about these seizures yet. If he starts having them all the time, it's going to be a totally different lifestyle. But I don't think that'll be the case. God, I hope not."

"Yeah, well." She took a long breath and toyed with her bracelets. "I just hope this isn't the beginning of some kind of regression." Cheryl stood and paced around the room, then sat back down with a huff. We'd seen regressions before. Just when we thought he was making progress with some kind of therapy, all the things he'd learned would be forgotten and, even worse, he would sink to an even lower level of withdrawn dysfunction. It was heartbreaking. Cheryl turned to me and studied my face. "Did you remember to give him his Wellbutrin?"

"Sure did."

"And his omegas and his probiotic?"

"Absolutely. I even took a probiotic myself." I smiled, trying to lighten things up. Anger would solve nothing. That was clear.

"Good for you." Cheryl sniffed. "Well, we'll have to see if it's safe to take the Wellbutrin along with the Dilantin."

"I still think he's doing better on that than on the Buspar," I said.

"Maybe." A hand went to her neck, rubbing it. "Yes. Thank God, he's off that Klonopin. It made him way too lethargic."

"I agree."

We were always chasing a variety of medications, hoping for something that would actually keep the peace in his mind.

I gulped my coffee, which went down lukewarm. Cheryl picked up the magazine from the table and returned her attention to it, flipping pages.

"By the way, Dr. McCain gave me Tommy's latest report on the Briggs Language test," she said a minute later.

McCain was Tommy's school psychologist and the Briggs was just one more attempt to try to assess Tommy's developmental progress so that we could decide on goals and objectives.

"And?" I raised an eyebrow.

"It basically showed minimal progress. After all the training we've done with him. Minimal progress," Cheryl hissed. "Can you believe it?"

"Well, you know what I think?" I leaned back in my chair and stretched out my legs. "Big deal. We're raising a child, not a test score. Who cares about those scores anyway?"

A hint of a smile broke on her face. "You know, you're right. He's not graphs and numbers on paper, not at all, and once he gets to Acorn, we should start seeing some real improvement." She touched my hand for a moment before pulling it away. She spoke softly. "Look, Chris. It's all for Tommy. You have to know that. I really believe Acorn's the best plan right now. We have to help him as much as we can. I'm sorry."

"I know, Cher," I said, feeling sorry too, feeling like I should just give up and let her have her way, tired of fighting. I touched her hand back. "I know."

TOMMY'S CLOUDY EYES and pale face set me on edge. I stood next to his bedside, leaning over him. He had a small, private room just off ICU. The curtains were closed around us, forming a kind of room cocoon. The humming whir of the AC kicked on. A water glass with a bent straw in it rested on a table next to his bed.

"Daddeee." He turned his head my way, but refused to give me eye contact, his eyes dodging my own and a lump of sadness lodged in my throat. Wetness filled my eyes, my vision blurring. The world itself seemed to suddenly melt down.

"I'm here, son, right here." I took his hand and held it, kissed the top of it. I knew he'd feel I was invading his space, but I did it anyway. I couldn't help it. His hand felt so fragile, so impossibly tender, smooth skin. I recalled his baby hands, marvelous and perfect, his baby smile, free and wide. He pulled his hand away.

"Does your head hurt? Does your—"

"Where." He didn't ask it as a question. Propped up in the bed, he looked at the tube running from his arm, then gave me direct eye contact. "Where."

"You're in the hospital, Tom-Tom. It's where doctors take care of you. But don't worry, you're going to be fine." I forced a fragile smile. "You had a time-out. You needed a rest, that's all. You had what they call a seizure. A bit of a break time." I smiled again, and this time my smile didn't feel so tight. "Nothing to worry about, okay? When we see Max, we'll tell him all about it."

"Max," Tommy said. "Max." His eyes met mine, but just for a moment. "Hosp. 'K."

Cheryl entered the room, her face contorted in an explosion of worry. She rushed toward Tommy like the motherly freight train of affection she was. I thought: *a force of nurture*. I moved back and stood against the wall, watching her, feeling like a second-class parent. Since the divorce, so many times I felt as if she and Tommy were the sun, and I was the orbiting planet. I had no idea whether I was a close Mercury or a distant Neptune.

"Tommy, my darling. My sweet boy. Feel better?" Her tender Mommy voice was perfect and reassuring, hitting just the right notes.

Tommy's words fell on my ears. His face was impassive, rigid. "Mommy, Daddy." He drew his tongue around his lips, north, east, south, west.

"Ah! You're up." A red-haired nurse, all smiles, bounced into the room. She checked Tommy's IV, then took out a blood-pressure cuff. "I'm going to wrap this around your arm, okay? It won't hurt. I promise."

"No, no, no, no touch." Tommy pulled away when she tried to wrap the cuff around his arm.

"It's all right," I said. "She's just trying—"

"Nooooooo." Tommy drooled and shook his head, closing his eyes. He sucked in his breath and tightened up his body as if he could somehow hide from her.

"Oh, Tommy," Cheryl said. "Don't worry. The nurse just wants to find out how you're doing. It's okay, baby doll."

"Ouuuuu . . ." He shut his eyes, balled his hands up in tight fists, and held his body rigid while the nurse proceeded to inflate the cuff. She was aware he had autism. Everyone on the floor knew.

"That's a good boy," I said once the procedure was done. "Are you hungry?"

Tommy didn't answer.

"No problem," the nurse said. "B.P.'s fine. We'll get a tray up here pronto. What does he like?"

"Peanut butter and jelly?" Cheryl asked. "And no crusts. And if they can cut it into squares, that would be great. Squares and circles, actually."

"I don't see why not." She raised an eyebrow as she smiled.

When the nurse swept out of the room, Cheryl put out her arms toward Tommy. "Hug?"

Tommy's expression grew smug. "Okay. Hug okay."

I stood back as Cheryl gave Tommy his version of a hug, a quick body-to-body press, practically over before it started. He sniffled and she quickly wiped his nose with a tissue from her purse. Mothers and their ever-ready tissues, a universal relationship: Wherever there was a mom and a child, tissues were not far behind. She sat down with him on the bed. I just realized that I'd rushed out of the house so fast, I'd forgotten Mister Backpack and suddenly felt like I was missing an appendage. I was that used to having the thing around.

"There you go, Tom-Tom. There you go," she said softly. "It's all going to be all right."

"Mommy."

"Yes, I'm here, darling. Mommy's here."

Cheryl beckoned me to come closer, pulling me into their orbit. I joined them next to the bed and gave Tommy a quick hug as well. We were now, the three of us, only inches apart—physically anyway. Our family, reuniting. It felt incredible.

"You're such a good boy," Cheryl whispered. "Yes, you are. Such a good, good boy. Isn't he, Chris?"

"He's the best." I said brightly. I did my best SpongeBob imitation. "Totally, the best kid in the whole pineapple. They're always talking about Tom-Tom at the Krusty Krab, you know."

"Daddeeee," Tommy said, dropping a brick-word on my heart. He licked his lips again and drooled, his face forming an impassive expression. "Dadddeeee."

"Hey, there, Mister Tommy," I said as SpongeBob SquarePants. "You doing better now? Everybody at Bikini Bottom's rootin' for you."

But I couldn't get him to laugh. Cheryl gave me a smile, though, and then wiped at her misty eyes. A throaty, nervous laughter came out of me. I couldn't help it.

"Guess what we're going to do as soon as we get out of here?" Cheryl said.

"Wanna go," Tommy said. "Go." He gave Cheryl his Tommy-smile, fixed and unnatural, covering his teeth with his lips.

"As soon as the doctors say it's all right to leave," Cheryl said. "We'll go home and watch *Star Wars*. You know, the one with the clone battle? And how about some cookie dough ice cream to eat while we watch the movie?" Cheryl gave Tommy a grandmotherly smile, pasting an all's-right-with-the-world expression on her face. "How's that sound, Tommy?"

I frowned. I wanted him to come home with me. It was still the weekend, Sunday afternoon, and officially, he was still in my custody. But I didn't say anything. Why cause a ruckus at this point?

Tommy dittoed my silence. That was his answer, the best he could do. Who knew what he was really thinking? My shoulders sagged. I felt so frustrated.

"'K," he said finally. He shrugged. "'K."

I found myself moving closer to Cheryl without even realizing it. And then, suddenly, Cheryl and I came together and hugged, so unexpectedly, and yet, it seemed, so inevitably. After seeing our son writhe the way he had, our emotions were burned raw, and it was as if all our defenses came down at once. At that moment, we needed each other. That was all there was to it. I soaked up the feel of her body, lingering against me for comfort. The smell of her, the memories.

"God, Chris," Cheryl whispered. "Seizures now. One more problem to deal with."

"We'll work through it," I said, trying to maintain a steadfast outlook, though inside, I didn't feel that way at all.

Her sudden closeness took me back to the warmth of when she was mine, those once upon a time days and nights. Now, we were just existing parent to parent. We would always be connected in that sense. Still, all that had lived between us for so many years washed over me as we continued clinging to each other, the in-and-out-tides of what we'd shared, what we'd lost. I felt somehow wounded yet slightly healed by her nearness simultaneously. Losing a marriage is like losing a child that you never get to see grow up, you never get to witness its full maturation and there's always a hole inside you as a result—no matter what you tell yourself. As our embrace ended, remorse and hurt and sorrow slivered through me, one after the other. Tommy started to drone to himself, turning inward, oblivious to the turbulence around him, to what was going on.

"Oh, Chris," Cheryl whispered. "Let's not be angry. It isn't worth it." She clutched my shoulders.

"I know, I know," I said. Tears came to my eyes as our two-year-old divorce seemed suddenly a lifetime ago, Paleolithic.

AFTER TOMMY HAD EATEN lunch and rested a while longer, the doctors said he could be discharged if his baseline bilirubin tested negative. Bilirubin was a measurement of his hemoglobin for medication purposes. That was the odd thing about hospitals. Your life could be a total emotional wreck, but if your baseline bilirubin tested negative, out the door you went. We'd talked to the billing department and signed the papers. The bill would go to Cheryl's gold insurance program, which was fine with me.

Cheryl and I went to the first-floor foyer of the hospital as directed, then twenty minutes later, a tall, curly-haired orderly wheeled Tommy to us. We stood near the front entrance, visitors passing in and out. I felt jittery and distraught as I watched him appear. Sitting in the wheelchair, he was motor-boating away, biting both hands. A senior citizen at the information desk stared at Tommy as well. I stood a foot away from Cheryl, who was checking her phone. A heavyset man passed us, carrying a dozen roses.

"There you are," Cheryl said brightly as we both walked up to our son. "Ready to go home?"

Tommy didn't answer. He shook his head right and left, which could have meant anything, still picking at his fingers and drooling. Color had returned to his cheeks, and I felt relieved. I quickly handed him a yellow token as Cheryl looked on.

"Tok," he said, fingering the token.

"Yes, that's for being a good boy. Max sure misses you. He told me himself." Then I pulled out Bugs Bunny from the contents of my vocal drawer: "That's right, doc. Missing you all day long, yuk, yuk, yuk."

Cheryl started to send a text message, and then Dr. Whitaker joined us one final time, his smooth-shaven face grim. He'd ditched his white coat, and now wore slacks and a white shirt, his glasses in the shirt pocket. He'd written two prescriptions for Tommy, and as he handed them to me, Cheryl yanked them out of my hand. I didn't try to stop her, but it made me feel angry. "I'll take these," she said.

The doctor offered his final advice in a somber tone: "We've figured out the proper dosage of Dilantin for him, but we'll continue to monitor him and do more blood work. Call my office tomorrow and set up your next appointment in one week. As far as taking the Wellbutrin, I'll need you to decrease the dose."

"Thank you, doctor," I said.

Finally, we were good to go, back to the real world, back to our reverse Disneyland. Cheryl, Tommy, and I made our way outside through the automatic doors, the orderly pushing the wheelchair with Tommy in it. What an adventure. I would have much preferred the public library, the puppet show we'd planned on.

I felt frustrated. I knew that Cheryl had talked about taking Tommy with her, but since my weekend visitation time wasn't finished yet, I wanted him to come home with me. It just seemed right. Since her car had broken down, I was assuming she'd get an

Uber. Having followed the ambulance to the hospital, my car was parked in the hospital's complex parking system, lot E-2, orange, about a hundred miles away.

As we walked outside, the sun washed the streets and sidewalks in a rain of light. It suddenly all seemed surreal, and I blinked and tried to adjust my eyes to this other-world and this new life I had stepped into with seizures in it, seizures that could arise anytime, anywhere.

The hospital's outdoor entrance was fronted by a horseshoe-shaped drive. We stood at the curb where other people were waiting for their rides. Cheryl shaded her eyes. I stood on one side of the wheelchair, Cheryl on the other. The orderly still maintained control.

"Wade should be pulling up any minute," Cheryl said. Then she pulled out a compact mirror and started to check her makeup, applying lipstick. She smoothed her hair. "Tommy and I will wait here for him and then go with Wade."

"Wade?" I asked, raising an eyebrow. "Who pray tell is Wade?"

"You remember Wade, don't you?" she said casually. "You introduced us yourself. We've sort of been seeing each other."

"What?" I cocked my head. "You mean Wade Dudley? Are you serious? You're seeing him?"

"Don't look so astonished." Cheryl put her makeup back into her leather purse.

I'd worked with Wade Dudley at Focus for about a year, and yes, I remembered the moment I'd introduced him to Cheryl. We were at Ed Ryerson's house in La Jolla. It was a party, a celebration, really, for landing an important account. The music was loud and when Wade brought Cheryl a drink, he did a little Michael Jackson moonwalk imitation, which made Cheryl roar. We were still married, then. The guy was obnoxious. Everybody knew that. Fairly successful, though.

He was great at sticking his nose into someone else's deal, glomming onto it, and then making it look like it was his.

"Fine. Whatever." I hung on an icy pause, and then: "Look, Cheryl, I'd like Tommy to come home with me. The weekend's still not over and I still have time with him. So, can you at least wait with Tommy while I go get my car?"

The orderly, whose skinny frame made him look like he was about to blow away, remained behind Tommy looking uncomfortable, playing with his watch band and tapping his right foot.

"No need." Cheryl took hold of Tommy's wheelchair. "Tommy's coming home with us. I promised him a movie and ice cream."

I stopped her and put my hands on the wheelchair, nodding at the orderly to step aside, which he did. I spoke sternly. "I know what you promised, Cher. But I have every right to want him to come home with me."

"Well, he's not." She glanced at the orderly and grabbed the wheelchair herself.

I couldn't believe her. We'd just had this intimate bonding session, the three of us, and we'd felt close—at least momentarily, but now she was acting like a witch, with this Wade guy and her persistent possessiveness. I felt let down, unwanted. I couldn't believe she'd act like this.

She tried to maneuver Tommy's wheelchair away from me, but I grabbed on, refusing to let go. She fought back, grappling against me, trying to unlock my grip on the chair's side handle. She shoved me with her hips and I pushed back. The orderly jumped back and didn't say a word, but his eyes were wide, and he stood there rigid as he rubbed his pockmarked face.

"He's coming home with me!" I'd had enough of this BS. "It's still my weekend with him, dammit!"

While we were fighting over him, Tommy was sitting in the wheelchair, biting his hands and droning, locked away in his private world. He seemed unbothered by the fuss. Completely oblivious, actually, tone deaf to the complex sounds of human emotions, even ones as confrontational as ours. Truly, his autism was a kind of emotional deafness.

Cheryl roared. "No, he's not!"

And then Wade pulled up, driving a white Jaguar XJR, four-door sedan. We both looked his way. The man of the hour. His car looked brand new and instantly, it was as if the jealousy button in my heart had been pressed, the alarm rung. I swallowed hard, but the thick lump in my throat wouldn't descend. Wade push-buttoned down the window on his car, his round face breaking out in a huge grin.

"Hey, sweetie," Wade said to Cheryl. "How's it going? Is Tommy all right?"

"Hey, babe. He's fine." Cheryl reciprocated with her own equally brilliant smile, standing straight now and smoothing her hair, pretending I didn't even exist. God, they were in love. I could practically smell the romantic tension between them.

Emotional termites started gnawing on the walls of my stomach. Cheryl walked quickly to the car. She opened the back door of the Jag where a sturdy car seat awaited, one of those deluxe models, with mounds of foam padding, all snapped in and everything. The nerve. She had a car seat in Wade's Jag? She'd been carrying on with Wade and I hadn't known a thing? How could she? I had to step back and take a deep breath.

I studied the white Jag, which I noticed already had a slight ding on the side, then, keeping my grip on the wheelchair, my eyes found the driver. Wade looked like he was about to say something, his lips parted, but in the end, decided not to. A blue VW pulled up behind Wade, waiting in line to pick up someone else.

"It's four o'clock," Cheryl said, glancing at her watch, her eyes lit with anger. She put a hand on her chest as she just stood there next to the open door, showing me the car seat. "He needs to come with me."

"Radar's still at my house and he wants him," I said, trying my best to keep my voice calm. "I told him we could tell Max about what happened. I think he should come home with me. I'll bring him tonight around eight. Weekends are *my time*. I can keep him as long as I want."

"Really?" Cheryl glared at me. "You think so? Tommy?" She paraded back to where I was standing with Tommy and once again tried to maneuver me out of the way. I momentarily lost my grip on the wheelchair. Tommy still appeared undisturbed by the all the fuss. "He's coming with me!"

She made some headway in the direction of the car, but I stopped her, yanking on the wheelchair, which tipped for a scary moment. Yikes!

"No!" I said as I struggled with the wheelchair. "I'm sick of you always getting your way on everything. He's coming home with me, dammit!"

"Christ." Cheryl rolled her eyes, took a long breath, and spoke softly to the orderly, who was waiting on the wheelchair to take back into the hospital. "I'm sorry my ex is such a lunatic."

He just shot us a tense smile.

"You are so damn intractable," she said to me. "Ugh!"

She let go of the wheelchair, pushing it slightly in my direction. Her crimson cheeks flared as she headed toward Wade's car, adjusting her blouse.

"Stay with me, Tom-Tom," I said, taking a breath.

"'Kay, Daddy."

"You're being a good, good boy. Daddy loves you."

"'Kay."

Maintaining my firm grip on the wheelchair, I turned my attention to Wade, who had been watching our little tête-à-tête with his face all tightened up, as if he'd smelled something rotten.

"Hold on, Tom-Tom." I handed him another token. I glanced at the orderly, who looked uncomfortable, his face turning red, his eyes pinpointed.

"Daddy, Mommy!" Tommy said. "Go. Go."

"Yes, in a minute, okay? Are you okay? Can Mommy and Daddy talk just a minute more?"

"'Kay, Daddy."

I turned to the orderly. "Can you please watch him a minute more?"

"Sure," he said in a soft voice, shrugging. "No problem."

I moved closer to the Jag and Wade shot me a good-natured grin. The guy was a real piece of work. A red patch of burnt skin stretched vertically across his Roman nose—too much San Diego sun, probably from driving his boat around.

"Chris, you remember Wade, don't you?" Cheryl tried to sound casual as she climbed in the car on the passenger side and clicked on her seatbelt.

Wade's good-natured grin turned cocky. "How you doing, Chris? You're looking well."

"Mommy, Daddy." Tommy's voice inched higher in pitch. "Mommy, Daddy stop." He banged his hands together like cymbals.

"It's okay, Tommy," I said, turning back to face Tommy. "Mommy and Daddy are just talking."

"Daddeee, Mommeee. Fine. Fine. Fiiiiine."

I tried to keep myself together. I looked over at Wade again. He snapped off his shades, revealing eyes as green and clear as Caribbean waters.

Wade extended his hand through the open window and I found myself shaking it, his grip exactly as I remembered, a "real man's" grip.

He had huge hands and baseball bats for arms and a square face with a jaw that could serve as a doorstop.

"Wade." It was the only word that found its way out of my mouth. Me, mister eloquence, mister voice-over guy. *Wade.* The awkward moment stretched lengthwise and sideways simultaneously. "How's biz?" I asked, not knowing what else to say. I glanced at Cheryl who, now sitting in the passenger side, narrowed her eyes at me.

"Not bad. How about you?" He gave me that famous all's-well-with-my-world San Diego grin.

"I'm making it." I squinted.

"Hey," Wade said. "Loved your work on that Presto Burger ad by the way. I thought it was great." Then he mimicked my routine, doing a bad job too, blathering out a deep, manly voice. "You like it fast? You like it hot? That's preeeestoooo!" He laughed. "Loved it! Here's my card. Let's keep in touch."

"Thanks." I hated to admit it, but I was appreciative of the praise. I glanced at his card. WC Productions. Evidently, he was freelancing, too.

"I want him home by eight," Cheryl said sternly, her red-hot eyes gunning me down.

"Sure," I said. "Not a problem."

Wade gave me a friendly nod, push-buttoned up his window, then gassed away, the two lovers heading off into their own version of a happy ever-after future, leaving me once again, in reverse Disneyland with Tommy still in the wheelchair. He was now looking up at the sky and pointing to a bird that was flying above us.

"Can you wait with him while I go get my car?" I asked the orderly.

"Sure thing," he said.

"Tommy," I said, trying to get his attention. "You wait with the nice man and I'll be back. I'm going to get the car."

"Daddddeee," he said in his monotonic way, forming his imitation smile and breaking my heart in the process. "Dadeeee." Wade and Cheryl; what a pair.

Chapter 8

"So, tell me, Tom-Tom." I pulled past a slower car as we drove back to Weller, cruising down the interstate. Three thankfully uneventful weeks had transpired, and Tommy, safely secured, clutched Radar and Monkey in the backseat. "Does Wade play any fun games with you? What do you think about him? Is he fun? You want to tell Daddy?"

So far, he'd had no more seizures, which was absolutely great news. Dr. Whitaker had evidently found the proper dosage—at least for now, it seemed. Whitaker and I had talked on the phone and I'd ended the call feeling satisfied with all that he was doing for Tommy. I'd called Rachel and told her about the seizure as well. I thought it only right that she should know. She sounded completely sympathetic. I felt grateful that she understood, glad that she was on my side. Truly, the seizure issue was something we'd have to closely monitor.

But as usual, there were other issues to deal with in my whack-a-mole life. Earlier that morning, my attorney had told me over the phone that the date for the hearing had been set. Cheryl was definitely going to sue for sole custody so that she could take Tommy to Houston without my permission, and so, the game was on. Talk about pissing me off. But anger would do nothing at this point. I would have to sharpen my wits and guard against all the attacks she would throw at me. She would try to prove that I was standing in the way of Tommy's educational development and his best interests. I would have to fight for him to stay in San Diego so he could be with the chimps, fight as hard as I could. What lay ahead made me feel as if I were standing at the foot of a tall mountain, preparing to somehow climb it. But climb it I must. It was time for complete inner resolve.

Evidently, Cheryl believed she had a strong case. She was the mother, after all. Didn't mothers know best? Mark reassured me that he felt we had a strong case, too.

"Can you tell Daddy what you and Wade do?" I asked softly as I continued driving.

"We play. Play."

"So, what do you play?" I kept my voice light.

I wasn't surprised that Tommy hadn't mentioned Wade to me. Tommy was too withdrawn to even understand what a new relationship was. Still, I needed to investigate, do a little father-sleuthing.

"Can you tell me, Tommy? Do you and Wade play games?"

After a long pause, Tommy dropped another word: "Ball."

"You mean ball games? Like what?"

"He . . . ball . . . throw."

"Oh, well, that's good." I ran a hand through my hair, trying to maintain my calm. "You know, Daddy can play ball with you too." I'd tried playing ball with him countless times. He'd never shown much interest. We were both silent, and then a minute later:

"Oooouuu." Tommy whimpered and I stared at him through my rearview mirror, my gut roiling. He was frowning and I saw lines of sadness around his mouth as he shifted in his child seat.

"What's wrong, Tom-Tom?"

"Ooooouuuu . . .Wade not you, Daddy. He not . . . youuuuu . . ." Tommy's words were suddenly laden with real emotion; completely unusual for him. "Wade not . . . youuuu, Daddy." It sounded like a plea, which reached into the depths of my fatherly heart and touched it like never before, deep in its most inner recesses. I couldn't help it. A single tear wandered down my cheek. I wiped it away. Tommy wanted me over Wade, of course he did. But what could I do?

"No, he's not me. He's . . ." I didn't know how to continue. The world seemed to suddenly spin. I felt completely mixed up, hanging upside down. Hurt and angry.

And then, as if mustering his words with all his might, Tommy spoke the best way he knew how: He leaned forward, extended his arms holding Radar, and let his stuffed pet rub the back of my neck, which tingled against the feel of it.

"Daddy, you," Tommy said in a low, soft voice. "Want . . . youuuuu."

It was my turn to be speechless. His words rumbled inside my heart, breaking it like glass. Oh, God.

"Oh, Tommy. And I want you too," I said, my voice breaking. "I'll always be here for you. You know that." It was as if I'd suddenly swallowed a sad pill and its effects quickly spread throughout my body.

In the rear-view, our eyes met, direct contact, then my son said it all: "You, Daddy. You."

I nearly lost it right there. Tommy would be going to Houston over my dead body.

WHEN WE ARRIVED AT Weller, still trying to handle in my mind what Tommy had expressed in his own unique way, I saw a Channel 2 news van parked outside the door to the main office. Their slogan was printed in blue on the van: *We keep you up-to-the-minute.* Pictures of Monica McReary and Randy Dowell, the hottest news anchors in town, were wrapped around the truck, both flashing their whitest, brightest smiles. Shootings, muggings, robberies—they handled it all.

What was Channel 2 doing at Weller? As I climbed out of my car, something else drew my attention: I spied a helicopter sitting about a hundred yards away, parked in a vacant field.

Tommy pointed at the van as I unhooked him from the backseat and he climbed out of the car. "Two, Daddy. Two." Then he returned to humming and murmuring again. I wiped dribble from his lips with a tissue from Mister Backpack. He blew his nose into another tissue.

Staring at the news van, I said, "Come on, son. Let's go talk to Dr. Simmons and see what's going on. You okay?"

Tommy nodded and I looked him over, afraid that I might find the glimmerings of another seizure about to happen. I used to fear tantrums. Now, I had something even worse to reckon with.

With Mister Backpack slung over my shoulder, we followed the pathway and walked up to the building. Holding Radar close to him, Tommy looked down at the ground, walking by my side, but continuing to keep his distance from me as usual. Once again, the fact that he wouldn't hug me or let me even hold his hand brought a sadness to my heart that I couldn't ignore.

When we opened the front door and stepped inside the office, a stocky, black-haired male reporter was in the midst of interviewing Rachel, while a large muscular cameraman in a headset shouldered a Channel 2 camera, its red light on. A lone assistant had her eyes on a computer in a far corner. Rachel kept fiddling with her hands as she spoke, her eyes darting nervously with every sentence.

"What we do here is . . . uh, basic research on nonhuman primates." She spoke haltingly, glancing at me as we entered.

"So, about this autistic boy. What can you tell us?" The reporter cast his eyes at Tommy and me as we walked in. "Is that him? Is that the kid?" The reporter rushed over to me and thrust a microphone in my face before Rachel could reply, the camera man following.

"Mike Bloomfield, Channel 2 news. Is this your son?" His brash attitude made me instantly dislike him.

"No comment."

"Is he autistic?" He waved the microphone at me like it was a weapon and this was a news hold-up. I felt accosted.

"I really don't have a comment." I shook my head.

This Bloomfield was a real piece of work. He wasn't just dressed in a suit, he looked as if he'd been finely tailored and primped like some fashion model about to hit the runway.

"Is it true your son actually speaks to chimpanzees?"

"Can we turn that camera off, please?" I said, growing angrier by the minute.

"Is this your son? What can you tell us?" His dark eyes drilled into mine.

"Look." I rose to my full height, towering over the shorter reporter. "You want the truth? Here it is. I'm not going to tell you one damn thing, all right?" I pointed at the door. "So, you may as well just climb into your van and head on back to your TV station because the news here is that there's no news for you."

Bloomfield turned to Rachel. "Care to comment?"

"No further comments," she said.

Bloomfield's eyes meandered over to my son. He motioned to the camera man to turn off the camera, then knelt down to Tommy's level, moving closer. Tommy backed off and screamed. He bit his hands and kicked, whirling around. "Ouuuuu. Oooouuuu. Ooooo . . ."

Bloomfield's eyes went wide. "Let's go, Rudy." Then he turned to me and stood to his full height. He spoke over Tommy's motorboating. "Just remember, if there's news here, it *will* come out, one way or the other. It's always better if you give your side of things before that happens."

"The door's that way," I said.

"Oooouuuuu...Way...way...way..."

When the reporter and his cameraman were gone, Rachel said, "Did you get my text? I tried to warn you."

"No. I didn't get it." I checked my phone and there it was: a waiting text message. I had turned off the ringer and hadn't felt the vibration when the text message came through.

She explained. "Evidently some YouTube video of your son at the zoo and the chimps staring at him has gone viral." I recalled the pimple-faced teen recording Tommy that first day at the zoo and how I'd thought about stopping him, but didn't. *This is so rad.* Of course. "It's gotten tons of hits and your ex's attorney—" Rachel stopped when I held up my hand.

"I get the picture. Trust me."

Tommy held Radar and suddenly struck himself on the cheek. We both looked at him.

"Tommy, no," I said. "Don't do that."

He motor-boated back at me.

"Weller's come up with an official statement that we're prepared to give if necessary, explaining that we are a research facility and that yes, we are considering doing research with an autistic child as part of our experimental protocol, but no, we don't believe the boy actually speaks to chimps," she explained as my eyes lifted from Tommy to study her face. "But you know how the media is. Always snooping around. I had no idea he'd actually show up like this, totally out of the blue."

"Are you all right?" I asked.

She was still breathing hard. The color had drained from her face. "Yeah, sure. I just need a moment. Let me go to the ladies' room. Be right back."

Speaking to Radar, Tommy went into a nonsensical stream of pseudo-words.

"Hey, Tom-Tom, what are you saying to Radar? Maybe you could tell Radar your ABC's." I spoke in my Mister Rogers voice, soothing and easy, hoping to get a response.

But Tommy ignored me, dropped Radar to his side. Head down, he put a finger into his mouth and sucked on it. Another finger went up his nostril as a sad heaviness tugged at my heart. Then he smacked himself on his cheek and gnawed on his knuckles.

"No, Tommy, please don't do that."

He looked down as if he knew what he'd done was wrong.

"Noooo," he said. "Nooooo."

When Dr. Simmons returned a few minutes later, I said, "Why can't guys like that cover real news, like for instance, the exorbitant salaries that TV reporters are paid?"

She laughed. She seemed in control now. "I know," she said. "He's clearly on a power trip of galactic proportions. You know, short man's syndrome? Anyway." She blinked and let out another long breath. "Let's go." She beckoned me and Tommy forward with a wave of her hand. "We're all assembled and we need to get this show on the road."

We walked out the door, passing through the courtyard and heading toward the buildings, Tommy at my side mumbling to Radar again.

"By the way, I was wondering. Is there no room for a compromise of some sort between you and Cheryl?" Rachel asked.

"Well, there've been letters and counter-letters." I rubbed the back of my neck. "My lawyer and I were trying to get Cheryl to agree to chimp therapy for a year and then see what happens. And if there's no result, then I would agree to try the Acorn School."

"What did she say to that?" she asked. Her eyes meandered over Tommy and Radar and then she looked at me.

"To translate the legalese—hell, no!"

"I see."

"Actually, the court date's been set. Cheryl wouldn't even agree to mediation. Her lawyer wanted a hearing with a judge and nothing else and she knows the law well enough to make it happen. My attorney just notified me this morning. It's going down one month from now. May 12th, to be exact. Friday. 10:30 a.m."

"It's really going to throw a wrench into things, isn't it?" She pinched her lips together and wrinkled her brow as she touched my shoulder.

"More like a bomb." I sighed.

"Then we'll just have to work as fast as we can to show that Tommy is benefiting from the chimps," she said with determination in her voice. "This is most disconcerting."

"Chimpies?" Tommy said. He gave Rachel a free-flowing smile, flicking his fingers.

"Oh yes," she said. "And we have a big surprise for you today."

"'Prize? 'Prize?"

"Yes, indeed." She nodded eagerly. "We want you to meet someone very special. Let's go. Actually a few special people, just this way."

I grew worried that Tommy might have a meltdown in front of these new faces. And I hoped that he wouldn't start convulsing and seizing up.

Instead of heading toward the play yard, Rachel led Tommy and me toward a building fifty yards away, to the left of the barn. It was a brick edifice about the size of a four-car garage, set back all on its own. The sign on the shiny metal door said: Research A-12.

We entered a green-walled conference room, with sophisticated-looking machines resting against one wall. I was so surprised that my hand went to my mouth and I gasped in awe. In the room sat three other white-coated scientists, along with Dr. Evans, all studying notes and staring at the equipment. And at the head of the conference table sat Carly Yates herself. The real deal. I couldn't believe it.

I recognized her instantly and grew breathless. How many times in your life do you actually get to meet a famous billionaire? As soon as we stepped in, all eyes turned our way. I ushered Tommy in slowly, not sure how he would react.

Then I looked beyond Ms. Yates, into the adjoining room, about twenty feet away and separated by a thick glass wall. Something even stranger than the appearance of the famous Ms. Yates made me draw back. I did a double-take and blinked. I couldn't believe it, but a fully-grown adult chimp sat on a chair doing what I guessed all smart adult chimps did in their spare time:

He was standing at an easel painting.

Chapter 9

Ms. Yates stood and stepped forward to meet me and Tommy, while the scientists remained sitting around the conference table. Tommy moved away from her, hands in mouth now, head down. He cuddled Radar, motor-boated, and spun around. Then he smacked himself.

"Tommy, no," I said. "Please don't do that."

But he was completely in his own world and didn't seem to even hear what I was saying.

"It's a pleasure to meet you, Mr. Crutcher," Ms. Yates said, extending a hand to me after she'd studied Tommy. She spoke in that familiar Boston accent of hers.

We shook hands and I felt my face turn red. For a minute, I grew speechless, a rare moment for me indeed. "Ms. Yates. I'm—I'm honored."

Her reassuring, thin-lipped smile was unable to put me at ease. As my hands clammed up, a sudden shyness overtook me. I was basically in a mild state of shock. I studied her piercing blue eyes, her broad forehead, her round face, on which she'd applied just a smattering of makeup. She wore a simple navy-blue dress belted at the waist; the ring on her left hand was the giveaway—it was huge, unfathomably expensive looking.

I sensed a kind of fiery dynamism that orbited around her, something that none of the photos in the newspapers or the shots on TV could reveal. She didn't just look at you, she absorbed you, subsumed you, her entire being fully engaged in the present moment.

"I'm so excited about this," she said, giving me a wide-open smile. "This has got to be one of my most interesting projects ever." She looked down at Tommy, who was fidgeting now as he turned and stared again at the adult chimp. She apparently knew not to try to greet him or touch him. I guessed she'd been forewarned. "He's such a beautiful little boy. I know you're proud of him."

"I am." I swallowed, again at a loss for words. "Tommy, can you say hello to Ms. Yates?"

Tommy gave her a quick look, and then a deep, robotic: "Hello."

"Hello to you too, Tommy," Ms. Yates said. "He's so precious!"

"Hello . . . Fine . . . Hello . . . Fine." Tommy repeated himself a minute more as we watched him, then sucked on the backs of his hands, which I gently tugged from his mouth.

"One of the reasons I was so drawn to this project was because I have a nephew who's autistic," Ms. Yates said. "He's also eight years old. I see how much he struggles. He's pretty severe. My sister and her husband are out of their minds with worry." Her brow wrinkled. "If this research can offer just a small window into how people with autism think and behave, I'm all for it, not to mention what it could possibly mean for our understanding of the nonhuman primates. Dr. Dunn? Am I right?" Yates turned to a shiny-headed bald man with a smooth-shaven face and a jutting jaw.

"Absolutely. This is truly groundbreaking work. I'm pleased to meet you as well," Dr. Dunn said in a smooth voice as he stood, then came over to me. He was hardly more than five feet five inches in shoes. But his dark eyes were sparkling and filled with what seemed to be a giant intelligence. We shook hands. "Morris Dunn. Pleased to meet you. I'm a neurobiologist and autism researcher from Berkeley, and I'll be working with Tommy to make sure he advances as much as possible through chimp therapy. I must tell you, we are extremely excited." Dr. Dunn looked down at Tommy, who was now whirling around.

They were excited? I was through the roof. I had no idea that Dr. Simmons had assembled a team as impressive as this. She hadn't even given me a clue what she'd done. "Thank you," I said, gushing. "Thank you so much."

"The pleasure is all ours," Dr. Simmons said, looking at me directly in the eyes. Her firm look said it all: You and I are in this together, every single exploratory piece of it.

"Monk," Tommy said.

I reached into Mr. Backpack and handed Tommy his other stuffed animal friend, which he took in his outstretched arms. Immediately he started mumbling to it as if he were passing along secrets, then banging Monkey against Radar. I looked at Dr. Dunn who gave me a winsome smile.

"I see he's strongly attached to them," Dr. Dunn said.

"Yes, he is."

"I'm hoping we'll be able to move him away from his interest in things and turn his focus on people," Dr. Dunn said. "This will be our ultimate goal."

"My ex just thinks this chimp business is nothing but something for Tommy to obsess on," I said., "She just doesn't buy into it like I do."

"Well, I don't see it that way at all. Of course, no one knows for sure," Dr. Dunn said, looking down at Tommy, then at Ms. Yates, and finally at me, "but after studying the videos and seeing him now in person, I firmly believe he'll be able to use this so-called obsession in a positive way so that he can learn to relate to humans through the chimps."

My heart thrummed. So, I wasn't such a fool after all. I now had an expert on board. Cheryl had no idea what she was up against. I had power and money on my side now.

After I'd been introduced to Dr. Osikawa, a short man from Japan who was in charge of the fancy equipment lined against one wall, the third scientist stepped forward. This man's expression was serious, almost pained.

"Mister Crutcher, my name's Carl Rekulak." He spoke with a British accent and had a square face with protruding cheekbones, a scar zigzagging across his dimpled chin. Tall and rail thin, with his pale, whitewashed face, he looked undernourished. His thinning white hair was slicked back and he had long sideburns with a silver mustache. Probably in his early fifties. "I'm very glad to meet you."

We shook hands.

"In the next room, Mr. Crutcher," Dr. Rekulak said, his voice even and low, "is a chimpanzee named Albert." He paused, cleared his throat, then said, "Albert is like no other chimp in the world, you see. He's a unique animal few people even know about."

I raised an eyebrow. "How so?"

"Awbert!" Tommy cried. It was as if he'd been waiting for the chimp to be named. "Awbert! See Awbert." Tommy spoke rapidly, excitement coursing through his voice.

"You'll see why I say this soon enough," Dr. Rekulak said with a quick smile.

"Well, if you all will excuse me," Carly Yates said, looking at her watch. "I really wish I could stay, but I'm afraid I need to get going. I have a meeting in LA with my Noah's Ark people in about an hour and a half. I just wanted to stop by and meet Tommy personally. Sidney," she said, turning to Dr. Evans and speaking firmly. "I want a full report as soon as possible."

"Absolutely," Dr. Evans said, nodding.

Before I could even say goodbye, Ms. Yates swept out of the room.

"Dr. Rekulak's one of the top researchers in our field," Rachel touched my shoulder briefly and explained when Ms. Yates was gone. "One of the most authoritative primatologists in the world. He's lived in the forests of Tanzania studying chimps for the past twenty-five years, and has extensive documentation of chimp communication, both gestural and oral. He's given his entire life to exploring nonhuman primate communication and has come all the way from Africa to meet your son."

"I'm entirely grateful," I said. "Thank you." We exchanged looks.

"It's my pleasure," he said giving me a flick of a smile. "This is too interesting to pass up."

A minute later, the whir of helicopter blades overhead made me prick up my ears. Ms. Yates's mode of transportation; pretty cool. I wondered if she flew herself. Knowing what I'd read about her, she probably did.

"Awbert." Tommy gave Monk and Radar back to me, and I placed them into Mister Backpack as he raced up to the window and peered through the glass. He began flicking his fingers like crazy. We all watched him. "Awbert. Awbert sick."

The window appeared to be one-way since Albert didn't seem to notice us.

"He's right," Rekulak said. "Albert is sick. And it's such a tragic story. I should make you aware of his history before we go further. If you don't mind."

"All right," I said, then turned to Tommy. "Tommy, we're going to meet Albert soon, but first I need to hear what the doctor says, okay?"

"'Kay. Fiiiine." Tommy shook his head back and forth, then seemed to lose his balance before righting himself. He put a hand to his head, the same spot where he received the blow from Turtle Boy, then rocked back on the balls of his feet as he looked down.

"Are you okay?" I asked.

For a moment, he said nothing as my throat turned dry. Another seizure? No. It couldn't happen now. Then: "Fiiiine," he said and turned to me and gave me direct eye contact. "Fiiiine, Daddy."

Relief let loose inside me. "Good. I'm fiiiine too." I smiled. "When you're fine, I'm fine."

Tommy continued staring at Albert, scratching his head, then an ear.

Rekulak began, speaking in a dry, somber tone. "You see, Albert's history is long and complex. And unfortunately, very sad. I rescued Albert from a biomedical lab about three years ago. He was abused there and basically tortured by the researchers. He'd been captured from the southern region of Gombe in Tanzania as a young chimp and brought to America for AIDS research. We estimate his age to be around 40. When the biomedical lab was finished working on him, experimenting and extracting information from his body, they stuck him in a cage to live out the rest of his years. It was an experience beyond misery. Torture, really."

"Sounds horrible." It hurt just thinking about it. "How did he even survive?" I looked at the chimp, who continued to peacefully paint.

"He barely did," Rekulak explained. "He suffers from a heart condition now, and most likely post-traumatic stress syndrome. I have him on a tranquilizer to keep him calm, though he still has a hard time falling asleep. After rescuing him and putting him through rehabilitation and education, I discovered Albert's marvelous and unusual talents. He's an incredibly quick learner."

"Chimpie, Daddy," Tommy said. He ran back to me and pointed, then grabbed my hand. I loved it when he willingly touched me. "Chimpie hurt." And he didn't have that robotic voice inflection.

"Yes, Tommy. Albert isn't feeling well, I'm afraid."

"Oh." Tommy looked down and grew silent. "Awbert hurt."

"In fact, as it turns out," Rekulak continued in his dry, sad tone, "this chimp has proven to be the most advanced nonhuman primate ever encountered. He literally knows hundreds of signs, paints sunsets and trees, and even renders fairly accurate depictions of flowers. The primatology community has kept him a secret from the public. We don't want the news of him getting out until we've thoroughly studied him, but in terms of chimp intelligence, you're looking at a true genius. His receptive language skills are incredible, his photographic memory unparalleled. When we learned of Tommy's chimp communication skills, we were all dying to have your son meet Albert. He's been living at Weller for the past three years."

"Well, I'm amazed," I said. "I really am. I don't know what—"

"Daddy," Tommy said. He started tugging at my pants. "Albert no free."

"What do you mean?" I said, kneeling down to him, surprised that he'd talk about such an abstract concept.

"Chimpie," he whispered. "Chimpie . . . He no free. He want free."

"Yes, Tommy," Dr. Rekulak said. "Albert's not free for now, but one day we plan to let him live out his final days in a sanctuary in Mexico."

"Albert free now!" Tommy said, stomping a foot. "Now!"

"It's okay, Tommy. Albert's here to meet you and to talk with you. This should be fun. We want to see how you talk to Albert."

"Tommy?" Rachel said gently, looking at me before continuing. "Would you mind if we put this special hat on your head?"

Rachel pointed to an electrode cap sitting next to a complex-looking machine in the corner of the room. The cap was made out of dark-blue rubber and had electrodes patched through it. What appeared to be a small antenna, a short wire with a bulb on the end, was attached at the top.

"Hat," Tommy said in his monotonic way.

"Yes. It'll be fun to wear. Let's let your Daddy wear it," she said.

Rachel gave me the cap and I pretended to put it on, though it was a child's size and would not fit me. I let it sit on top of my head to show that it was harmless. Tommy bit his hands. He started to drool as he peered at it.

"See?" I said. "It's fun!" But this needed to be more than fun, I thought as I tensed up inside. So much of Tommy's future was riding on this research. I had to show some kind of developmental benefit so that I could counter Acorn—or else Tommy would be on his way to Houston and my dream of successful chimp therapy would be out the window.

"This hat will help the chimpies," Rachel said with a bright smile. "And Albert wants to see you wear it."

"'Kay," Tommy said. He touched Rachel's hand. "Help," he said. "Yes, help."

"Great!" I said. "And this is for being a good boy."

I handed Tommy some tokens. He carefully placed them in his pocket as Dr. Osikawa took the cap from me and placed it on Tommy's head, adjusting it in place. I was surprised he let them do it without a fuss. It seemed like Tommy was starting to appreciate the tokens more lately, that they might actually be working to my favor.

"Help chimpies," he said.

"Yes, for chimpies. So we can learn."

"Know," he said. "Know."

"Yes, that's right," Dr. Rekulak said. "I think he gets it. Great!"

We all studied Tommy as he put on the hat. That was my boy, all wired up to help us explore his own mind. What a trooper!

"Dr. Osikawa?" Rekulak said, speaking to the Japanese scientist. "Shall we?"

"Wireless communication," Dr. Osikawa explained to me, gesturing to the largest machine, which he rolled in front of him. "We watch in here when your son is with Albert. Like portable MRI. Very advanced."

He clicked it on and the high-tech device bleeped and blipped. Graphs of various colors appeared on the monitor in bright detail.

Dr. Osikawa began twisting dials and punching buttons. I stood next to Tommy, my arm around his shoulder. He was letting me touch him and a sensation of lightness floated across my chest. After a few moments, with the other scientists watching and taking notes, he finally gave Dr. Rekulak a nod.

"Look at this," Dr. Osikawa said. "Already we see reading."

Rachel explained. "This machine maps blood flow in the brain. It allows us to pinpoint oxygen and blood consumption, showing us regions of stronger and weaker activity. The more oxygen and blood consumption in a certain area of the brain, the greater the activity."

"Ah, the default-mode network," Dr. Rekulak said, staring at the machine. "Of course!"

"What?" I said. "What's that?"

"It's really quite remarkable. Tommy is showing major activity in the pre-frontal cortex. It's just as I'd presumed. This is the area of the brain that controls feeling and intuition. This is, no doubt, what's giving him his empathic abilities. It's all lit up."

I looked down at Tommy who had a finger in his mouth. I smiled inside. This was getting more than interesting.

REKULAK OPENED THE door and allowed himself, Tommy, me, and Rachel into Albert's room. Echoes of the chimp's loud, ragged breathing rebounded from wall to wall. A musky chimp odor invaded my nostrils, and for a minute, I just had to stop walking and almost gagged. Tommy didn't seem to mind, though, and neither did Rekulak or Rachel. They were real chimp-heads, I guess.

The aging chimp, whose hair was mostly grey, scrutinized us with dark, liquid, roving eyes, accompanied by a crooked twist of his lips, and what looked to be genuine self-consciousness. I could immediately tell he was living with pain. His movements at the easel,

I now saw, were slow and careful, as if he had arthritis. He contorted his face when he moved, wincing and groaning in pain.

I felt like he was not only watching us, he was *aware* in his mind he was watching us. Unlike say, a shark, or any other animal with that two-dimensional gaze. The way he turned and peered directly at us, examining each and every one of us with a kind of bemused curiosity written on his wrinkled face, spoke clearly of a greater intelligence than I had seen in Mikey or Obo or the chimps at the zoo; truly, this was a special being. He almost seemed more like an aging chieftain from some primitive human tribe than a chimp.

Putting down his brush, Albert slowly and creakily got up from his easel and shambled toward us. When he reached our party, standing just a foot away from us, he scratched his head and for some reason, reached out one hand to me, not to Tommy, nodding his head several times.

Then he flicked his hands in the air, making a sign, and Rachel interpreted: "Who?"

She signed back to him while telling me the meanings of her gestures. "Boy. Son. Man. Big Man."

Albert spread his mouth wide open. He signed, "Boy. Good. Big Man. Good."

When Tommy started signing, Albert shrieked, "Eeee, eeee, eeee, ahhhhh, ahhhhh, wuuuu." The long blare grew louder, ending in what sounded like an exclamation mark.

Dr. Rekulak reared back and then matched him: "Eeee, eeee, eeee, ahhhhh, ahhhhh, wuuuu." And then added: "Ahhhh!"

I had to give him kudos. As a voice-over talent, Dr. Rekulak really seemed to have his "chimpese" down.

"What did you two say?" I asked Rekulak. It sounded like a shouting match to me.

"I gave him a hello or 'welcome' cry." Rekulak wasn't a happy man. His dark eyes looked bereaved, as if he'd seen something too horrible to ever forget.

I looked at Rachel, who stood closest to me, then back at Rekulak. "So, chimps do communicate then."

"Yes," Rekulak said. He gave me flicker of a smile, but it was hardly more than reflex. "Communication is a deeply embedded part of their society. The more I've studied these nonhuman primates, the more I have seen the depth and breadth of their communication. Communication in the chimp world is partly based on survival and necessity, but also, part of it is based on what I would call culture, finer things, beauty, happiness, even a religious belief in a spiritual being."

"You mean they have an understanding of God?" I asked, incredulous.

"Absolutely. I've seen chimps perform rituals and worship. They create simple stone structures that seem to symbolize something close to the mystical."

"Wow," I said.

"Much of Dr. Rekulak's research has been to compile an essential chimp language dictionary," Rachel said. "He's spent years matching squawks, chatter, bellows, shrieks, and gestures with actual concepts and meanings. He's established fifty-six real definitions thus far, and every year we move closer to true communication with these primates. It's completely exciting."

I noticed that two cameras hung on the walls videotaping everything. Of course. This was a momentous occasion. The waiver I'd signed had included a statement about using cameras to record Tommy's behaviors. I was on board with that.

Albert began focusing in on Tommy's finger flicks, his eyes glued to the gestures. And then Albert signed and shrieked. "Eeeeee . .

.uuuuu . . ." Tommy shrieked back as well. "Eee . . . Uuuuuuu . . . ohhhhh."

"What are you saying, Tommy?" I bent down next to him and tried to get eye contact.

But Tommy gave no indication he'd even heard me. He and Albert were completely in their own orbit now. Tommy's signing was faster than I'd ever seen before. He pointed toward the door and then signed "Out. Out." Albert shook his head and signed, according to Rachel, "Hurt . . . body . . . me. Rain. Trees. Tall. Sky."

Dr. Rekulak's flushed face alerted me to the incredible nature of this brand new linguistic relationship flowing right before our eyes. My skin tingled.

Tommy squawked at Albert. "Eeee, ahahahah, ooooo!"

Albert squawked right back. "Eeeee, ahahaha, oooo!" Then Albert touched Tommy's hand and started pounding out rhythms in it: beat, beat, beat, pause, beat, pause, beat . . . Albert shook his head and shrieked. They continued like this for at least five minutes, Albert beating his hand into Tommy's, the rhythms constantly changing.

Finally, it was as if the communication had ended when Tommy turned to me and looked straight into my eyes. "Daddy, chimpie he say he . . . happy I here. He say he good here. He smile me. Me and I say I want him better. He say . . . we all same . . . same. . . fam . . . eee . . .ly . . . Daddy. Peoples, chimpies. Fam . . . eee . . .ly . . . See?"

I blinked, not knowing what to say. I was so taken aback. I gave a bark of uncertain laughter. "Really? He says that?" I turned to Rachel and Rekulak, whose eyes were wide open. We were all stunned. Was he simply making this up?

I didn't think so. I thought about how Tommy had known the chimp at the zoo was pregnant. Still, the skeptic inside me said that there was no way a boy could really and truly understand what a chimp was thinking. But in a way, it didn't really matter. Tommy was talking, his fluency was improving, and being around the chimps was bringing him out of his shell. It was all happening right before my eyes, obvious as the back of my hand. We were excavating emotional treasure.

"Daddy, chimpie . . . bad days remember," Tommy said as eloquently as I'd ever heard him speak. His grammar wasn't the best, but surely, it would come around too, wouldn't it?

"Bad days?" I asked. "What do you mean?"

In a flow of words, Tommy pronounced: "Chimpie say he want tell human peoples many, manies . . .things."

"So, what does Albert want to say?" Rekulak asked. His tone was grave as he focused intently on Tommy.

Tommy's eyes shifted right and left, then up and then down, as if he were using his eyes to draw the information down from his brain, receiving transmissions, then shuttling the ideas into his mouth and out to the world.

"He say . . . He say . . . He say," Tommy took a long breath. "He say . . . chimps see just one." He held his first finger in the air. "One. See? Chimps see every . . . thing and . . . one . . . Humans see many manies. Can't see one." Tommy spread his arms wide, trying to elucidate what he wanted to express.

"Yes!" Rekulak said. "I understand." He spoke directly to me. "Chimps see globally, in fields of awareness that come to them all at once, whereas humans see the world one step at a time. This car, that stop sign, this cloud."

Rachel said, her scientific personality full bore, "This could very possibly be an actual verification of chimpanzee thought processing, right Carl? What we had always surmised, but never knew for sure. Jungle processing, an evolutionary skill, the ability to see many things at once in order to maintain safety."

"Tommy either hyper-focuses on a tiny detail, or sees globally as well," I said. "And if too much information comes at him at once, he can't handle it. Is his brain working in jungle mode, similar to Albert's?"

"It could be a possibility," Rachel said. "This is the connection we've been looking for. The relationship between chimp processing and the processing of an autistic child. Perhaps they are more similar than we ever thought."

"He want talk you, Daddy. You," Tommy said, tugging on my hand now, his eyes bright and alive. "Awbert want you."

"Me?" I pointed to my chest. "But why?"

I turned toward Dr. Rekulak for reassurance, and when he nodded, I stepped forward and gingerly extended my hand, trying to make friends. Albert reached out his hand, which was hairless and clammy, his palm cold and leathery-rough, his thumb set farther apart from the thick and wrinkled fingers.

"Nice chimp," I said. "Good chimp."

I was about to draw my hand away when Albert latched onto it and, before I could stop him, shoved my hand into his mouth. He moved so quickly—too quickly—there was no getting it back. Albert held on with a strength that seemed supernatural, the power in his jaws as mighty as a steel bear trap. He owned my hand. I knew it wouldn't take much for him to clamp down to the bone. My heart suddenly boomed in my chest as my knees grew wobbly.

"Don't worry," Rekulak said, his voice calm, as if this were the most ordinary thing in the world. "Albert doesn't bite. He's only getting to know you. He realizes you're the father of the boy, you're Big Man, and this is his way of introduction."

Rachel added: "Albert's a very formal guy, a kingly chimp, and everything's done right and proper according to his ways, which I'm sure are genetically implanted in his memory from thousands of years back."

I wasn't totally reassured.

"We humans shake hands or even kiss them," Dr. Rekulak said. "Dogs lick hands. And chimps put hands in their mouths. Different strokes for different species. Relax."

But I couldn't relax. Sweat dribbled down my face as my breathing quickened. Rachel gave me a reassuring smile, but the moment lasted an ice age as the kingly chimp ran his teeth over my hand, lightly touching my flesh, feeling it, examining it. His teeth felt hard as marble, but they weren't sharp. I winced, squeezed my eyes closed.

"Friendly sort," I said when he finally let go of my hand. Most dads watch their kids play baseball in little league. There I was, for the sake my son, letting a chimp take my hand in his mouth. Wow. Rachel gave me a paper towel and I wiped my hand.

"That was the friend-to-friend gesture," Rekulak said. "Hand in mouth, running it over with his teeth. You're on his good side already. You must have a way with animals, Mr. Crutcher."

"Guess it kind of runs in the family," I said with a shrug, thinking of my father's intuitive way with horses, relieved that I had my hand back.

Albert rubbed his shoulder against my side, then, without another word or gesture, shuffled back to his chair and started painting again in long brushstrokes, wholly focused on the task at hand; a regular Chimp Van Gogh.

Tommy and I stepped closer to view Albert's handiwork.

An array of color-bottles and paint brushes rested on a small table next to Albert's poster board on which he now drew horizontal lines of yellow and black, merging them into light brown toward the bottom. If there was symbolism or logic to his painting, I could not figure it out.

Tommy scrutinized the drawings and fidgeted.

"Home," Tommy said, looking at me and giving me gorgeous eye contact.

"What?" I asked. "What do you mean?"

"Home. Home." He pointed at Albert's painting, then at Albert. "Home."

"You mean Albert's drawing a picture of his home?" Rachel asked. Both of the doctors had moved toward the painting as well and were watching Albert's work.

Tommy nodded. "Good home. Happy."

On the top half of the poster board, Albert started painting reds and yellows and blues, blending them together in the same manner as he'd done the yellows and blacks.

Tommy said, "Awbert. Making sun and sky. Awbert . . . member," Tommy said, looking at us all as he pointed to his head. "'member."

"Remember?" Rekulak asked.

Tommy nodded and stood on his toes. "Yes. Home. Jungle. Big, big trees. Sun. Sky. Sun. Down." Tommy spread his arms wide.

"Good job, Tommy! You know what Albert's painting," I said, going along. "How do you know?"

"Oooohhh . . . good job, Awbert!" Tommy exclaimed, mimicking me and praising his new friend. Was my son actually trying to be humorous?

Albert stopped painting, looked up, grunted, and then signed, "Talk-boy," according to Rekulak. He grunted again.

"He's designating your son," Rekulak said, "naming him."

Then Albert pointed to Rachel who explained, "Talk-woman." Albert nodded.

Just as Albert returned to his painting, Tommy emitted his low vowel sound, "Ooouuu. Need Radar. Radar, Daddy."

I pulled Radar from Mister Backpack and handed it to Tommy.

"Awbert, look," he said. "Look!"

Tommy showed the Beanie to the chimp, who lifted his head from his art, gazed at it, scratched his head, and screeched. He studied it a while longer and made a sound like a snort. Tommy emitted a series of *varooommm*s and started flying Radar, lifting the pet over his head and zooming him around in the air. Albert watched intently but didn't seem to know what to make of it. When Tommy zoomed Radar close to the chimp's face, Albert backed his head away, nostrils flaring.

"Fly," Tommy said. "Fly."

Albert grunted and signed "bird" as translated by Rekulak.

Tommy mimicked the sign for bird and zoomed Radar around some more. When he tried to hand the Beanie to Albert, the chimp pushed it away. According to Rachel, Albert signed, "No me," and returned to his painting, keeping his eyes glued to the paper in front of him, his brush swishing across the scene.

Tommy hung his head and let his Beanie drop to the floor.

"What's wrong, Tommy? Did Albert hurt your feelings?" I asked.

"No free," he said softly, barely above a whisper. "Awbert no free. Awbert sad."

"Are you sad because he won't take Radar?" Dr. Rekulak asked.

"Awbert no like Radar." He gave himself a whack right on his forehead.

"Tommy!" I took his hands and held them to his sides. "Breathe. Relax."

Tommy tilted his head toward me, his eyes wet as he opened his mouth. I was sure he wanted to say something, but the words wouldn't come. Instead, he wrestled himself free from my grip and began to suck the back of his hand, which I pulled away. Still, he brought it right back up to his mouth.

Then he spoke in a soft but fierce whisper, "Now, Daddy. N-o-o-o-o-ow."

I had never heard him say this word before all by itself before, uttered with such strange intensity.

"N-o-o-o-o-ow. See?" Tommy repeated.

"What do you mean? Noooow. See?" Rekulak echoed Tommy's utterance, then tapped a fist against his lips as he tilted his head to one side. "Tell us more."

Tommy shook his head, the cap slightly shifted, and Rekulak gently re-adjusted it. Tommy's whole face screwed up into an impossible collage of flesh, distorting his features as much as his mind sometimes distorted reality.

"Chimpie," he said.

"Yes?" I said, encouraging him.

"Now! See? See?"

"I'm sorry, I don't see," I said. I shook my head and frowned.

I watched as Albert chose black and painted with long, broad strokes. Then he shrieked and tore up the paper and threw it across the room.

"Albert!" Rekulak cried. "No! Settle down!"

Rekulak signed to the chimp, gave him a hug, and talked soothingly to him. He placed a new poster board in front of him, and the chimp, calming down, began to paint his lines, horizontal and then vertical, in just black now.

"Cage," Tommy said. "No free. No go," Tommy said, his face turning red. "See, Daddy? Awlbert sad." Tommy pointed to him. "He wants now. But . . . but . . ."

"What do you mean when you say 'now'?" Rachel asked.

Tommy took a deep breath and then precious words tripped out of his mouth, syllables dancing in the air. "Now-ing, Daddy. Now. . . ing. Awlbert now-ing. This time, here, now. See?"

"Go on," I said.

"Now . . . ing. But hooooman-peoples go back . . See? Back . . . And . . . peoples go . . . front, too." Tommy pointed forward and then pointed back. "See? Front. Back. But chimps . . . Want NOW! Now-ing, all the time," he said. "See?"

"You mean being now? Right this second? In this moment?" Rachel asked.

Tommy nodded and hugged himself.

"I think I'm starting to get it," I said. "Chimps live in the now, in the moment. Of course. That's probably what gives them their photographic memories, too. They only see what's in front of them. Reality sprays an entire picture at them, instead of the way we look at the world, taking in things one by one, this and that."

"Awlbert ... hurt ... Awbert lost NOW. Hurt! Remember. Paint black lines. No free."

My heart turned over. No free. Tommy seemed to be talking about being in the moment, in the now, when the past and future drop away. Albert couldn't be happy in the Now, the way he should be, because of his painful past. Was Tommy "no free" as well? Locked up in the cage of autism? Of course, he was. I knew I would never give up until I'd found the key and opened his cage. This was my obligation. There simply was no other way. I held my breath to find out more.

"So how do *you* think, Tommy?" I asked, kneeling down to his level. "Are you front and back, or are you ... Now?"

He stamped his foot once again, preparing to say something as he worked his jaw, opened his mouth, and shut it. His eyes shone and he cupped his hands in front of him as if he were waiting to catch water, cradling his ideas with his hands. Finally, he had the words.

"I cage too, just like Awbert, Daddy. Hurt. Hurt bad sometimes. I know now, Daddy. Now." He shook his head. "No like . . . back. No want front. Just want ... Now! Can't talk." He lowered his head. "Like other peoples."

"It's okay, Tom-Tom," I said, putting an arm around him as he inched closer to me, my eyes moistening, my heart breaking. He didn't resist my touch. "Listen," I said, "we *all* have thoughts, humans have all kinds of thoughts. Some good, some bad. It's okay to think about past and future. Front and back. It's fine."

"Fine? Fine? Fine? Fine?"

"Yes. It's fine! Sometimes it's fun to go back and front. That's what people do," I said, trying to reassure him.

"Back front?" Tommy said.

"Yes! You can go places in your mind, think up things, see? Sometimes back and front is fun! Future. Past. Back, front. They're fun. Daddy has fun with front and back. So can you, Tommy. Past, present, and future are all good. That's how you talk better."

"Okay, Daddy," Tommy said. "Varooom." *Flick, flick. Flick-flick.* "I talk now. Okay?"

"Yes, you do!" My pulse raced. I was making a connection here, forming a linguistic bridge, just like Tommy was doing with the chimps. I couldn't believe it. This was as close to a miracle as I'd ever gotten.

"So, what can we do to help Albert, then?" I asked a minute later.

Tommy once again tried to give Radar to Albert, who rejected it a second time.

"Free," Tommy said. "Free."

"Freedom?" Rachel said.

"Free!" Tommy said. "Free! Albert need free."

"You mean like outside?" Rachel asked, pointing to the door. "Back in the forest?"

"No. Free!" Tommy exclaimed. Then he formed his lips in an O and spouted the words: "Like . . . like . . . Granna."

For a moment, we were all silent as we contemplated this concept.

Granna?

"Wait," I said, rubbing the side of my face. "I think I get it. I think he's saying that Albert's sentenced to live the rest of his life in a worn-out body, no matter whether he's indoors or outdoors. I'm not sure it's just about being imprisoned," I continued, thinking about how we'd explained his grandmother's death to Tommy. "I think Albert needs to be free in a different way."

"And what's that?" Rekulak asked, brow furrowed.

Rachel looked confused as well.

"Albert wants to be free from his pain," I said. "That's the kind of freedom he's talking about. Freedom from this world." I shuddered when I said it, looking down at Tommy who was nodding at me, as our eyes connected: "Albert just wants to die."

"Yes, Daddy," Tommy said. "Albert want die. Soooon. Free. No cage no more."

I shivered, hearing the words drip from my son's mouth. I caught Dr. Rekulak's eyes and there were tears in them. The next thing I knew, he was breaking down and sobbing, covering his face with his hands. I stared at him, stunned. I didn't know what to say. Pain, suffering, that was Albert's life; pain and suffering at the hand of man. So, who was the real animal? Wasn't that a fair question? I was on the verge of breaking down myself.

"Oh, Albert," Dr. Rekulak said, "my poor friend. Such a journey you've taken. And to think of all that's been done to you. It's so cruel. So very cruel."

God, the ache inside my chest felt like a stone that suddenly sank into my stomach. Rachel and I traded glances, that same breeze of understanding passed between us, and when she reached out and touched my hand, I caught a trace of mistiness in her eyes. She tried to give me a sorrowful smile, but couldn't make her lips turn up. I also wiped away a tear. I felt our connection deepen, that breeze of understanding blowing just a bit stronger.

"It's true," Dr. Rekulak said, gazing at Albert, whose head was down, panting hard now with pain. "So very sad and so very true."

Tommy held Radar tightly. "Ouuuu . . . drrrrrr . . ." He closed his eyes and turned within, not picking up on the grief that was suddenly circling the room.

Chapter 10

On Monday, two days after the Weller visit, which was probably the most extraordinary event of my life—I still couldn't get over it—I found my father in the backyard, standing high on a ladder and cleaning leaves from his gutter, wearing large garden gloves. The ladder was shaking, his legs, trembling. The good news was that there were still no further seizures from Tommy, thank God, and I sent Whitaker a note of thanks to his email.

"Dad! Get down from there." I stormed up and placed my hands on the ladder to stabilize it. "You want to kill yourself?"

I'd come to check on him and tell him everything I'd seen with Tom-Tom and Albert. There was another reason, too, which nestled deep inside of me.

"I'm fine," he growled. His lined face contorted into the frown of frowns. "You don't have to worry about me." He grabbed a handful of leaves from the gutter and slung them to the ground, just missing my head. "I was cleaning leaves from gutters before you could even walk."

But when he reached out again for another bunch of leaves, his legs trembled even more and for a dire moment, his upper body slanted and the ladder perilously shook.

"Dad! Watch out!"

"There." He barely righted himself. "Man, it's a mess up here."

"Would you please get the hell down?"

When he finally climbed down, he was breathing heavily. He mopped his brow with a white handkerchief, then tipped his ball cap back on his head. His face was as pale as wax.

"Next time call me and I'll help you," I said angrily. "Are you trying to wind up in the hospital or something?"

He didn't say a word. He had a way of going to the Tommy-side too. He studied me as he rubbed his leathery neck, his skeptical frown telling me I wasn't fit to even be the water boy on the ball club of gutter cleaners he ran.

He tromped over to his bed of roses in the middle of the backyard. A beautiful array, cordoned off by a knee-high wooden fence. He bent down to a red rose and took a long, deep sniff. I stood next to him, my nerves still on edge.

"Now, that's what I call nice," he said in his rough voice. "Yes, sir."

I bent down to smell the roses as well, taking a long whiff. Then I took in the yard, the weeping acacia tree and the two pear trees that grew full and tall. I'd played many games of army with my neighborhood friends under that acacia tree. I was always a restless kid, couldn't sit still to save my life. I also did puppet shows and experimented with all kinds of voices, using socks at first as hand puppets and creating short plays. Kids all over the neighborhood would come to watch. It turned out I had talent to make people laugh with my voice at a young age. Go figure.

Dad took care of his roses as if they were his children. He turned on the serpentine-shaped soaker hose nestled on the ground in the rose bed. "About two inches of water a week." He didn't look at me. His gravelly voice sounded like a stream of words pouring over rocks. "Deep soaking's best. Helps to firm up the canes." He stroked a few petals. "Love these Betty Priors." He stood back, admiring them. Then he lumbered over to the garage and, hunched over, returned with some clippers and delicately clipped away a few misaligned stems. For a long moment, a sad silence hung in the air between us, and then: "Know what day this is?" He kept his eyes on the roses; he still wouldn't dare take his gaze away.

A weighty sadness fell around my shoulders, emotional shoulder pads. I took a long breath before answering. "Of course, I do."

"Well . . . You think I'm going to get all upset over it?"

"Hell, no. Not you. That's not your style." Our eyes refused to meet.

"You're right. And that's why I keep these damn roses. They remind me of your mother. They're here for her."

The moment hovered like a big grey rain cloud. Neither of us spoke for a while. This was the second anniversary of my mother's death. We refused to look each other in the eye, two men needing their distance, uncomfortable with expressing their emotions, especially in the presence of each other. I couldn't remember the last time I'd ever hugged my father. "I brought over some hearing aid batteries, Dad," I said finally.

He put a hand to his ear and twisted one of the dials on his hearing aids. His scowl deepened. "Hate wearing these damn things." He turned off the hose and studied me like only a father can. Finally, our eyes met. He grumbled: "What the hell's wrong with you?"

I flinched. "What do you mean?"

His face crumpled into a collision of skin against skin. "You look, I don't know, different. Better. You're even standing straighter. And I don't see that wimpy expression in your eyes. What's got into you?" He flashed me a nanosecond of a proud smile. "Know what? I like it."

"Thanks." I could feel it myself, a new resolve inside me. Tommy's chimp therapy was bringing out the best in me. I was taking charge, changing, just like my father had said: *I was doing something.* Maybe I could bring my dad one day to Weller. Who knew? They might want to put him under that MRI cap and read his brain as well.

"Well, whatever you're doing, keep it up." My father took off his gloves, then clapped me on the back.

We entered his house through the creaky backdoor. My father went straight to the fridge, handed me a beer and grabbed one for himself. Local IPAs. Coolwater Brew. He took a long pull. Two empty beer cans stood on the counter, pictures of log cabins on the silver labels. I blinked and shook my head. And he'd been up on that ladder? Was he kidding? He was an accident waiting to happen.

He was drinking too much, but what could I do? Restraining my dad was like trying to cage the wind.

I tossed the hearing aid batteries onto the kitchen table.

"Could use one of these little buggers right about now." He growled. "Thanks."

My father took off his hearing aid, searched around the kitchen for his bifocals, found them next to the phone book, and put them on. After taking the sticky tape off the battery, he attempted to replace a tiny silver battery inside the aid with a new one. His hands tremored, hardly able to perform the fine motor task—the silver battery was as small as a collar-button—but I knew better than to try to do it for him, even when he fumbled. I didn't feel like getting slapped or yelled at.

"There, goddammit." He got the battery in, inserted his hearing aids back into his ear, then cranked them up. "Better." He sighed heavily. "Gettin' old, Chris," my father said, taking off his bifocals. "Don't let it happen to you. It's no fun. Let me tell you that. Back's killing me today too. Must be arthritis."

"Well you had no business up on that ladder, that's for sure."

He waved a hand in the air and grumbled. "Fuck that shit."

My father led me to his den and snapped on a light. The curtains were closed on this beautiful day, and a distinctively sour odor made my nose itch. Books and magazines, candy bar wrappers, and beer cans were scattered everywhere. The day after I cleaned up, the place became as much of a mess as ever.

"I know what you're thinking." He pointed to his head. "Order here." And then he pointed to the room. "Chaos there. That's how I like it."

He finished his beer as he studied the picture of my mother on the wall above us. The heaviness of her passing tromped all over my heart.

I knew my father would want me around today—would expect me around—even though he would never admit it. I felt an aching in my chest that seemed to dig into my very soul.

In the photo, my mother's golden-brown hair was cut short. She was standing beside that weeping acacia in the backyard wearing capris and a white blouse. The picture had been taken ten years ago at least. There she was, perpetually smiling at us. It was a real smile, not one of those fake expressions people put on just for the camera these days with their selfies. To my mother, life was full of *real* reasons to smile, good food, friends, swimming in the ocean in the early morning, music, the stars. She didn't have to pretend to be happy; she just was, and other people could sense it. To her, life wasn't a series of problems at all; it was a gift, she used to tell me. How my mother had lived with my crotchety and moody father for so long was still a puzzle to me. Still, my parents' marriage had been largely successful. A yin-yang type of marriage that seemed to work. Whereas Cheryl and I . . . Why couldn't we have stuck it out and found a way to continue loving each other even in our darkest hours?

"Two damn years now," he said, his voice starting to tremble as he plopped down in his green lounger and hunched over. He adjusted one of his aids. "Seems like yesterday, doesn't it? She'd be seventy-seven today."

Tears welled up in his eyes. When one trickled down his cheek, he wiped it away with his thumb.

"Goddammit!" he said, covering his face with his hands. "Hell."

I'd never seen him cry before. His stoicism at the funeral had been unflinching. He was finally letting go at least a little, and I understood completely. This was good for him. I missed Mom so much. Her touch along my shoulder when she knew I needed consolation, her lilac smell, her infectious laughter.

"I . . . I never said this," my father spoke slowly, gazing at her picture from his lounger, his voice suddenly soft, "but she told me before she died to make sure I did right by you and Tommy or else she'd meet me in heaven and ream my ass out." He laughed and then one more tear dribbled down his cheek. He pulled out his handkerchief and wiped his eyes. "Goddammit. Crap!"

He had liver-spot splotches on the backs of both hands, and his fingers were gnarled. His face was a ragged road map.

Time was the great eradicator. We're all like leaves, green for a while, turning to yellow, brown, then crumbling to dust on the ground. I would lose my father next. I sighed. It was just a matter of time.

My father went to the bathroom as I clomped around the room straightening things. When he flushed, the sound of the toilet reverberated in the house. Old plumbing. Somewhere a pipe rattled as if a ghost had been woken up. God only knew when one of those ancient pipes would simply give way. Keeping this house up was a huge expense. I put books in place and gathered up beer cans and bottles. He plodded into the room and rubbed his lower back as he plopped back down in his lounger. This was a future version of myself, whether I liked it or not.

"Goddamn back," he said, swigging his beer. "Ain't worth a shit anymore."

"We all get old, Dad."

"Here's to old age," my father said, raising his bottle. "It sucks."

As I kept straightening the room—thinking about getting out the vacuum next—I came across a book of Wordsworth poems lying on the table next to his chair. I stopped and stared at it. My Dad read poetry? Wordsworth? When I opened the book with its dog-eared pages, a sheet of white paper fell out. Scribblings in pencil.

"What's this, Dad?" I asked.

"What the hell do you think it is?" He growled. "It's a goddamn poem."

"I see that. Did you write it?"

"Yeah." He shrugged.

I laughed. "Since when did you start writing poetry?"

"Just read it," he said.

"Are you kidding?"

I could hardly make out the scribble.

"Just read the damn thing."

"Fine."

Our time upon this earth before we die, is no more than the blink of an eye.

All I know is there's the Great Unknown, and that dash they put between

two numbers on a stone.

Yes, the moon and stars are laughin' at our entrance on the stage

as the roar of youth soon becomes a whisper as we age.

We're just here blind-walkin' 'round this temporary home.

It all comes down to a dash between two numbers on a stone.

"Dad," I said. "You wrote this?" I held the paper in front of him.

"Yep." He nodded and scratched his stomach, then took another swig.

"I like it, but it's so somber. Is it about Mom?"

"Yep." He blushed as he took a sip of beer. I'd never thought I'd see my father embarrassed about anything.

"But Mom was more than a dash, don't you think?"

He looked at me with sad eyes. "I was talking about time, son. In terms of time, that's about all any of us are."

"Well, anyway, it's a cool poem. We should laminate it."

"Suit yourself," he said, taking a long pull on his beer. "Want to watch some TV?"

"Before we do, I need to tell you the latest about Tommy," I said. "Go for it."

I told him everything I'd seen with Albert and Tommy, the entire research project. My father listened intently, and I could tell he was impressed.

"So, his name's Albert, huh?" my father said. "Hmmm. With a name like that, he's got to be smart."

"More than smart, Dad," I said. "That chimp is wise."

"And Tommy started talking a lot?" he asked.

"You should have heard him. It was amazing," I said. "I still get shivers thinking about it."

"Well, keep it up. Maybe it'll help. You never know."

"I plan to."

"How's Cheryl these days?" he asked, turning to me and once again using his dad radar to plumb my face. He came to like Cheryl and was saddened by the divorce; took it hard though he wouldn't say so.

"Fine," I said. "Cheryl's Cheryl. What more can I say?"

I didn't want to tell him that we were going back to court, that she wanted to take Tommy to Houston and put a knife in my heart at the same time. I didn't want to upset him; not today, anyway. Besides, it was my problem, not his.

Chapter 11

Some folks' lives are dashes, for sure, but some of us live in a world filled with exclamation points, one after the other. That's how *I* felt, anyway, when I turned on the TV to Channel Two for the six o'clock news that evening, only to discover my own personal family drama aired out for all to see, dirty laundry on the screen. I'd just gotten out of the shower and was dressed in jeans and a t-shirt, watching TV in my bedroom, hair still wet. Right before my eyes, the anchor babe shifted from a murder in the San Ysidro area of San Diego to, "and in other news . . ." And there it was: Mike Bloomfield, perfectly tailored in a blue suit, black hair slicked back, interviewing Cheryl and Gloria Beaman inside Cheryl's home.

Beaman was dressed in red as if to underscore her bad-ass attitude toward anyone who dared to get in her way. Cheryl was in a sea-blue dress that clung tight to her body—maybe too tight.

"So, you're alleging Mr. Crutcher is using this so-called science experiment at the Weller Institute to manipulate your autistic son to the point of abuse?" Bloomfield asked, after explaining to his audience the dilemma between me and Cheryl.

Abuse? What? Was she kidding me? Anger slivered through my mind.

"That's correct. He's doing this all for monetary gain and . . ." Cheryl stood with her hands behind her back, looking uncomfortable in front of the TV.

I stopped toweling my hair dry and felt the water drip on my shoulders and shirt. Breathless, I couldn't move as I continued watching. I sure hoped my dad didn't have the TV tuned to this station. Chances were low since he hardly ever watched the news. It was sports, usually, or not at all.

" . . . and he's denying my son the best treatment possible, a school for autistic children in Houston. Plus, he's endangering my son by allowing him near chimpanzees. These animals are powerful and there's absolutely no reason for my son to be near them. Just last year a chimpanzee ripped into a caretaker's face for no reason at all, nearly killing him. There have been other incidents like this as well. If this isn't abuse or close to it, I don't know what is."

I clenched my fists. I felt like throwing a shoe at the TV.

"And there's no truth to the rumor that your son actually talks to chimps, then?" Bloomfield asked.

They were standing in Cheryl's den, a Salvador Dali print hanging on the wall behind her. Angels floating up to heaven. Weird. She'd gotten it in the divorce. We'd picked it out together on a romantic trip to Sausalito when we were . . . oh, hell!

"I think the answer to that question is in the question itself," Beaman said, a grim voice with ice around the edges. "Obviously, there is absolutely no truth at all to that absurd notion. How could one even prove such a thing?"

"So how do you explain the online video that's gone viral?" Bloomfield pressed.

"It's complete nonsense, most likely the result of video tampering," Beaman shot back.

The interview ended, followed by Bloomfield's summary, the fireplug of a reporter staring directly into the eye of the camera.

"We are awaiting the father's side of the story," he said in that dry journalistic tone, "but so far, he has refused to return our phone calls or to make a statement. Can an eight-year-old autistic boy talk to the chimps or not? That is the question. This is Mark Bloomfield, Channel 2 News. Now back to you, Stacey."

Another perfectly dressed anchor came on. "Thanks, Mark. And in other news . . ."

Bloomfield had called me once and I'd curtly said, "no comment," then hung up on him. His other calls went unanswered. I wasn't about to talk to him.

I went to my computer to pull up the now-famous video I hadn't seen yet, waiting five seconds to see it because some ad for a hair product was attached to it. The video showed just what had happened: Tommy at the zoo that day, *This is so rad* . . . the big chimp staring at Tommy and swaying. I should have known. Never trust anyone under twenty.

The video boasted over a million hits and two hundred plus comments. Viewers were slugging it out over whether humans could actually talk to a variety of animals, chimps, birds, dogs . . . I scrolled through the comments as a vein throbbed on my neck and my stomach knotted up:

There is no way in hell a kid can talk to a chimp! Lulujones246

Everybody knows that parrots have a high intelligence. I talk to my Birdie-girl every day and she talks back. We discuss all kinds of things. SaraPrincetongal

I communicated with a chimp once. He said he was dying for an organic banana. HumblePoet

And on and on.

At 10 a.m. the next day, a harried Cheryl called and begged me to take Tommy so that she could keep a major appointment with a client. She said it was life or death.

"After killing me on TV like that?" I said, my voice stern and thick with anger. "Are you crazy?"

"Beaman made me do it, Chris, you have to believe me. I didn't want to. It was her idea."

"Well, it's a lousy thing to do. Who does she think she is anyway, Gloria Allred?"

"I'm sorry. I know. She's over the top. I tried to get her not to do it. What can I say?"

"You could have tried to stop her, and not said all those awful things you said."

"Stop Niagra Falls, Chris? Same thing. So, can you keep him? Please? I'm on my knees here. I have a major appointment I can't afford to break. The client has to see me today or he's going to cancel. I swear. He's a real headache, but this deal is worth a ton."

I thought about saying no, of course, just to get back at her. I recalled how I'd been offered that job by Marty Ackerman a while back, that spur of the moment thing, but couldn't take it because I couldn't find anyone to watch Tommy. Cheryl was out of town as were her parents, and my father had refused. Tit for tat?

But I actually looked forward to being with Tommy. And suddenly, something struck me. I was going to visit my attorney that day and it would be great to bring Tommy with me, so they could actually meet.

"Mom and Dad are out of the country and—" Cheryl went on.

"Hell, okay," I said. I knew the story well enough. "I just can't believe you sometimes. Bring him over. How's Wade by the way?"

"Great." At the mention of his name, her voice changed from somber to light. "Just landed a new deal with Pepsi. He's in Houston scoping out housing."

"I'm sure." I swallowed hard and for a moment, lost my sense of where I was. I blinked rapidly. Wade waltzes away with Cher and a great job in Houston. And as for me . . . I'm left holding the emotional bag—alone.

When Cheryl and Tommy came to my front door, the drop off was quick and mechanical. Only Max showed any excitement, bumping his nose against Cheryl's hand, begging for attention. I had nothing to say to her and she had even less to say to me. With Tommy around, we played the part of friendly exes. We might have even won an award. Plastered on smiles, stiff and quick responses. The whole enchilada.

After she left, Tommy played with Max in the backyard. An hour later, he was climbing into my car, clutching Radar and Monkey, and my mood lifted.

We headed straight to Mark Hyman's office. Mister Backpack came with us as well.

Tommy seemed more distant and quiet than usual. Though he was carrying both Radar and Monkey, one in each hand, he still managed to suck on his hands and then slap himself as we made our way into the building. New places created so much anxiety for him.

"Radar and Monkey don't want you to gobble up your hands." I did my infamous SpongeBob: "Let's go, my little starfish, no hands in mouth, all right?"

"'Kay."

Thank God, it worked. He took his hand from his mouth and relief washed over me. I wasn't sure why, but when it came to Tommy, SpongeBob SquarePants—that absorbable little fellow—seemed to yield more results than any of the best psychologists.

We stepped into the Drake Building in downtown San Diego. Mark shared an assistant with two other attorneys on the twelfth floor. Black-haired with dark-framed glasses perched on her nose, she offered me and Tommy leather chairs in the waiting area. I put Monkey away for him, hit the coffee machine down the hall, and brought out a juice box from Mr. Backpack for Tommy.

"I hope you don't mind me bringing him," I said to Mark when he called us into his office for our second meeting. "Had no other choice."

Mark shrugged as if he was always welcoming autistic children and their dads into his office. "No problem at all. He's what it's all about."

"Tommy, sit quietly next to me so that I can talk to the man, okay?" I said softly.

"'Kay, Daddy." He didn't look at Mark. He just zoomed Radar in the air, looking everywhere but at this new man-person across from him, murmuring away in the process. He got that way sometimes, simply blanked out everything in his field of vision except for one detail, focusing solely and exclusively on that.

"Chimpies, Daddy?" he asked suddenly. Then a new question that startled me. "See Rach'l doc?"

"Rachel?"

He shook his head. "Want see Rach'l doc!" he said. "Rach'l doc . . . see . . ."

I was surprised at this reference to Rachel. Tommy normally didn't talk about anything that wasn't in his immediate presence. Other than "chimpies," of course. His wanting to see Rachel made me realize what an impression she was making on him. I had to smile.

"He's cute," Mark said, studying Tommy, who was now quietly playing with Radar. "Ooooouuuu . . ." "So, you know all about chimpanzees?" he asked, trying to get Tommy's attention.

But Tommy quickly looked away. Spittle dribbled from his mouth, and then he hit himself, gave himself a good thwack right on his left cheek. I felt the sting inside my gut.

"Tommy, please," I said, feeling embarrassed.

"Ooooouuuu . . ."

I put a hand on his knee to try to calm him, but he pushed it away. I got him to settle down with a picture book about chimps, which I'd withdrawn from Mister Backpack. He thumbed through the book quietly. Mark, looking relieved, dove in, getting right to the point.

"So." He leaned forward, staring at me from behind his neatly organized desk. "I've been studying custody law regarding special children like Tommy. The suitability of the parents is one of the key points. So, tell me all you can about Cheryl. I need to know as much as possible. She's going to paint you as the unfit father. We need to fight back."

"Let's see," I said, letting my mind roll back in time. "There was that DUI two years ago with Tommy in the car. Her father got her a big lawyer to help her through it. Still, she had to pay a fine and do public service."

"Really. Interesting. She's a drinker?" he asked.

"A wine enthusiast, Mark." I took a sip of coffee. "But with all the stress she's under, she depends on it to keep her sanity. I mean she's no alcoholic, I don't think, but she does like to tip back a few—been that way ever since I knew her."

Mark scrawled with black ink on a yellow legal pad. He rubbed his brow. "Drinking and driving with the son in tow. I'll check on the details. Anything else?"

I looked at Tommy who was now pinching Radar's nose, a line of spittle glistening from his chin. I grabbed a tissue and wiped it away. He sucked on his hand. "Drrrrr . . . Ouuuuuu . . ." He shook his head right and left.

"Let's be good, Tom-Tom," I said and gently removed his hand from his mouth. Mark watched silently. I caught a look of sympathy in his eyes.

"Actually, there is something else," I said, turning back to Mark. "An accident on the playground when she was watching him. Tommy was three at the time. He fell from a swing and busted his lip. He needed stitches. I'm sure we can find a medical report on it."

As Mark jotted down some notes, I gazed out the window for a moment, then expressed my greatest fear, my heart beating hard. "What do you think about her statement that chimps are dangerous and she has every right to take Tommy to Houston?"

"Chimpies!" Tommy said.

"I saw it on TV," Mark said. "I made a copy of the interview. The thing is, your best bet is to just let her rave. All you care about is the judge's opinion. It's Beaman who loves this kind of thing, getting in the news. She lives for the camera. She's no doubt eating this case up, loving every minute of it."

"So, it's no big deal?" I leaned forward.

"From a legal standpoint, no."

Relief rippled through my bones. "Got it." I noticed a picture of Mark hanging on the wall with some buddies, dressed in camouflage with rifles at their sides. They were holding up a buck. This was good: A lawyer who liked to kill things. I was impressed.

Still. I couldn't get the image out of my head of Beaman and Cheryl on TV. Gloria Beaman was a superstar. She'd trounced my attorney in our divorce proceedings. She was known throughout California. It was said that Hollywood executives shook in their expensive Italian leather shoes when they heard her name.

"Our best bet is to prove these scientists of yours at Weller can truly offer something special for Tommy," Mark said. "From what I've seen, you have some real experts on the team. This Dr. Rekulak appears to be a rather famous primatologist. I've seen some of the videos of Tommy interacting with the chimps and they're incredible. So, they're still gathering data?" Mark leaned back in his chair, his eyes wandering over Tommy who was now quiet, looking at his picture book.

"Yes. Dr. Simmons said they should be finished in about two weeks."

"Good. Having Carly Yates involved won't hurt either." Mark sighed. "Look. I know this is going to be hard for you. I'm a dad myself. I love my daughter like crazy. I know at least a little bit about how you must feel. The good news is that I really think we're going to be able to give the judge some excellent factual evidence that will swing the decision your way."

I smiled. This was exactly what I wanted to hear. Happiness, warm and joyful, surged through my chest.

"Well, keep in touch," I said. I just noticed it: on the shelf behind him was a family picture. Mark smiling with a gorgeous wife beside him and their daughter. She looked to be about Tommy's age. This was good; a family man who could understand where I was coming from.

"Will do."

Tommy and I made our way to my car, which was located a block away from the office in a parking garage. Tommy walked beside me, head down, latching onto Radar. My mind flashed back to Tommy's seizure at the hospital. His body twisting and contorting. He was just so vulnerable. And yet, so far, no further seizures had occurred. It had been six weeks since that first miserable attack and he hadn't had any others since then. I was thinking that maybe we had truly gotten this issue under control when, suddenly, my cell buzzed.

"Mr. Crutcher?" The woman sounded troubled and already I could tell the news would not be good. My throat constricted.

"Yes?"

She spoke with a hesitation in her voice. "This is Belinda Samuels and I'm, I'm a, uh, a nurse at Sharp Memorial Hospital."

"Yes?"

"I'm calling because your father was involved in an accident about two hours ago. Can you come to the hospital as soon as possible, please?"

"An accident? What happened?" I gripped the phone.

"He fell on his kitchen floor and he's bruised his hip pretty badly. It could even be broken. We're not sure yet. He called 911. An ambulance brought him to the emergency room."

My mouth grew dry. "I'm on my way."

TOMMY AND I, WITH MISTER Backpack on my shoulder, arrived at the emergency room entrance fifteen minutes later. Tommy didn't seem to take in the surroundings and didn't associate it with the kind of place where he'd had his seizure. But this didn't surprise me. He seemed to be indifferent to most environments he found himself in.

I spoke with a tall, black-haired nurse who said she'd have more information as soon as possible. Then we were ushered into a waiting room with a TV on the wall broadcasting CNN news, something about Afghanistan, Anderson Cooper looking end-of-the-world grim as usual.

Finally, the nurse called us back and we stood at the door to my father's private room, Tommy next to me carrying Monk now, quiet and withdrawn. I was always amazed at how he was able to draw an invisible bubble around himself and dive inside.

My father was sitting up in bed, a white bandage across his forehead. His right leg was wedged into a sling. I stood there, staring at this father of mine, who suddenly seemed so small, a fragile autumn leaf of a human being, and I surged with love for this man who knew me better than anyone else alive. He watched me make sock-puppets as a child, inventing different voices for each of them. He was the one who actually encouraged me to go into the voice-over business. And he was there the day I burned my finger on a grill. I was six years old and raced crying into his arms. Why did I run into *his* arms and not my mother's? I never thought about that until now.

A nurse was checking his blood pressure and my father's eyes were closed as she worked.

"Okay, Mister Crutcher," the nurse said when she was finished, laying her stethoscope down on the table next to his bed. "It continues to be a bit high, I'm afraid—180 over 90. I need to notify the doctor."

"Oh, Christ. There's nothing wrong with me," my father grumbled.

"Dad," I said as I stepped into the room. Tommy followed behind me like a shadow, a mini-me.

My father and the nurse both turned our way.

"Pop," Tommy said, pointing at my father once he'd taken his hand out of his mouth. "Pop hurt." He spoke in his robotic style, detached as ever, like a scientist identifying a leaf.

"Dad," I said, furrowing my brow. "What in God's name?"

He growled: "I don't want to hear a goddamn thing."

The nurse gave me a knowing smile, as if to say she too knew about relating to aging parents.

"I'll leave you alone for a while," she said, lowering her eyes. "We'll have Dr. Anderson do a consult for the BP." She turned to look at Tommy. "What a cute son!"

"Thank you," I said.

"Goodness, he's a doll." But I could see that she recognized his far-away stare and knew enough not to try to engage him. She gave me a compassionate look and a sad smile.

"Who cares about my goddamn blood pressure?" my father said when the nurse had left the room.

"Dad, it's high," I said. "You need to take care of that."

"It's not that high," he said. He adjusted his aid on his right ear, it squawked, and he re-adjusted. "These doctors don't know what they're doing."

"Right."

I took off Mister Backpack and set him down in a chair in the corner.

A knock on the door, and then: "Hey, everybody." A short man with a mustache entered. Fiftyish. He was wearing brown slacks and a white shirt with a tie, a smile on his face, bushy eyebrows that needed clipping. "I'm Doctor Brady."

We shook hands. "Chris Crutcher," I said.

"Nice to meet you."

"Meet, meeeeeet, meet," Tommy mimicked. Dr. Brady turned and stared at Tommy for a moment, clicking his pen.

"And who is this gentleman?" he asked.

"That's Tommy, my son," I said, smiling back at him.

"Hello, Tommy," Dr. Brady said.

"Meet, meeeet, meet . ." Tommy continued repeating.

"Very cute," he said. Then, without missing a beat, Dr. Brady stepped over to my father. "How you doing, Mr. Crutcher?" he asked.

I already felt embarrassed and my father hadn't even started speaking yet.

"I'll be doing a lot better once I get out of this so-called hospital," my father said. His angry tone made Dr. Brady cock his head and he smoothed back his grey hair.

"Dad," I said. "Settle down."

Dr. Brady rubbed the side of his smooth-shaven face. "Anyway, from the X-ray it looks like you've got a badly bruised right hip and sprained right ankle, Mr. Crutcher. Nothing broken, actually, which is a kind of miracle." He turned to me. "He was pretty loose when he fell."

"Loose?" I asked.

"I'd downed a few beers," my father said. "So what?"

I rolled my eyes. How could I ever move to Houston with a father like this?

"What am I going to do with you, Dad?" I turned to the doctor. "A few weeks ago, he was out cleaning leaves from the gutter, standing high on a ladder. He'd had a few then, too." I turned back to my father who eyed me with a scowl. "What were you doing this time, Dad?"

"I was fixing the plumbing under the sink. Pipe broke and water went everywhere. Totally surprised me and I slipped and fell. Should've known. Pipes in that house are as old as Moses. Look. Just take me home and let me be," my father said. "It's a goddamn free country, isn't it?"

"Let you be, huh?" I stepped closer to the bed, sizing him up. I looked at Dr. Brady, then stared at my father. "You mean let you kill yourself on your next home improvement project?"

"Pop hurt," Tommy said. We all looked at him.

"Okay, no more home improvement. I promise," my father said.

"No more cleaning gutters?"

"Promise."

"No more being your own in-house plumber?" I asked.

"Fine, goddammit. Do you realize how expensive a goddamn plumber is these days? How was I to know that pipe was about to blow? I've been fixing leaks under sinks..."

"Yeah, I know. Before I was born. Maybe we should talk about selling the house and—"

He spoke threateningly, "Don't you dare!"

Dr. Brady cleared his throat. "Is there anything else you need from me?" Dr. Brady asked. "We'll need to stabilize his BP and do some blood work, too. I can release him tomorrow." He faced my father and spoke louder. "I need to prolong your stay, Mr. Crutcher, for observation for one night. It's medically indicated."

"Tomorrow?" my father gasped. "Are you kidding me?"

"No sir," Dr. Brady said. "Trust me, it's for your own good."

"A whole night in this hell hole?"

"Yes, sir. Just consider it a night off, a vacation. You need it."

"I don't need crap," my father said.

Dr. Brady gave me a quick nod, scrawled some notes into the chart he was carrying, then hurriedly left the room, closing the door behind him. He seemed a tiny bit afraid of my father and I couldn't blame him.

"Okay, Dad," I said, folding my arms across my chest, "I hope you've learned your lesson."

"Sure could use a beer right now," my father said. "Call the nurse's station and see if they can scrounge one up."

"I'm sure you—"

"Beer, beer, beer," Tommy mimicked. "Beeeeer . . ."

We both laughed. "Look at you, Dad, you're already giving my son ideas."

"A chip off the old block, that one," my father said with a smile.

Minutes later, someone else knocked on the door. Three quick raps. I was thinking it was another nurse. Man, I was so wrong.

"Can I come in?" The voice outside the door was unmistakable. It was Cheryl who stepped into the room, a look of concern on her face, carrying a fruit basket wrapped in yellow plastic, her purse slung over her shoulder. I just stood there, my jaw dropping as my stomach flipped over.

"Mommy," Tommy said. But he didn't rush up to her the way a normal child would. He merely stated the fact of the situation, then returned to playing with Monkey, spinning him around on the floor.

"What are you doing here?" I asked. But she moved right past me as if I hadn't said a word, and came up to my father's bed. She smelled like citrus and soap. She set the fruit basket on a table near the window.

"For you, Ralph." Her voice was sweet and endearing. "How are you doing? Are you all right? I was so worried about you."

"Oh, for an old grouch, I'm doing lousy as hell. For a dead body, pretty good." My father shifted in bed and snorted.

I was dumbfounded. How did she even know?

Cheryl laid her purse on a chair, bent down, and kissed my father on the cheek, then smudged away her lipstick mark with a laugh.

"You're tough as nails, Ralph. A little fall on the floor won't hurt an old steel man like you. Maybe a few dings on your rear bumper. You'll be fine."

She looked beautiful, dammit, her auburn hair tied back and worn off to the side. Blue dress, pearls, earrings to match the pearls, and black heels. Her complexion was flushed with color. But not just beautiful. She looked goddamn happy too, a fact that made me cringe.

"Mommy. Chimpies, Daddy? Chimpies fun!" Tommy said.

"Are you being a good boy for grandpa?" Cheryl asked, taking in Tommy, her motherly eyes inspecting him. She put her hands on her hips.

"Fine," Tommy said. "Fiiiine."

"How'd you know, Cher?" I asked.

"The hospital called me," she said, eyeing me at last, running a hand through her hair. Her tone of voice was now a little less sweet. "I'm still on the emergency call list for your father."

"That makes sense," I said. I made a mental note to have her taken off the list.

I told her the story and Cheryl listened with a sympathetic look on her face. As I spoke, my father scratched his head and stared straight ahead, looking like a schoolboy who'd been found cheating on an exam and was now sitting in the principal's office.

I had to admit it: My father and Cheryl had always gotten along well. They were both die-hard Padres fans and had even gone to several games together through the years. Cheryl was one of the few people who could actually light my father up, make him smile. The divorce had crushed my parents, but I think it hurt my father most of all. I still hadn't told him about the upcoming hearing. I had to do it at the right time. Luckily, he hadn't seen the story on the local news.

"Chimpies," Tommy intoned, that one word, spoken in his monotonic way, dropping from his mouth, carried emotional dynamite.

"No, son. Not now, okay?" I took a gulp of air and looked at Cheryl. Her eyes darkened for a moment and she let out a thin sigh.

"No chimpies," she said sternly. She shot me an angry look, pursing her lips.

My stomach hardened. *We'll see about that.*

"Chris, can you step out into the hall with me and Tommy?" Cheryl asked a few minutes later after we'd talked to my father some more.

"Sure," I said, wondering what she had in mind.

We left my father grumbling at a no-nonsense technician who had come in to take some blood and entered the hallway. The scent of rubbing alcohol and something like paint or fingernail polish wafted through my nostrils. A doctor in a white coat quickly passed us, moving as if he were on roller skates, his face pale and grim. He was followed by an old man with a walker and an oxygen tank, accompanied by what could have been his granddaughter; yellow dress, twenty-something, a caring look on her face.

Tommy shambled next to me, pulling on Monk's ears. Dribble ran from his mouth and I wiped his mouth clean with a tissue I kept in my pocket for just such purposes. I'd left Mister Backpack in my father's room.

"Talked to Dr. Whitaker by the way," Cheryl said, fingering her pearls as we moved as a unit down the hall.

"And?"

"He thinks we have a good handle on the seizure issue," she said. "He changed the medication slightly again, but so far, everything seems okay on that front. The last EEG looked good."

"Yes, I know. I spoke with him as well. Let's keep our fingers crossed."

Her voice turned grave when she spoke again. "Chris, there's something I need to tell you."

We continued walking, passing the nurse's station and then heading toward the end of the hallway, which was probably fifty feet off. Two female workers dressed in blue scrubs hurried past us. Someone dropped a metal tray in the distance and I jumped.

"Go ahead. I'm all ears," I said. I didn't like the wary sound of her voice, but surely, things couldn't get any worse—or, could they? Did she know something else about Tommy that I was about to learn?

"Anyway, the truth is," she paused, gathering herself. She stopped walking and I faced her, Tommy at my side still playing with Monk. She spoke the words softly so that Tommy couldn't hear. "I just wanted to tell you that, well, I'm . . . I'm pregnant."

My head jerked back as if I'd just been rear-ended in my car. So. It could get worse. I grew disoriented, dizzy, this Merry-Go-Round life of mine kept circling faster and faster. "What? Are you fucking kidding me? You're telling me this now?"

"See, Wade's landed this great job in Houston with Creative Media and . . ."

"Wait . . . What? Houston? Did you say Houston? You mean where the Acorn School is?" I was dumbfounded.

"Yes." She nodded. "So, it looks like we'll be moving there together, once the courts reach their decision. I thought you should know."

Once the courts reach their decision?

I was stunned and felt as if I'd been hit in the chest. How could she be so blind?

"I mean we want to keep you in the loop, of course," Cheryl went on. "We'll have no problem with you coming for visits, any time you want. Really. No problem at all."

I gasped; sputtered. A sudden internal coldness made me stiff with anger. "So, that's what this Acorn School's all about." I was fuming now. "I should have known. It's all coming to light, isn't it, Cher?"

"What are you talking about?"

"You just went and found yourself a private school in Houston so you could come up with an excuse to move there. The truth is it all boils down to nothing more than your love life."

Cheryl's lips turned downward as I spoke and a bead of sweat broke out on her forehead. "That's not it at all," she said, waving a hand in the air.

"Sure, it is. But let me tell you something. If you think you're going to just pop this guy in as my replacement and . . . and . . . live happily ever after with our son in tow, you better think again. There is a research grant from Weller right this minute and the truth is—"

"Research grant?" Cheryl snorted. "For those chimps of yours? Look. If you want the truth, here's the truth for *you*." Her face flushed with color as she stabbed my chest with her finger.

But before she said anything further, for some reason, we both looked down at Tommy at exactly the same time. Tommy. Our shared responsibility, no matter how much we disagreed. He was continuing to murmur and hum to himself, oblivious to the emotional depth charges we were slinging at each other over his head. Suddenly, he spun around and kicked a foot out, then spoke some nonsense words to Monk. I distinctly heard him say the word, "chimpies."

Cheryl continued. She lowered her voice as she looked in my eyes. "My attorney and I are going to totally prove that Acorn's in Tommy's best interest and that this chimp business of yours is just one plain piece of pure one hundred percent bullshit. I'm going to do what's best for Tommy. This is *all* for Tommy and nothing else. That monkey business is laughable. Any judge will see that."

"Then be prepared for some ass-kicking evidence."

She narrowed her eyes at me. Tommy continued whirling around, still seemingly oblivious—or was he? He squeezed Monkey to his chest and cuddled it, wrapping his arms around it. "Ouuuu . . ."

"What I want to know is," I said, "which came first, Cher, the chicken or the egg?"

She stiffened and blinked rapidly. "What? What are you talking about?" She wiped away some hair off her face.

"Which was it? Acorn, then Wade? Or Wade, then Acorn? Tell me the truth."

"Jesus." She sighed and rolled her eyes at me. "You're more of a fool than I thought." Cheryl frowned. And then I couldn't help it. Even in the midst of our all-out anger, even as our emotional guns aimed and fired, I found my eyes roving to that angular scar on her right eyebrow; a childhood injury; she'd fallen off a swing and bumped her head there. I used to kiss that sweet place and pretend I could heal it; this, of course, was in our romantic era, pre-apocalyptic. A different time and place. God! "Look, Chris." Her angry voice ripped me back into the present. "Here's the truth. I found Acorn entirely on my own, *months* before I got serious with Wade, okay? The school's amazing. It's just complete coincidence that Wade's moving to Houston. Actually, he was originally going to work in Austin. But he made some adjustments so that we could be together. There's no way I would just up and take Tommy if I didn't think it was for his own good. You know that, right? You know what kind of mother I am." Her eyes fixed on my face.

I did know, of course, and sighed. She was right. She *was* Tommy's fiercest advocate. The one who did so much more research than me, and who knew all the statistics, who knew practically everything about autism, the one who'd spent countless hours staying up with him at night, training him to use the bathroom over and over again, who took care of his Activities of Daily Living, teaching him for hours the nuances of "hello-goodbye," trying various behavioral programs with him, the one who'd practically knocked down educators in hallways to make sure Tommy received the right classes and therapies.

I had to admit it. I believed her. I knew Cheryl too well. She would never just chase a man. She was too strong of a woman for that. And Tommy was her life.

"Okay, I believe you. I'm sorry. You're right."

And then, crazy as it was, I realized that I still loved her in some unexplainably, unforgettable way. From the first time I laid eyes on her at a party in Santa Barbara, where we'd literally bumped into each other and she'd spilled wine on my shirt, right up to now. But I hated her as well in a way, hated her for the turmoil she was causing in my life.

Basically, I couldn't make up my heart.

"Okay, apology accepted," she said.

"When are you due?" I asked., feeling flummoxed. Still, I had to know.

"Six months. It's a girl."

"Well, I guess I should say it," turning on a brief smile, "congratulations."

"Thank you. Now, let's just go back and talk to your dad and smile and pretend all's well with the world," she said.

I had no choice but to agree. "Fine."

"Fiiiine, fine, fiiiine, fine . . ." Tommy mimicked.

We both looked down at him, and then our eyes met, collided this time. Sadness seized me, gripping me with emotional pain.

Houston, we have a problem.

Chapter 12

Two days later. The aroma of fresh-brewed coffee. The Marina Café. 2:30 p.m. Espresso machines huffing out cloudbursts of steam, and the smell of freshly baked chocolate-chip cookies filling the air. That smell drove me back in time to the cookies my mother used to bake.

It was just another paradisiacal blue-sky day in San Diego, "Plymouth Rock of the West," as it's called, a place well chosen by Spanish settlers long ago.

But dark clouds rolled all over my mind. Cheryl was now pregnant by Wade Dudley—of all people!—and threatening to take Tommy with her when they moved to Houston. I just couldn't let that happen. I had to fight. There was no other way. I had to stand up for what I knew in my fatherly bones was the right thing.

It all still blew me away—elephant-sized problems, impossible to get my arms around.

I was sitting at a two-person table near a window that held a sweeping view of the bay, a pair of teens next to me staring at their phones and drinking huge frappuccinos. When Rachel stepped through the door of the coffee shop, I waved to her.

She wasn't wearing her lab coat and the professional, scientist persona had vanished. Instead of being tied back, her blonde hair was down around her shoulders. She was in a blue blouse, jeans, and heels. She struck me as head-over-heels attractive.

We were meeting to go over the data the scientists at Weller had amassed. At first, we'd planned on me going out to Weller, but when she said she was going to be in this part of town, we decided on this location for convenience.

"Thanks for coming," I said, standing and shaking her hand. "I've been waiting for this moment for what's felt like an eternity."

"Sure. Of course. Not a problem." She pointed to the computer she was carrying. "I have all the information right here so that you can give it to your attorney."

After ordering—me, a mint mocha and Rachel, chai tea, and we would share a chocolate-chip cookie—we returned to our seats at the table, our chairs facing across each other. Sailboats and windsurfers rode the waters outside while Tom Petty poured from the speakers. Cheryl's favorite, "I Won't Back Down."

Did that not sum her up? But couldn't that serve as my theme song as well?

The espresso machines continued huffing in the background as a baby wailed from the opposite side of the room.

Rachel turned on her computer, waited for it to load, then opened up the files. "Look at this, Chris," she said. She took a bite of her half of the cookie. I scooted my chair around the table, closer to her, and she angled the computer screen my way so we could both view it. Colorful graphs and data points flashed on the screen. "Following chimp therapy for four weeks," she said, "Tommy has shown thirteen percent improvement in linguistic syntax at the core level. His fluency has yielded big improvement, phonemically and syntactically. We even caught him using strong inflection when talking to Obo, which indicates improved emotional intent.

"When we combine the signs and movements in slow-motion shots, the communication session with Albert, and the improvement in his vocal patterns every time he's with the chimps, I would have to say we have an extremely compelling case here. He's definitely improving in his expressive language skills while interacting with the chimpanzees."

This was good, really good, and a heady sense of weightlessness rose inside me. But a new problem quickly dragged me down: Two weeks ago, Beaman had convinced the judge to issue an injunction that served to block Tommy from seeing the chimps further until a final decision in the court had been made.

"But is it proof?" I asked. I sipped on my mocha and downed a piece of the cookie. I felt the sugar rush kick in.

"I'd say it is," Rachel said thoughtfully. She took a sip of her drink. "We're doing an analysis of his speech levels at Hillwood to compare, too. We talked to a speech pathologist who worked for the school and got his records. But overall, it looks pretty solid. Dr. Dunn will testify as an expert witness regarding Tommy's improvements. He's already talked to your lawyer. Wait a minute. I almost forgot. Check this out."

As I took another drink, she quickly clicked on an icon on the screen marked stat. Seconds later, a different program flashed on the screen. "We use this program called Word-Flash with the chimps," she said, "but I think we can adapt it for Tommy, too. It's a statistical program that tracks sign language behaviors in terms of duration, complexity, and frequency."

"Cool," I said. "It looks impressive."

She nodded. "It provides rigorous details." She paged through the application, which allowed for all kinds of data inputs and calculations, far beyond my understanding. "We can chart word frequency and intermittency, and we can track the chimps' behaviors too, and any effort they make to communicate with him. We can also input all the other data we've accumulated into this application."

She entered some hypothetical figures to show me how the program worked.

"This is great," I said. "Really detailed. Total quantification."

"Exactly." Rachel nibbled on her cookie, then leaned back in her chair. "I thought you'd like it."

"I love it. Can you put all of this on a flash drive for me so that I can give it to my attorney?"

"Already done." Rachel smiled as she reached into her purse. "Here. Ready to go." She handed me the drive. "I'll also ask Mark if he wants me to download everything to his email. It's an awful lot of data, so I'll check with him first."

"Great. I'll be anxious to hear what he has to say."

Finishing my coffee, I gazed out at the harbor. A huge cruise ship passed by in the distance, sun sparkling on its bow.

"Are you worried?" she asked. I felt her eyes lingering on me, trying to read me.

I sighed. My gut roiled all of a sudden, rippling waters within. "Of course, I'm worried. How could I not be?"

"It'll work out." She smiled and her eyes shone brightly. I wondered if all of this was merely a science project to her, another day at the office, or was she getting involved on a level deeper than that. Her tone of voice was sympathetic. "You'll see. It has to work out."

"God, I hope so. This whole thing—Weller, the chimps. You don't understand how much this all means to me." My hands suddenly grew slick. "I can't tell you how grateful I am that Weller opened its doors to us and has been so receptive. It's meant the world to me and Tommy. I want to thank you for that."

I'd received the check for the first twenty-thousand dollars—split between me and Cheryl—payment for the first three months, more to follow after future visits, and that had helped immensely as well. Filled up my financial gas tank. Weller had come through as promised. The money was a godsend.

"This is important work," Rachel said, growing serious. "Primatologically speaking, it's major. Rekulak can't stop talking about your son. If you win the hearing—which I'm sure you will—he's even talking about inviting you and Tommy to Africa to let Tommy interact with the chimps on a sanctuary. This would really give Tommy a chance to explore his intuitive abilities, don't you think?"

"Absolutely. That would be amazing!"

Rachel gripped her hands firmly around her cup of chai. She had lovely hands, a pianist's hands, long and slender. Then she put her computer away and for a moment, we both sat in silence, just staring out the window toward the blue water.

"So, how in the world did you become a primatologist?" I asked. "It's almost as odd as being a voice-over actor."

She smiled. "My father was a vet," she said, "and so I used to hang around his office and help out. I loved being around the animals he treated. Dad had connections at the local zoo in St. Louis, and once I was old enough, I started volunteering there. When I took care of the chimps, I couldn't get enough of them. I was completely hooked. They're the most amazing creatures on the planet as far as I'm concerned."

"You know, I'm coming to think that myself."

She nodded. "Most people don't realize it, but studying chimpanzees is like going back in time and looking at ourselves in our earliest stages of development. It really is. Anyway, after graduate school, I lived in Africa, observing chimps in their natural habitats. Best years of my life, actually." Her eyes lit up.

"I'm sure." I leaned back in my seat. "Tell me more," I said.

"You can't imagine the peace, Chris." I watched as her blue eyes softened. "The Gombe rainforest in Africa is like nothing else in the world. And when you live and work there long enough, just being in that environment and breathing it in, something happens to you. It changes you, takes hold of you. You see and hear differently, and you feel differently, too. We'd have bonfires on the shore of the lake at night and baboons would come right up to us, eyes alert, so wild, but tamed by their interaction with the many scientists who'd come before. It's frightening and fascinating at the same time."

"Wow. It sounds awesome." I was entranced.

"One thing I learned was that all these cities we've grown up in, you know?—the air-conditioned houses, cars, the smell of exhaust and the traffic noise? We just don't realize how much all of that changes us, takes us away from who we really are—the natural human beings we're designed to be.

"But when you're in the rainforest and if you stay there long enough, you find yourself getting stripped down to a much more basic mentality. And that's when it's so much easier to take one moment at a time. You live more easily, more simply. You even see more clearly. It's like you finally go from black-and-white to seeing in real living color."

I was enthralled. "It sounds amazing. It really does."

"All I can say is that, when you immerse yourself in the rainforest, the air, the water, the life force around you," she spoke slowly now, her eyes sparkling, "this new self emerges inside you and you learn to somehow expand that self outward into the world. You become part of your surroundings in a way you never could in concrete-and-steel America."

Her words heightened my senses. I was totally aware of the sound of a passing car outside, the feel of my cotton shirt against my skin, the cadence as well as the content of her speech. The cacophony of background noise in the coffee shop seemed to fade away.

"And that's why I think chimps are so much more advanced than we know," she said, taking a long breath.

"How so?"

"Because in their natural environment, in the rainforest, they experience what I'm talking about all the time. They understand this kind of clarity naturally. They're geniuses in being in the moment. And this awareness goes well beyond language. It's about seeing and hearing and feeling the whole of things, not just the parts. Language slices up nature into sections and divisions, it categorizes, but when you let go of seeing the world through the lens of language, you're left with nature as it is, as a whole." She shook her head. "Yes, chimps have language as well. But their brains don't allow their language patterns to overwhelm their sense patterns, their ability to be in the now and to soak up what's going on around them. To immerse into the whole."

"Fascinating. That's what Tommy was talking about too, I think."

"Yes. Exactly." She leaned forward. "He doesn't even need to go to the rainforest. His brain is wired in such a way that when he's around the chimps, his heightened activity in the prefrontal cortex allows his awareness to supercharge. This is the story of all savants."

"So, a deficiency in one area of the brain allows for a super-ability in another area," I said.

"Right."

"What if chimps could teach us about this other way of seeing and hearing?" I asked. "What if we could learn from the chimps about the importance of the moment without having to go all the way to the rain forest? What would they impart to us? And what if Tommy could help lead the way?"

"I know," she said, putting a hand on her chin. "I've thought the same thing myself. That's what's so exciting. Jane Goodall once said that if she could look at the world through the eyes of a chimp, even one such minute would be worth a lifetime of research."

"Wow. Interesting."

She finished off her drink. The background music in the cafe changed to a mellow rock hit from the seventies.

"Actually, I may be going back to Africa soon," she said, her voice turning brighter.

"What? Really? When?" I was taken aback by this sudden news and squirmed in my seat.

"I'm involved in research sponsored by *National Geographic*. And if the funding comes through, I could be leaving fairly soon." She grinned. "I'd give anything to get back to Gombe."

"And you'd abandon your Weller chimps?"

"For this, yes. Of course." She laughed. "It would only be eighteen months to two years. Weller would find a replacement for me while I'm gone."

I was surprised that it was such an easy choice for her. "But what about managing Tommy?"

She looked away. Things turned awkward all of a sudden. "We'll find the perfect person," she said finally. "I promise."

The perfect person? I wasn't so sure. "But Tommy's glommed onto you. Remember how he took hold of your hand that first day? You're the one he wants to see. You seem to make him comfortable. You have a way with him."

"I know, Chris, I do." Her face colored. "That son of yours has really touched me. He's just plain adorable. But of course, you know that." Her eyes suddenly misted as she smiled at me, a smile that seemed to plumb the rushing waters of my heart. I looked down at her hands, which rested on the table, suddenly aware that I was yearning with the urge to touch her hands and hold them in mine.

"Thank you," I said, holding my urge in check.

"But you have to realize. It's not just me, Chris. It's the whole team. Think of it this way. Tommy needs to learn to adjust to all kinds of people. He can't just hyper focus on one person."

I exhaled slowly. My eyes lingered on the water in the harbor, sunlight glimmering on water, but now I hardly saw it. "Okay," I said. "Maybe you're right."

She had a point. And yet, she was the one who had eased my son into the group of chimps and had formed a kind of bridge for him in the first place, showing him the way. And now she might be leaving? It still just didn't seem right.

We left the coffee shop and strolled to her car, an eco-sensitive red Prius parked down the street, next to a barber shop called "Uncle's." Citified humans of all shapes and sizes traipsed past; this was our jungle and we Home sapiens had adjusted accordingly, carbon dioxide enhanced. A car honked; brakes screeched; we were used to the noise, the smell of a big old dump truck's noxious fumes, the sights of kids flying past on skateboards. Buildings all around us, a concrete and steel world. And yet, a breezy wind flowed against my face, telling me that no matter how deeply entrenched in the city we were, nothing will ever obliterate nature.

"You look troubled," she said as we stood next to her car. She pushed a button on her fob and her car's lights flashed, doors unlocked, like an animal waking up, opening its eyes. She put her computer in the backseat.

"I am." I sighed and shoved my hands in my pockets. I wasn't good at hiding the emotions on my face. Voice-actors portray emotions on the job and off. We have to be emotionally transparent and in this fake-it-till-you-make-it society, transparent isn't always the best way to be. Besides the breaking news about Africa, which I was still trying to digest, I was worried about the hearing. "I don't know. I just keep going back to the fact of how hard it would be to take Tommy out of San Diego and just drop him in Houston. Children with autism resist change and even regress when they're confronted by change and this would be the biggest change of his life. But how will I know that argument's going to work?" I shrugged. "It seems like I'm just throwing my cards on the table only to see who has the best hand."

"I understand. I know nothing's certain. But look at it this way." We faced each other as the wind blew a strand of hair across Rachel's face. In the light, I saw that her blue eyes were flecked with bits of green. Beautiful eyes. "We have Carly Yates on our side, all these scientists, we've got some amazing data and the videos. You'll see.

Tommy will be with the chimps in the end, and luck's going to turn your way."

Luck.

She had no idea about my relationship with that crazy coin-tosser.

In the end, it was going to come down to what the judge decided. One person, one decision. That was the entire ball of wax. There was no other way around it.

"Talk to you soon, okay?" Rachel said. She touched my shoulder, and for a small moment, leaned closer to me. "And don't fret so much. It's going to be fine."

"Sure. Of course. You're right." I turned on my best smile for her, but it didn't change the trepidation I felt inside. And then I said it, what had been on my mind for quite a while. "And thanks again for everything, Rachel, no matter how it works out." I spoke sincerely. "Really. None of this would have happened if you hadn't opened Weller up to me and Tommy from the beginning. You could have easily just turned us away, but you didn't. You got involved and you've helped my son more than you know. I'm completely grateful."

She laughed. "It's been my pleasure. And you know what? You've helped me too, Chris. You've actually rescued me in a way, though I'm sure you haven't realized it."

"I have? How?" I furrowed my brow.

"Before I met you and Tommy, I was jaded about so many things outside of Gombe. I can't help but wonder if we've all become cut-off and somehow disconnected from each other. I mean have people lost their ability to care? So much hatred and cruelty in the world. Terrorism. School shootings. You name it. In a way, things are really bad. But then when you came along, seeing you with Tommy, the way you care for him and love him, well, it showed me another side to life that I had totally forgotten about. The best side. Here."

She stepped forward and wrapped her arms around me and gave me a long, enduring hug. "Thanks," she whispered in my ear.

Our bodies found their own way, drawing closer. Contact. Her touch sent an electric tingling through me that turned my stomach into a butterfly cage. Finally, we let go. I just stood there, blinking, not knowing what else to say. Feelings speak louder than words.

"See you soon," she said a moment later.

"For sure."

She got in her car and eco-drove away. I stared at her red taillights as they faded into the distance.

I turned and walked away, thinking that Rachel had become more than just a friend in all this, she'd become my ally. But now, something else was becoming clear. Tommy and I were digging our emotional hooks into her. And we were pulling her in by her heart.

RACHEL AND I MET UP again as the hearing approached and I was a mess of nerves. But I wanted her to reassure me one more time that everything would work out.

Amazingly, she agreed on a date of sorts, saying that she did have a hole in her schedule, and I brought Max along for reinforcement. We strolled around downtown San Diego. We found a smoothie shop on First Avenue, not far from the marina, and sat outside in the gorgeous weather. Max laid at my feet, his nose actively in search mode, wagging his tail.

"It's going to be all right," Rachel said, drinking a green smoothie. "Don't look so down."

"But how can you be so certain?"

"Because I just am. Once you start talking about Tommy and how much this chimp therapy benefits him, he'll rule your way. I'm positive."

"Well, I wish I could share your view."

"Look," she said, grabbing my hand. "You have to believe. You love your son. You're going the distance for him. It's going to work out. Trust the universe."

Interesting take. I hoped she was right.

I felt my anxiety lessen as we continued walking and talking. She told me about her parents who were living in Arizona now, her sister, a physician, who lived in Savannah, Georgia, who she hardly ever got to see.

We stopped at an antique shop along the way, and after tying up Max, we went inside. I examined a pile of old *Life* magazines, ran my hand over a nineteenth-century oak table, admired an early 1920s chair made in France, the legs gracefully curved. Then I found Rachel, who was examining a pair of tall crystal candlesticks etched with ornate flower designs sitting on a shelf.

"You like them?" I asked.

She said nothing, just continued studying the candlesticks, then blinked her eyes and turned to me.

"What did you say?"

"I asked if you liked them."

"Oh, yes. Very much," She pushed some hair behind her ears. "They remind me of the pair my father gave my mother on their twentieth anniversary. I was about fourteen. I remember the way the sunlight hit them and how pretty and soft everything looked when they were lit. I thought it was so romantic." She lowered her head shyly.

"They're beautiful," I said. Studying the flower designs on the candlesticks made me think of the roses my father carefully raised. Were those roses engraved on the candlesticks too? I couldn't quite tell. Still, I couldn't help but wonder if life would ever present me with a long-lasting relationship as well, one that was sustaining and caring and deep.

Chapter 13

D r. Brady warned my crotchety father that drinking alcohol would slow the recovery of his bruised hip. But did he listen to the doctor's advice? Hell, no.

He needed rounds of ice—no heat—ibuprofen, and rest. He'd been instructed to wrap an elastic bandage around his upper leg to compress the swelling and to elevate his injured hip above the level of his heart to decrease swelling and pain. The bruise was bad. He had pain all the way to his toes, along with numbness all down his leg. At first, he could hardly get around, then finally graduated to the school of advanced cane-ology. I was surprised by his resilience, the old codger. But he kept on drinking.

Cheryl was right. He was tough as nails, wood, even steel.

Insurance paid for an aid to come to the house every Tuesday and Thursday. Dahlia, dark hair, brown eyes, a big-boned woman with a Caribbean accent. She had gotten the cane for him. Made of dark wood with all kinds of animal engravings on it, coolest one I'd ever seen, but he hated the cane and threatened to burn it.

On a windy Saturday, two weeks after my father's accident, I brought Tommy with me to see him. Max came along as well as did Mister Backpack.

"Pop." Tommy gave my father direct eye contact, standing in front of him in the den. "Pop. Hurt." My father sat in his green lounger, a glass of beer in his hand, froth still at the top, his leg elevated on a chair with two pillows and an ice bag planted on his hip. The house smelled muggy and I went to open a window. "Pop."

Tommy's lips still held traces of the peanut butter sandwich he'd just eaten. Of course, I'd cut it up into the special shapes he'd demanded, one half a square, one half a circle. Tommy stared at my father, and then shook his head right and left. "Pop."

"What's he want?" my father asked, looking at me. "Game's on in an hour. Today we're going to win. I know it."

"Pop. Pop." Tommy evidently was fixating on my dad. "Pop," Tommy said again. "Pop. Pop. Pop."

"Pop loves you," my father said.

"Pop. Pop. Pop."

"Why don't you go outside and play with Max, Tommy? Pop's not in such a great mood," I said.

Tommy headed out the back door, slamming it hard behind him. The house shook.

"Jesus!" my father cried. "Don't slam the door!" He reached up to his hearing aids and adjusted them. Just like with Tommy, loud sounds aggravated him. "Crap." He took a long swig from his beer. "When will he ever learn not to do that?"

"Not sure," I said.

"So." My father took another swig, put it back down on the table, then crossed his arms over his chest. "That hearing. I can't believe it. You and Cheryl. What a perfect mess." I'd put off telling my father for as long as possible, but finally filled him in on the entire custody situation over the phone.

"I'm a nervous wreck," I said. And I was. The past few nights, I'd hardly been able to sleep. I hated to go down Ambien Highway, but it could happen after all.

"Well, I hope you stick it to her. Come on. Let's go outside. I need a little sunshine. Tired of sitting here all day."

Dad brought his leg down off the pillow, took off the ice pack, and groaned in pain. "Good thing I'm on ibuprofen," he said.

He stood shakily, took his cane, and he and I trudged outside. I was amazed that he left his beer behind. Outside, the scent of rain hung in the air. Max, spying us, moseyed up to my father and licked his hand, tasting it, sniffing it. God only knew what kind of information he was deducing through his amazing olfactory senses. Max paid no attention to me. He loved Dad absolutely. There wasn't even a question as to who he favored more.

"Now I'm limping like you, old boy," my father said with a coarse laugh, scratching Max behind his ears. "I sure am."

Max barked as if he understood, as if he were saying, "Welcome to the club."

"You're a good ole fella," my father said. "You're my boy!"

We sat down in green lawn chairs and I got an ottoman from the house so my father could prop up his leg. I scanned the fenced-in backyard. The weeping acacia looked beautiful, green and lush, and Dad's roses, pink and red, were lovely as always. Tommy was lying underneath the acacia. He had both Radar and Monk in his arms. He was looking up at the sky. A flock of birds flew above us, forming that infamous V pattern, one bird in the lead. Tommy's motorboat sounds reached my ears, though I was sure my father didn't hear it. Tommy was always happiest off by himself.

"Writing any more poetry, Dad?" I asked.

"Hell no." He spoke as if it was the last thing on earth he would ever do, waved a hand in the air.

"But you should. You're good. I think you have talent."

"It doesn't come that easy, all right?"

I didn't want to argue. Nothing comes easy: good poetry, protecting your autistic son, or anything else.

We both studied the sky, grey clouds forming, clumping together like cotton balls. Then he looked straight ahead, refusing to turn my way. His grainy voice softened and I detected a slight quiver. "Sure do miss your mother, though."

"Me, too," I said. My heart leapt in my throat. *Anything worth doing is worth doing well.* She always used to say that. I could hear her laughter in my head, her playing piano, her bright, bubbly laugh.

"Feels so empty around here," my father said. "Hate to say it, but some days, I wish I was with her. Why not? What do I have to live for anymore, you know? I mean, really."

"Don't say that, Dad," I said. "You've got the Padres. You've got Tommy. And me."

"The Padres and Tommy I can handle. You, I'm not so sure." My father gave me one of his rare smiles, then as he looked at me, his eyes moistened up. A trembling hand went to his face and he lowered his head. "Your mother's in a better place, though." He looked up. "Yeah. I'm sure of it." He was more introspective and quiet than I'd ever seen him. This was interesting. Maybe that fall knocked some sense into him.

He rubbed his bruised hip and groaned. He tapped his cane against the ground. "Oh, hell, I'm just one old fool."

"No, you're not, Dad," I said.

I looked out at Tommy as Max raced to him, barking at him. Tommy stood and clapped his hands, egging Max on.

"I was the kind of husband who never saw life through her eyes, you know? It was always about me. I still don't understand how she put up with me all those years. And now that she's gone . . . We don't know what we've really got till it's gone, do we? And then it's too late to do anything about it," my father said. He put a hand on my shoulder. "Here's my advice. Enjoy that boy." He pointed at Tommy, who was now spinning around and laughing at some inner joke. "He's the best thing you've got going."

"Look, Dad." I pulled out my cell and showed a video of Tommy and Albert, which Rachel had sent me. Tommy, signing to Albert, Albert, signing back. Tommy explaining what Albert was painting.

"That's my grandson!" my father said, laughing. He slapped his knee. "That's a Crutcher through and through, all right. He knows those chimps inside and out."

After a while, Tommy walked over to us and stood before my father.

"Pop," he said. "Pop. Fall."

"Yes, I fell all right," my father said. "Right on my tush."

"Tush?" Tommy repeated. "Tush?"

"Yeah. Tush."

We both laughed at that. Then my father said, "You sure like those chimps, don't you, Tom-Tom?" my father asked. "Do you see pictures in your mind when you're with them? That's what I did back on the farm in Georgia when I was with the horses. Pictures." My father pointed to his head. "Pictures in here? Is that right?"

Tommy nodded eagerly. "Pics," he said and formed his lips into that pseudo-smile, mechanical. "Pics. See." He closed his eyes and opened them. "See, Pop . . . See! See!" He actually reached out and touched my father's hand.

"Yes. I see," my father said. Then a minute later, when Tommy was playing with Max, he said, "You better win that hearing, that's all I can say. That boy is depending on you to stay with those damn chimps of his. He's got no business going to Houston. He needs those chimps and that need of his is written in his DNA."

"I'll do my best, Dad."

But his eyes dug into mine, and then he spoke with an edge of fear in his voice that surprised me. "What if your best isn't good enough?"

I didn't have an answer for that and my shoulders grew tight.

"You want an old man's advice?" He shifted slowly in his seat and groaned.

"Sure."

He growled: "Go for the goddamn jugular."

Chapter 14

May 23. A windy and cloudy Thursday afternoon.

The time had come to fight for my beliefs. To stand tall and stand my ground.

I made my way downtown to the Family Law Court building on Sixth Street. It's a dumpy 1960s two-story brick structure near the El Cortez Hotel. I wore a fine grey Joseph Abboud Italian-made suit and a silk blue tie, both of which I'd recently purchased with my increased income. I needed this coat of armor to bolster my nerves and up my self-confidence. My stomach quaked and blood pounded in my ears with every step I took. I'd used a brand-new razor to shave, wanting to get my face as smooth as possible, but nicked myself on that difficult groove, the philtrum, between my nose and my upper lip. It had taken ten minutes for the damn thing to stop bleeding; such a nuisance.

I plodded up the marble steps, almost missing the last step and nearly falling on my face. I felt like a fool. Three reporters lined up to meet me. I knew what to say—nothing. I would be mute and distant as a star. It wouldn't be hard given the circumstances, even for a vocal talent like me.

"Mr. Crutcher, is it true your son speaks to chimpanzees?" Bloomfield led the charge, microphone in hand. The guy was incorrigible and full of himself. He was really getting on my nerves.

"No comment."

Another microphone came forward, held by a black-haired female reporter from Channel Six. She asked, "Your ex-wife alleges that you're harming your son. How do you feel about that?"

"No comment."

I elbowed past the reporters and made my way into the courthouse. I found the courtroom and saw Mark sitting at the defendant's table, going over his notes. He stood when he saw me, his face drawn tight with concern. Dressed in a dark-blue suit, looking sharp and camera-ready himself, Mark pressed his lips together and frowned.

"You ready for this?" he asked.

"You bet," I said, heart fluttering.

There was a nervous edge to Mark's voice that worried me. Was there something I didn't know? Some new angle he wasn't telling me about? Was Cheryl also suing Weller? I wondered if Rachel knew anything at all about that. The possibility had entered my mind.

Tommy was staying with Cheryl's parents, who had enlisted the help of an aide from "Care Now," an agency that specialized in disabled children. I swallowed. Right about now, I was sure her mother and father were talking in front of him about how I was the worst thing that could have happened to their darling daughter. Who knew? Maybe I was. I'd gotten along with her parents fairly well, and felt comfortable around them, though there was always a certain amount of mildly expressed reservation toward me. I'd felt it mostly from Cheryl's father.

The reporters were finding their seats, each and every one as attractive as a model in a Ralph Lauren ad. A few witnesses sat on Cheryl's side of the courtroom, well-dressed and professional looking, most likely Acorn representatives. On my side sat grim-faced Dr. Osikawa from Weller. I was grateful to see him. But where was my expert witness, Dr. Dunn? Rekulak and Rachel weren't there, either. Then I spotted her coming in along with Dunn and I breathed with relief. I caught Rachel's attention and she gave me an encouraging smile. Then, before finding her seat, she came up to me and put a hand on my shoulder. I felt comforted by it. I turned to her and our eyes met. God, I needed her there.

"Good luck," she said.

"Thank you. I'm going to need luck and anything else I can get my hands on."

"You're going to do fine."

She gave me another encouraging smile, and as she walked back to her seat, in came Gloria Beaman marching alongside Cheryl. What a pair. Tall and lean, built like a professional tennis player, Beaman was truly hell on heels. She was wearing a purple sheath dress with ruffled sleeves, a white blazer on top, a gold necklace. Hardly any makeup. Her black heels clattered on the floor. Think Cruella Deville as an attorney. My throat constricted at just the sight of her. Basically, she gave me the willies and my hands grew slick with dread.

Cheryl wore a beige dress and pearls, her baby bump grown now to near-hill status. Our eyes met for an eternal second and everything else faded away. It crushed me, seeing her all lawyered up and pregnant by another man.

Cheryl and Beaman took their seats in the front at their desk, along with Beaman's assistant, a short, squat woman dressed in a dark suit. I wiped my slick hands on my pants. Where was Mark's assistant? Oh, yeah. He didn't have one.

I was hoping my father might show up. I ran my eyes around the room. Nope. A minute later, there he was, sliding quietly into the back of the room and taking a seat, cane in hand. He'd been getting up and around more and more lately. I smiled. Unshaven, wearing a ball cap, he didn't even look at me. I tried to make eye contact, but he only stared straight ahead—not even a nod. At least he'd come. I was hoping that Belinda, his caretaker, had driven him. Finally, she entered the courtroom and sat down next to him. She'd probably had to park the car.

The square-faced bailiff announced, "All rise." Judge Joseph Korbovitch entered the room. An exceedingly tall man in his sixties. Korbovitch strutted with his chest out toward his high seat beneath the State of California seal. A court stenographer was set up near the witness stand with an American flag to her side. Since this was a hearing, there would be no jury.

"Ms. Beaman," Korbovitch said, adjusted the sleeves of his robe. The judge's voice was smooth, silky, as if he worked as a piano bar singer during the weekends. "Are you ready to proceed?"

Beaman said something to her assistant, put a hand on Cheryl's shoulder, then rose to her full height. "Yes, Your Honor, I am ready." Beaman's voice, confident and sharp, rang throughout the courtroom. Since Cheryl was the one initiating the petition and we were the respondents, Beaman was allowed to go first.

She started out simply enough, summarizing her client's objectives: to gain full or sole custody in order to leave the state and take Tommy to a private school in Houston. Then she said, "I'd like to call Ms. Cheryl Bridgewater to the stand."

Cheryl took the stand, sitting on a chair to the right of the judge. Beaman quickly established Tommy's age and his psychological history, then asked, "Ms. Bridgewater, can you explain your present position to the court and how it relates to the child in question?"

Cheryl crossed her legs, took a long breath, then began. "As Tommy's mother and shared custodian . . ." Cheryl looked toward Korbovitch, who ran a hand through his unkempt grey hair. She paused before continuing, her voice breathy and soft. "I am trying to do the best I can for my son, a child with autism. I want to enroll him in the Acorn School in Houston, Texas. Its programs have been the subject of various studies published in professional journals and have been proven to offer. . . "

"I object, Your Honor," Mark said. "Ms. Bridgewater is not an authority."

"Sustained."

"So, basically, you believe this school shows potential for your son?" Beaman asked.

"Definitely." She nodded. "And Dr. Norman Kaplan, a child psychologist at UCLA that you'll hear from later, agrees."

"And what's keeping you from taking your son there?" Beaman asked.

"Even though all the science and the therapists . . ."

Mark said, interrupting, "*All* the science and therapists, Your Honor? Really?"

"Please restate, Ms. Bridgewater," Korbovitch said. He wiped his bent nose with a handkerchief.

"Even though several therapists who have seen Tommy agree that this would be an excellent school for my son's educational development, my ex-husband," she pointed at me, "has refused to agree to this move. He has his own ideas."

This was going to be nasty business. Tommy's opening up with the chimps, that look on his face when he was with them. I had to keep that in the forefront—always.

"Would you explain what your ex-husband's ideas are?" Beaman asked.

I closed my eyes for a moment. My stomach exploded with anxiety and I started shallow breathing, shoulders moving up and down with each breath. I drank some bottled water. I was on the verge of a panic attack. Things had just started and I was already unraveling, a spool of emotional yarn coming undone.

"He wants Tommy to have what I guess could be called . . ." She nearly choked on the words, "some kind of crazy, I don't know, chimpanzee therapy. He thinks it's good for Tommy. I think it's a disaster." Her face flushed red.

"Could you tell us why?" Beaman asked.

"A chimp and a child simply have no reason on earth to be together." Cheryl scanned the courtroom, then looked directly at the judge. "Number one, it's dangerous, and number two, my son received absolutely no benefit. In fact, it made him regress."

"Both of these issues are conjecture, Your Honor," Mark said. "Ms. Bridgewater is not an expert."

"Please refrain from speculation, Ms. Bridgewater," Korbovitch said.

Beaman addressed Cheryl. "Would you say your ex-husband is obsessed with your son interacting with these chimpanzees then, Ms. Bridgewater?"

"Absolutely. That's all he cares about, getting Tommy and those chimps together. He's brainwashed my son. I really think he has."

I clenched my teeth.

"Your Honor, please," Mark said, his voice stern.

"Ms. Bridgewater," the judge said, rubbing his brow, "the court is only here to learn the facts. Allegations about brainwashing cannot be substantiated, or can they?"

"No, Your Honor," Cheryl said.

"Then please stick to the facts."

"Yes, sir."

"Can you tell us what you know about the Acorn School in Houston?" Beaman asked, moving closer to where Cheryl was sitting.

"Of course. They have small class sizes, documented cases of real progress, one-on-one therapy, and even groundbreaking techniques that truly seem to have validity. If I can't get him in that school, if my ex keeps blocking me every step of the way . . ." Cheryl sniffled, and then out came her prop—the tissue. She dabbed at her eyes theatrically, but still, it was effective. "I just don't know what I'd do. I'm obviously doing everything I can to ensure that my son is afforded the best therapies and education possible. He needs this school. There's nothing like Acorn anywhere else. Believe me." Cheryl turned to the judge. "I've checked everywhere."

The judge rubbed the side of his face. He made a few notes.

Beaman had Cheryl explain how she had taken Tommy to doctors and therapists throughout his life. She painted a picture of a mother totally involved in raising a developmentally challenged son. I couldn't disagree with that. She was a great mom. Involved, committed.

"Would you say Chris was a cooperative parent when it came to raising Tommy?" Beaman asked.

"Hardly. When I wanted to try the Lovaas method with Tommy, for example?" Cheryl said, "my ex was completely against it. We argued for days." She frowned.

"Do you think it's because he just doesn't care?" Beaman raised an eyebrow.

"Objection!" Mark said. "Completely subjective."

"Sustained."

"Have you ever refused to bring Tommy to your ex-husband's house for his weekend stays?" Beaman continued.

"Only if we both agreed that he shouldn't come for some reason." Cheryl twisted in her seat and glanced my way.

Beaman handed a document to Korbovitch, who took it from her, slipped on his bifocals, and perused it.

"Your Honor," Beaman said, "I'd like to enter into the record this psychologist's report on Cheryl Bridgewater's interview as Exhibit B-14. I believe you'll find the evaluation from the psychologist very positive," Beaman went on. "Ms. Bridgewater doesn't smoke, has no history of mental illness, no problems with drugs or alcohol, and plans to marry a man of means and good standing in the local community."

Beaman strode from the bench to the witness box, turning her thin lips upward in a smile, flashing her white teeth. She looked benignly at Cheryl as though she were about to address Mother Teresa. I clasped my hands together, pulse racing.

"Raising an autistic child is difficult, is it not, Ms. Bridgewater?" Beaman asked sympathetically.

Cheryl hesitated a minute before answering, dabbing her eyes with the tissue. "Extremely." Her voice quivered. "No one knows what it's really like until they experience it. It's a twenty-four seven obligation. Completely unpredictable. One day he does fairly well, the next, he can be a total terror. The simple fact is that Tommy needs me completely in his life, and I need to be there for him."

My muscles tensed. I leaned closer to Mark, whose head was down, writing. "I need to be there for him too," I whispered. Mark nodded.

"I love my son," she went on. Her voice quivered. "I'm desperate for him to have the very best. Any mother would feel the same way. The truth is, mothers know best. It's just a shame I have to fight...." Cheryl dabbed back another tear. She heaved a sigh. "That I have to fight my ex-husband every step of the way so that I can do . . ." another sigh, "what's right for my son."

"Thank you, Ms. Bridgewater," Beaman said. "No further questions."

Mark stood and approached Cheryl, standing about two feet away from her. He folded his arms across his chest and began his cross-examination.

"Have you ever withheld Tommy's visitation with his father?" he asked.

Cheryl jerked her head back as if she was offended by the question. "Of course not."

"Were there any times in your relationship when you've been angry at Mr. Crutcher?" Mark inched closer to Cheryl, who shrugged.

"Answer the question, please," the judge said. His smooth mellow voice made me think he was about to break out in a song. "We can't transcribe body language."

"Can you give us an occasion?" Mark asked. He glanced at the judge, then stared at Cheryl.

"Your Honor, I object!" Beaman said with a snarl on her lips. "Irrelevant and immaterial."

"Goes to the whole motive for this hearing, Your Honor," Mark said. He waved a hand in the air.

"Overruled," Korbovitch said. "Please answer the question, Ms. Bridgewater."

"An occasion?" Mark prompted her.

"Well, then . . ."

"If you're having a hard time thinking of one, may I help?" Mark produced a document and handed it to the judge and another copy to Beaman.

"Your Honor, I've just given you a copy of the testimony from the divorce proceedings between Ms. Bridgewater and Mr. Crutcher. I'll read from my copy," Mark said. He cleared his throat. "And I quote from Ms. Bridgewater's words: 'I want to make sure Chris sees Tommy as little as possible. Is that so hard to understand? Is it? Well, is it? Yes, I want him to suffer. He deserves to suffer. He's done nothing but block me every step of the way. It's because of him that our marriage failed.'"

"Are these your words?" Mark asked.

"Yes," Cheryl said. She suddenly looked shaken, her face turning pale, her lips drawing tightly together. "But they were spoken in the heat of a divorce."

Mark continued reading from the transcript. "'What's wrong with Tommy is Chris's fault. And I don't want him to ever live it down.'"

I remembered those words clearly during our divorce proceeding. She'd spoken with venom too. I rubbed my forehead, then took a drink of water. I felt anger bubbling to the surface and did my best to push it down.

"Were you angry at Mr. Crutcher then?" Mark asked.

Cheryl said nothing. She cocked her head back, as if she were about to tell Mark to go fuck himself. Lines of defiance traced the edges of her mouth.

"Answer the question, please," the judge said.

"Yes." For a moment, she looked down, then gazed full on at Mark, then quickly eyed me. I gave her a mean stare, our eyes locking like horns.

"Angry because you blamed him for Tommy's autism?"

"But that transcript was from a different time," Cheryl said. "I'm not angry now. I just want to do what's right."

Mark walked a few feet away from Cheryl and paced for a few seconds. Finally, he said, "Is it fair to say that this very same anger is behind your desire to take your son to Houston? Don't you want to see Mr. Crutcher *continue* to suffer?"

"I . . . No! That's not true."

"It's not?"

"I want the best for Tommy."

"And the worst for Mr. Crutcher?"

"Yes! I mean no!" She turned red-faced.

Beaman shot to her feet. "Your Honor, I object! The respondent is leading the witness."

"Overruled, Ms. Beaman."

Beaman sat down, turned to her assistant, and whispered in her ear.

Mark approached Cheryl again. "Ms. Bridgewater, don't you believe that a father's place in the upbringing of his son is extremely important?"

Cheryl nodded. "Of course."

"You say, 'of course,' so why didn't you allow more visitation during your first custody decision? Why did you fight Mr. Crutcher's access to his son?"

"I . . ."

"You wanted to restrict his visitation, did you not?"

"No. Yes. Some, yes."

"Why did you want to restrict Mr. Crutcher's access to his son?"

"Because . . . Tommy needs me." Cheryl turned to the judge. "He does need me. He can do without Chris."

It hit me hard and deep, right in my emotional solar plexus. How could she even say those words? Did she really believe that? That I was dispensable? I started squeezing the life out of my water bottle without even realizing it. The plastic made a loud crinkling sound. The judge scowled at me. Beaman even looked my way.

"I guess you don't think a father's place in his son's upbringing is so important after all. Is that right?" Mark asked.

Cheryl blinked rapidly. "I'll admit it," Cheryl said. "I was hard on him, all right? But I'm always thinking of Tommy in everything I do. I may have gone a little overboard, but I had good reasons. I know what's best for my son." She glared at me. She spoke emphatically. "Chris doesn't even have a clue as to what Tommy really needs or what would be best."

"So, you admit you went overboard."

Cheryl paused before answering. She spoke softly. "Yes."

"And what's going to make us think you're not going overboard now? What's going to make us think you're not mainly out to get your ex right now, and that Tommy's care is secondary?"

"Because this is totally different. The Acorn School's the perfect place for Tommy."

Mark switched gears. "You're pregnant, aren't you?"

"Yes."

"And the father of your unborn child, the man you intend to marry, just happens to have accepted a position in Houston, right?"

"Yes."

"So, could we say that the real reason you want to go to Houston is to be with your fiancé?"

"That's part of it, yes, but the main reason is so that Tommy can have the best possible schooling."

"But isn't it a bit convenient? The location of the school and your fiancé's new job being one and the same?"

"I learned about Acorn before I even started dating Wade."

"Have you ever been convicted of a DUI, Ms. Bridgewater?" Mark asked.

I leaned forward in my seat. She murmured the word. "Yes."

Mark took a breath and eyed Korbovitch, who seemed preoccupied with a thought. His eyes looked distant. Mark said, "And was your son in the car when you were stopped while driving under the influence?"

Cheryl took a long moment before answering, eyes shifting back and forth. Finally, she said in a soft voice, "Yes."

"And so, you say mothers know best?" Mark asked. He caught Korbovitch's eye.

"Look. I'd had two glasses of wine that afternoon, okay? I'd just won a bid for a major job in La Jolla, and I was celebrating with some friends. I picked up Tommy from his after-school therapy session and I ran a red light. It was a huge mistake, I admit it. But I've made restitution, I've paid the fine, I've gone to the traffic safety classes, and I did public service. It occurred three years ago. I don't see why you should even bring it up."

"But it was a DUI with your son in the car, was it not?"

Cheryl looked down and her shoulders sagged. "Yes."

Mark let the information sink in. "And one final question, Ms. Bridgewater. Did Tommy have an accident at a playground while you were supervising him?"

The surprised look on Cheryl's face made me hurt inside. I winced. I hated bringing this memory up, airing it out like this. "Yes. But it was—"

"Can you tell us about that incident?"

Cheryl suddenly looked away. A hand went to the side of her face and her brow narrowed. She didn't reply to the question.

"Ms. Bridgewater? Can you tell us?"

She spoke slowly as her cheeks inflamed. "I was with a friend, all right? Another mother, and we were watching our sons play on the monkey bars." Cheryl swallowed and sunk down in her chair. "So, I turned around to talk to my friend for no more than a second, and, the next thing I know," she looked squarely at Mark, "he was on the ground."

"Did he require stitches?"

"Yes. It could have happened to any mother. We aren't perfect."

"But Mister Crutcher must be perfect?"

"Yes, no. Oh, I don't know." Cheryl's exasperated voice tripped through the courtroom. She scratched her wrist. "All I know is that chimps are much more dangerous than playground mishaps."

"No further questions."

The judge dismissed us and I sat there, talking to Mark. I tried to sense how he was thinking it was going, but he seemed hard to read. I knew my own face was an open book, total desperation written all over it. We walked out together into the hallway and Mark departed with a clap on the shoulder, saying, "Keep the faith." Not much else.

Sure. Why not?

I spotted my father and Rachel waiting for me, standing side by side. They were talking together as I approached them. I was surprised. My father hardly talked to anyone.

"Don't look like such a hound dog," my father growled, leaning on his cane as I approached. "You're going to win this thing. Don't worry."

"So, you met Rachel, I see," I said to him.

"Yep. Told her all about how I used to see pictures in my mind too."

"Your dad's quite the character," Rachel said with a smile.

"A bit rough around the edges," I said.

"Look, I need to get home," my father said. "Got a ball game to watch." Then he winked at me. "I like her, Chris," he said.

I felt myself blushing, then spoke the first words that came into my head. "I do, too." I smiled at Rachel.

My father departed, latching onto Belinda's arm, and then it was just me and Rachel, who shot me a pained look. "God, Chris, this must be so hard for you. I can hardly stand it in that courtroom. I imagined something a lot less intense. I had no idea it would be like this."

"So, how do you think it's going?" I asked. I was eager to know her thoughts.

But now she was silent. She muddled her brow. "Not sure. That judge is so hard to read."

"I know."

We walked outside together, shuffling into the San Diego sunlight, which was as bright as ever. Emotional explosions kept blowing up in my mind. The fear of losing Tommy. Gloria Beaman and her legal tactics. And now what my father said about Rachel right in front of her. *I like her.* He was never so quick to compliment someone. Amazing.

The sounds of heavy traffic rose around me. Fortunately, the obnoxious reporters were nowhere to be seen. Clusters of people, some well-dressed, some in t-shirts and jeans, were coming in and out of the courthouse. My heart pounded hard. Divorce. Custody. I realized that this was a world in itself that went on day by day. It was like a factory that welcomed people in, stamped them with legal decisions, one way or the other, then spat them out.

"We'll get through this," Rachel said. "I know it's hard. But we have so much evidence, remember. The judge has to see our side of things."

Our eyes met, that same breeze of understanding that I'd felt before, passed through us again. I knew it.

"It's hard, Rachel," I said. "Really hard."

"I know."

We hugged, expressing our feelings of trepidation the only way we knew how. Further words seemed useless as our bodies spoke to each other with a newborn sense of togetherness, intimacy, and need.

When we finally pulled apart, I looked deep into her eyes. Rachel said, "I didn't think I'd get so involved in this, Chris. It all started out as merely a research project, you know? But now, see . . . I had no idea what was going to happen when I took hold of Tommy's hand that day. I thought I was walking him into the play yard, but you know what? He was the one who was leading me—straight into a new world. Straight into your arms."

Touched deeply by her words, by her caring and understanding, I stroked her hair and plumbed the depths of her eyes. They seemed bottomless, endless as the natural beauty in Gombe. "Are you saying this is more than science between us?"

She nodded as the blue-green emotional oceans before me sparkled with tears. We hugged again.

THE NEXT DAY I WAS much too nervous to eat breakfast, so I relied on only a large cup of dirt-black coffee to get me through the morning. I couldn't stop thinking about Rachel and what she'd said. That this was more than a mere science project to her, that Tommy had taken her hand and led her into my arms. Wow. Heady stuff. Was this really happening? I felt excited, but at the same time, unsure. She was leaving for Africa anyway. Who knew what would really happen between us?

Max kept pacing around me, reflecting my own anxiety. He wouldn't leave my side. He wasn't swishing his tail and he kept licking my shoes for some reason. I left him in the backyard with his bowl of food and water.

"See you later, buddy," I said. "Got some major BS to get through today."

Max just eyed me and then laid down, whining. In his own way, I was sure he knew that I was in bad shape, that something was definitely up.

Wearing a navy-blue blazer and grey pants, I made my way up the steps to the courtroom, where once again, reporters aimed questions at me, firing one after another. The silence I retaliated with was the perfect weapon; they hated the sound of it.

I didn't see Rachel. My father was sitting in the back with Belinda by his side. This time he gave me a quick nod when our eyes met. I didn't know what to do—I wanted to talk to him for emotional support, but I was afraid to go near him as well because he might say something that would piss me off. Let's face it, a fire provides warmth, but it also burns. I chose to stay away.

Wade, wearing a dark-blue suit, was talking to Cheryl. He had a hand on her shoulder. I had no idea how he was taking all this, but I wondered if he was now having regrets about getting involved with a woman with an autistic child. He looked caged in, his eyes darting right and left. Trapped. Every so often, he pulled at his collar.

I was sure he'd rather be sailing in wide open spaces. *Having fun now, Jaguar Man?*

The bailiff called us to order, and I once again took my seat next to Mark. Korbovitch marched into the courtroom, black robes, all business. Taking his seat, he whipped off his bifocals, which were perched on the crest of his bent nose and penetrated the room with a stern glare.

"Ms. Beaman," he said. "Please begin your questioning."

"I would like to call Dr. Norman Kaplan to the stand," Beaman said.

Kaplan stepped up to the stand with quick confident strides, silver hair slicked back from a large forehead. He was a local psychologist who specialized in autism. Everyone in the autistic community knew him. A very conventional thinker. I was sure he was not going to support my side.

"Dr. Kaplan, please tell the court what you saw when you investigated the boy in question at the chimp institute," Beaman said.

"Actually, I visited Tommy Crutcher at both Hillwood, his conventional school, and at the chimp institute." Kaplan's soft voice had a way of demanding attention. Wire-framed glasses gave him an edgy but intelligent persona. "I wanted to compare the differences in Tommy's behavior in the two different settings."

"Go on."

"My conclusion was that I saw no real transferability that would benefit the boy's best interests." He folded his arms across his chest and spoke emphatically.

Was the man blind? How could he say that? I grabbed a pen resting next to me and tried to squeeze the ink out of it.

"Explain, please."

Kaplan formed a V with his hands. "You see, even if Tommy were to somehow communicate with these chimps, I believe this kind of activity would fail to ultimately improve Tommy's relationships with

humans, children, or adults. Given what I know about autism, I see
Tommy's focusing on chimps as a kind of escape mechanism from
human relationships altogether and thus a hindrance."

His words fell like hammers on my ears, pounding my eardrums.

He had it totally backwards! Tommy was *much* more
human-friendly when he was with the chimps. I sagged in my chair,
wanting to stand up and shout this man down, while Cheryl, sitting
across from me next to Beaman, was eating it up. She leaned forward
as Kaplan spoke and then wrote down a few notes of her own. Then
she turned my way, looked at me, and death-stared me down.

"I see," Beaman said. "So, these chimps are limiting his ability to
progress toward better human interaction in your opinion, then?"

"Yes, I believe so. I can tell he enjoys it there at Weller, and
it certainly de-stresses him, if you want to call it that. But as a
therapeutic interventional tool, I think it has severe limitations. I
would have to consider any such evidence merely anecdotal at best."

"Thank you, Dr. Kaplan," Beaman said.

"Mr. Levy?" Korbovitch said.

Mark stood and fired up the computer that cast an image onto
a wall-mounted monitor, its screen visible for the entire courtroom
to observe. This was the moment when, for the first time, Tommy's
talents would be seen somewhere besides Weller.

"I'd like to play a video of Tommy interacting and relating to the
chimps," Mark said.

The judge nodded. "Go ahead."

Mark clicked a button on his computer and the video began.
He'd set up a monitor that faced the courtroom, so that all of us
could view the screen. Tommy's young voice came through the
speakers, and just hearing him speak in his own unique way made
my eyes wet. I blinked and pressed my hands together as I held them
under the table, my eyelids growing hot, my chin trembling. Cheryl
sat immobile, refusing to even view the monitor.

"Daddy say good meet you, Awbert. Chimpie old. See Obo. He meet me in place and we talk much. He good chimpie."

Cheryl glanced my way. My stomach turned to jelly. I read in her look an iron-willed determination. My hands grew slick. I'd never seen her so fierce. Beaman reviewed her notes as if what we were doing didn't even exist.

"Chimpies . . . play. See . . . my . . . See. Chimpies love play. They be fun. Obo want show you here . . .every . . .thing."

Mark stopped the video. "How would you compare those rates of fluency with the ones observed at Hillwood, Dr. Kaplan?"

Dr. Kaplan coughed. "The boy's speaking, for sure, but there's no consistency, no real communication. It's just words."

"Words?"

"Yes, words!" Kaplan furrowed his brow. He leaned forward and nearly spat it out. "A child cannot communicate with a chimp and a chimp cannot communicate with a child beyond a few signs or things like that. If you think there's any way that this could ever in a million years help an autistic child speak better or learn better or . . ."

"Surely, sir, you must see at least some fluency, do you not?"

"No, I do not! These are random words. Those chimps are just drawing him out because they're playful. He's getting lost in their world. What I want to see is real communication with human beings! That's what Ms. Bridgewater cares about, and it's what I care about too, what any *normal* parent would care about."

Korbovitch wrote down some notes and looked off into the distance in a state of contemplation. The sinking feeling in my stomach told me the video had not brought the kind of clear result we'd intended.

Korbovitch dismissed us for the morning. It was 11:30.

I went to lunch at a place called Lucy's, a bar/restaurant down the street. I wanted to be alone.

Jazz music from speakers filled the air. It was a dark place, dimly lit, and the atmosphere suited me fine. Waiting for my food, I pulled up a file on my cell's video mode. There was Tommy getting his first haircut, three years old. He was sitting so still for the barber. My eyes grew misty just watching. It was amazing. He'd stopped droning, too, sitting there like a little champion. We'd bribed him with the promise of ice cream. For some reason, it actually worked. Another video: Tommy and I in the park. *"Swing son,"* I was saying as I threw him the ball and he held the bat on his shoulder, just like I'd taught him. He was five then. Cheryl was recording it. The ball went past him and the bat didn't even budge off his shoulder. I laughed. No, a pro ball career was definitely not in his future.

Sometimes I just saw this hidden person inside him, and I knew this Other Tommy was dying to come out, the way he'd suddenly turn to me and look up at me so out of the blue and alive, wanting to connect with me, trying so very hard, so innocent. This was the normal Tommy, the one that could have been normal as any other child. It tore me up, knowing it would never happen, that the normal son of I'd hoped for would never emerge.

One more episode: The day he was born, 5:47 p.m., the nurse, the doctor, Cheryl's mother and me in the room. Cheryl looked beautiful and exhausted, the smile of accomplishment on her sweaty face. Tommy squirming with his eyes shut and a finger in his mouth, so new to this world, so ready for anything. He was such a beautiful baby boy, lips, chin, ears, all perfectly formed.

I'd never been so proud.

"CHERYL. PLEASE. PLEASE don't do this," I called to Cheryl, who was up ahead of me on the way into the courthouse the next morning.

I touched her shoulder and she swung around. The San Diego weather had lost its mojo and had turned coolish, low sixties, and clouds were blowing in from the east just like the clouds that were blowing through my mind.

"Have some mercy," I said.

Cheryl stopped walking and turned to me, her face all made up like a mask, her armor against the world. I had luckily found her without Beaman. When our eyes met, I wobbled on my feet. I rubbed the back of my neck. A car horn honked from the street. An airplane soared above us. The wind blew Cheryl's hair and she pulled it back from her face.

"I need Tommy in my life too," I said. "Don't you see that?"

"I'm seeking full custody, Chris. That's the only way—"

"That's just Beaman talking! You couldn't really want that! To separate me from my own son? To break up our bond? You know I can't move to Houston and leave my dad. You know he needs me too much. You know how close Tommy and I are—how could breaking us up be good for him?"

Cheryl sighed. She looked right and left. "I have to go inside now."

"Cheryl, please. Be reasonable."

But she turned and walked away and I stared up at the increasingly cloudy sky and just stood there, shaking my head. She'd become a totally different woman. I felt so lost with her now, completely disconnected, and I saw no way that I'd ever get any kind of a relationship back, which was sad, since we were Tommy's parents. Who had more influence over her—Beaman or Wade?

When the hearing resumed, Mark called Dr. Dunn to the stand. This was the moment I'd been waiting for. After establishing his credentials as a Ph.D. from Berkeley, a neurobiologist and autism researcher for many years, Mark asked him, "Dr. Dunn, can you tell us about the benefits that the boy in question is receiving as you view this video from a neurologist's perspective?"

"I clearly see major benefits," Dr. Dunn said, sitting up straight in his seat. He looked out at us through clear brown eyes. "I see the chimps bringing Tommy out of his shell, making him more alive and happy. I also studied his behavior at Hillwood and the fluency charts, and what we just witnessed looks like an immense improvement in fluency. Tommy, in the presence of the chimps, appears to be released from his mental shell."

"So, you see chimp therapy as potentially beneficial for Tommy Crutcher?"

"I do."

"And would you recommend that the father be allowed to pursue this approach on reasonable scientific grounds?"

"I would."

Mark glanced at Korbovitch who pursed his lips together and tapped a pencil on his desk. God only knew what he was thinking. "And may I ask why you don't recommend the Acorn School?"

"Well." Dr. Dunn paused for a moment. "I've examined the data that comes out of the school, and some of it troubles me. Sample scores are skewed to make findings appear more positive than is really the case."

"Interesting. Can you give us an example?"

"Yes. The TOLD—Test of Language Development—was administered, but only five subjects were chosen to participate in a yearlong study. And the actual testing sequences had been rearranged to benefit each child's test-taking abilities. I hardly call that valid or conclusive. And there are no long-term studies to show that the eclectic approach used at the Acorn School is more successful than a simple public education classroom-style learning environment."

Dunn was hitting all the right buttons. I relaxed in my seat and felt the beginnings of a smile crop up on my face. I was hoping that Mark would play the doctor for all he was worth.

"Any other information you would like to provide?" Mark asked.

"Actually, there's also the issue of separating Tommy from his father," Dunn continued. He stroked his chin, his eyes landing on me. "That could be highly stressful given the close relationship between this father and son. I've interviewed both Tommy and Chris Crutcher, and it's clear that a loving bond exists between them. If they were to be separated by a move to Houston, I believe it's quite possible that negative consequences would result."

Beaman chose not to cross-examine. She whispered something to her assistant again, then looked down at her notes.

FINALLY, IT WAS MY turn to take the stand. Once I was seated, Mark summarized a psychologist's report, which he handed the judge. The report stated I had been interviewed and appeared to be a caring father; there was no evidence of my shirking weekend custody, no proof of my engaging in any behavior that would be considered harmful to my son, no sign of drug or alcohol abuse, sexual abuse, or irresponsibility.

When Mark asked me to describe a typical weekend with Tommy, I talked about taking him to the zoo, trying to help him improve his language skills, listening to him, giving him stimulating toys in the hope that he'd respond. I tried to express the depth of our bond, how much we meant to each other.

When Beaman whispered something into Cheryl's ear, I stopped talking and blanked out for a moment. My mind spun.

"Would you do just about anything for Tommy?" Mark asked finally.

"I would do whatever it takes to help him." I glanced at Rachel.

"And isn't that why you engaged in the chimp therapy, as a means of helping your son?"

"Yes."

"How did your idea for chimp therapy come about?"

"We were at the San Diego Zoo," I said. "Tommy showed an uncanny ability to communicate with the chimps. He seemed to do it by gestures and natural instinct. I was really taken aback and from there, I found the Weller Institute."

"And did you see improvement when you took your son to Weller to interact with the chimps there?"

"I certainly did."

"And you were paid a stipend by Weller?"

"Yes." I nodded. "Both me and Cheryl. The money went toward Tommy's needs, mostly. I didn't take that money and buy a new car or anything like that at all. Plus," I turned toward the judge, "Weller gave Tommy a ten-thousand-dollar educational fund."

"Yes, the fund has been noted in the file. Your Honor," Mark said. He faced the judge. His voice rang throughout the courtroom as he pointed at the monitor. "At this point, I'd like to present a video that shows Mr. Crutcher's son, first as he tries to participate in a classroom activity at school, and then, as he interacts with chimpanzees. It will clearly demonstrate why Mr. Crutcher felt that being around the chimps was helpful to Tommy. The two scenes involved were taped within a month of each other, as you can see by the dates on the film. They—"

"Objection! Relevance!" Beaman bellowed. Her loud voice sent shivers through me. "Video footage as described by counsel is not germane to the central question of this hearing, namely, whether the father is engaging in dangerous child-raising practices, and ultimately, whether Acorn is in the best interest of the child."

Korbovitch rubbed the side of his face as he leaned back in his chair. "I understand your reasoning, Ms. Beaman, but I want to see the video. This hearing is about the child's best interests. I think the video may shed further light on several questions I've been formulating. Mr. Hyman, go ahead and introduce the video."

"Thank you, Your Honor. This is an observational video made about a month before Tommy first interacted with the chimps."

I'd made this video after asking the principal at Hillwood and explaining the circumstances. We'd received waivers from all the parents involved in the shot.

As the video began, Ms. Sullivan at Hillwood was talking to four children about the pictures they'd just drawn as they sat around a table. When she called on Tommy, he didn't say a word and flapped his hands in front of his face. When she tried to engage him, he rocked back and forth, made motor noises, and showed no facial expression other than a stony stare.

Next came a scene with Tommy at the chimp compound. He was standing at the entrance to the enclosure, watching the chimps with a precious smile on his face.

"Look, Daddy, you look. Chimpies! Like chimpies, Daddy. Like lots."

My voice resounded in the courtroom. *"Yes, Tommy, they're really cool."*

The next scene was with chimps playing in the background while Tommy cooed with Obo in a corner. Holding his hand, Tommy led Obo to a table and handed the chimp pieces of watermelon. After eating, he reached out and stroked Obo's face, and Obo reciprocated. While Mikey hooted in the background, Obo stretched his lips, showing his teeth, and Tommy did the same.

This relaxed, animated child was so unlike the one in Ms. Sullivan's class. My eyes moistened watching it. Surely, the judge would see the difference. My breathing quickened as I fiddled with my watch on my wrist. This was my reason why. Something tingled at the base of my spine, the whisper of a feeling, the voice of hope.

Cheryl only frowned as she watched from her seat in the courtroom. Tommy circled a stick through the air, waving it like a baton as he jumped up and down. Obo watched him, then did the same thing when Tommy handed him the stick. Tommy spoke some words and Obo appeared to listen intently, knowingly shaking his head.

"Bird . . . Tree . . . Dog . . . Hug . . ."

Obo yammered and shrieked.

"Look, Daddy," Tommy said. "Chimpies! All around! Love chimpies!" He waved his arms to take in the whole playground.

"I see, Tommy. It's wonderful, isn't it?"

Mark freeze-framed Tommy's smile for a few moments. And such a smile! Pure delight blossomed all over his rosy face. My heart plummeted into my stomach.

I turned around and stared at my father who gave me a knowing nod as Mark sat down.

"What's your occupation, Mr. Crutcher?" Beaman said when she stood to question me.

Nerves got to me. I couldn't find my voice for a minute and sat there, unable to say a thing. "I-I-I'm a . . . " And then finally, I managed to spurt with hesitation: "a, uh, well, a voice-over actor."

A mild laughter filled the room.

"I see." Beaman raised an eyebrow, pausing before continuing. "So, would you consider yourself an expert in primatology?"

"No."

"In child psychology?"

"No."

"Would you consider yourself an expert in the study of autism?"

"No."

"In special education?"

"No."

"How about psychiatry?"
"No."

"Neurology?"
"No."

I crossed and uncrossed my legs, looking around the courtroom. All eyes were watching me, Cheryl, the reporters, my Dad, everyone. I felt as if I were a museum exhibit all of a sudden, "Dad Under Duress," a real piece of emotional art. I froze in place.

"And yet you've chosen to expose your son to this unproven, so-called chimp therapy," Beaman continued, "putting your son at risk with these dangerous animals and based on what?"

"Objection!" Mark said. "Personal accusation that's not fact based."

"Sustained. Please, Ms. Beaman," Korbovitch said. "Stick to the task at hand."

Beaman turned her back on the judge.

"So, you don't see the risk of chimp therapy but you have absolutely no expertise in this area? Are you aware of the documented cases around the world of chimps attacking humans?" She grabbed a sheet of paper from her desk. "St. Louis Times. March 2014. Chimps assault zookeeper and bite his neck and hands. London, England. December 2015. Two chimps escape from a lab and maul a janitor. The list goes on, Mr. Crutcher. Is this what you want your son to experience?"

I caught the anger on Rachel's face when Beaman. Described the chimps as dangerous. She looked stricken.

"Look. I know Tommy," I said. I took a breath, feeling the emotions rise. "I know him through and through. You've seen the video. I'm not imagining this. The chimps are one-hundred percent helping him. He's not afraid of the chimps at Weller and has no cause to be afraid."

"So, you consider yourself the expert here as Tommy's father?" Beaman said.

"In a way, yes."

"But you were being paid by Weller as part of their research grant?" Beaman asked.

"Yes."

"And are you still being paid?"

I waited a long moment before answering. "Yes."

"And that money is not influencing you in any way?"

"No, it's not."

"But you said the money is *mostly* being used for Tommy. Can you define mostly?"

I hesitated before answering. "I put the money to work in the best way I knew how." I looked down, feeling blood rushing to my face.

"So, you basically received an income from Tommy's endeavors. And you didn't spend any of the money for our own needs, like for instance, paying the mortgage?"

"Well, of course, the money was available and yes, I did use some of the money for my own needs."

"I see. You're out of work, Mr. Crutcher?"

"Off and on."

"You need the money. Right?"

"Yes." I couldn't lie. "But I used the money to pay the mortgage so I'd have a home for Tommy as well. That money impacted Tommy as much as it did me."

"So, don't you think it could be said that the main reason you took your son out to Weller wasn't for some abstract psychological benefit for your son, but simply because you would receive a very good income?"

"No! That's not it. This was all about Tommy's welfare!" I clenched my fists, scrunching up my jaw.

"So, if it's all about your son, as you say, aren't you concerned with the fact that you're ignoring the conventional psychologists and neurologists and pediatricians," Beaman went on, "people who've spent years studying autism? How can you be so sure that you're the expert when you can hardly hold a job in your own field?"

When I looked up, my hands knotted together, I saw a ferocity in Beaman's eyes that resembled the eyes of a tiger about to attack. Something about them wasn't even human.

But I wasn't going to back down. "If Cheryl thinks she's the expert because she's the mother, then I have every right to think I'm the expert because I'm the father. Don't I?"

A chuckle went out across the courtroom. My heart sank.

"You've also taken him to see an adult chimp, right?" she asked.

"Yes."

"What was the purpose of that visit?"

"It was a remarkable experience for him."

"Remarkable?"

"Yes, my son could tell us what Albert was thinking by looking at the chimp's paintings."

"My, that's incredible, Mr. Crutcher." She raised her eyebrows, mock-grinned at me, and made sure the judge saw her wide-eyed incredulous expression. "But of course, you're the expert, right?"

"I'm the boy's father. But it's not just me. Dr. Dunn has also testified as an expert that the chimp visits are beneficial. The entire Weller Institute has geared up for Tommy's chimp interactions."

But I caught Korbovitch sizing me up with a skeptical eye before he took more notes.

After I sat down next to Mark, Beaman presented two more witnesses from Weller, child psychologists, but they didn't offer much evidence as far as I could see, just an explanation of these so-called studies that seemed bogus and contrived to me. But the judge listened carefully and actually asked a question or two himself before they'd finished. Then Mark presented Rekulak, Dr. Evans, and finally Rachel, all explaining their expertise and testifying as to the benefits of chimp therapy.

Dr. Rekulak stated that Tommy was providing remarkable insights into the mind of nonhuman primates and as a primatologist for the past twenty-five years, "I've never seen anything like this my entire career. Never." Rachel also hit the ground running, saying that her observations regarding Tommy's chimp affinities had gone far beyond her expectations. She reiterated the studies as presented by Dr. Dunn, showing fluency rates as Tommy's speech progressed while in the presence of the chimps. The judge listened to these expert testimonies with interest.

The biggest moment was when Carly Yates herself took the stand. Mark hadn't told me she was even coming. Talk about a media sensation. The reporters went wild. Ms. Yates entered the courtroom just as the judge was going to end the session. Mark kept looking at his watch, wondering if she'd arrive. When she got on the stand, she explained all she'd gone through with her own autistic nephew. She praised me and Tommy and told the judge that the Weller Institute had an amazing opportunity with Tommy.

"This is the kind of research that is unparalleled," Ms. Yates said. "To deny Tommy and Weller the chance to see this research through would be a black eye on science itself."

"Thank you for coming," Korbovitch said when she was done.

Ms. Yates left the courtroom with two assistants following her. Reporters breathed down her neck, taking pictures, shoving microphones in her face. As far as I could tell, she appeared totally used to it, nonplussed, taking it all in stride.

I felt that we'd presented as good a case as was possible. The only problem was that Beaman had put up a damn good case herself. Basically, I'd bet the farm and I was exhausted. Bolts of anger rushed through me at the system itself, the need to even go through with this hearing and to face off with Cheryl, forced to sever my relationship with Tommy's mother in an ugly confrontation.

Even if I won, which seemed more like a coin toss than anything else, I was still going to lose so much.

Chapter 15

The day of Korbovitch's decision left me jangling inside with the kind of fear I hadn't known since the awful day of Tommy's diagnosis when he was two years old. My entire body ached. I felt like I was coming down with the flu. My nerves were frazzled. Knowing that Rachel was going to Africa only added to the pain. She'd told me yesterday over the phone. I tried to sound casual as she talked, but inside, I was churning away.

Putting Max out in the backyard after a long, farewell hug, Max's ponderous eyes on mine, I left the house in a fog, got in my car, and forgot how to get to the courtroom. My breathing came hard and fast. I panicked. I was that lost emotionally, geographically, a human being sitting at a red light at an intersection I couldn't recognize. Devinshire Street, something like that. I didn't know which way to turn—the story of my life. I had to stop by the side of the road, take a few deep breaths, and get my bearings.

Twenty minutes later, I was sitting in the courtroom as it started to thunder and rain outside. I was wearing my best dark-grey suit, waiting for the judge to appear. Each moment felt like it was ticking away; a time-bomb. Mark sat next to me, shuffling papers, checking his phone for messages.

"You did your best," I said to him, my lips dry. I swallowed some bottled water and nearly choked.

He put a hand on my shoulder. "We both did our best. It's out of our hands now."

My father sat stiffly in the back on the courtroom, accompanied by Belinda. He looked straight ahead, refusing to make eye contact with me. This was his way. Just like Tommy, he had a hard time with eye contact as well. We'd talked several times about the hearing over the phone, but all I could tell him was that the verdict was completely up in the air.

The Weller staff was present, Dr. Dunn, Rekulak, Dr. Evans, and Rachel. They all looked pensive. Beaman, for some reason, appeared relaxed. For the first time, a smile broached her face as she talked to Cheryl. Did Beaman know something I didn't? I wouldn't be surprised.

The usual reporters were lined up in the back as well. The possibility of Tommy "talking" with chimps was still a newsworthy fire they were trying their best to blow on and inflame. Evidently, their bosses still saw ratings possibilities. Several spots on TV had been aired and I'd learned that the TV stations' phones were blowing up with calls from San Diegans wanting to know more about the story. Was national news next?

Korbovitch finally trooped into the room, which suddenly grew stone quiet. My stomach turned over. With his black-robes on, he sat down in a huff and put on his bifocals. Surely, this was just another day at the office to him. For me, it was the biggest day of my life. He peered out at us, his face stern, his grey eyes burning with judicial resolve.

He silently read through his notes for what felt like an eternity, flipping through papers. Finally, he spoke in his smooth voice, a voice that I could now mimic fairly well. "I believe both sides have done a reasonably good job presenting their arguments," Korbovitch said. The judge looked at Cheryl, Beaman, Mark, then finally at me, his eyes lingering on me, studying me like I was some crazed father-creature from the wilds of suburbia. "However," he finally continued, "the benefit of the boy is what I must think of first and foremost, not the father's or the mother's wishes. Truly, this has been his hearing."

The judge ruffled some papers, his brow so wrinkled no amount of emotional ironing would help.

"I've read all about this Acorn School in Texas from various sources, including psychologists' data, general news articles, and, of course from the data provided by Ms. Beaman," he said. "The expert opinion seems to show real merit and validity. I've perused their research, and even though it's a new school, I must say, I'm impressed."

He rubbed his chin, then the side of his face. My entire body quivered.

"The father believes in a radical form of therapy," Korbovitch said, "and he's presented documentation as to possible outcomes for the child, but the problem is that his research, if you could call it that, is based on only one child. I've consulted with an independent professor of psychology from UCLA and she agrees. This kind of protocol is too much in its infancy to make a sound decision regarding its efficacy.

"And yet in regards to the singularity of this particular child, I've viewed the videos of the boy while he's in the presence of the chimps, and quite honestly, not only as a judge but as a father and grandfather, I've never seen anything like it. Truly, the boy appears more relaxed, inquisitive, and definitely more fluent when he's at the chimp compound. The chimps do seem to have a positive influence on him. And he seems to truly have some sort of uncanny influence over the chimps as well."

Yes, of course. Hearing these words made my eyes grow misty. I peered over at Cheryl who sat stiff, leaning forward in her seat, her face grim. I turned to Mark and put a hand on his arm, holding on like a rescue line, holding on for dear life.

"Of course," Korbovitch went on, shifting down into a more somber tone, "I must say, there is the question of safety, and there's also the question of transferability, that is, will the boy's so-called success with the chimps flow over into human interactions?" Hearing this new, grave tone of voice, my heart fell into my stomach. I rubbed the back of my neck as if a spider was biting my flesh. "Again, I must think of the boy first and foremost, and I must think of the long term." The judge cleared his throat, took a sip of water from the glass resting next to him.

Korbovitch folded his hands in front of him as he leaned forward in his chair, which suddenly squeaked. My head throbbed. I started wondering if the judge had taken Cheryl's pregnancy into account—a mother with a new baby trying to handle her autistic son in a new city.

"Though the two parents do have shared custody," he went on, "the primary caregiver is the mother. She has been adjudicated primary custody of the boy during the week, the father only on weekends, and more extended periods during the summer. Given the mother's not altogether irresponsible background, plus the fact that she is pursuing a course that follows more than anecdotal documentation, I must say she clearly has the more conventional argument for the overall long-term needs of the child. As I see it, her argument has the greater merit, and, in the end," he took a long pause, looking around the courtroom, down at his notes, then said, "that is the argument that stands." *No! No!* Therefore, after due consideration," he paused for another long moment as I thought my heart would pound its way out of my chest, "I've decided to render a verdict for the petitioner, Ms. Cheryl Bridgewater. I'm going to allow her the relocation she requests in the name of the child's best interests."

No! I couldn't believe it! My lungs collapsed. *It can't be! No!* I felt totally betrayed by the system, angry and sad simultaneously.

"I will, however," Korbovitch said, "reexamine Tommy's progress at the Acorn School after one school year. I am granting sole custody to Ms. Bridgewater so that she can pursue the educational opportunities she has in mind for her son. This will not restrict the father's visitation rights, however. I want to make this clear, Ms. Beaman." He turned toward Beaman. "Though I'm awarding sole custody to the mother, the father will still be granted his usual weekend time with his son, and it is strongly recommended by this court that the father move to Houston as well, if at all possible, to be close to his son during this time of transition." Judge Korbovitch signed the decree. "Thus, shall it stand, this day, Court of Family Law, San Diego County, California."

"Bullshit!" I heard from the back of the courtroom and swung around. It was my father, standing up now, aiming his cane at the judge like a gun. "Pure and plain bullshit!"

Korbovitch pretended he didn't hear as he gathered up his notes.

I pounded the desk with my fist. Dots clouded my vision. My heart beat wildly, an animal inside my ribcage. I was on the verge of passing out, my mind whirling. This was the way it was going to be? It seemed impossible, and yet, there it was. I felt the weight of abject failure drag me down, straight to despair and utter loss.

"It's only for a year," Mark was saying as Korbovitch stood, took off his bifocals, and left the courtroom.

"Fuck this!" I said. I flashed with anger.

"Chris. Look at it this way," Mark said, his angular chin set rigid.

"We lost, dammit! What other way is there to look at it?"

"I know. I know. But who knows what'll happen after the first year?" He put his arm around my shoulder as we remained sitting.

"Are you kidding?" I looked at him straight on. Eyes wet with misery. "It's a lifetime." I could hardly breathe. A weird noise blurted out of me. "A year is a fucking lifetime. I won't be able to see him when he's gone. Won't be able to watch him grow, nothing. I failed him and the chimps. I failed, goddammit!" I sliced a hand through the air. "He had a chance to really come out of his shell, and now that chance is gone. I won't be able to move to Houston. Not with my Dad here. Who will take care of my father if I leave for Houston?"

"I still think you're taking it worse than it is."

When I looked past Mark, I suddenly realized that Beaman was glaring at me with fire in her eyes, standing beside her table as she gathered her notes. Cheryl stood next to her, a thoroughly pleased expression on her face that drove daggers deep into my heart. I felt both hatred and fury whirling, spinning around in my mind.

"You'll get through this," Mark said.

But I hardly heard him. My ears felt clogged. My mind fogged over. My gut roiled. I watched, feeling like a total loser, my lips parted, as Cheryl gave Beaman a big hug and Wade, still with that stupid burnt patch of skin on his nose, rushed down from the back of the room to be with them, a joyous grin splashed all over his ruddy face. The winning team. I felt disgusted.

As she let go of Cheryl, Beaman's eyes collided with mine. "Do you really think you could beat me? Me? Gloria Beaman?" her angry eyes were telling me, yelling at me, really. "Who do you think you are, anyway? I eat ex-husbands like you for breakfast." Her lips curled into a devil's smile. A sneer that sent hammers of misery pounding through my heart.

"I want to appeal," I said to Mark as I forced myself to turn away from Beaman's mesmerizing glare.

"We can only appeal if we find some kind of technical error the judge has made. In this case, I don't think that's possible." Mark started stuffing papers into his briefcase. He suddenly turned cold, even callous, and I was stunned. He looked like an attorney ready to head to his next client.

I lost.

My life was over. I felt like dying; ready to go cage-less.

Chapter 16

After the hearing, we all met in the grey-walled hallway. I was surrounded by my team: Evans, Rekulak, Rachel, Osikawa, Dr. Dunn, Mark, and my dad. Hardly any words were spoken. It was as if we were in mourning. We were all in a state of shock. Not even Carly Yates' presence had swung the decision our way.

"You tried," my father kept saying in that gruff, sandpaper voice of his. "You stood your ground. I'm proud of you. That judge has his head up his ass."

"I let everyone down, Dad," I said. My shoulders sagged.

"No way!" He shook his head. "You did the best you could. That's all you could do."

We both had tears in our eyes and then, the impossible happened: We came together in a father-son hug as the others watched, gathered around us. My father and I had hardly ever hugged, but now, it was as if we were drawn to each other by an invisible cord. I felt my body shaking, overwhelmed, resting my heart for solace against him. I needed his rugged father-love more than ever.

"You stood up for what you believed in, Chris," he said, clapping me on the back. "That's important. Don't you forget it."

"Are you going to be all right?" Rachel asked.

"I'll be fine," I said. "I just need to be alone for a while." I put a hand to my chest. I could practically feel the ache inside my heart. It was taking me over, subsuming me with despair.

"Are you sure?"

"Yes." I turned to her. "I'm sorry, but I just want to be alone."

As soon as I left the building, dodging the annoying reporters in the process, I hit the bars with a vengeance, starting around three-thirty in the afternoon. I didn't care. If my dad was a drinker, then I was a drinker too. That was all there was to it. Grey clouds and a slow and steady rain suffused the day. Sitting alone at the bar inside Polite Provisions on 30th Street in North Park, tasting my first Jack Daniels on the rocks, I couldn't help but recall the look on my father's grim face, how he was all choked up, how I'd never seen him so shaken. After all I'd done, Tommy was going to Houston and my father might never see him again. This realization made the hurt I was feeling even worse. Tommy was going to be separated not only from me, but from his grandfather as well. The man with the mental pictures. I felt suddenly numb, zombie-like. It had all turned out wrong. I'd been unable to make it work. I'd failed everyone.

I got home around 9 o'clock, so drunk I had to take an Uber, leaving my car in the parking lot of some bar on Twelfth Avenue. I had to take care of Max after all. To my great surprise, Rachel was waiting for me in her Prius, she was parked right in front of my condo. I certainly didn't want her to see me like this, no way, wobbling around after too many shots, head spinning. I'd hardly eaten, either, just some wings and chips. I was so messed up as I staggered to my door.

I checked my phone for the first time since I'd left the courthouse and realized there were five voice messages and three texts, all from her.

"I'm worried about you."

"Where are you?"

"Are you there?"

"Let me help you inside," Rachel said, trying to put an arm around me as I staggered up the front steps. I dropped my keys on the ground next to the walkway, picked them up, then dropped them again, and lost them. She turned on the flashlight app on her cell phone and found the keys for me. I felt dizzy and nauseous. In the distance, a dog barked as a plane flew overhead.

"What do you want, Rachel?" I asked, moving away from her. "I told you I wanted to be alone."

"I really don't think you do. I want to help you."

"But why? It's over. I lost."

She looked like a blur to me as she handed me my keys, then, when I could hardly grab them, took them from me and opened the door herself. As we both stepped inside, she switched on the hall light.

Max was in the backyard and started barking, hearing me enter the house. I got a call on my phone and for some reason I took it, thinking, praying, hoping it was Beaman, telling me that Cheryl had changed her mind and all was forgiven. I was a fool.

"Mr. Crutcher, I'm Frank Reynolds from Channel Four News." He spoke rapidly, nearly out of breath. "Can you give me a statement about how you feel about the custody decision?"

"Don't call me—ever!" I quickly hit end.

When I let Max inside for his food, he dove at me, whirling around, doing his song and dance. He shook his body like a canine James Brown. He barked and leaped up at me, his two front paws on my chest.

"Down, boy," I said.

"I'll feed him," Rachel said. "What's his name?"

"Max."

"Come on, Max." She snapped her fingers, and before I could stop her, led Max into my kitchen and poured some food for him. I snapped on my lights in the den, found my couch, and just plopped down on it. My head pressurized like a balloon about to burst. My heart ached. No more Tommy sitting next to me on the couch. No more watching him being happy with the chimps.

I was near throw-up time, a quarter till.

"I kept texting you and calling." Rachel stood over me after feeding Max, arms folded across her blue blouse. She frowned. Concern was written all over her face. "Why didn't you answer?"

"I turned my phone off. Didn't want to talk to anyone. God, Rachel, you don't have to be here. Really. It's over. I lost Tommy and Weller lost their project. What's done is done."

"Oh, Chris." She put her hands on her hips, then brushed some hair off her face. "I'm so sorry."

"Hey, don't worry. You've still got Africa," I said, kicking off my shoes. "You should be ecstat, ecstat . . . oh, hell. Whatever."

"Will you go to Houston and follow them down there?" she asked, sitting down next to me on the couch.

It was the question that had been pounding inside my brain ever since I'd lost the ruling, throbbing like a headache. But the answer was clear.

"And leave my eighty-two-year old aging dad to fend for himself? Honestly, I don't see how." I looked away. I felt my face turning red. "He has an aide that his insurance is paying for and she comes three times a week. But that's going to end soon. We can't afford anything like that without insurance. There's no way I could just leave him on his own without some kind of assistance. Besides, even if I went," I continued, my eyes getting misty, "I'd have no idea if I could find a job in Houston. I can barely make ends meet in this town where people know me. In Houston, I wouldn't have a shot. I got this offer in Atlanta a while back, but that was a lucky break. I wouldn't have any guarantees in Houston at all."

There went the money from Weller, too, out the window. Gone.

"I can't believe that judge," I said.

"I know," Rachel said.

"I'm going to fix you some coffee."

"You don't have to."

"I know I don't have to."

She gave me a sorrowful look, then left me on the couch and went to my kitchen. I heard her opening drawers and shelves and pouring water into my coffee pot.

"Cream and sugar?" she called from the kitchen.

"No. Just plain black as my life right now."

A few minutes later, she returned with a cup, which she handed me. I took a long sip as she sat down next to me again. The coffee helped. Coffee. Life. Somehow, they were inextricably linked.

I stretched my legs out and thought of something that made me smile. "You know, this is crazy but when Cheryl told me she and Wade were moving to Houston, you know what the first thing that came to my mind was?"

"What?"

"I felt like saying to her, 'Stick it up your Astros.'" I laughed, staring into space. My drunk brain was drawing all kinds of weird associations.

"That's punny," she said.

I looked at her. "Yes, it is, isn't it?"

We were both silent for a long moment. I stared at my hands, but felt her eyes on me, studying me.

I looked past her, studying the Voice Arts awards on my shelf. They blurred and multiplied in my vision.

"God, Chris. That judge just destroyed the most important breakthrough in primatology in years. Does he even realize that?" she said.

I looked at her. "Does Carly Yates know?"

"Yes, and she's livid. She told us she was sorry she hadn't offered one of her own lawyers to help out."

"Wow, I had no idea she would have done that. Mark was okay, I guess. He tried." I shrugged. "But whatever's the case, it's over. I should have known the odds were against us."

Max wandered in the den and smelled Rachel, gathering information. He bit on his hindquarters and gnawed at himself, then sat down on the floor at our feet. He whimpered, then came up to me and tried to work his way onto my lap. But I pushed him off and then he poked his nose into Rachel's hand. She started scratching him behind his ears.

The next thing I knew, I was in the bathroom, throwing up.

When I returned to the den after washing my face with a cold towel, wobbly but feeling lighter, Rachel was still sitting on the couch, staring at her phone.

"Are you going to go now?" I asked.

She sat up straight and blinked. "Are you going to be okay?"

I nodded.

"I'm not so sure about that," she said.

I AWOKE ON THE COUCH, a bundle of arms and legs and body strewn everywhere. I had no idea what time it was. I felt hot and cold simultaneously. My emotional thermostat was all screwed up, as if my thalamus and my hypothalamus were having an argument. God, my throat was dry and my tongue was sticking to the top of my mouth. I heard Max scratching himself. The San Diego sun streamed into the den and I quickly closed my eyes and groaned.

My head pounded as the thought of the hearing and of losing Tommy sledge-hammered into me. I didn't want to get off the couch. A ton of emotional bricks weighed me down. My cell phone was lying on the end table and I reached for it and clicked it on: 11:45 a.m. Great. Nearly noon. Then I saw a note sitting on the table, no doubt from Rachel. I made myself get up and read it: "Gone to work, will call you later." I had no idea what time she'd left, if she'd slept here, or what.

This woman, I realized, would always be going to work, if not at Weller, then off to Africa or somewhere else where another exciting opportunity was waiting. Tommy and I were important to her, no doubt about that. But her career came first. Wasn't it obvious? The probability of us actually working out was slight to nil and this hurt, another door slammed in my face.

Max barked at me. He sat on his hind legs, giving me the feed-me, let me go pee guilt look. "Okay, dammit. Just a minute."

As I stood and got my bearing, I looked around my den, the emptiness of my house, my life without Tom-Tom, without the hope I had for him, and the realization of my loss hit me even harder, flooding me with despair.

Christ!

Max barked, rattling me out of my reverie, and I went to the kitchen, got out the bag of dog food, and fed Max who ate with a vigorous appetite. Then my cell phone rang.

"Mr. Crutcher, can you give us a statement on—"

"Leave me the fuck alone!"

This was what I got for making a fool of myself in court.

I let Max outside and quickly shut the door. I ate some oatmeal and fired up a pot of black organic coffee, then drank three cups before I even knew what I was doing. Ten minutes later, I let Max back in. He sniffed my hands and stared in my face, tongue out, questioning me with that doggie look. Where's the lady from last night? Where's Tommy?

Sadly, I had nothing positive to say. Rachel was going to Africa, Tommy, to Houston. And I was remaining here in San Diego with my dad.

Staring out the window with Max by my side, Rachel moments slid through my mind: The way Tommy had taken her hand so willingly and easily during that first visit, amazing both me and Cheryl, how Rachel and I had swung Tommy like a monkey between us, all of us laughing. That "breeze of understanding" that passed between us when we'd talked about Tommy and what he needed, her profound scientific explanations of Tommy's abilities, how she'd opened up to me about her life in the rain forest, made me see and feel her experiences. Basically, she'd drawn me into the chimp world and offered hope for my son. But what had I given her? What had I done for her?

I'd given her Tommy. I'd drawn her into Tommy's world, and as a consequence, my own as well.

Maybe she was torn inside about going to Africa, though she hadn't expressed it. Maybe it wasn't the easy-breezy decision she'd made it out to be.

I led Max to the den and he licked my hands and my face, rubbing against me, then bowled me over. I lay on the floor and we wrestled. "At least I have you." Max barked and then sat on his hind legs, staring at me, tongue lolling.

"What, boy?"

He whined and looked around the room. Then he left my side, raced upstairs, and came down with a Beanie Baby in his mouth. He dropped it at my feet, then looked deep into my eyes. He barked, then whined.

It was Blackie, an old, worn-down Beanie bear with lots of rips and tears and food stains. Tommy used to play with Blackie when he was little, but for some reason, gave up on the black bear when he got Radar. My heart rattled inside my chest just looking at the stuffed pet.

"Oh, Max. You miss Tommy too," I said, hugging him. "Yes, you do!"

Max barked.

"No, he won't be back, Max. That's the thing."

The last I heard, Cheryl and Wade were moving in about two weeks. Tommy had been enrolled fully into Acorn.

And then I lost it right there, the brutal realization slamming against me. I sunk into a hole, eyes wet, head pounding, heart completely broken into a thousand emotional pieces, too fragmented to ever put back together, Chris Crutcher mini-me's, everywhere, I was shattered like glass.

"He won't be coming back, Max," I said, my voice tight. "Not anytime soon, anyway."

Max looked around and whined, then he gave me one long doggie stare and lay down next to me, edging his body against me as a source of comfort. Overcome with sadness, I cuddled him in my arms.

THAT AFTERNOON, I SPIED a thick book on custody law sitting on my coffee table. I'd bought it several weeks ago and had read through it from time to time. I opened it up in the kitchen, sunlight streaming through the window. I thumbed through it, trying to understand all the variables of appealing my case. But as I read, I only got more confused. It appeared that Mark was indeed right: Unless there was a chance to show that Korbovitch had made some kind of technical error, my hope for an appeal was mostly nil. But wasn't his entire verdict a technical error? He'd made the wrong decision, dammit! Wasn't that enough?

Then the next thing I knew, I was walking like a zombie upstairs to my bedroom. It was five-thirty. I took a shower and crawled into bed, Max lying on the floor next to my bed. I fell asleep hard and fast.

When I woke up, it was nearly nine p.m. and suddenly, the urge hit me hard. Something needed doing and it needed doing now. Before I even thought about it, I was throwing on a pair of faded jeans and a t-shirt, putting on my shoes, and then, without even calling, I was driving over to Cheryl's house in my beat-up Altima.

Dark outside with only a sliver of moon, it was starting to sprinkle again just as I pulled up to the curb.

Instead of going to her door, I crept up the long driveway to the side of her house and peered into a side window. The rain fell harder, splattering me, but I didn't care. I wanted to see how this new "family" was making it. I just needed to know. I banged my knee against the side of the house and had to muffle a cry.

I hid in the shadows until the pain subsided and then peeked into the window. Tommy was sitting on a couch watching TV with Wade, one finger in his nostril. Radar sat next to him, propped up against him, his constant pal. My heart boomed witnessing this sight, just seeing Tommy there, with Wade. I clenched and unclenched my fists, my jaw stiffened. Sweat streamed down my face.

Burnt-nose Wade switched on a lamp and grabbed a magazine, then suddenly turned and looked out the same window I was hovering at. I didn't think he saw me, but still, I quickly slid away. When I got my courage up, I peered through the window again. Wade was thumbing through his magazine, while Tommy continued watching TV.

Cheryl had switched the room around, or the TV was new—something looked different. And boxes were everywhere. Small ones, large ones, no doubt evidence of her getting ready to move. The sight of the boxes made my heart freeze up.

But it was the lamp that got to me. That goddamn safe-looking piece of shit lamp with the yellow light. So damn homey. And normal. And . . . My breaths came fast. *I* should have been on that couch. As Wade continued thumbing through the magazine, Tommy actually leaned against him for a moment.

But wait a minute . . . Tommy appeared well taken care of and this new thought made me gasp. After all, he had a stepdad, who appeared to be if not loving, at least kind and considerate. Cheryl would give him a brother or sister. She would surround our son with love. And there it was. Presto: a new life. It was the light of that lamp that said it all. This was Tommy's new home, and it was a place where I, Chris Crutcher, wasn't wanted.

I slouched under the window as a tear fell down my cheek and an ache the size of Texas filled my heart. Maybe this Acorn School was the answer after all, and I was just standing in everyone's way. Cheryl and Wade were going to make it. Wasn't I the one who wasn't needed? Hadn't a new relationship formed? Suddenly, Wade stood and came up to the window, a suspicious look on his face, and I moved to the side, standing next to a row of bushes hidden from the sight line of the window.

I slugged through the increasing raindrops, head down, thunder booming above. My hair was wet as were my shoes, which were covered with wet grass. I made it back to my car, popped the trunk, and grabbed a towel before getting in the car. I wiped my face with it, then called Cheryl on my cell.

"Put him on the phone, please," I said when Wade answered.

"Sure thing." His smooth voice rattled me.

But finally, I heard Tommy's voice. "Huh?" Tommy said. "Huh?"

"Hey, Tom-Tom. It's Daddy." Yes. Daddy! For whatever I was worth. "How are you? You doing okay? You having fun?"

"Daddy! TV, Daddy." The sound of his voice, the closeness of it in my ear mixed with his innocence felt like it was singeing my soul.

"That's good," I said. I tried not to breakdown. "What's on, son?"

He breathed into the phone, but he didn't answer.

"Listen, there's something I want you to know."

"Huh, Daddy? Daddddeeee." He was pressing his mouth against the phone so close I could practically feel the sound of his voice inside my ear, his breath against my face. So close and yet so miserably far away . . . I'd heard it said that love's the shortest distance between two hearts. Maybe for most people, but not for me, not right now.

"Huh?"

"I want you to know that somehow I'm going to get you back with the chimps, with your friends, Tommy." My hands shook. "That's a promise, Tom-Tom. I don't know how yet, and I don't know when, but it's going to happen, okay? Even if you're at the new school. Don't you worry. Maybe there are some chimps in Houston. Don't give up. I'm working it—"

"Chimpies?"

I was sure he didn't even understand me. But I rattled on. "Yes! I swear it! Somehow. Do you understand me? I won't give up, Tommy. I'll never give up. You're my—"

"Daddy, can I—" Then he was gone.

"Okay, that's enough," Cheryl said, her stern voice like a slap in the face.

"I have every right to talk to Tommy over the phone." I spat out the words.

"Okay, Chris. Let's make a deal. Every night at eight you can call if you want. Okay? But not about those damn chimps."

"Fine. And Cheryl?" I asked.

"Yes?"

The question popped into my head. I hesitated, staring up at the sliver of moon that peeked out behind the clouds, then spoke softly. "Can I ask you something kind of silly?"

She sighed, telling me how tired she was of dealing with me. "Fire away."

I spoke with a fragility I'd never felt before, a sudden tenderness that arose from somewhere deep inside me. "Just wondering . . . "

"What?"

"Who combs his hair before he goes to bed?" My heart palpitated in my chest as the words poured out of me. "I'm just curious."

"Who—What? What do you mean? What are you talking about?" she said.

"Doesn't he ask for it at his bedtime? Someone to comb his hair?"

Cheryl was silent, and then: "No, he doesn't," she snapped. "Goodbye, Chris. And please don't start harassing Tommy about the chimps again. It's over. Just give it up. You lost. I won. It's done."

I was unable to move when the call ended. I closed my eyes as the rain splattered against the roof of my car. I could almost feel my son's soft hair against my fingertips, and I could hear the pulsating urgency in his voice when he'd said, "Hair, Daddy. Hair."

The hair combing was our thing, Tommy's and mine. It was *our* special time together. Irreplaceable. He needed me, his *real* father, after all.

Chapter 17

After I begged and pleaded, appealed to her heart, while at the same time, promising that I would do as much as possible to stay out of her life, Cheryl granted us one final visit with Tommy's friends. Tommy and I drove out to Weller on a Tuesday afternoon, about a week before Cheryl and Wade would travel to Houston. As soon as he came in contact with the chimps in the play yard, Tommy's beaming face, his blue eyes alive with light, and his flicking fingers told me he was completely immersed in what he loved most. Rachel wasn't there. She was getting ready for her trip and had to go to L.A. for a meeting with the staff of *National Geographic*. But Marcy was with us, standing next to Tommy as he interacted with Mikey, Obo, and SeeSaw.

Of course, I'd struggled with letting Tommy say goodbye, thinking perhaps I shouldn't even push for it. Why cause the pain that I was sure would follow? But in the end, I decided he had the right to say goodbye to his best friends, he needed to say goodbye, he needed one last time with them, and I would regret it if I didn't follow through.

"Obo. Here!" I said. "Here!"

Unlike the others, Obo stayed in the corner, hiding his face with his hands.

"He's been regressing since Tommy stopped coming around," said Marcy, who was standing next to me. She frowned, arms folded across her chest. "We really don't know what to do."

Tommy marched toward Obo like a disappointed parent and plopped down in front of the chimp. Obo lowered his head and bit himself, then raced to the other side of the enclosure. Tommy followed. Self-confident Seesaw strutted over to Tommy and got in his way, beating his chest and then racing up a tree. Tommy studied Seesaw, tapping a foot on the ground, and for a moment he seemed to forget Obo. Rose came up to Tommy and put her arms around him. Tommy finger flicked. Rose, a new chimp introduced in the compound, sat down on the ground, curled her toes up, and stretched her mouth wide.

"Rose want fun," Tommy said to me and Marcy. We were both in the play yard, supervising Tommy's every move. "She like fun."

Cheryl had broken the news to Tommy, informing him he was going to a school in a different city, but I doubted Tommy even made the connection that the chimps would be gone from his life. I wondered if he even comprehended the idea of moving to another state. She'd left me with the task of telling him he wouldn't see his friends again.

And that I would be gone from his life too. At least for a while.

Finally, after Tommy had gotten his fill of the chimps, the time came for us to leave the play yard. Sadness walked across my heart. How was I going to do this?

"Tell the chimpies goodbye, Tommy," I said. "You won't be seeing them for a long time, I'm afraid." The sadness of this thought made my eyes get misty. It was miserable. *You may not be seeing me for a long time, either.*

The pain of it all flashed through me.

Tommy looked down, then gazed around the play yard.

"Bye, bye," he said. "Bye."

The chimps shrieked at him. Except for Obo, they all trudged up to Tommy, fumbling over each other, shrieking and scratching. They gestured, pointing, waving their arms, then huddled around my son, playfully bumping into each other in the process. Tommy hugged them back, one at a time, Mikey, SeeSaw, Rose. God. I hated it. The entire dream, gone, Tommy's hope to fulfill his unique ability, taken away from him. I blinked back a tear. And Weller too. Dr. Evans had returned to Washington for his job there. The entire program, scrapped. Rachel had found her replacement, according to Marcy, a primatologist named James King, Ph.D., who would continue working with the chimps while Rachel was gone. She said he was an excellent researcher. Then a new thought occurred: With Tommy gone to Houston, would Rachel still be drawn to me once she returned from Africa? And then again, maybe she'd extend her stay there; maybe she'd loved it so much in the land of the Gombe rainforest that she wouldn't return at all.

"There you go. And now we need to leave them, okay?" I said.

Tommy looked up at me and gave me direct eye contact. "'K."

We walked out of the play yard, went to the cleaning room and washed our hands, and then I escorted Tommy back to my car with Marcy joining us. Surprisingly, Tommy didn't pitch a fit when we departed. He seemed to accept the conclusion of the visit with understanding, even a bit of maturity, and I was relieved.

"What's the latest on Albert?" I asked Marcy as we passed through the courtyard, then out the door that led to the parking lot. Tommy followed behind us. "Oooouuu . . ." I'd lost him to his inner world.

"Oh, poor Albert," Marcy said. "He's getting even sicker, I'm afraid, and Dr. Rekulak's unable to transport him to the sanctuary in Mexico."

"Really." I rubbed my chin.

She whispered so that Tommy wouldn't hear. "He's too fragile it seems. So he's staying by Albert's side, nursing him as best he can, basically waiting for him to die."

"Oh. That's too bad." I frowned. I recalled how Albert had moved me with his wisdom, his gentleness, his keen perception of his surroundings, and drew a sad breath. Poor Albert. He was the best.

Finally, Tommy and I told Marcy goodbye, and then alone with him in the parking lot, the chimps shrieking in the distance, I bent down to Tommy's level. Other than the shrieks of the chimps, the underlying quiet of this out-of-the-way area seemed to almost have an intelligence of its own, deep and rich.

We were standing next to my car, that old man with metallic arthritis. It was time for me to give Tommy the heartbreaking news, that he'd no longer be seeing the chimps and that I would, at least for a while, be out of his life when he moved to Houston. How cruel could it get?

But he had to know.

The sun burned hot on my back, the blue umbrella sky wide, high, and omniscient. I wanted to scream at that sky, but I fought to keep myself under control.

"Daddy, chimpies fun," Tommy said. He gave me direct eye contact, then put a hand in his mouth. He stepped a bit closer to me. He took a satisfying deep breath.

"They are fun, but you know what? There are other things that are fun, too. Like puzzles and games and playing outside."

Tommy fidgeted, looked down, then put a hand in his mouth.

I forced myself to continue. "Remember that school Mommy talked about where she wants you to go?"

"School."

"Yes. The Acorn School."

"Go." Tommy looked right and left, then swirled around. He thwacked his face and I grabbed his hands and placed them at his sides.

"No, son. Please don't do that." I took a breath. "Anyway, you're going to go to that school soon. But what you need to know is .

. . ." My voice, my instrument, my moneymaker, suddenly stopped working, as if the mechanisms ground to a halt. I swallowed. Finally, I pushed on. "What you need to know is that Daddy won't be coming with you, at least for a while anyway. It'll just be you, Mom, and Wade. But that'll be fun, won't it?" I felt sweat trickle down my sides under my shirt.

"Daddeee," Tommy said.

"I'm sorry, Tommy."

"Daddy. No."

"No, I'm sorry. Daddy, no. I am really sorry, but your mom has made it so . . ." Could I really tell him? I could hardly breathe.

He seemed to get the message: "No no chimpies."

"Well . . . Maybe again someday. I'm going to work on that, for sure."

Tommy turned away from me, looking back at the chimp enclosure.

"But I'll come to visit you soon," I said, forcing a smile on my face. "That's for sure."

He said nothing, just licked his lips, that long around-the-world circle that he made. I knew he was trying to say something, but the words wouldn't come. It was as if life itself was punching me in the gut.

"For now, it'll just be you and Mom and Wade and the new school, okay?"

Wade and Cheryl had married a week ago, tied the knot in a small ceremony at the courthouse, and honeymooned at the Venetian overnight. Second time around for both of them. I guessed you just kept on doing it until you got it right. At least for some people anyway. Tommy had stayed home with a nanny who was trained for dealing with autistic children. I'd had a job and wouldn't have been able to keep him—even if Cheryl had wanted me to.

"I'm so sorry, Tommy. It's just the way it has to be. At least for a while." A lump lodged in my throat.

"No chimpies." He hung his head, shoulders drooping. "No . . . chimpies."

"No."

Then he gave me excellent eye contact, long and lingering. He inched closer to me. Sweat had formed across his upper lip and creases lined his forehead. That ever-worried scowl was planted on his face, but this time the worried edge seemed even more apprehensive. He grabbed my hand, uncurled my fingers, put his hand in mine, and locked it together.

"You, Daddeeee."

"I know, Tom-Tom. I know."

"Youuuuu . . ." He creased his face up into a look of longing. Intense desire.

"I'm so sorry."

My breaking heart creaked and ripped, tore apart against the power of emotionally bitter winds. Tommy whimpered, a rare tear came to his eyes, as an emotional cannonball ripped through me.

"Youuuuu . . . Daddeee . . ." His lower lip trembled.

"I'm so sorry, Tom-Tom. Just so sorry."

"Dadddeeeee . . . Youuuuu . . ."

I could hardly catch my breath. I'd never felt so helpless.

Chapter 18

J ust one day later, after I'd drifted off to sleep, I received the wake-up call of my life.

It started out as an undecipherable sound, a strange, unrecognizable aural sensation that was drifting through my consciousness. Surely it was part of a dream: bells and gongs, a tambourine? But then . . . I realized it was my cell lying next to my bed on an end table and I grabbed my phone and answered in a mumble. The clock's red numbers said 11:13 p.m.

"Hello?"

"Chris. It's Wade." But this didn't sound like the smooth Wade I knew. This man's tone of voice was raw and frightened. I quickly shot up in bed.

"What's wrong?" My heart leaped into my throat.

"It's Tommy. You need to come to Harborview. Something's happened."

"What?"

"Just come to the emergency room as fast as you can. Your son had a seizure. Just come."

I jumped out of bed and threw on some clothes. Stomach churning, I banged my knee against a chair, but the pain was nothing compared to the walking fear that stepped in and around my spine. We thought we'd beaten the seizure issue. Tommy hadn't had one since that last episode at the hospital. The meds were supposed to be working. And now this? I woke up Max who was lying on his side next to my bed and put him in the backyard. Then I raced out the door.

Sheets of rain deliquesced along the mostly dark, empty streets as I drove to the hospital as fast as I could. I found Cheryl huddled in the corner of a waiting room in Wing B of the emergency room while Wade stood over her, rubbing her shoulders. They were alone in the white-walled room, which was filled with several wooden chairs, some lamps, and a TV on the wall. Mercifully, the TV was turned off.

"Tommy's unconscious," Cheryl said when she saw me, her voice shaking so badly she could hardly get the words out. She tugged at her oversized blue sweater and as she did, I suddenly realized how far along she'd gotten. Her stomach was around volleyball size. This pregnant Cheryl looked older than the pregnant Cheryl I'd known with Tommy, new lines around her chin and her eyes.

"He won't come to. He . . . He . . ." Her voice quaked.

"What? Was it the seizure? What are you talking about? Talk to me!"

"He's in intensive care," Wade said gravely, filling in. He swallowed hard, his voice shaking. Wade's face formed a grip of pain, tight jaw, dull eyes, pinched lips. Wearing grey slacks and a yellow golf shirt, his ruddy complexion had turned white-cheese pale. He sported at least a two-day growth of beard. "The doctors are working on him. We've been waiting here, just waiting for an update, for something. So far, no one's told us a thing."

Cheryl kept rubbing the round ball of her stomach, her eyes looked animal-wild. Her auburn hair falling on her shoulders, normally always so well-coiffed, was now uncombed and unkempt. I stared at her stomach. What would her *new* child be like? Would she have the perfect child she'd always wanted? All I knew was that Cheryl's unexpected pregnancy left me feeling bitter and even angry.

I couldn't help it. Deep down, I basically felt replaced, though I would never admit that to her face.

"Intensive care? How? What happened?" My voice was barely above a whisper as my limbs grew so shaky I had to plop down in a chair. She and Wade probably would have a perfect child and it didn't seem fair at all.

"He had another seizure, and he fell backwards and . . ." Cheryl's voice turned crazily soft.

"Yes?"

"I—I tried to catch him, Chris, but he hit his head against the chest of drawers in my bedroom." She stared into space. "The fall knocked him out, see, and then . . . then he didn't come out of it." She glanced at Wade, took his hand.

Wade continued. "We tried to get him to wake up. We did everything we could. It's been," he swallowed, looking up at the clock on the wall, which now read 1:15, A.M., "what, two hours now?"

"Probably closer to three," Cheryl said.

"Why didn't you call me sooner?" I was seething inside, hands clenched.

"We're sorry. We weren't thinking," Wade said. "We were panicked."

I felt completely left out, not needed in this newly assembled family, and it hurt badly.

"The back of his head was bleeding." Cheryl whimpered.

"Jesus!" I shot up out of my chair. "What?"

"It just got out of control," she continued, her two hands twisted together. "He'd come into my room around nine o'clock and before I could stop him, he started having a tantrum, a major fit right there in front of me and Wade. He started throwing things and saying he wanted to see you and the chimps. He was yelling that he didn't want to go to the new school. 'No school! No school! Want chimpies.' That's all he said, over and over again. I, I couldn't console him. He broke a lamp. He kicked me in the stomach, Chris. Right in the stomach as I was trying to wrestle him down. It was awful."

"Jesus!"

"His face got all red. He spun around, then started having a seizure, but when he fell, he hit his head on the dresser. So hard." Our eyes met. There was a rainbow of pain in her misty eyes, all the various modalities of hurt. "I'm sure he knocked himself out when he hit the dresser. He was lying on the floor. We . . . we couldn't rouse him." She sobbed and her shoulders shook. Out came a tissue from her purse. "We did everything we could think of. We pinched him, yelled in his ear, poured cold water on his face. Nothing helped."

"God." This was miserable. Unbelievable. I wanted to scream at the universe for allowing this to happen. But who would actually listen? Suddenly, a dam broke in my heart and the next thing I knew, I was flooded with despair.

A door swung open and a large white-coated doctor with a heavy growth of salt-and-pepper beard shuffled in. He was pro-football size with big shoulders and a thick neck. If he couldn't cure a medical issue, he could at least knock it to its knees. We all turned to him as if his white coat were magnetized.

"Mrs. Dudley?" he said in a deep baritone. Cheryl looked up through her tears. "Mr. Dudley?"

"I'm the father," I said quickly, glancing at Wade, Mister Jaguar. "I'm Chris Crutcher."

"Fine. I'm Dr. Thomlinson. Let's sit down, all right?" Dr. Thomlinson sat down next to Cheryl and I pulled up a chair next to him. Wade remained standing. A cold blast of air conditioning blew on top of me. I gazed hopefully at the doctor whose massive hands made the pen he was holding appear as small as a toothpick.

"I'm afraid your son's still unresponsive." Thomlinson was so large and yet seemed so empathic by the gentle sound of his voice that, for a moment, the coexistence of these two characteristics in one human being made me blink. "At this stage," he said, "I'd call it simple obtundation, which just means reduced alertness combined with excessive tiredness or hypersomnia." He rubbed his thick beard. "But we're monitoring his brain stem along with an EEG, and we're keeping a close eye on his blood pressure. The good news is there's just a small amount of intracranial swelling. The seizures he's had also add a measure of cerebral instability unfortunately. For now, however, I'm going to say that it's still only temporary loss of consciousness and that, hopefully, arousal's just around the corner."

"I want to see him," I said quickly. "I need to see him."

"We all need to see him," Cheryl said. "Can we?"

"Of course." Thomlinson stood, signaling for us to follow him.

Wade, Cheryl, and I stood and followed Thomlinson down a long, winding corridor, and then through a door marked: "Authorized Personnel Only." Walking along a tiled corridor, I was moving in a fog, passing nurses writing on charts or on the phone or softly talking to each other. The astringent smell of antiseptic wafted through my nostrils. The lights were bright in the hallway, making me blink. The air felt cold, too much AC. Finally, we stopped at Tommy's dimly lit private room. The door was open.

Standing next to Cheryl, I sucked in my breath. I couldn't believe it. My heart plummeted into my gut and I grabbed my chest in despair. My son was lying on a long, raised-up bed under a white sheet and brown blanket, his eyes tightly shut. I blinked rapidly. Surely, this was just a dream. There was a bandage on the back of his head and an intravenous line going into the top of his left hand, the clear-liquid glucose drip-bottle hanging above him. As soon as I saw him like that, this Other Tommy, motionless, nearly devoid of life, I Arctic-froze. He was so still and so far from me, farther than he'd ever been, distant in a brand-new way. For a minute, my mind closed down. I felt faint, my head swirling. My mouth fell open and gaped.

"Jesus," Cheryl moaned. "Christ."

Wade gave out a short burst of a cry. Cheryl hugged Wade.

So, this was how Cheryl had taken care of him? The chimps were dangerous? When he'd fallen and hurt himself right inside Cheryl's own bedroom? It was inconceivable. A wave of nausea rolled through me.

You, Daddy. You.

The machines standing guard next to his bed beeped. Lights flickered. I stepped gingerly forward. But it was as if I wasn't walking at all, but floating somehow. I found myself elbowing past Cheryl and Wade to the bedside. Soon, Cheryl and Wade stood behind me. I nearly lost my balance.

"Dr. Whitaker's on his way," Thomlinson said, standing next to me. I felt his breath on my neck.

Whitaker. The pediatric neurologist, the doctor who had assured us he'd gotten the seizure problem right, that it was medicinally managed. I bent down next to the bed and whispered in Tommy's left ear; such a beautiful ear, perfectly formed, the tip as translucent as a rose window.

"Tommy? This is Daddy. Can you hear me, son? You've got to hang in there, okay? Daddy's here with you. I'm right here. I'm right beside you and I'll never ever leave you. I love you. You know that, right? I love you so much."

Once again, as it had been through so much of his short life, the only response I received was silence. It was almost always silence with him, but this was the deepest and most unfathomable I'd ever heard.

Leaving Wade's side, Cheryl hesitantly approached and stroked Tommy's cheek. She felt his forehead. I let her have her space and backed out of the way.

"He feels cold." She bent down and kissed him on the cheek, a motherly kiss suffused with love. "It's Mommy, sweetheart," she said softly. "I'm right beside you too. Are you all right? You're going to come out of this, Tommy. I love you."

Suddenly, one of the machines next to Tommy's bed started beeping loudly, warning lights flashing. Another machine with a long tube attached to a square box kicked in, beeping as well. Dr. Thomlinson observed the readings with a grave look on his face and dark, worried eyes.

Just then Dr. Whitaker rushed into the room. His broad forehead wrinkled, his angular jaw tight. Here was our final defense against our ultimate fear. He stepped toward the machines, turned off the warning indicators, and read the numbers.

"Brain activity's decreasing," he said, his expression impassive. "Brainstem-evoked potentials are latent as well."

"What's that mean?" I demanded. But gazing at Tommy so still on the bed, I pretty much already knew.

Dr. Whitaker's voice was gentle. "Basically, it means this isn't hypersomnia any longer."

"What is it, then?" Cheryl asked.

It sounded as if he was speaking through water, the words far away.

"I'm sorry to say, but your son has slipped into a coma."

"Oh, God!" I cried. "No!"

Cheryl put her hands to her face and sobbed, leaning against Wade who moved to comfort her. I turned away and felt the life being squeezed out of me. Life. Such a precious and fragile thing. Jesus! Darkness was everywhere, my mind clouded over, and I nearly fainted right there on the spot.

EMOTIONAL CHRONOLOGY; time is a circle.

I'm holding a hose and Tommy stares at the running water as it puddles in his hands. We're in the backyard, he is only three years old, and the averted look in his eyes has washed away that healthy child we'd hoped for. But then, for a moment, it's as if the longed-for child emerges and he turns his head to me, eyes shining now.

"Water, Daddy. Water." A clear voice, clear and rich with young life.

And I let the water puddle in my hands too, sparkle in the sun, and then we touch hands and the water splashes together as drops fly everywhere.

Tommy gives me that healthy smile that comes so easily to all the other children. And he laughs spontaneously, just leans back his head and laughs. For a brief moment, standing before me is a child without autism, one small emotional interval of time when the light shines through, when the candle burns bright.

And then it's gone.

Chapter 19

I was standing in Tommy's room at two in the morning of the same day, watching over him. I was a nervous wreck, falling into a hole of sadness covered by emotional quicksand. The even more painful news: there was nothing I could do for him, not one damn thing. The hospital staff had put a cot in the room for me to sleep on, but I didn't touch it. Every so often, after walking around for a while or pacing, I'd step toward his bed, bend down next to him, and whisper in his ear, hoping with all my might that he'd respond to my words. "Tommy? Can you hear me? It's dad. Can you hear?"

There was not even a flicker of movement.

Exhausted and weak, feeling sick to her stomach, Cheryl decided to check into a nearby hotel with Wade for the rest of the night. She texted me about ten times saying how miserable she felt and that she couldn't sleep, and that Wade had conked out beside her. I told her I couldn't sleep either. In the state I was in, I could barely even think.

I stayed at the hospital, hanging out next to Tommy in his darkened room, experiencing a kind of fear that went beyond anything I'd ever known. The remainder of the night was a desert. Alone with a son in a coma. I didn't feel tired and yet I felt dead tired. Dread circumscribed my heart. Every time I looked over at Tommy, so still on the bed, I shivered within, a fist of pain pounding inside me. When I went to touch his forehead, I was unable to control the shakiness of my hands.

Finally, from the window in Tommy's room I watched the night gradually fade as the sunrise appeared, newborn gradations of orange and red surfacing in the distance.

I would have to wait until the morning to give my father the news. I found myself texting Rachel though, and telling her what had happened. She didn't respond. She was already on her way to Africa, I assumed, possibly in flight.

At around 7 a.m., as Tommy continued lying motionless, it struck me that I'd completely forgotten about Max, and so I called the maintenance man for my condo and explained the situation. Thank God, he answered. He said he'd take care of Max until I was ready to come back home. I was grateful for that. Poor Max. He'd probably spent the night in a state of high anxiety. I always came home for him—but not this time.

As the morning wore on, Tommy's breathing grew noticeably shallower, which destroyed me. I felt as if I were in a fog as I stayed by his side, my entire world subsumed by parental pain. At ten a.m., I switched off with Cheryl and Wade and went home where I showered, changed clothes, and checked on Max, who was outside in the backyard. Poor Max. When he saw me, he jumped all over me, nearly attacking me with his canine love; such sloppy licks.

"Tommy's in a coma, Max," I said. "He's really sick." Saying the words out loud, hearing them spoken, felt miserable.

Max barked and mewled, then sniffed me all over, licking my hands.

How could I even begin to explain what was happening? I couldn't. I said goodbye to him, looked into his sad eyes, and quickly returned to the hospital.

At eleven, the doctors began what they called, "The Endo-Process," and Cheryl, Wade and I were asked to leave the room. They planned to hook Tommy up to a respirator and insert an endotracheal tube through his mouth. The three of us stood outside his room. We watched as more machines with dials and lights and digital readouts were brought into the room.

As the doctors continued working on Tommy, Cheryl, Wade, and I went to the lunchroom. Hospital visitors surrounded us as well as men and women in blue scrubs. Chatter filled the air, but we ate in silence, all of us worn out. I still hadn't slept. There was nothing to say. I felt like a zombie. Cheryl and Wade were both on the verge of tears, pale-faced. Sad.

Around one o'clock, I found an out-of-the-way garden in the hospital's courtyard and sat on a white iron bench. The courtyard featured a gurgling fountain, some overhanging shade trees, and several rose bushes. Songbirds chirped nearby from shade trees. On another bench, a small child in a yellow dress with a yellow ribbon in her hair was lying in her mother's arms. The mother looked pregnant. I gazed at them, but hardly registered the scene before me. Without sleep, I was having a hard time concentrating. I was a human sponge absorbing nothing but liquid pain.

A helicopter passed overhead, its engine clacking.

I yawned. I looked up at the sky for help, guidance, then closed my eyes.

I couldn't help but ask the question, sitting there on that bench: Was there an honest to goodness meaning to life? Were we just purposeless random events colliding against each other? Why would the logic of the universe, if there was such a thing, want Tommy to experience the kind of pain he was undergoing?

I looked at the roses and my father's poem came to mind: We're all just a dash between two numbers.

No! I couldn't buy that. We were more than that. We had to be. Each life had *meaning.* We were here to *do something.* To make sense of the world around us through our actions, to improve our own lot and the lots of others around us, even if it was only in some small way. It couldn't all just be random chaos, could it?

And yet I thought of Tommy's pale face and still body lying on the bed. His shallow breathing. His near lifelessness. Why? What was the purpose of that?

I FINALLY CALLED MY father to relay the news, and that afternoon went downstairs on the hospital's first floor to greet him. He was sitting in the lobby drinking from a Styrofoam coffee cup in his trembling hands. Belinda had driven him over. When he spied me, the mask of negativity and defiance he normally wore dripped away like wax. He stood with the help of his cane and clapped me on the back. A glimmer of tears filled his eyes.

We walked down the hall together and found an isolated spot, two chairs by a row of vending machines in a hallway that led to billing.

"Can I see him?" he asked. My father was unshaven and wore a stained white shirt; cracked lips, hairy nostrils, a gold watch encircled his wrist, but the band was too large for his frail wrist. He'd changed; but in his own mind, he'd stayed the same. As far as he was concerned, that watch-band still fit perfectly.

"Sorry, Dad. They won't let anyone in his room but me, Cheryl, and Wade."

My father's shoulders sagged. For a minute, he closed his eyes, trying to get control. "I can't believe it, Chris. First your mother, and now this. Hell, it's like the whole damn world's falling apart." He frowned, scowled, his face drawing tight. He slugged his coffee down and finished it off, then made a face. "This stuff tastes like crap."

"Dad, I really don't need to hear about the bad coffee." I grew angry.

"So, what's the goddamn prognosis anyway?" My father coughed. "Shit. Go get me another cup of this crap, will you?"

I went and poured him another cup from the nearby coffee machine, then handed it to him, black. I poured a cup for myself. The coffee was awful, but in a sordid way, it was just what I needed, matching the way I felt.

"They can't say," I said when I sat down again. "It doesn't seem like they really know a whole lot. It seems like 'wait and see' is their only mantra. Those seizures of his made his brain more vulnerable when he got that blow on the head. That's what the doctor said anyway. I don't know. It sounds logical, I guess."

Seizures, brain trauma, coma. A deadly triumvirate, indeed.

I hung my head and sighed. I was on the verge of losing it right there. Wait and see was simply the frickin' worst kind of mantra there could possibly be. I clenched my jaw. "Tommy just doesn't deserve this. Isn't the autism bad enough? I don't know . . ." My voice trailed off. The fear, the dread hit me all at once. My gut turned hard and I put my face in my hands scrubbing my face with my hands. Then I looked at my father. "Ever thought about just plain giving up, Dad?"

My father drained his cup, crushed it, and threw it against the vending machine with surprising strength. He leaned forward and grabbed my shoulders with his hands, squeezed hard. "Now you look at me and you listen good, goddammit! We have got to *believe*, Chris. There's no way in hell we are *ever* giving up on him. Do you understand? That boy of yours is going to pull out of this goddamn hole he's in right now and come out alive." His raw voice was like a slap in the face, waking me up. "And don't you dare think otherwise. It's going to happen, all right? We've got to set our minds on this. There's only going to be one outcome here." He threw up his first finger, signifying one. "One fucking outcome, all right? And don't you forget it!"

The crazed glint in his eyes reminded me of Rocky Balboa's manager, the old man in the first and second Rocky flicks. For some reason, that crazed look made me more hopeful, uplifted. I had no idea why. It was nuts, but his grumpiness actually made me feel a little better.

"Okay, Dad."

"Look. You just go back in there and be with him, you hear me? And remember, it's just like Yogi says: it's not over till it's over." He stood slowly, leaned against his cane. I stood with him. "Damn drive over here was a mess. Sat in traffic for a half hour."

"Are you sure you're okay, Dad?" I asked, shoving my hands in my pockets.

"Don't worry about me," he said, then turned and slow-walked down the hall.

But I do, Dad. I always do.

LATER, I SPIED WADE standing in the hallway outside Tommy's room without Cheryl. He said she'd gone down to the lunchroom for something to eat, "for the baby." I motioned for him to come with me, and together we stepped inside Tommy's room, which was set at a cool temperature and was quiet except for the dull whir of the machines next to the bed. It was just the two of us, not even a nurse around. Wade's face was a collision point of grief. He rubbed the back of his neck. He basically looked like he'd gone through hell and back. He was a far different man than Mister Jaguar.

"How's Cheryl?" I asked softly.

"She's a mess. How are you?"

"Totally fucked," I said.

"God, Chris." He threw his hands in the air. "I can't believe this is happening. He's such a sweet kid. I'm devastated. By the way, everyone down at Focus sends their regards."

"Well, that's nice." I shoved my hands in my pockets. Focus. Ryerson. They were thinking of me. That was good to hear.

"Yes, I thought so."

Suddenly, Wade closed his eyes and bowed his head. "Please God," he said, "please help this little boy. Give Tommy back to us. Please, give him life. Hear us, Lord. Hear our prayer."

Wade opened his eyes and a single tear ran down his cheek. He wiped it away with his thumb. He sniffled. "Never had any kids of my own, you know." He sighed heavily. "But here I am, a second-stringer compared to you, but a father, nonetheless. Strange, isn't it?"

"Very."

Wade gulped. "I never thought I'd . . . I never thought I'd love him like I do." When he turned away from me, his broad shoulders shook as he wept, covering his face with his hands.

I put my arm around him and we hugged. My skin tingled at the surprise of Wade's raw emotions, my heartbeat raced. In that moment, I knew that Wade would make a good father for his own child with Cheryl.

LATER THAT AFTERNOON, I stepped out of the room for a break just as Cheryl walked in, scraggly hair, pale face. It was an emotional collision. We just stood there, the two of us, then turned toward Tommy. I suddenly didn't know what to do with my hands. Being with Cheryl in the same room set me on edge. I stiffened.

"Where's Wade?" I asked with a brittle edge to my voice.

"He had to check on something for work," she said. "He'll be back later."

I actually didn't want to be around her. If she hadn't been so adamant about the chimps, if she hadn't upset him so much, maybe Tommy wouldn't be in the position he was in. I felt like someone had drilled holes into my mind, allowing for extra bolts of pain. But maybe I had a part to play in it as well. If I hadn't brought him to say goodbye to the chimps . . . Maybe he wouldn't have gotten so upset. Guilty feelings stormed through me.

"Nothing's changed," I said gravely, then left the room, my pulse racing. *Especially, you.*

A minute later, I nearly collided into the one person I never thought I'd see again, and then a whole lot changed.

Chapter 20

Rachel.

I fell back against a wall and gasped, not believing my eyes as I blinked and shook my head. Hair down on her shoulders, wearing jeans and a blue blouse, the troubled look on her pale face told me how badly she was feeling. I stared at her as if she were a resurrected body. My hands grew slick and I gasped again, gawked at her. "I thought you'd be in Africa by now. Or at least flying there."

Her face was red, and she sniffed and wiped her nose. "How is he?" she asked.

"The doctors are saying wait and see. There's nothing for us to do. It's horrible. What can I say?" I swallowed hard. "You didn't go to Africa?"

"I couldn't."

"Why not?" I blinked at her, still finding it hard to believe that she was standing in front of me.

"Not after I received your text." She took a long breath, her hands shaking. "I got it while I was sitting on the plane in SF before it took off for Tunisia. I dropped my phone, I was so surprised. The next thing I know, I'm grabbing my bag and telling the stewardess I need to get off—emergency."

"But what about your opportunity? *National Geographic* and all that? Your research?"

She shook her head. "I postponed. I called them up and told them what was going on, that I had a friend whose son was in a coma, that I was too shaken up by it all, and they totally understood.

0

 5

They said I could come at a later date. I mean, Tommy. Jesus! I'm a mess of nerves now anyway. I can't do anything until I know what's going to happen. Besides, I'd be miserable. I couldn't be in Africa with Tommy in a coma. Are you kidding me? Now, is there anything I can do to help? Anything at all?"

"God, Rachel," I said, the words flowing out of me as we hugged. "I'm so glad you're here."

I became a fountain of emotions, joyous, happy, a sense of warmth flowing through my chest. My ally in all this was back. I wasn't alone anymore.

ACTUALLY, THERE WAS something she could do to help me out.

At 3 a.m. the next morning, I awoke with a start. I was lying on my cot next to Tommy's bed, when it hit me.

My plan. I had to try it. It was so simple, and yet, it seemed filled with possibilities.

I threw on some jeans and a shirt and shoes and raced out of the hospital, literally ran two blocks down the street, and knocked on the door of Rachel's hotel room. She was staying at a Hilton. I had to tell her. I didn't care what time it was.

"Look," I said, as soon as she let me in. My hair was disheveled. I was out of breath. I'd been wearing the same jeans and blue shirt for the last two days. There was a coffee stain on the shirt. I didn't care. She was in a pink nightgown.

"What is it, Chris?" she asked.

I swallowed, gathering my thoughts. "What if Tommy heard chimp voices played to him through headphones?" My voice grew excited the more I thought about it. "What if he could hear his friends speaking to him right in his ears? We'll record Obo, Mikey,

Rose, SeeSaw, the whole gang of chimps at Weller on an mp3. If I can't take him to the chimps, then I'll bring the chimps to him. What do you think?"

"Let's do it," Rachel said quickly. The redness in her eyes told me she'd been crying. "I think it's a great idea! I'll download some files into a recorder and bring it over first thing in the morning. I'll add some Gibbons singing in a forest too. They sound beautiful."

And then, around eleven that morning, Rachel rushed to meet me in the lobby of the hospital, carrying an mp3 player. She looked mournful, on the verge of tears, red-faced.

"Thank you," I said. We hugged for a moment, bodies close, and I felt swept away by her nearness. Then I rushed the mp3 player up to a young nurse who was attending to Tommy. She placed the player on the stand next to Tommy's bed. She then carefully slipped headphones over his ears. I watched as the nurse turned on the player and then chimp sounds that Rachel had recorded flowed through the headphones: their chatter, their cries, their shrieks.

Surely, if anything was going to bring him back to life, it would be the chimps.

But when the hour recording played out and nothing happened, my spirits fell. Tommy lay still as ever. Comatose. His face white, barely breathing.

"Again," I said to the nurse. "Please. We'll play it until we wear this thing out."

Cheryl looked like a wreck when she entered the room. Her pale, hollowed-out face and sad eyes said it all. She rubbed her stomach and then twisted her hands in front of her.

"What are you doing?" she asked. Her weary voice was distant, full of sadness.

"I'm playing chimp sounds into his ears." I didn't care what she said or thought. There was no way she was going to stop me.

"Chimp sounds?"

"Yes, their voices. I want Tommy to hear them."

Instead of getting a negative reaction, she surprised me. She touched my shoulder as tears swelled in her eyes. "Okay. Fine. I'll do anything at this point."

I kept playing the sounds again and again throughout the rest of the day and into the evening. Doctors and nurses came in and out, checking machines, and reading graphs.

Five hours later, I was still standing next to the bed, playing the chimp sounds in an automatic loop of desperation.

"Tommy! Do you hear the chimps?" My voice boomed, deep and resonant, as my limbs shook and I barely contained a scream. "Tommy! Can you hear the chimps? Can you move a finger, a toe? Anything? Tell Daddy that you hear your friends! Can you tell me?"

Still, Tommy remained silent as ever. Lost to me.

Lost.

AND THEN, BEFORE I even knew it, an entire week had passed. Nothing had changed. This was the week from hell. But I wasn't going to give up. I was going to keep on playing those recordings no matter what. Then, five days later, on a rainy Friday morning, thunder breaking all around, Dr. Whitaker called Cheryl and me into a wood-paneled conference room on the second floor.

I knew what this was about. My stomach churned, my chest tightened into a fist as I walked into the room and sat down in a chair across from Dr. Whitaker. I started hyperventilating, quick, shallow breaths that forced my shoulders to rise and fall.

Cheryl was weeping softly, covering her face with her hands, as she sat down next to me.

The room was wood-paneled with large medical textbooks lining the bookshelves. Titles like: *Endothelial Management*, and

Vasodilation of Arterial Nerves. There were two pictures on the wall, artwork of hunting scenes.

Dr. Whitaker's grim expression told me the entire story.

"Thank you for coming," he said. His lugubrious voice only frightened me more. "I'm waiting on two other people to join us."

I nodded. Cheryl continued weeping, her hands on her stomach. I'd asked her if she wanted Wade to join us, but she'd said no. This was between Tommy's biological parents; I agreed.

Finally, two men entered the room. One was tall and grey-haired, sixtyish, and he introduced himself as Dr. Edgar Cornwell, hospital administrator. The other man was a social worker named Adam Hudson. Shorter with bony facial features, he gazed at me, then Cheryl through soft brown eyes. He clutched a large brown folder and placed it on the table in front of him. I stared at that folder as if it were a bomb. The two men took their seats around the table.

As soon as Hudson began pulling out papers from the folder, Cheryl bent forward, her shoulders shaking as she sobbed. I reached for her hand and she grabbed it and squeezed. We looked at each other and suddenly, it was as if a wall broke down between us. All our old differences fell away, melted down. Her hand was my last remaining support system, its flesh, its bones, holding me up. And I was hers.

I recalled when she'd let go of my hand at Dr. Garman's office, the day when we'd first learned of Tommy's diagnosis. Tommy was two years old then.

"Your son is on the autism spectrum," Dr. Garman had said. "I'm so sorry to have to tell you this."

I'd tasted acid in my throat just hearing that word.

When Cheryl had let go of my hand that day, it was as if she had let go of us, our relationship, so that she could give her all to Tommy. It wasn't hard to tell what our future would be.

But now, we'd come full circle.

"When someone has been in a coma as long as your son has, twelve days now," Dr. Whitaker said. I was unable to meet his eyes. "Unfortunately, you see, the brain begins to deteriorate. As it loses oxygen, the brain reaches a point where we must question the future quality of life. Therefore, we need to make certain recommendations and create a management team for all kinds of likelihoods. It's hospital policy. I hope you understand."

"Don't people stay in comas for years?" I asked, "and then they suddenly, you know, come out of it?"

"Well, you hear of isolated cases," Dr. Cornwell said, as he shifted in his chair, his tone of voice even and calm, "miracles, really. But the reality is that when the brain succumbs to the comatose state, it can tend to lose certain basic functions that are beyond re-vitalization."

Hudson took over even more delicately, his sympathetic eyes burrowing into mine. I could tell that this was their go-to man. The guy to which they turned to deliver "the news." "We're sorry. We're more than sorry. But even if your son were to somehow return to us, you see, even if that were to happen, there's a good chance that at this point, it would be unlikely he'd have the kind of neurological function that would give him a quality life." He paused, letting his words soak in. "This is a very difficult situation for all families, of course, and it's totally understandable for you to want to discuss this serious matter from every conceivable angle. Let me suggest that you two take some time today to talk. Here's my card."

Slowly, with a somber look on his face, he passed one to me, one to Cheryl. "We're here to answer any questions you may have." Then he pulled out a large envelope. "In this packet, you'll find all the necessary materials needed to make an informed decision, including an end-of-life consent form you'll find that spells out in detail . . ."

"No!" I exploded forward, shoving the papers toward Hudson. I roared: "No, goddammit! He's coming back to life, he's going to come out of this coma, do you understand me?"

I was a drowning man, but I forced my way up and out of the office, barely able to see because of my tears, barely able to breathe. I dashed into Tommy's room, a collage of emotional chaos. I worked with new dedication and resolve. A nurse was standing next to Tommy and I pushed her out of the way and then snapped on the mp3 player, placed the headphones over Tommy's ears, and again played the sounds that had inspired my son so easily, lit him up like emotional neon. *Please God, help me! Please!*

The nurse quickly exited the room. She saw the crisis written all over my face. I just stood there, alone.

Cheryl edged into the room. I grabbed her hand again, squeezed it and she squeezed back before letting go. We didn't speak a word. I was gasping for air, sucking it up as if it were coming in through a straw. We both just stood there, watching Tommy's impassive face as the sounds continued playing through the headphones, chimps shrieks, chimps cries, chimp moans. He was barely breathing. Silence. It was always silence with him. I cranked up the volume of the mp3 player to its loudest possible setting. But Tommy still remained in his own world. Lost to us. Maybe even lost to himself this time.

We drew closer together to the bed, heads nearly touching. Cheryl's tears dropped onto Tommy's pillow. Mine mingled with hers. She put a hand on my back and rested it there. I didn't even think she realized she was doing it.

"What should we do, Chris?" she said finally.

Tommy's smiles and laughter when he was with the chimps, that life inside of him, so strong . . . And now . . .

You, Daddy. You . . .

I couldn't find my voice, the one thing I'd always relied on.

"Do you think the doctors are right, that it's time to let him go?" she said.

I slowly turned to her. "I can't let him go." I spoke in a hiss. "I'll never let him go. I don't care what the doctors say."

Cheryl started rubbing her stomach and for some reason it took me back to when she was pregnant with Tommy. I blinked, feeling suddenly transported in time. She was such a proud mother. And I was a proud . . . Oh, God! I rubbed my forehead and looked around the room, looking for something to ground me. I couldn't find a thing.

"I don't know, Chris," she said, her voice quivering. "Christ! I just don't know!"

An hour passed and Tommy continued to lay still. Another hour. Nothing. We stood next to each other, together and alone simultaneously. I felt like the floor of my world had just lost its foundation.

I stepped out of the room and Cheryl followed me. We found a pale-faced Rachel sitting on a chair in the hallway, staring down at the floor, her hands knotted together. Wade had to leave for an important job, Cheryl had told me, though he hated to go. She said he was totally distraught.

I had no idea how they'd let Rachel into this unit. But I didn't care. I didn't care about anything. My body was numb. I was a bomb about to explode. When she spied us, she quickly rose to her feet and grabbed my arm.

"How is he?" she asked, desperation in her eyes.

I shook my head. Dots floated before me. Despair. A future without my son. I grew wobbly on my feet. It was more than I could take. "No movement. Nothing."

"Oh, Chris. I'm so sorry." A hand went to her mouth and tears streamed down her face. She sobbed into her hands. "What are you going to do?" She looked at Cheryl, then me.

"I don't know . . . The doctors . . ." I said, but my voice trailed off.

I couldn't go on. I just stared into space, holding onto Cheryl's shoulder for support as Cheryl held onto me. We were tumbleweeds, human beings blown around by the wind of parental pain. I lowered my head. "The doctors . . . they . . . want . . ."

I couldn't finish my words and we all just stood there. No one said a word. What good were words anyway? Grief spoke for us, circled the three of us, a real thing, choking my heart. Finally, Cheryl said, "Come on, Chris. We need to get back in the room."

"Yes," Rachel said. "I'll be here waiting if you need anything."

I nodded and gave Rachel one last sad look.

When we returned to the room, the light from the window had slowly shifted, making slanted shadows appear. We both stepped close to the bed and stared down at our son. His face was still passive, a complete blank. I couldn't take it. This wasn't life. This wasn't anything worth living for. Maybe the doctors were right. I just didn't know.

Chapter 21

That night around 6 o'clock, Rachel brought us Greek take-out as we continued waiting for any signs of Tommy awakening; sadly, he didn't stir, even with the chimp sounds playing over and over again. Rachel told me I had to eat, that I needed some sustenance, but food was not what I wanted or cared for. Wade, who had returned from his job, and Cheryl could barely eat, either. Rachel looked destroyed, was barely able to contain herself, and didn't stay long. None of us had much to say.

Then the next day, I went to see my dad at his house and told him what the doctors were advising. Sitting in his lounger with a beer next to him, my father grew silent, hearing the news, then wiped a tear from his eyes. His face turned pale.

"Godddammit," he said, fiddling with his hearing aid. "I had to let your mother go too." He wiped a tear away and sat up in his chair. "I don't know, Chris. It's the hardest thing you'll ever have to do. Come on. Let's go outside." We walked outside together, my father breathing hard as we walked, and stood next to his roses, clouds passing by overhead. The roses—his children, in a way—were as beautiful as ever, well taken care of. It was as if they were blossoming proudly for the world to see and enjoy. I sniffed one and inhaled the sweet fragrance; natural perfume. Nice and . . .

Dad put a hand on my shoulder and the next thing I knew, I was just plain sobbing. I couldn't help it. I leaned against him and he put his arm around me.

"Oh, Dad. This is awful."

His gruff voice in my ear seemed to echo his words from my childhood when I had a nightmare and he came into my room and sat next to me; just like I sat next to Tom-Tom when he was having problems sleeping. And then I thought about combing Tommy's hair, that look in his eyes; our special time together when he'd allow me into his space. The pain of it all hit me all at once.

"You just have to do what you think is right, Chris," my father said, pulling me out of my sad reverie. "There's no easy answer for this. Go with your gut, son. God knows that's the only way. Just listen to your heart. It'll talk to you if you listen hard enough. But don't you dare rule out the possibility that you deserve a miracle too. And that maybe this is your time." He put a hand on my chest. "Listen to your heart." And then we both came together in a tight, father-son embrace. I felt his tears and the roughness of his unshaven face against my cheek.

"Sure, Dad. Sure."

I shivered inside and knew I'd remember this moment for the rest of my life, regardless what happened. And when he was gone . . .

I returned to the hospital, shaken. Devastated. Cheryl and I continued checking on Tommy and still, all we saw was our little child in bed, slowly slipping away from us. It was probably the worst moment of my life. Agony tore through my heart and soul.

That night, I thought about what the doctors had said. Should I take their advice? I'd lost my mother, my father was frail and aging, not long for this world, either, and soon, if Tommy passed, I would be alone—without a family.

Perhaps it was all meant to be this way. Who really knew? Once again, I felt like screaming at the universe, angry as hell, yet baffled by it all, befuddled by that vast conspiracy that seemed to put us on this earth, then removed us without offering even a hint as to why.

I fell asleep at nearly two in the morning, sobbing in my pillow; afraid; looking for answers and finding none. Rachel called me at three in the morning and asked if there had been any change. She said she couldn't sleep. I hated with all my might giving her the only answer I had.

I woke up around six in a fog. For a minute, I didn't know where I was. Then a second later, everything hit me and all the pain and suffering I was enduring came slashing back. I was sleeping in a room down the hall from Tommy's room. I scurried out of bed, put on my clothes, and immediately went into Tommy's room and stared down at his face. He was as still as ever. Dammit! In a fit of desperation, I started playing the chimp sounds again. I refused to give up. Cheryl came into the room about 6:15 looking pale and hollow-eyed and we both stood next to his bed, our belief that we, as parents, even with all we'd done, had still somehow failed our son. But still, I wasn't going to let this go down without a fight; the fight of my life.

And then it happened:

As the chimp sounds continued playing, Tommy's eyes started to flutter. Or was the movement just my imagination? His eyes went motionless for a minute, until . . .

Another movement of his eyelids. I was stunned.

"Look!" I said to Cheryl, grabbing her arm. "Look!"

"Is this real?" she asked, her voice quivering.

I sucked in a breath. Again, he blinked several times and we both watched, incredulous. Then Tommy's right hand which was laying straight by his side, started moving, and his fingers, slowly at first, and then with more direction, formed into a curl and then, he moved his arm up and down his side, moving . . . At first, I didn't even realize what he was trying to do, but then it hit me: It was the sign for "chimp!"

I slowly and carefully removed the headphones. I placed my mouth next to his ear. My heart was racing, my limbs shaky.

"Tommy!" I shouted.

Cheryl bent down next to him as well. "Tommy! Can you hear us?"

We both took turns calling him, desperate now, begging, pleading that he move his arm again. I could hardly breathe. And then, as if a spirit had invaded him, his eyes still closed, Tommy raised his right hand in the air and placed it back down. Then he raised his left hand.

"I can't believe it!" Cheryl said. "My God!"

"Tommy!" I said again. "Can you hear me, Tom-Tom? It's Daddy. I'm right here. Can you hear me, son?"

"Can you hear us, Tommy?" Cheryl said.

When the EEG spiked, Tommy's heart rate increased. Another monitoring machine emitted a long buzz.

"Can you . . . "

Tommy's eyes flew open.

"Tommy!" Cheryl said. "We're right here for you, darling. Oh, Tommy! Are you with us?"

Tommy blinked again, and then turned his head my way. His sweet eyes landed on mine and then moved to Cheryl's. Direct eye contact for both parents. *Mommy! Daddy!* Cheryl fell against me as Tommy reached out his hand, edged his little finger next to my hand, then signed even more boldly, his fingers curled up, moving against his side: "Chimp. Chimp."

"Yes, chimpies!" Cheryl said, tears falling onto Tommy's face as she stared at his hand. "Yes, son. Chimpies! You like those chimps of yours, don't you? Oh, Tommy! Once you get better, darling, Mommy will take you to see the chimps every day if you need it, every single—"

I couldn't believe I was hearing her say that.

Two nurses burst into the room. Whitaker followed. He pushed buttons on machines, checked readouts, and gave orders in abstract medicalese. All I knew was that Tommy's eyes remained open, and he moved his head left and right again, and when he looked at me he again held my gaze, then he looked at Cheryl and held her gaze as well. Again, he made the sign for chimp.

"Let's do this," Whitaker said to the staff after scrutinizing one of the machines and twisting a few dials. "According to the readouts, it's safe to extricate the tubes." He turned to Cheryl and me. "Can you give us a few minutes? We'll need to scrub down for this procedure."

When we stepped out of the room, we were both shaking. Delirious with joy. Cheryl wrapped her arms around my neck and squeezed me close to her. I felt her hot breath against my ears, her tears against my skin. I was overflowing with gratitude, elation, and relief was a hand that seemed to lift me up on the shoulders of unstoppable happiness. Cheryl's body against mine felt warm and tender; we needed each other so much right then—more than we'd ever needed each other before.

"He's back, Cher, he's back!" We hugged again, warmly, tightly.

"Thank God!"

I couldn't wait to tell my father.

I laughed out loud. Maybe if you screamed loud enough at the universe, perhaps someone actually heard what you were saying, and then did something about it.

Rachel approached us and my heart beat hard at the sight of her. I couldn't wait to give her the news.

"What happened?" she asked, her eyes wide open as she watched Cheryl and I embrace. "What's going on?"

"He woke up!" I cried, turning to her. Overwhelmed, I could barely speak. "He's . . . he's back! He woke up from the coma!"

"Oh, my God!" she said, jumping up and down. "Really? Really?"

Cheryl and I both shouted, "Yes!"

"And it was those chimp sounds that did the trick," Cheryl said, wiping tears from her eyes as she gave Rachel a long, body enveloping hug, her face flushed with color. "The first thing he did, after fluttering his eyes, was make the sign for chimp."

"You're kidding." Rachel stepped back, surprised.

"No. We're not. Not at all."

Later, when the tubes had been taken out of his throat, Cheryl and I stood next to Tommy's bedside, and he turned to us and whispered the one word he had signed, the one word that, for him, said it all: "Chimpies. Chimpies."

Standing there next to his bed, I closed my eyes and it was as if all the adrenaline that had kept me going through the dark days and nights finally drained away. I crashed. Unable to stop myself, my lights went out, and like a puppet that had lost all its strings, I crumpled to the floor.

Chapter 22

On a clear day at the Weller compound, the sky infinitely blue, Tommy was finally back with his friends once again. It had been six months since he'd emerged from his coma. The doctors had been amazed by his recovery, which apparently hadn't been slowed down by his autism, though I was afraid it would. He'd had to re-learn how to walk at first, but he'd progressed quickly with physical therapy. He'd also suffered from amnesia for the first two weeks out of the coma but had recovered from that as well. His communication skills, of course, remained low, but the doctors said no other cognitive harm had been done. God, were we grateful.

Obo, Mikey, SeeSaw, and Rose all welcomed Tommy with a kind of self-composed gentleness, touching him with careful hands, looking him up and down. They sensed what he'd been through. I was sure of it. Standing among the chimps, his gang, Tommy closed his eyes for a second and just breathed it all in. The fact that he was really and truly back meant everything to him. He clapped his hands and jumped up and down. I had never been happier.

Marcy stood next to me, supervising, a bright smile on her face. Rachel was in Africa. We talked every so often via Skype and I kept her up-dated on Tommy's recovery. She'd be back in about eighteen months, she told me, a long time, but not forever. I missed her, of course, and she missed me and Tommy, she said, but her career called and she was where she needed to be—for now. We kept emailing each other at least twice a week. No way was I going to let our connection end just because she was on a different continent. I was hoping that we would only grow closer with time.

A smile lit up Tommy's face, a golden, heart-filled, real smile, the one I had yearned to see. When Tommy sat down in the middle of the chimps in the play yard, the chimps gathered around him, getting re-acquainted.

"Chimpies! Miss me," Tommy said. He laughed, a normal child's laughter that sent my spine tingling with joy.

Carefully, Tommy hugged Obo, who had joined the gang after a little reluctance.

"Chimpies happy see me, Daddy," Tommy said. "They know happy today. Beautiful."

I wiped back a happy tear. Words flowed out of him. Strings of words. It was "beautiful."

Cheryl texted me: *"How's he doing?"*

"Great! He's really talking again! And the chimps love him to death! How's your baby girl?"

"Cute as could be!"

Cheryl had given birth to Clarissa, a beautiful six-pound baby, and she and Wade had decided to stay in San Diego for Tommy's sake after all. No more Acorn School. We were back to shared custody status too. Cheryl had dropped her lawsuit and had petitioned the court to return to our original agreement. The court had agreed. Gloria Beaman actually sent me a note of congratulations. I couldn't believe it!

And even more good news: Two weeks ago, I'd talked to Dr. Evans and he was preparing to start the research program again with Tommy and the chimps. Dr. Dunn would be back on board and Carly Yates would give us her approval and financing.

Cheryl gave her blessing and I was overjoyed. She planned to help with Tommy in chimp therapy as well. Even after all she'd done against me, after all she'd put me through, I couldn't deny the importance of maintaining our connection as father and mother for Tommy. After all, we were still joined together at the hip when it came to Tommy—till death do us part.

Chapter 23

Another connection loomed just as important: Tommy's and Albert's.

Tommy and I were at Weller in the room with the one-way mirror once again later that afternoon. Tommy was standing in front of Albert who was sitting at his chair in front of his easel. Albert was wearing a diaper that fit snugly around his bottom. Albert raised his hand, Tommy raised his as well, and the two of them put palm against palm. I never grew tired of watching Tommy relate with the chimps. Especially with Albert. They had the ultimate connection, boy and chimp. I smiled broadly.

"It's the pain," Rekulak said, rubbing Albert's shoulder. "Chronic pain so intense I can't seem to relieve it, even on his best days. And his heart's failing. Nevertheless, I'm so glad you've come. Albert's been asking about Tommy so much, signing Tommy's name, at least twice a day. You wouldn't believe it."

"Tommy, would you like to talk to Albert?" I asked.

But Tommy was silent. He shook his head.

He and Albert began to sway together, back and forth, left, right, gradually gaining more and more momentum. Albert was taller than Tommy, but not by much. Finally, as if the hypnotic spell was broken, Tommy stepped even closer to Albert.

Albert said, "Hoooo . . . Eeeiii . . ." He stretched his lips.

"Is there anything you want to tell Albert?" I asked Tommy. "Anything at all?"

Albert wailed and the sound reverberated throughout the room, eerie and primitive. I felt it in my bones. Then Albert grabbed his stomach. He seemed shot through with pain. My stomach churned.

Tommy put his face against the chimp's broad chest. Albert lowered his head and wrapped an arm around Tommy's shoulder, then the two hugged in a long embrace.

I kneeled next to Tommy. "Tell us more about old Albert," I said.

"Awbert want . . . free, Daddy," Tommy said. He gave me direct eye contact. "No cage. Awbert want . . . free!" Yes, I understood, as Tommy had hinted before. Freedom meant the final phase, beyond the body.

Ultimate cagelessness.

"So, this was what he meant by Albert being free," Rekulak said. "It wasn't about putting him in a sanctuary at all."

I nodded. "No. He meant Albert's dying. How astute was that?"

"Completely astute," Rekulak said, his eyes falling on Tommy's face. "I'm amazed at his understanding." He put a hand on my shoulder. "I kind of think Albert was waiting for Tommy to come back before he died."

The chimp groaned. His body quavered and flinched. Then he gave a loud cry of pain. He rested his head against Tommy and snuggled close. Albert's body shook one final time. Heaved.

Rekulak's eyes were brimming with tears, his face contorted in grief. He sighed with sadness. "Oh, Albert," Rekulak said. "Goodbye, my friend."

"So long, Albert," I said. The poor chimp. I shed tears myself. My chest felt like it was caving in with sorrow. What a hard life he'd led, this close cousin of ours, so many of his difficulties caused by human beings. It was such a shame.

"Awbert!" Tommy cried. "Want free!"

Albert closed his eyes and went limp, peace at last descending on his face.

Peace at last.

"Awbert no cage no more," Tommy said, turning to me. He spoke louder. "Awbert free."

"Free," Tommy said. He looked at me for a quick slice of a moment, lowered his head, then sucked on the backs of his hands.

Ah, life. What a strange and unfathomable mystery you are. Does our inevitable passing lead to ultimate freedom? Or is it only a path toward another prison made of dirt or ashes?

I'd come so close to losing Tommy.

Sure hope my Dad finds peace when his time comes, too.

Chapter 24

As time passed, the voice-over jobs started to come back more and more—Wade even helped me land a major job for a chain restaurant—and I was finding enough to keep me afloat. With the Weller stipend now back on, all in all, I was making it, if not doing fairly well.

Then, sometimes a son has to do what a son has to do.

I decided I needed to move in with my dad. He still refused to sell the house and move into assisted living, and when he fell in the den about a month ago—his second fall—I knew I had no choice. He hadn't hurt himself, thank God, but I couldn't take any more chances. Since we couldn't afford a live-in aid, I was the next best choice. I put my condo on the market and it sold in less than a week! It actually felt good to get out from under the payments. I'd even made a small profit on the sale.

The day came for me to move in. I'd packed all my stuff into a U-haul, which I pulled behind my old man of a car. I parked at the curb of my father's house and was getting ready to haul my belongings inside. I'd sold all my furniture and my TV and was basically down to what was left of my material life: my clothes—never really owned a whole lot of clothes—my liquor bottles, and a few pictures and paintings. It was time to return to the Essential Chris Crutcher. Back to my Roots. Something like that. I had to smile.

The weather was San Diego fine, another temperate afternoon, just like the one at the zoo when Tommy had first showed me his unique ability. There are lots of things to complain about in this world, but San Diego weather isn't one of them. It was a Saturday afternoon. Tommy was with me, helping me move. Max was on a leash tied to a pole in the front yard, watching our every move, tail wagging.

Before I started hauling my stuff in, I looked around and just took a long breath. A slow-moving red car clattered down the street. Then a bicyclist waved at me as he passed me by. I waved back. It was a great neighborhood, really, North Park, full of shade trees and memories, my childhood home. Mrs. Rosenkrantz still lived next door, at least ninety-five by now, her mind still sharp. I used to mow her lawn. The two dollars she'd give me was a fortune in my twelve-year-old eyes.

I knelt down to Tommy's level and gave him the news. He was carrying Radar in one hand.

"This is where you'll come on your days with me now," I told Tommy.

"Good, Daddy. Like." Tommy clapped his hands. "Like lots."

I did a cartoon character, Dexter, one of Tommy's fav's. "Me too, Tom-Tom. Lots. Me thinks this place'll be really and really really nice!"

Tommy laughed. "Fun, Daddeeee . . . You fun."

Tommy had returned to Weller several times, and with the chimp therapy he'd undergone under the guidance of Dr. Dunn, he was definitely coming out of his shell, just as I'd known he would. Cheryl and I had worked out a schedule so that Tommy could go to school at Hillwood in the mornings, and then I would drive him out to Weller in the afternoon, Mondays, Wednesdays, and Fridays. Sure, it was a long haul, but it was so worth it. He was giving me lots of direct eye contact now and his speech was improving, for sure. He spoke with longer sentence patterns, though far from perfect, and there was a bit more emotional inflection in his tone. I couldn't have been happier.

Later, after moving everything in, I left Tommy outside to play with Max in the backyard and stepped inside. My father, who had watched me carry things in for a while, who hadn't offered to help move even one thing, was now asleep in his favorite old chair, his jaw dropped and his head turned to the side. He had berated me on how long it took for me to move everything in.

"Can't you go any faster than that?"

A nearly empty beer glass rested next to him on the table. The Padres were on TV. I was glad he'd just missed a run scored by the Mets. I had to smile.

I spotted a piece of paper next to his chair; another poem! I slowly read the words, once again written in his scrawl:
The meaning of existence
lies not in who you are, or will be,
but in who follows after you.
No greater thing there is than a child to watch over,
to raise like a rose,
its human petals emerging in the bright sunlight of your folly, your guidance,
your sun and shadow,
the soil of your love as rich as the tenderness you cultivate.
For this is your future, your hope,
which harbors your past in its bones.

Wow! Beautiful! He'd answered my question! So, *this* was his meaning to life after all. I stared at the scrawl again with tears in my eyes, and felt the rumblings of an earthquake in my heart no Richter scale could ever measure. Raising Tommy is, was, always will be the meaning to my life, for sure. We were all a dash, me, Tommy, Cheryl, Rachel, everyone, but we were an important dash, a meaningful dash. That was because our actions had consequences, ripple effects that reached out into family, friends, future generations, ultimately, the world.

I sighed and tried to wrap my heart around it all, feeling a rush of love run through me, and how great and large almighty love was. Love, the ultimate ripple effect.

EPILOGUE

"Often, it's not about becoming a new person, but becoming the person you were meant to be, and already are, but don't know how to be."
–Heath L. Buckmaster

Tommy takes his time as Zutu slowly stands and shrieks. Zutu is a wounded chimp recently placed in the sanctuary. He walks but in a halting stop-and-start way, one arm hanging limply from his side. Tommy watches his every move, helping him, a natural-born assistant. The chimps here in the Congo are all living deep inside the sanctuary where there's plenty of forest and room to roam. They are free and safe. A poacher had tried to capture Zutu, hurting him, but the chimp had escaped. Now he is safe, too.

Tommy smiles and coos at Zutu, and the chimp shakes his head. He shrieks. The chimp moves closer to Tommy and actually whispers in Tommy's ear.

"Daddy, Zutu has secret," my son says to me.

"What?"

He moves next to me, takes my hand, and pulls me down to him. When I bend down to his level, he whispers in my ear, "Zutu misses his brother."

Zutu's brother had been lost to the poachers.

"Really?"

Tommy nods.

Two years after the coma, Tommy is flourishing in this sanctuary in the Congo. We live in a complex of two concrete buildings and a series of huts, and the sanctuary itself is nearly 300 acres. We are here for three months, a summer retreat for us. Rachel had arranged it. I'd left my father back home with Belinda, who would be his live-in aid until I returned to the States. Dad is taking care of Max and nursing more beers, I'm sure, partying it up in his own way. I tried to Skype with him once to tell him how me and Tommy were doing, but he couldn't figure out how to work the computer and all I heard was, "This goddamn bullshit thing . . ." before his voice faded away, a bit worn with time and a touch even more ornery as well.

All of the workers at the sanctuary, native Africans, both men and women, are astounded by Tommy's uncanny ability to communicate with the chimps, using a combination of mental pictures, signs, postures, and who knows what else. Dr. Rekulak has assured me that Tommy will still play an important role in chimp studies for a very long time as well.

All I know is that Tommy is happy here and his human speech is greatly improved. It's still not perfect, but it's come a long, long way.

Rachel strides over to us. She looks radiant, her smile is wide, suffused with the richness of being here. Her eyes are bright, filled with an inner vitality. She's just gotten back from a visit to the rain forest in Gombe. I can't take my eyes off her. Her hair is longer now, reaching to the middle of her back. I can see the effects of being in the Gombe written in her eyes, in the lightness of her walk, the happiness blossomed all over her face. Just like she said in the coffee shop when we met to discuss the Weller data, I see how Gombe changes a person, teaches them to see in living color and to dwell in the luxury of the present moment.

"Time for dinner," she says. "Are you guys ready?"

"Absolutely." I tingle inside just seeing her, being with her in Africa. It feels incredible.

Rachel has packed sandwiches and a bottle of wine. We climb into a jeep, Zutu sits on my lap, and we head to Nawango Beach, to tree-lined, windswept ocean and pure white sand. Tommy, Rachel, Zutu and I sit down to dinner on a blanket on the sand.

"We have to get ready for your Mommy," I say to Tommy who takes a sandwich from Rachel. She's cut it into a square especially for him. "She's coming in two weeks." Cheryl's still all for the chimps, and her new child, Clarissa, seems healthy as any normal two-year-old. We're all entirely grateful.

"Goodie," Tommy says quickly, a special light sparkling in his eyes and real emotion flickering on his face. "Talk good for Mommy. Show. Me and chimpies now. Show .. every .. her ... thing!" He gives me a broad smile, just like any kid; and my heart surges with a rush of joy and love for him.

Tommy and Zutu sway with each other. Then Tommy signs and Zutu shakes his head up and down in sympathy.

Rachel and I uncork the wine, pouring two glasses of an African cabernet.

"Damn good," I say. We raise our glasses and clink them together. She's been sending me strong signals of attraction lately, a bit of flirtation here, a touch there, and all I can say is: I plan on sending a few signals of my own. Those candlesticks that she'd loved in that antique shop? I went back and bought them two days later and was planning to surprise her with them tonight.

I gaze out into the open ocean, admiring this great white beach, old as life itself, this water and this blue uninterrupted sky. A flock of birds soars above us, gifted with their natural-born ability to fly away from predators.

"Me love you, Daddy," Tommy says, turning to me, giving me beautiful direct eye contact.

"And I love you too, Tom-Tom. So very much! This big." I spread my arms wide. Rachel looks on, smiling.

"This big, Daddy?" Tommy says, spreading his arms wide too, his voice full of emotion.

"Yes!" I stretch my arms even wider. "All the way to the moon and back. This big!"

We all laugh. Then I get on my knees and he runs into my outstretched arms, not even hesitating. It's happened at last—I can hug him and he hugs me back. It feels so good to hold my little boy next to me, clutching him tightly. I give him a long, warm embrace. He doesn't resist. My heart swells.

My own fight to rescue Tommy has taught me so much, but this most of all: We have to stand up for what we believe in. We have to go the distance, to fight the odds, if we want to make a change. In the end, it's worth it, though while you're doing the fighting, it certainly sometimes seems like it's just easier to give up.

Has Tommy's autism been healed? Not at all. He still stares from time to time. He still goes into his own world and sinks his teeth into the backs of his hands. He still hyper-focuses. But he's come such a long way. The most important thing of all to me is that I just want him to be who he is in all his uniqueness, his special "me-ness."

I think Tommy is on the way to becoming that person. He's found the best spot on the planet for him, where his unique abilities make the most sense, where a happy and positive future stretches before him.

No, he won't be staying past the summer for now. And yes, he'll be going back to school in the fall. But at least for now, this place can bring out the best in him. I am proud and overjoyed to be here with him, where he can be who he is—for surely, Tommy Crutcher is like no other boy.

Made in the USA
Columbia, SC
06 November 2020